M000206563

SALVATION

DAWN OF WAR DUOLOGY

BOOK ONE

A. M. Hawke

Supposed Crimes LLC • Matthews, North Carolina

Published in the United States.

ISBN: 978-1-944591-35-9

www.supposedcrimes.com

This book is typeset in Goudy Old Style.

To Kat, whose love for this book helped make it the best it could be.

Acknowledgments

Thanks to the many people who helped with this book in some way. If you think this means you, it probably does.

And as always, thanks to Theo and Kat. For everything.

CHAPTER ONE

"So." THE visitor's lips curled like he tasted something sour. "You're the man they call the Destroyer."

Malek nodded. He expected nothing less from the reigning Seraph of Aerix. "In the pits, they call me by that name."

"In the pits." The Seraph laughed. "Where barbarians rip one another apart because people like watching them die."

Malek ignored the insult. He'd never been to Aerix, but he knew enough not to argue.

The few people he knew who'd been there said the sky was still blue, blue and so bright it stung the eyes. And the Seraph had his own tower, a gilded finger stretching up into the clouds, piercing the bright sky.

Malek was used to the factories of Dis. They built for longevity and sturdiness, not for beauty. And Dis's skies hadn't been blue for generations. A stream of black smoke belched from the foundries and smelters. Soot encrusted everything, and neither cleaner nor polish nor solvent could remove the most stubborn grime. It filled the cracks between the wall tiles and clung to the light strips in the walls and ceiling.

The Seraph was cleaner. Which meant he hadn't been here long.

Like most people from Aerix, he was tall and thin, too tall and thin for his features to be natural. But despite his eerie thinness, his body was packed with sleek, lean muscle. The light from the ceiling strips shone on reddish hair framing a delicate, angular face. His lips, though, were thick and full, too thick for such dainty features.

Sensual, maybe. Malek guessed that was the point. But he'd gone too far with whatever alteration had given him such pouty lips, and they looked wrong on his face.

You're exaggerating. Malek smirked.

The Seraph's eyes were even more striking. They were blue, a neon blue too vivid to be anything but artificial. Malek looked closer. Streaks of azure bled outward from the edge of the iris, a sure sign that their color had been altered.

Malek's smirk deepened. He'd had plain eyes too, once, brown and unremarkable. His one concession to vanity had been to dye them black. The same slight ring of color that bled blue into the whites of Soran's eyes made Malek's irises look big and dark.

In the pits, they called him Destroyer. Why not look the part?

"The pits sit just three levels below where we stand," Malek said. He tapped the ground with his foot. "So don't forget your manners, Soran. Seraph of Aerix or not."

Soran cocked an eyebrow. He moved around Malek, sizing him up. Staring at him like a trainer sizing up a new recruit or a buyer studying the features of a new hovercar. Malek growled. He'd snapped gawking fools in half for less.

But he'd brought Soran here to forge an alliance, not for a petty brawl. And feeding Soran's arrogance might help him get it.

As for Soran, had his eyes always been blue? Maybe he'd only brightened eyes that were already pale, as social status demanded. He was, after all, a prince.

But brown would be more interesting. Brown was the color of soil. No high-ranking Skyknight would be caught dead with eyes the color of the ground.

"Lord Malek!" called one of the guards.

She had short-cropped hair and dark brown skin. And like him, the pits had left her with scars. The most prominent was a long diagonal line slanting just under one eye. Her altered muscles bulged, and angry energy crackled over the surface of the blade she held.

Malek smiled. Loyalty like hers was always useful.

But at the moment, the hostility only made things tense. "Stand down. The Seraph is my guest."

Soran snickered. The woman muttered a curse in the dialect of the pits and lapsed into silence.

"Barbarians," Soran said again. "And you're the man who leads them."

He reached slender fingers toward one of Malek's arms, his fingertips just barely touching the skin. "Impressive. But you have so many scars. No Skyknight would let an enemy get close enough to mar him that way."

"Any pit fighter who got that close would crush him."

Malek hadn't fought many Skyknights. He hadn't had much opportunity, since few visited Dis. But the few who did had proven difficult opponents. Their reshaped bodies mimicked the starships they piloted: light, nimble, and deadly.

But the alterations came with a price. The alterations that made them so agile made them delicate as well. Grinning viciously, Malek lunged.

Soran twisted away from Malek with unnatural speed. "You'll have to do better than that, brute!"

His gloating became a high-pitched howl of pain.

Malek knew better than to try to catch him. He'd only meant to grab at Soran's arm as he dashed by. And that, he'd managed, slower reflexes or no. From there, it was only a matter of twisting Soran's arm just hard enough to make sure he'd notice.

But Soran was a warrior and a sovereign to boot. Pain didn't stupefy him for long. His free hand reached for a weapon hidden in his boot.

Malek's alterations heightened his senses and augmented his strength, but that didn't make him as fast as a Skyknight. He turned his body to protect his chest from the inevitable cut.

Pain blossomed in Malek's upper arm. He welcomed it.

Going anywhere in Dis unarmed was as good as a death sentence, whatever banner of peace someone came under. If Soran hadn't managed to sneak a weapon in here, he wouldn't be worth meeting.

Malek twisted Soran's arm again, harder this time. Soran screeched, the sound stinging Malek's ears. Malek grabbed at the wrist that held the dagger and forced Soran's hand back until he snarled and opened his hand. The blade clattered to the floor.

The guards rushed toward them, alarmed. Malek shook his head.

"I have everything under control," he called to them. "Leave."

"But my Lord!" the woman stammered. "He—"

"Leave. The Seraph is no threat to me."

Still muttering their misgivings, the guards glared at Soran.

"Now!" Malek ordered.

No sooner had the door hissed shut behind them than Soran twisted his wrist free and whirled on Malek as best he could, striking out with a thin fist.

"Savage! How dare you!"

"Remember, Seraph: the opponents who gave me those scars are dead."

Soran lowered his head to meet Malek's gaze, his brows knotted in anger. "You want an alliance, and this is how you go about proposing it?"

"If I meant to harm you, I would have done more than twist your arm."

Soran's eyes glittered. "Understood."

Magnanimous in victory, Malek let go. Soran moved his shoulder, his teeth still gritted against the pain, struggling to get comfortable again.

He glared, his face inches from Malek's. Suddenly aware of his nearness, Malek remembered his circling earlier, his appraising, intense stare. His wound twinged, a sharp sting, and he grinned.

Soran's lips parted. Sensual, indeed. In some circles, Skyknights' altered bodies were famous for their beauty. Some said they'd altered their nervous system as well, heightening sensations of all sorts. Including pleasure.

Malek doubted the people who'd spread those rumors knew any of it from experience. Still, from the way Soran had looked at him before...

And was looking at him now. "Malek the Destroyer. Lord of the deathmatch arena. Undefeated and unstoppable."

Malek chuckled and looked down at the dagger on the ground. It gleamed brighter than any weapon Malek had ever used.

Soran's gaze followed Malek's. That full mouth curled into another mocking smile. "Or so your band of rabble claims."

"Rabble? You sound like someone from the Senate. Talk like that is beneath you."

"The Senate? I have nothing in common with that pack of fools."

"I don't think you do." Malek chuckled. "You're a prince. They are a pack of bureaucrats, in love with their own stagnation."

Soran threw back his head and laughed. "Aerix is a city of warriors. And Dis is a city of brutes who fancy themselves fighters. Tell me again why I should be paying attention?"

"Aerix is beset on all sides," Malek answered. "Do you really think no one else has noticed it?"

"Beset on all–?" Soran reached out a hand and pushed at Malek's chest. Malek grabbed at his wrist.

Soran's eyes narrowed. He squirmed in Malek's grip. "Aerix has always stood alone. We rule the skies. No one can touch us. Certainly not the Senate."

"You do. But the skies you rule are shrinking, Seraph."

Soran turned his head and scoffed. Malek reached up to cup his chin, gripping it with the gentleness of carefully restrained strength. Soran blinked in surprise or indignation, but made no move to resist.

"I was speaking to you, Soran. You would do well to listen when I do."

"We rule the skies, yes. And the Senate builds nothing but hovels, hugging the ground–" He stopped. Most buildings in Dis stood low to the ground, and Malek had him by the chin. "No offense."

Malek released him. "None taken. But the Senate isn't just jealous. They're greedy."

"Greedy?" Soran drew back, practically prancing, as he let out another high trill of laughter. "Don't tell me you think that the fools in Feris or Corian could get close enough to Aerix to plunder it!"

"That's exactly what I mean."

"But we have wings of Skyknights, trained from youth to defend their city with their lives. Really, for a man who calls himself 'the Destroyer'"—he glanced at the doors the guards had left through—"you strike me as more paranoid than frightening, 'Lord' Malek."

Malek gave Soran a mirthless grin. "You're right. The Skyknights of Aerix are the last of a noble breed. There's nothing like them left on our planet. There hasn't been for a long time."

Soran's eyes widened. "Praise, Malek? After I've spent the afternoon scoffing at your city, your followers, and even—" He glanced at the slash across Malek's arm and the red streams dripping from it.

"You and I are not so different, Soran."

Soran pursed his lips. "Aren't we?"

"We both lead cities of fighters. We both remember a better age. An age when our world's armies were feared across the galaxy."

"Across the galaxy..." Soran began. Then he stopped. "What does that have to do with you, pit fighter?"

"Don't tell me you can't guess."

"Dis is an overglorified factory town with a few gladiators in it. A handful of people who kill other athletes for show aren't an army."

"Dis is a factory town now. That doesn't mean it always was."

Soran scoffed. "Malek the Destroyer, scourge of the death pits and amateur historian?" Soran smiled. "I'd forgotten about your little hobby."

Malek waited. Better to let Soran figure that one out for himself.

"Tell me something," Soran went on, "that band of thugs who broke into the Great Library of Delen a few years back—"

"It was necessary."

"Of course it was," Soran said in the sing-song tone of an adult humoring a child. "And now you're going to tell me that Dis had some illustrious past?"

"You've heard the theory, I think."

Soran stepped back, startled. "I've heard of the speeches you give before the pit fights. I thought you were just trying to make bloodsport sound legitimate." He shook his head. "I had no idea you believed cheap conspiracy theories."

"Conspiracy theories, Seraph? Or something the Senate wants us to forget? The Senate tells us we belong in factories, in foundries, in mines."

"Yes."

"And yet, what does everyone talk about?"

"The deathmatches."

"Precisely."

"Because Dis is filled with undisciplined brutes who can't keep from ripping each other apart. What is that supposed to prove?"

Malek dropped into a fighting stance. "I told you before. I have no interest in hearing the Senate's lies out of your mouth."

With a fluid motion, Soran mirrored Malek. "Fine. But if you try to tell me your people don't like killing each other, I won't believe you."

Now it was Malek's turn to laugh, harsh and mirthless. "I'm not saying they don't. I'm saying they deserve better targets."

"Better targets? You can't mean—" He stopped, and his lips curled into a grin even bigger than his smirk from before. "You want to start a war."

"Start a war? Of course not. But I expect one to find me, sooner or later. Or, more accurately, I expect one to find you."

"So you do think those fools plan to attack Aerix." Soran shook his head, chuckling. "Maybe you are a conspiracy theorist."

"I think the Senate is prying into Aerix's business. I don't think that's a coincidence." Malek's mouth set in a grim line. "And I don't think the Seraph of a city known for its fighters writes off threats as conspiracy theories. You're not a profligate fool of a prince, Seraph. Don't pretend to be one."

Soran tensed. Malek ignored him. "Your warriors patrol the skies over Aerix more often nowadays. And fly further. Just last week, the Senate's soldiers caught a wing flying almost to Corian."

"They were off course. Their Wingleader's navigational systems were malfunctioning."

"Of course. And no one else in the squad said anything."

Soran glared.

Malek stepped closer to him. "Tell me, leader of the Skyknights. If the towers of Aerix stand alone, as they always have—if the Skyknights would just as soon watch the 'groundlings'' cities rust—what were they doing there?"

Soran made a strangled sound and stared down at the floor. "Corian has been strengthening its garrison. I wanted someone to keep an eye on it. Skycaptain Tanth is one of my best flyers, and clever besides. If anyone could have managed to fly there undetected—"

Malek nodded gravely.

Soran paced again. He stepped around Malek, who matched his movements. "But what's all this to you, Lord of the Pits? Corian hasn't threatened Dis."

"Don't play the fool, Seraph. Like I said, it doesn't become you."

Soran snickered. Malek kept talking. "Corian is nothing special, just as you say. Aerix is the stuff of legend. What would give them the courage to aggress against a city bristling with starfighters?"

"Backup," Soran ground out. "From someone greater."

Malek spread his arms wide, as Soran had earlier. "Then you do understand."

Soran sidled up to Malek with effortless grace. "Oh, I understand perfectly, gladiator." He pressed a thin-fingered hand to Malek's chest. "But why should I trade one danger for another?"

"We are no danger to you." Malek grabbed at Soran's wrist and wrenched his arm away. "Not unless you force my hand."

Soran winced. "No danger? Now you're playing dumb, Destroyer."

"Am I? I didn't call you here to make an enemy."

Soran ignored him, pulled away, and paced. So he was nervous after all. His movements were too quick to be natural even when he did nothing but walk across a room.

Then he turned, a fey gleam in his too-bright eyes. "Aerix stands alone. Aerix has always stood alone."

"I know."

"So suppose your little theory is right. That Corian does attack us, and that the Senate sends its legions as backup." His hand moved, a violent gesture of disgust. "Suppose I call you and your barbarians. Suppose you rush to my aid. And suppose that, together, we drive them off."

Malek waited.

Soran's lips pursed into a venomous scowl. "Well, then not only have I made enemies of people who think they rule the planet, but now, for the first time in generations, Aerix is in debt. To you. Really, now, Lord of the Pits, do you think I don't know what you want?"

Malek laughed, a pure, rolling sound that echoed through the room. After years of clawing his way to the top in the pits, and years of running them after that besides, very little had the power to honestly surprise him.

"What I want?" Malek said. "Do you think I'm no better than the Senators and their pawns? Aerix is the one thing on this planet worth preserving. If you think I want to take it from you, you haven't heard a word I've said."

Soran's lithe form was a blur. Malek planted his feet as it streaked toward him, pitching backward as the blow caught him in the chest. Light as the Skyknights' altered bodies were, their speed made up for it.

But Malek couldn't afford to lose this sparring match. He barreled forward, wrapping his arms around the slender frame in front of him and squeezing.

Soran thrashed against him. His fists beat against Malek's shoulders and back. Once, he reached down far enough to strike at Malek's cut. Struck with sudden inspiration, he opened his hand and then clenched it into a claw, digging at the wound.

Malek roared in pain and pressed harder, tightening his grip. *So you think we're savages who have no self control?*

Coughing from the pressure, Soran gave a soft, high whine. "I yield," he said finally, his blue eyes shining as cold and bright as the dagger he'd dropped to the floor.

Malek let go. "I've said it several times now. I won't say it again. I am not your enemy, Seraph of Aerix. If I were, you would be dead."

"Fine." Soran's body was still tense. Whether from readiness to fight or from pain, Malek couldn't tell.

"Think it over. If your pride will allow it."

Soran twitched. Then he tossed his head. "I'll think about it. If those dunderheads behind the door don't try to kill me for not worshipping your every word."

Malek frowned. "You're underestimating them."

Soran smirked. He glanced toward the dagger on the floor and bent down. But he didn't pick it up, and only walked to the door. "Keep it," he called over his shoulder.

Malek waited for the doors to close behind Soran and looked down at the dagger. The blood it had drawn streaked it, ruby on silver, and he stared at it a moment. Then, slowly, he lifted it up.

The floor had already dirtied it, and even his grip would smudge the gleaming hilt. He shook his head. That was a shame.

He glanced over at his arm and at the line of red smeared with the prints of Soran's fingers where he'd dug his nails in.

Remember, Seraph: The opponents who gave me those scars are dead.

And yet Soran had wounded him, had scored a line across his right arm, a talisman and testament, and had not died for it.

He could have it altered, smoothed away by the doctors and medics who served the gladiators. The vain ones sometimes had that done, eager to show off their chiseled bodies. The insecure did it too, not wanting anyone to know just how many of their fights had been close calls.

Malek was neither.

"I'll keep it," he told the room. He tucked the dagger into a band around his uninjured arm. "I'll keep them both."

CHAPTER TWO

LIGHT STREAMED through the oval windows of the meeting room. It bathed the room in brightness, gleaming against the metallic filigree of the walls, table, and chairs.

Soran loved it, most of the time. One of the perks of being Seraph was the chance to live and work in the highest—and most beautiful—tower in the city. Even the plainest of the meeting rooms had been designed to dazzle and awe anyone the Seraph invited in.

The window reached nearly to the vaulted ceiling. Thin, twisted metal framed it, sculptured shapes that caught the sunlight and glowed with it as if aflame.

But the best thing about the windows was the wide expanse of sky they opened into. Unlike the districts of the Molten Belt, where the belch of factories choked the skies and left them in perpetual, sooty twilight, the skies of Aerix were blue, streaked with the trails of the starfighter patrols and the thin wisps of clouds. Towers rose into the air, their designs almost as elaborate as that of the Seraph's own Tower.

Even so, the daylight flooding in through the massive windows illuminated a visitor that Soran doubted would prove worthy of it. He scowled.

It wasn't that Senator Derell was especially ugly. Compared to a Skyknight, everyone was ugly. And in any city but Aerix, he would be tall. The formal dress of the Senate fit well on his frame. A sweep of salt-and-pepper hair framed his long face. He had an aquiline nose—probably modified to make it more pronounced—and large, bright eyes. They caught the light from the window and fragmented it, an alteration that made his irises almost iridescent.

By any standard but Aerix's, the Senator looked regal.

But regal or not, Derell should never have been let in here at all. Official insignia winking in the bright light from Soran's windows didn't change that.

"Seraph of Aerix," Derell began. "It's a privilege and a delight to visit your city. Even though I'm here on unpleasant business."

"I bid you welcome, Senator." Soran twisted his frown into a flawless grin. "It's not every day I have occasion to meet with one of you."

Derell glanced out the window and then back at Soran. "I'm hoping that what I have to say might change that, Seraph."

"That's a bold thing to say, Senator."

"Is it?"

Soran blinked, the picture of innocence. It helped to be young.

Derell leaned forward, abandoning all pretense of gawking at the view. "We've heard that you left Aerix recently. Something we've rarely seen you do."

"That says more about your spies than about me. I'm familiar with your world."

"With all of it? I'd think that some cities' skies would be...unpalatable to Skyknights."

"Most." Soran scowled. "But do tell me what it is you're dancing around, Senator."

"Very well." Derell's fingers twitched against the table. "Our sources tell me you paid a visit to the Molten Belt recently. Specifically, Dis."

Soran chuckled. "I go where I please."

"I'm sure. But tell me: what business does Aerix have with a city of violent thugs?"

"Malek the Destroyer called me there."

Derell winced. Soran studied him—the shifting of the fingers, the rapid blinking of the eyes. Had he expected to hear that answer, or had it surprised him? Soran couldn't tell, and not being sure intrigued him.

He opened his mouth wide in a parody of an engaging smile. "I was curious, so I met with him. That hardly makes me your enemy. Still, your little garrison in Corian suggests that perhaps you think I am."

"Some of my colleagues do. I'm not one for jumping to conclusions." Derell spread his arms wide. "Not about a city like Aerix. I'd hate to see it threatened just because a few other Senators feel uneasy."

"It's good to hear that some in the Senate have cooler heads than others."

"But I can't convince them to stop rattling their sabers without a reason. So give me a reason to help you, Soran. What exactly is the king of the barbarians after?"

King of the Barbarians. Soran couldn't mask his grin. It suited Malek perfectly. And the pompous brute would hate it.

He thought of Malek's body, thick with muscle. Some of it came from alterations, but the Seraph felt sure the rest came from old-fashioned sweat. Malek liked the old ways, if his fascination with history was any indication.

But he certainly didn't look like he'd stepped out of a legend. He cropped his dark hair close for the fights—practical, not patrician. Those fights had scarred him, had tanned and toughened his brown skin. He looked more suited to the factories than to palaces. Even the pale imitations of palaces he might someday build in Dis.

Lines creased his forehead and brows, testifying to the harsh environment in Dis, but also to his long career in the pits. Most of Dis's gladiators died young. The smart ones lasted long enough to retire, and did so once aging slowed them down past what modifications could correct.

Malek hadn't bothered to smooth out his flaws, however attractive it would have made him. His brows were too thick, for one. Still, the dark lines they created accentuated the black irises. Probably the only feature Malek had ever altered.

As imperfect as the rest of his face was, Soran had to admit that the dark eyes stood out against it. And the tight set of his mouth was almost elegant. Soran had heard Malek laugh, seen him smirk, watched him frown or smile. But the mouth barely moved, its edges tilting up or down. It looked like the mouth of a statue, cold and immense and untouchable. Even wreathed as it was by the steely gray of poorly-shaved stubble.

"King of the Barbarians, indeed." Soran licked his lips. "Did you know that his followers call him 'Lord'?"

Derell's eyes widened. "No one has used a title like that in generations. We've made sure of it." He blinked. "Er...no one outside of present company, I mean."

"No offense taken. My title is 'Seraph,' not 'Lord.'" Soran slid a hand under the table and pulled one of his blades from his boot. Then he held it up to the light, making sure that Derell saw it.

Seeing him tense, Soran threw it into the air. It shimmered as it rose and fell, the sunlight glinting off of it.

Soran waited. Then he moved, so quickly his visitor could hardly follow the movement. His fingers curled unerringly around the hilt of his blade.

Derell stared. Soran smirked. He held the knife for a moment and then slowly turned it, leaving its point hanging just above the surface of the ornate table.

"The Destroyer's pets are quite loyal," he said, as if nothing out of the ordinary had happened. "Though I think the woman who went for me had more brawn than brains."

"Woman?" prompted Derell, his gaze still fixed on the blade.

Soran tilted his head. Her gender mattered? Or was this fool driving at something else? Soran toyed with his dagger a moment, tossing and catching it, thinking. A *pack of bureaucrats, in love with their own stagnation.*

He frowned. Damn Malek's words for worming their way into his mind. And damn the voice he heard them in, too measured and even to belong to a mere savage. Where had he learned to speak like that?

Soran gripped the hilt of his knife. Its smooth solidity reassured him. "Dark brown skin, heavily modified, clearly a pit fighter. Almost as big as her 'Lord' the Destroyer. I'm afraid I didn't look more closely than that."

Derell relaxed into his chair. "Do you follow the pit fights?"

"You're a fan of the arena bouts? And here I thought the Senate was desperate to close it down."

"A fan? Hardly. But I do pay attention to what my enemies are doing."

"Wise enough." He tossed the dagger idly from hand to hand. "So what do you know about this fool who threatened me?"

"Nothing. Not for certain. But a few years ago, the arena's up-and-coming star was a woman, Vareth the Crusher. Dark skin, broad build. Muscular to start with, and modifications made her even bigger. Big enough to start rumors that she spent her winnings on growing ever larger."

Soran snickered. "Possible. She was hideous." Not like Malek, who at least understood proportions. "But what does that have to do with me?"

"I'm getting to that."

Soran scowled.

"Vareth's rise in the pits was meteoric. Few matched her raw power. Or her skill."

Too big to overpower, Soran could see. But skilled?

"After only a year, she won against legends who'd lasted far longer. She fought the arena's best so often and so consistently that everyone expected she would face Malek someday."

"If she had, she would have died."

Derell's scowl matched Soran's. "Probably. As I said, I don't follow the fights."

"Of course you don't," Soran cooed. "But when I visited Dis, she was very much alive. Serving as a security guard. Hardly a job for the arena's best."

"Not quite. Think, Soran. You're a trained fighter in a world where peace has lasted for generations, thanks to the tireless efforts of the Senate."

A pack of bureaucrats, in love with their own stagnation.

If Derell noticed Soran's silence, he gave no sign. "The only other warriors left are our soldiers and his gladiators. You're the leader of the Skyknights. Do you really think he entrusted escorting you through Dis to one of the Arena's security guards?"

"Point taken. But Malek fancies himself a warlord, cut from the cloth of the Old Empire." Soran pursed his lips. "What use would he have for someone who refused to face him?"

"I'm not saying he forgave her, Seraph. I'm saying he spared her."

Now that was interesting. Soran leaned forward. "A rising star in the pits, at the height of her fame, disappears. And shows up again at Malek's right hand."

"Precisely."

Soran threw back his head and laughed.

"He's recruiting, Seraph," said Derell. "A hand-picked fighting force, made up of the best gladiators in his ring."

"And how did you find that out?"

"We've known Malek's been doing this for years. We've even compiled a list." Derell drew a small tablet from a pocket. He tapped it and its screen flared with light.

He slid it across the table to Soran, who picked it up and touched a finger to it. Names slid by, the glyphs shifting. Names, scrolling aside to reveal each fighter's epithet in the arena and then switching back again. The Crusher. The Silent. The Fearless.

The list wasn't long. Not for someone who expected trouble. But it was a start. Soran's fingers curled over the tablet, greedy and possessive. "Is this all of them?"

"No. But the arena has plenty of victors, and it's impossible to know who's left and who's died. Especially if Malek is trying to make sure we don't find out."

"And you want me to help you find out."

"No."

Soran frowned.

"Asking who they are is petty, Seraph. We'd never come to you with something so insignificant."

"Then what do you want?"

"'Who' doesn't matter. Not really. 'Why' matters."

"And you don't know why, do you?" Soran crowed. "You know he loathes you. Anyone can see that. But you don't know what he has in mind."

Derell winced. "No. We don't."

"And you think I do." Soran laid his blade on the table, drawing his thin fingers away from it with an exaggerated, slow motion. This was fascinating. And more useful than he had expected.

"We think you do. Or better said, we think you will, if he keeps confiding in you."

"Confiding in me? He wants something from me. Wants something from Aerix. That doesn't mean I know his plans."

Derell's hands tightened into fists. "Maybe not." He glared at Soran, and then smoothed his face into a calm, benign smile. "But he does want something from you."

Soran splayed his fingers on the table, near the hilt of his blade. "And if he hopes to get it, he'll have to reveal something."

"Exactly." Derell's smile looked more sincere now. And hungrier.

"We argued during my visit. I think I disappointed the pompous fool. But he did want me to think things over." Soran laughed. "I'll go back, and inform him that I have."

He lifted his hand from the table and extended it to his visitor. Derell shook it. "You do realize that what I can do for you depends on what you bring back to us."

"Of course." His smirk never wavering, Soran pulled his hand back. He picked up his dagger, ostensibly to put it away.

The hilt in his hand felt infinitely better than the sweat on Derell's palm. Clean and real and like holding it completed his hand, his wrist, his arm. He closed his eyes, letting himself exult in it.

He remembered the feeling of resistance as his blade sliced through skin, the bright line it scored in a sinewy arm, thicker than any he'd seen here in his home city. He remembered the red of the blood as it filled the cut and spilled over in testament to his triumph.

The Destroyer had struck first, but Soran had drawn first blood.

"Then—then we have a deal," Derell said, his voice faltering.

Soran opened his eyes. The light in Derell's iridescent eyes brought him back from the memory he'd lost himself in. Back from the dim, choked air of a faraway city to the place where he belonged. From the Destroyer's home and the darkness that wreathed it to the tall windows of his meeting room and the blue expanse of sky beyond. To the sunlight streaming in, yellow fire on the metal of the ornate windowpanes.

"We do." He stood, fixing Derell with an intense stare. *Now leave.*

"Excellent. I won't keep you. I know that the Skyknights value their privacy and their solitude."

"We do," Soran said again, the smile still plastered on his face. "But your visit has been useful. For both of us. And I hope you've enjoyed yourself." He turned to the window, looked out at the expanse of sky and clouds and the silver streaks of his Skyknights' starships as they zoomed by overhead.

Derell's gaze followed his. He walked to the window and stood near its edge. For a brief moment Soran had the wild thought of pushing him out and of calling Malek to brag about it.

But nothing is that simple. He imagined Malek's dark eyes, glinting with triumph. *Not even for those who commit themselves to fairy tales.*

Besides, he still didn't know which side would win.

"Enjoyed myself? Of course I have," Derell said, still gazing out the window. "When the time comes, contact me using the pad I gave you. The communication link there is heavily encrypted."

"I will." *Now get out of here.*

"Very well. Farewell, Seraph of Aerix. I am sure my colleagues in the Senate will be glad to hear that Aerix has, in its own way, seen fit to join with us at last."

Soran's smile twisted into a scowl. The hand that held the blade trembled against the sudden hot impulse to strike. *You are the greatest of the Skyknights. You're faster than anyone in Aerix. Faster than anyone on this planet. A politician like Derell won't even see it coming.*

"You'll have what you want," Soran ground out, forcing his hand to stillness again. "And I'll have what I want—once your pack of soldiers is out of Corian."

"Understood. I'll do everything I can for you, Seraph." The iridescent eyes glittered. "Your city truly is remarkable."

Because scum like you hasn't touched it.

Derell stepped toward the door at last. Soran sighed with relief behind his back.

The doors slid shut with a hiss. Soran picked up the tablet, scrolled through names and epithets. He tapped the screen again and a picture of Derell appeared. Glyphs brightened and darkened again, showing the communication link.

Soran tucked the tablet away in a pocket. It radiated heat, hummed close against his skin.

It would prove useful, no matter what he decided to do with it.

CHAPTER THREE

MALEK STOOD at a large table in the center of a room high above his arena. On the table, a massive hologram swirled, glowing molten-flame orange and crimson.

All of Dis lay mapped out in front of him. Every factory and foundry and business and home, every council hall and tall warehouse, every seedy bar and secret place that had long ago been transformed into a training hall for the arena complex, gleaming red-bright in the center of the city.

The room could hold large numbers of people, the table big enough for several to stand or walk around it. Tiered rows of seats ringed it, allowing many more a clear view of the hologram. Consoles glowed on the surface of the table, within easy reach of the seats. A few taps of a finger could rotate the hologram map, magnify parts of it, or even switch the display to another city entirely. Aerix, Corian, Feris. Even the Senate's capitol city, Delen, its domes rendered in unearthly green.

But for now, only Malek studied the projection. The great councils of war would come later. Right now, Malek was thinking. Thinking and waiting.

He looked down at the low ring that made up the Grand Arena. Buildings rose around it, housing everything from the gladiators and their medics to the security Malek had long since entrusted only to his own.

Not to his little set of victors. He would have had them supervise the pits if there had been enough of them. But even now, there were too few. Still, most remained here, some altered beyond recognition, some hidden in plain sight, overseeing the workings of the pits or the crowds that gathered in them.

It was beautiful. Or at least, it was now, presented in glowing miniature in front of him. The once-perfect order had been lost, lost with the technology that had died with the Old Empire.

Once, Dis's factories had built everything an army might need. Armor that only the strongest blades could pierce. Blades whose edges never dulled, built of light metal whose alloy had long been lost to time.

Or so the histories said. Malek shook his head, walked around the table, studied the hologram from all angles. So few of the old records remained. He couldn't always tell what was real and what was exaggeration, the scribes of an ancient civilization waxing poetic about the might of the greatest army the galaxy had known.

But some things still remained. Some people in Dis still built arms and armor, and Malek had no doubt those old descriptions in the histories showed why. And the Senate's forces still needed such things, even in their fabled new era of peace.

Malek scoffed. A bright new age, indeed. A peace bought with the silence of the warriors. Changed. Altered. Stunted. Fighting in the only place left to them: his arena.

Gladiators needed weapons too, and Dis's factories were still the best place to get them. They built everything, from hovercars to tables, and sold them across a planet that had once been theirs.

Malek stared. *How far we've fallen.*

The door behind him buzzed, a staticky chime. He recognized the note and waved.

At his signal, the doors thudded open.

"Kenn," he said. "Come in." He turned to face the newcomer, a young man whose lanky build shared more with the Skyknights of Aerix than the fighters in the pits.

The resemblance ended there. Kenn didn't stand nearly as tall as a Skyknight. And although his body had been altered almost as extensively as one of Aerix's warriors, it wasn't obvious. He'd needed those alterations for a far more private reason.

Malek's gaze flicked over to Kenn's legs. No trace remained of the damage an enemy's mace had done on that last fateful fight in the arena. Malek had to admit it was impressive. They'd even erased any visible scars.

But no reconstruction was perfect. Kenn could stand, walk, and even run, but he'd never return to the arena. Malek could see the damage when Kenn ran. The slight dragging movement of one leg behind the other, the faint twist as he moved.

Oh, he might survive to win a few more fights; agility wasn't everything. But someday his injury would slow him down just enough to prove his undoing. And Malek hadn't saved him just to watch him die five matches later.

He'd won that last match thanks to two things. One, a blade hidden in a pocket of his armor. Two, the best of his inventions, a metal helmet he'd worn in the pits and out of it.

He still wore the helmet, even though it made him easily identifiable. He made sure no one saw him by keeping to his lab near the arena, designing weapons and traps, and never leaving the grounds if he could help it.

Malek doubted he could physically remove the helmet. It followed the shape of his skull exactly, shimmering quicksilver where his hair should have been. A visor covered his eyes, golden and as close to mirror-shiny as anything could be in Dis. Only the line of his mouth showed his expression.

He could retract the visor, and usually did when meeting with his lord. Seeing it now, Malek frowned. "Kenn. You have information for me?"

"Yes, my Lord. There's something you should see." He turned away from Malek and tilted his head. Light streamed from his visor and projected an image in the center of the room, golden where Malek's hologram was orange.

Malek recognized a starfighter, sleek and pointed. It swooped across the far wall in a honey-golden blur, too large now for his city-hologram, but shrinking as it grew nearer, fitting itself to the city.

"That's a Skyknight's ship," Malek said.

"Yes, my Lord, it is."

"So our friend the Seraph did decide to come back."

"That isn't his ship. It's a standard fighter, used by low-ranking pilots."

Malek stepped toward the wall and stretched a hand toward the hologram. It froze as he approached, enlarging again as he traced its contours.

He saw at once that Kenn was right. The sleek ship bore no adornment, and only the standard wing-symbol of Aerix City on the side. Plain and anonymous. The sort of ship that patrolled Aerix's sky by the hundreds.

Hiding, Soran? Malek watched the light of the hologram swirl. "Then he doesn't want anyone noticing he's coming."

Kenn's visor slid aside with a hiss. Malek turned to look at him, studying his unobscured face. The thick black brows—the only clue to the color of Kenn's hair—creased in concentration. A frown twisted the deep pink lips. "It's my job to notice."

Kenn's eyes shifted in his sockets. His gaze alighted on the bright red line cutting a jagged path from Malek's shoulder to elbow. Medics had stitched up the wound, but Malek had refused any treatments that would speed the healing.

Or minimize the scarring.

Malek rotated his shoulders, feeling the injury itch, and looked back at Kenn. Caught, Kenn stared back for a moment. Then his eyes moved and he looked straight ahead, his expression smoothing.

Had someone told Kenn what Soran had done? He hadn't been present at that meeting. Vareth, perhaps. He frowned. He would have to remind her to keep quiet, even when provoked.

But Kenn had always been observant. It took cleverness and intelligence to win in the pits even after an opponent shattered your legs.

The corner of Malek's mouth turned up. If someone had cut open his arm in the pits, Kenn would have known about it. And while tempers in Dis ran short both in the arena and out of it, no one would attack the Destroyer himself. Not unless they wanted scars or worse.

Which made the source of Malek's scar obvious. Especially since Malek had recently started to wear a light, ornate dagger in one of his armbands. A dagger that clearly hadn't come from Dis. Whose silvery surface was steadily dulling to a soot-stained gray.

"That's not the Seraph's ship," Malek said. "But I think he's flying it, all the same."

Kenn nodded again. "But he hasn't contacted you. Unless you heard from him privately and didn't tell us."

Didn't tell them? There were plenty of people he wouldn't tell. He didn't need the staff of the pits gossiping about it. Or the City Council, bustling to welcome a visiting dignitary. All that would make his dealings with Aerix entirely too obvious.

And the Council could never handle Soran anyway. Malek snickered.

But Malek's elite were a different story. They heard every speech he gave to the masses who flocked to the pits eager for blood and excitement. They knew exactly what every word meant. "Chose not to tell you? You, of all people? The first of my chosen? The eyes and ears of my army?"

Kenn said nothing. He only returned Malek's gaze, never flinching, never blinking.

Vareth isn't the only one who dislikes you, Prince of the Air.

Malek walked over to the table and pretended to be closely interested in his hologram. For a long moment, he gazed at the ember-bright city, staring into the flames at its heart. Then he looked up, as if the thought had just occurred to him. The hologram's light glowed red against his skin. "Welcome him."

"Welcome him?"

"Anything he wants, ensure that he gets."

"But my Lord—"

Malek waited, a rumble of discontent the only sound he made.

Kenn's eyes moved to Malek's wound again. "I thought that you would want to welcome Soran yourself." The visor slid over his eyes, a golden shield, covering his emotions too late.

Malek looked at his reflection in the mirrored glass. He moved one of his arms, watching the dagger Soran had left behind shimmer as it caught the light. "I'm sure that's what he expects. A Skyknight's ship would never go unnoticed."

"You think he wants you to notice him."

"He's the one in that ship," Malek said again. He spread his arms wide, relishing the sting in his wound.

"But why would he hide?"

"I asked him to consider my offer. To contact me once he'd made his decision. Instead he hides. He's looking for something." Malek opened his hand and then closed it, clenching it tight. "Let him find it."

"My Lord? Are you sure that's wise? He never promised us an alliance."

Malek looked over at Kenn, at the bright metal covering his head and the dulled, once-shiny mesh of his bodysuit, half clothing and half armor. Metal plates lay atop some of it, protecting vital targets. A band of metal adorned his left shoulder, bearing a crimson circle. The device marked him as one of the Arena staff.

His legs, shattered and rebuilt, lay hidden and secret beneath a layer of mesh. In the light of a city like Aerix or the Senate's capitol, it would have glittered as he moved.

Kenn's victory had come at a high price. But his opponent had died first, thanks to Kenn's hidden weapon and his helmet's perfect aim. Malek had waited only long enough to officially announce Kenn the winner. He'd ordered his medics to save Kenn even as they'd carted the combatants' bodies off the arena sands.

If he dies, you die, Malek had said.

Stabilizing Kenn had taken a day. Rebuilding his body had taken weeks.

And when he'd finally awoken, the first thing he'd seen had been Malek's face. Malek had made sure of that.

He took a step toward Kenn now. "Do you remember when you pledged yourself to me?"

The visor slid upward with a hiss. Kenn's naturally dark eyes locked with Malek's altered ones. "You saved my life. You rebuilt my body. I could do nothing else." He looked down at himself. "I thought you wanted me for the pits."

"That would have been a waste. I had a better use for you."

"I expected to fight for you. To draw crowds. To invent weapons and use them in the arena. Instead, you pulled me from the pits and gave me a place here."

"Where you became my eyes and ears," Malek rumbled, a rough, contented purr.

Kenn inclined his head. A small movement, but from Kenn, one as formal as a bow. "It is an honor I can only hope to deserve."

Malek paused a long moment, studying Kenn's face. Then he walked over to the table, beckoning for Kenn to follow. "A greater destiny. Not only for you and for those I've chosen, Kenn." He spread out his hands, indicating the hologram of the city. "For all who would see their world reborn."

Kenn nodded. "When the time comes, all of Dis will take up our banner. All of the Molten Belt will stand with us. Will fight alongside us. For you."

"For themselves," Malek corrected. "With all the fury the Senate subdued. That is only right. That alone will give them what they truly deserve. But I want more than their rage."

"My Lord—you yourself have said—"

He raised a hand. Kenn fell silent. "They will remember what it means to fight. But that history is generations old, and there are only so many of them. A few thousand newly minted warriors won't retake a planet."

"Retake a planet." Kenn looked down at the hologram.

He reached one hand to his left shoulder and tapped at the metal plate there. Light gleamed from the spot where his hand had touched it, the ring symbol of the arena shining first fiery red, then cold, bluish white. The curve of the glowing symbol straightened, shifting into a single, straight vertical line. A point flared out at the top of it and formed a stylized spearhead, pointed straight upward.

Then the symbol darkened, as if the city's smoke had stained the metal black.

Long ago, Malek had taken the spearhead symbol as his mark. He'd worn it as a symbol on his armor, a stylized version of the first glyph of his name.

Other fighters used symbols too, particularly people who fought in teams. But Malek had taken a useful tool and made it something else entirely.

Kenn pressed his hand to his shoulder-plate again. The symbol flared white as it bent into its circle shape. The light dimmed to a fiery red before fading, leaving the arena's crimson ring behind.

"I am with you until the end, my Lord. All of us are. But from what I hear, Soran insulted you. Harmed you, if I am right about where your wound came from." His mouth set in an unforgiving line. "The Seraph is a formidable fighter. And I understand the advantage that the Skyknights would give us, should they ally with us. But we're yours. The Skyknights are not."

Malek chuckled. He turned from his red city to the amber starfighter on the wall. "The people of Aerix are our kin. When the time comes, he will remember that."

"My Lord." Kenn's voice was quiet. "I wish I could believe you. But this—I cannot understand it." He slid his visor over his face again. Its hiss filled the silence between them.

Then Kenn shook his head, a barely perceptible motion. In a surge of gold, the hologram of the Skyknight's starfighter winked out.

Malek looked at the empty space and thought of Soran. Of the slight body in his arms as he tightened his grip around it. Of the slim fingers, clenched into claws, digging into his open wound, desperate and cruel. Of the artificial blue of his eyes, overbright and glittering, garish and precious all at once.

Malek stepped over to Kenn. He wrapped a hand around Kenn's chin, as he had Soran's, only a few short weeks ago. "The Molten Belt will rise to my call when the time comes. But they are not enough. Not to root out the cancer eating at the core of our world."

"There must be another way. There will be others who rise with us, once we reveal the truth. There will be—"

"I don't want blind obedience," Malek said, his voice cold. "I want warriors. The best of the pits. Victors serve with their eyes open. But I didn't save you to see you defy me. Not when so much depends on securing this alliance."

Kenn was silent a long moment. Then he lowered his head in another formal nod. "He gets everything he wants. But I will have him watched."

Malek nodded and let go of Kenn's chin. "Of course. If you didn't suggest it—if you didn't insist on it—you would not be the man I saved all those years ago."

The visor hid Kenn's eyes and brows, but Malek saw one of his lips twitch. "Understood. He goes anywhere he likes, then. But nowhere without an escort. Or at least a spy."

Malek smirked. "No. Not quite. He goes nowhere without one of us."

"He knows about us?"

"No. I told him only enough to ensure he would come back." Malek looked at the hologram, imagining how Soran would look standing here beside him, alight with its red glow. He looked back up at Kenn, studying his own reflection's scars in the visor's mirror. "But it serves our ends. I want to show him where he belongs. What better way to do that than to surround him?"

"Indeed, my Lord," Kenn answered, his tone as formal as ever. "We'll shadow him without you, and inform you of anything worth noting." He leaned closer. "My team and I will miss nothing."

"I expect nothing less."

The first of my chosen. And the greatest, however broken his body once was. Unless someone else arises to surpass him.

Malek thought of Soran's thick lips and sarcastic smile. Of the feeling of his thin body when he'd wrapped his arms around it. And the hands, sharp, clawed as a bird of prey, digging into his wound, pain blossoming in the flesh as it tore and tore.

He closed his eyes. *You will come to me, Seraph of Aerix. As surely as this world will burn.*

Kenn cleared his throat with a faint, polite cough.

Malek opened his eyes again. "Go. Prepare for him."

He looked over at his wound, the edges of his mouth curling upward as he stared at the angry pink line of flesh. "He'll come looking for me soon enough."

CHAPTER FOUR

MALEK'S PEOPLE met Soran as soon as he landed. He stepped out of the borrowed craft to find them converging on him. And others staring, eyes bright with curiosity or cold distrust. How long had they been staring, waiting for his craft to touch down?

He pulled off his helmet, looking from one to the other long enough to realize that Malek wasn't among them. He shook out his hair and hissed. He'd felt sure that Malek would come, if only to snarl at him for not bothering to say he was coming.

But apparently Malek had other ideas. *Waiting for me to play by your rules, Lord of the Pits?* Soran smirked at the people moving toward him.

They didn't rush. All three moved with a purposeful stride someone from outside Aerix might even have called graceful.

Or perhaps you're playing along. Soran waved at them.

The smallest of the three led the group. He had a leaner frame than most gladiators. Still, Soran recognized him from the tight helmet clinging to his head and the golden visor over his eyes.

Soran couldn't remember his name. He'd studied Derell's list for a week now, poring over names and epithets. But remembering the specifics had gotten complicated fast. And even if he did remember them, it might not matter. Malek's little cadre of victors could easily change their names—and their bodies. Derell's little database offered no guarantees.

But a helmet like that wasn't something even a man with a new body could easily hide.

Hiding in plain sight, then. Soran favored him with a smirk and a nod. Was he just too arrogant to bother covering his tracks? Or was that helmet so important he'd take the chance that someone would notice him?

"My name is Kenn." He walked over to Soran and extended a hand. "Lord Malek sent me to welcome you, Skyknight."

Skyknight. Not "Seraph." Did that mean Kenn didn't recognize him? Malek would, but he'd decided not to show up. Who had he sent instead, and how clever was he?

Soran shook the hand Kenn offered. "I was told he'd come himself."

Kenn frowned. "He has the arena to oversee, and a bout of his own to prepare for. Had the Seraph announced your coming, he might have met with you."

"Fine," Soran snapped. "I have better things to do than dance attendance on a gladiator."

The others looked from Kenn to Soran and then back at one another. Then they stepped closer.

"The City Council sent us," said one, a man, gracing Soran with precisely the kind of smile Soran would have given him if he weren't so irritated by the news.

The woman beside him smiled as well. "Welcome. I'm Tena, and this is my brother Tor."

Glad for the moment to recover, Soran extended his hand to whichever of the two felt like taking it. "Eran," he said. The name belonged to a low-ranked Skyknight who had similar red hair. *Let's see if that fools anyone.*

The pair had paler skin than Kenn. The soot clinging to everything made it look ashen and gray. They had pale hair as well, a white-blond that fell to their shoulders, framing faces bearing matching smiles. Their eyes were the washed-out slate that passed for blue anywhere but Aerix.

Twins? Soran wondered. The resemblance seemed uncanny even if they were. They looked identical, despite one being a man and one a woman.

Alterations? Fashion? He couldn't tell. He ran through the list of victors in his mind, trying to place them. But he didn't recall any siblings on Derell's list. Which only made sense. What brother would want to face his sister in the Destroyer's death pits?

They stood taller than Kenn. Their bodies had the thick, well-muscled weight of fighters. Soran thought of what the Senator had said to him, mere weeks ago, about one of Malek's winners: *I'm saying he spared her.*

Were these two victors as well? Was that what Malek had spared them: the unthinkable possibility that someday they'd face each other in a fight only one could survive?

They all owe you, don't they, Lord of the Pits?

Or maybe these two weren't part of Malek's elite. Maybe the City Council had sent them tagging along behind Malek's representative because someone had to.

It didn't really matter, either way. From what Soran had heard, the City Council couldn't do so much as declare a holiday without the gladiators' approval anyway.

"Eran." The man's lip quirked. "You say the Seraph sent you?"

Soran grinned. "He did. But if the Destroyer isn't available for now, I might as well explore."

"If you care to visit the arena," Kenn said, his voice cold, "you have only to ask."

You have only to ask. Ask for what? For seats to an event, or for an audience with the man who ran the pits?

"Of course." Soran frowned, feigning offense. This could prove useful. It would give him time to explore the city, both the arena and the rest of it. To see whether the rest of the people here felt the same bitterness toward the Senate as the man who ran the pits.

And what they knew, if anything, about what Malek and his elite had in mind.

Soran looked straight at Kenn and spoke in as affected a voice as he could. "Surely that's not the only thing to do around here."

Kenn's lips twitched. Just as quickly, they smoothed themselves to stillness again. Soran waited, hoping that Kenn's next words would betray his emotions. But he said nothing at all.

"Of course there's more to do in Dis than that!" said Tena, stepping in front of Kenn. "We would be glad to show you around."

I'm sure you would. But don't be so transparent about keeping an eye on me. "That won't be necessary. I'm sure I can find my way around easily enough."

"At least allow us to show you to some decent lodgings," Kenn put in. "We had something prepared, in case the Seraph chose to visit."

Soran raised an eyebrow. That was new. It seemed the lord of the arena couldn't decide whether to irritate or flatter him.

"Lead the way," he said.

The room was clearly meant for him.

It wasn't fancy. At least not by Soran's standards.

The metal walls were thick, better suited to a barracks than a luxurious apartment. Or to one of the city's famous factories. The window looked out over a black, grimy sky and squat buildings. Their lights shone yellow and orange, feeble candles lit against the smog.

But for Dis? Malek had outdone himself. Twists of metal laced the window's frame and curled around the furniture. Soran had never seen anything from Dis decorated that way, and he could guess what inspired it.

How much did that cost you, Lord of the Pits? And how foolish would you feel if I really had sent one of my Skyknights instead of coming here myself?

He walked toward a mirror set against one wall. Compared to the flourishes of thin metal he was used to, the mock-filigree here looked blocky and thick. Still, it had clearly been crafted with care.

The designers had laced the curling designs with small lights. They glimmered blue, winking from the space between the swirls, as if the craftsmen had captured tiny slivers of a brighter sky and woven them into the pattern.

With a pang, Soran turned away. *You're not supposed to make me miss the sky.*

He turned away, toward the bed. It looked hard and uncomfortable. But the factory workers in this city probably slept on slabs of wood or metal. Once again, Malek had outdone himself.

The sheets on the bed were a pale gray. Discolored by the ubiquitous dirt? Or would anything too white dirty too quickly? Threads of pale blue wove through the fabric as well, and the bedspread glimmered, likewise iridescent.

You do know it's me. Soran reached out a hand to touch the bedspread. It felt rough, harsher than the cloth of his home, but that was only to be expected. *If I had sent someone else, he never would have seen this.*

He turned, suddenly alert. If Malek had this room prepared for him, no doubt he'd filled it with hidden cameras. He thought of the tablet tucked into his flight suit and frowned. He'd have to be especially careful about looking at it.

Which meant no looking up the twins. At least not here.

Still frowning, he moved into the bathroom, looked at himself in another mirror. This one took up nearly the whole of one wall. *All of this to win an ally in a war you want to start. Fine things. Not arms or armor or strategic support.*

He took one of the soaps from its dish and turned it around in his hand. It was rough, grit embedded in it to help scrub away the grime of the city. He raised it to his nose and sniffed, pursing his lips at the caustic scent of cleaners and the faint fragrance that couldn't mask it.

I'll smell like chemicals. And I'll only go back out into the dirt anyway. He cursed, scowling. Then he peeled off his flight suit, slowly and deliberately, staring straight into the mirror and smirking. For whose benefit, he couldn't guess. Probably not Malek's. Probably some lackey he'd assigned to keep an eye on his visitor. Maybe even Kenn.

He laughed, thinking of the mirror-bright visor. Of the eyes on him at the starport, shining with hunger. Licking his lips, he ran his hands down his sides and pouted in blatant invitation.

Whether Malek was watching or not, he'd hear about it. And an angry follower appalled by his display served his ends almost as well. His eyes glinting with mockery, he gazed at his reflection for a moment longer.

Then he turned away, walked into the shower, and turned on the water.

Just a few minutes after he'd arrived in the lobby, the twins had appeared to collect him. That meant something, no doubt, but Soran hadn't minded. Their sudden appearance gave him a way to avoid someone.

A woman had stared at him from the moment he stepped into the room. He'd stared back and her lips had pulled back in a sudden smile, nothing at all like the look she'd been giving him before that. She'd looked him over, and her mouth had twisted in a parody of a lascivious grin.

Whatever she wanted, he had no interest in giving it to her.

He'd asked the twins to take him out for dinner and drinks. He'd rejected their first suggestion. He didn't want them to impress him. As entertaining as it would be to let half the city wine and dine him, he'd come here to find out more than their fine things could tell him.

And therefore: this place, a gloomy bar the twins had told him the gladiators favored, pyramid-shaped, its walls covered with scratched videoscreens replaying highlights of various arena matches. Soran could barely hear them; so as not to compete with one another, they all played at low volume, audible only to those sitting nearby. Captions glowed below the screens.

The bar's patrons had been busy nursing drinks, watching bouts, arguing. But when Soran walked in, they turned. He caught whispers. One man wondered why he was here. Another said he didn't care, as long as he could keep staring.

A small crowd gathered around one monitor, projecting Malek's face.

Of course.

Soran walked toward them, feeling eyes on him from all directions. He'd worn the least flashy outfit he'd brought with him, but he had no way of hiding his slim build or his height.

"What are you doing here?" said a gray-haired man with a burly frame and scarred face. One arm ended at the elbow, and a metallic contraption jutted from the stump, half prosthesis and half weapon. With a whir and click of gears, it shifted, a blade peeking from the tip.

It wasn't quite a threat, not yet. Not when the blade hadn't locked into place. It twitched with its wielder's indecision. "Slumming,

Skyknight?"

Soran flashed the man a smile. "I'm sure I don't know what you mean."

The twins stepped in front of him. "He's welcome here for now," Tena said.

His mouth twisted into a snarl. "Fake little creature. What makes you think you can talk to me?" The prosthesis clicked, its blade locking into place. Soran's hand slid down toward his boot.

The old man shook his head, his weapon sliding back into its place with a metallic hiss. "Fine," he growled and trudged away.

The tension broken, the others drifted away too. The twins guided him into a far corner and sat down. He slid into a seat beside them and waited as they ordered drinks for themselves and for him.

"Thank you. I appreciate your help."

"Don't mention it," snapped Tor.

Soran took a careful sip of his drink, a bright orange liquid swirled with red. It burned as it went down. He coughed as delicately as he could, but the bright heat in his stomach wasn't bad at all.

He looked at the twins' impassive faces. This silence did nothing to further his aims. "Our visored friend isn't with us tonight. Not a fan of the rabble, or busy with something else?"

Tor shrugged. "Who knows what the Destroyer has him doing?"

"We don't pay attention to that." Tena scowled at one of the nearby monitors.

Malek's face filled it. His thick brows knotted in anger or concentration. Soran could catch only snippets of what he said, but watched the captions as they scrolled by.

"...and remember that this is more than entertainment. Some in this world would have us forget our strength. Our muscles, they tell us, are for toil. Our minds, for the work of building the things they need. But do any of them test themselves against us? The pits are beneath them, they say. But are they superior, or are they hiding?"

"That sounds more like politics than commentary on a sporting event." Soran forced a chuckle.

Tena's eyes narrowed. She leaned over and spoke in a low voice, barely audible over the noise of the bar. "Which would be why we made sure Helmet Head didn't come with us."

"Oh? How did you manage to convince him to stay behind? He seems...difficult to distract."

Offhand as he'd tried to be, the remark earned him two gray stares.

"Who knows? Malek doesn't let him out much," Tor said.

Soran glanced around. People drifted away from their tables and their arguments and gathered in front of the videoscreen. A few growled their approval in the harsh dialect of the pits.

And nearby, Soran could see a familiar figure, all knotted, dark muscle. She lifted her head, stared pointedly in his direction, and turned back to the monitors.

Vareth. Gazing worshipfully at her lord, no doubt. *And where were you when that fool threatened me?*

Not that it matters. Keep your secrets. I can always trick them out of you later.

He turned back to the twins. What had they been discussing? *Kenn.* "No, I don't imagine Malek does let him out much. Not with that thing on his head. Not unless he wants everyone to recognize him."

As quickly as they'd tensed, the twins relaxed, their mouths curling into pale half-smiles. They volunteered nothing more.

"But what about the two of you?" Soran asked. "Are you gladiators too?"

Tena snorted. "Not likely. Do you think everyone in this city is in the Destroyer's pocket?"

"Then you've never fought in the arena?" he pressed, leaning in.

"We didn't say that. Everyone does it once or twice." Tor tilted his head toward the monitor. "This is Dis. Who wouldn't want to be 'the mightiest in this world'?"

"There's also those winnings." Tena grinned. "But there's a difference between all that and—"

"And belonging here." Soran nodded. "Understood."

Those winnings? What did she use them for? It wasn't much of a lead. You could do anything with money. Soran frowned.

The twins were still talking, something about too few opportunities to fight as a team. Soran stood up and excused himself, just to see if they would object. But they nodded and let him go.

Soran sauntered over to the crowd near the monitor. He didn't bother to stay scarce. He had nothing to be nervous about now, not with the twins protecting him and Vareth half-watching out for him from the other corner.

"Maybe we ought to prove to them we are strong," a dark-haired man was saying.

"How exactly do you want us do that?" another shot back.

"He's just talking," said a familiar voice. Soran raised his head to see the man who'd threatened him spit on the ground. "He and that fool on the video feed both."

Belligerent, aren't you? Soran walked up to the man's table. "You seem unimpressed," He gave the man another of his widest smiles.

The man's blade clicked restlessly in its place in his prosthesis, and he cast a baleful glance at the twins. "If you're here to gawk at us, go do it in the stands. If you're here to laugh at him—" he waved at the screen with a flash of metal—"you can do that from home, too."

"Maybe I'm here because I want to know."

A cheer rose from the group around them. Apparently Malek had finished his speech. And apparently they'd appreciated it.

All but the man Soran was talking to. His face twisted in anger. He glared at the crowd. At the monitor, the crimson circle of the Arena logo flaring and fading to black.

"I thought everyone liked Malek the Destroyer," Soran pressed.

"We're fighters," the man said. "Fighters and builders. If he remembered that, I'd have no problem with him. Instead—" The metal-tipped arm swept wide. "The hell with them. All of them." He lowered his hand and looked at Soran. "And you, too."

"I understand wanting to be left alone."

The bladed arm waved at a chair.

Soran ignored him. "But most of this room is on one side or the other."

"You think any of us cared what they had to say until he started making noise?"

A woman from the crowd whirled around to face them both. Tight braids framed a chiseled face, and her brown lips were drawn tight. "The Senate thinks our lives are theirs."

"So?" the man said.

"You think the pits are our refuge. But I want to know why we need one."

"Why we—?"

"If the Destroyer's right, we used to—"

"Used to nothing. We used to fight in our pits. For our reasons." The man's blade clicked into its place again. "Now this fool comes in, trying to tell us what we are."

"He's telling the truth," the woman spat back. "Not that I'd expect a washed-up old fool to see that."

"Washed-up? That's rich, coming from a kid who gave it up."

Heads turned. Voices murmured.

"What kind of coward quits?" one said.

"And then tells us we don't need a place to run."

"Who's the one doing the hiding again?"

Soran winced. *Those cowards could bring this place down around your ears.*

The woman's shriek interrupted his private amusement. He looked over, saw her hands twitch.

Her body shook with rage. "Why you—you ignorant—idiotic—! You have no idea—no idea and no right! I ought to tear you apart, old man."

She froze, stared at Soran as though seeing him for the first time.

He grinned blandly at her. *I couldn't care less what you do to this brute. Supposedly, I'm on your side.*

"You have no idea," she said again.

Vareth's broad-mountain body rose from its seat. She laid a hand on the younger victor's shoulder. "They aren't worth the energy, Dia. Let them learn the truth at the point of a blade. Later. Come on."

"Wait," the dark-haired man called after them. "Some of us wanted to hear what you had to say."

Dia grinned, sharp and feral. Soran couldn't help but chuckle.

Then he heard Tor's voice behind him. "I think you've heard enough, Skyknight."

"Yes. I think I have."

CHAPTER FIVE

MALEK STEPPED into the ring to the roar of his name.

It surged through him as it always did. His hands twitched around the handle of his axe. Energy crackled over the edge of the blade, sharing his hunger.

It was almost a shame Malek had learned the truth. Almost a shame he could no longer lose himself entirely.

He spared a brief glance for the crowd. Kenn had informed him that a certain Skyknight would be attending. He'd also shown Malek some interesting footage from the cameras in Soran's room. Malek chuckled, remembering it.

But whatever he'd been doing last night, Soran was trying to be subtle now. Kenn had offered him a spot in one of the luxury boxes, and he'd declined. He sat in the crowd like anyone else.

Malek smirked, wondering how an aristocrat like Soran would like that. He'd be able to see without staring at the monitors ringing the arena, given how tall his modifications made him. And his eyes had no doubt been modified to improve his vision. That was one of the few modifications Malek had deigned to get as well, for its use in the ring. And in the war, when it came.

Modified eyes meant Soran might even see his scar, pink and bold and unashamed. And that he'd also see the dagger Malek had kept tucked into his armband since that first meeting.

By now, it no longer gleamed white. But he'd done his best to keep it polished, all the same.

He raised the axe high. The crowd shrieked at the display. He favored them with a half-smile and dropped into his fighting stance. Their din was strong as ever, but it faded from his mind. He'd given them what they wanted. Now he had to fight.

His opponent, a man named Fel, had the square, stocky build of a worker. His brown skin was pink with the burn of his factory's heat. The lattice of scars along his limbs testified to another life here in the pits.

The marks of many victories.

Braided hair fell to his shoulders, beads of metal woven into it, dark with the ubiquitous grime of the city. He held a club in his hand, its tip flaring into a flower of wickedly sharp points, the grooves between them glowing red with heat and giving off small plumes of smoke. A plain armor plate covered his torso, adorned with a simple sun design.

It was lighter than most soldiers' armor would be, built of thin, overlapping plates of metal. Bouts in the arena took too long if everyone hid themselves in the thickest armor they could find. That did little to impress a crowd. Still, armor so light had its vulnerabilities.

Malek recognized Fel's sunburst device. Malek's own helmet bore his spearhead design.

To his fans, it meant only his might. To his victors, it meant more.

Banners around the arena bore his device as well. As not only the favored combatant, but the owner of the pits, most of the audience wanted to see Malek anyway.

Fel's factory supplied weapons to anyone who wanted them and could pay for them. That included the Senate's army. Malek didn't bother with him. He had not only his own designers, but manufacturers producing what his revolution would need when the time came.

Fel had probably designed the armor himself. He wore a fancy gauntlet on one hand that extended to his elbow, the fingertips sharp points. The metal covering his hand bore another sunburst, its center a sphere and its rays radiating over his fingers and arm. They glowed the same fiery orange as the energized parts of his club.

That intrigued Malek far more than the armor did. *A force field generator?* he wondered, fixing his gaze on the glowing circles. *Or another weapon?*

He had little time to ponder the question. Fel bellowed. He lowered his head and dropped into a crouch, in wordless defiance of the thing both men had known before they stepped into the ring.

This is a waste. You're dead already.

Fel ran toward Malek, smoke billowing from his weapon. The energy in its cracks glowed bright. Malek stepped to the side and struck out with his axe. He wouldn't manage any serious damage, not with Fel's side protected by the armor. But if those circles did hide a force field generator, the shield would flare to life to protect him from the blow.

But the axe's edge only bit into Fel's arm as he raced by.

Not a force field, then. That was good. A crowd that had come to see the Destroyer fight didn't want to see such weakness. Malek could hear their shouts of approval, the rumblings of a hungry beast.

Malek would feed it. He had fed it since the beginning. Since the first time he stood on these sands and saw what he must be.

That sunburst is a weapon.

Fel whirled to face Malek and swung his club. Black smoke rose from it, the orange trails of energy hot and eager to burn.

Malek's axe met it. Lightning flickered over both weapons in a searing bolt of light.

With a growl of frustration and another billow of smoke from his club, Fel sprang back. Malek smirked and advanced.

Fel was no coward, shrinking away just because his opponent had drawn first blood. No one came this far if they were weak. But Malek could sense something in his movements, a quaking hesitation that promised the beginnings of fear.

The club crashed down again too quickly, too forcefully. Malek planted his feet again and parried the blow, his muscles straining against his foe's. Fel held firm, his might a mix of alteration and long years of toil in his factories. Gritting his teeth, Malek twisted hard, intending to turn his opponent's weapon aside. And to throw him off-balance, if he could manage it.

Fel snarled in frustration and pitched to one side. Malek kicked at him as he swayed. He fell to the ground with a heavy thud and a spray of gray sand. The crowd howled its delight. Fel struggled to his feet again. Malek raised his axe.

Fel's leg swept out to catch Malek's shin. Seeing the quick flash of movement, Malek stepped aside. Fel broke into a run, giving up for the moment.

Malek let him go. Kenn and his designers laced the pits with traps and hiding places, offering columns or shelves to hide in or behind. Sometimes artificial hills or peaks offered high ground to perch in, where those who favored spears or bows or stinging darts could lie in wait for the unsuspecting.

But there wasn't much of that today. There never was, not during Malek's fights. The audience didn't want to see traps. It wanted to see its Destroyer.

And Malek rarely used such weapons. The crowds wanted to see him cleave and tear and smash. He wore Soran's knife strapped around one arm, but didn't intend to use it. Only to send a message. *How does it feel to see me bear your weapon, Seraph of Aerix? If I did kill him with it, would that flatter you enough?*

But as well-made as Soran's dagger was, he'd be hard-pressed to get close enough for it to do much damage. If he needed to draw an opponent out of hiding, far better to use the smoke bombs at his belt.

Still, if he could drive the blade between the plates of Fel's armor, perhaps—

I'm getting ahead of myself. I have more immediate things to worry about than impressing a silly little prince who's playing hard to get.

Today's pit bore a few piles of twisted scrap metal big enough to serve as cover, but only two tall enough to serve as hiding places. These rose like twin mountains, one on either side of the pit. Malek glanced down at the ground, looking for blood drops from Fel's wound. Finding them, he lifted his head for the benefit of the crowd. He grinned and sprinted toward the nearer of the two mounds.

The dagger strapped to his arm felt hot against his skin. What was Soran thinking now? He thought of Soran's eyes, gleaming bluer than blue as he leaned forward to watch. The thought lent Malek speed, and he raced along the sands.

He slowed as he approached the mound. No one earned the right to face Malek the Destroyer by being a fool. He might lunge at Malek from out of nowhere. And those lights on his arms didn't bode well either.

The air in front of Malek flared orange, crackling with heat. He dove to one side, hitting the sands hard as a sphere of flame whizzed toward him.

Weapon, indeed. Malek hit the sand hard. It dug into his cheek and chin, and blood welled up from the scrapes. The crowd roared, half in awe of the pyrotechnics and half in protest.

Malek scrambled to his feet, keeping a wary eye on the mound, and darted away. An energy weapon would take some time to recharge.

He felt the shimmer in the air again and leapt out of the bolt's path just in time. Its heat seared his armor. He gritted his teeth at the heat, sure he'd find a red, angry burn there after this was over.

"Come out!" he bellowed. "Or are you so frightened you'll spend all day shooting at me?"

Laughter boomed from the stands, all around him. His hand twitched and slid from his axe to one of the smoke bombs from his belt. His fingers felt its smoothness and he murmured for just a moment before tapping a finger to the catch and tossing it toward the spot the flames had come from.

A fitting weapon, he reflected. It hissed, and the mound of metal became a pillar of black, caustic smoke. Carrying them was like carrying the soot of the city with him, twisting it into a weapon that would bring his enemies to heel.

Even from this distance, the smoke stung his eyes.

Good. It's only right for this ritual to bring pain. Even to me. Especially to me.

How long had it been? How long ago had he discovered the secret? He'd thought the same thing as all the rest: the weak perish so that the strong may endure. The people of Dis melted ore into metal and twisted metal into weapons and yearned to use them.

He'd courted that life eagerly. Each victory had told him *You are the strongest. You are the best. You rise, and others fall.* But a question came on the heels of that revelation. Should he rise alone? Who should fall to him? Whose blood should stain his blades and skin?

The pits offered no answer to that. You faced the one who challenged you. Simple. Elegant. Clean.

Or so he'd thought.

He knew what the others said: that your innocence died with your first victim. That killing in the pits changed you. Made you something new, something terrible and fearsome. That had changed him. Had sharpened his movements, his gaze, his mind. Hardened his body into a thing of muscle and speed and coiling force. Given him focus and drive.

But it hadn't corrupted him.

You are strong. You live. You rise. That was a pattern. A cruel one, but cruelty had never bothered him. Life itself was a rise and fall. Through bloody combat, he had risen to reign over the pits.

But what might he have been, in a world where the best ruled over more than a circle of sand? The question had refused to leave his mind. He'd returned to it, over and over. Driven to distraction, he'd had his men—even then, he'd had men, bound to him by loyalty and fear and awe—raid the libraries of Delen, just to answer the question burning in his mind.

It had taken them months of planning and months of raids to find the records. And what they'd finally found had been in pieces. Snatches of history. Fragments of poetry, hailing the great warriors of old. Half-missing entries in the journals of generals long forgotten.

He'd pored for years over those secrets. And when he'd finally put them all together, what he'd found had been another question: Who rises, and who falls?

The answer he had found had reforged him. As surely as his first bouts in the pits had. And someday he would share that answer with them all. Someday he would show everyone in the roaring throng that leaned forward in their seats, eager to see their Destroyer kill, just where they all had come from.

Someday, he would take away their innocence, just as the things he'd found had stolen his.

But not now. Not yet.

For now, he let the pits answer that question for him. For now, he let anticipation burn in his veins. For now, he laughed in triumph as Fel stumbled out.

Fel shook, his locks of hair flying in all directions. Malek grabbed his axe in both hands and sped toward his prey.

Fel swung the great club, still struggling to clear the smoke from his eyes. Malek dodged easily and raised the axe.

This ends now. Energy crackled over Malek's blade, its heat fueling his own hunger. This life was his to take, presented and offered, a sacrifice to his own strength.

The spectators' eagerness hummed through him, quickening his blood. Hunger of his own rose to answer it: the all-consuming desire for victory, for destruction, for his own exaltation.

He did not do what others did. He did not snarl in anticipation of his victory. He chuckled once, his dark eyes glittering, and brought the axe down.

It was only to Fel's credit that he brought the club up to parry the blow. As before, sparks flew from the weapons, a sparkling display of bright light. Fel pulled the club away for another attack, but Malek was ready for him. He kicked out at Fel's side with all the strength that remained to him.

Fel fell to his knees on the sands. The club fell from his hands and rolled away, wreathed in clouds of its own darkness. Fel looked up at Malek above him, and for an instant Malek saw fear there. Fear and weariness, as if Fel wondered what it meant to come so far, only to end here.

And now the pits claim you. Malek felt the anticipation of the crowd, a roar in his ears, a pulse in his blood.

It was easy, even now, to lose himself to this. The twinge Malek felt was the closest thing he knew to compassion.

He blinked it away. His pity wasn't for Fel. Fel had made his choice, as so many others did, to fight in these pits. And to die in them, if it came to that. And he'd known what facing the Destroyer would cost him.

But it was only now that Fel would truly understand. Only in the face of his one and only loss would he see the truth Malek had learned.

Does it pain you to see it, knowing you die for the knowledge? It pains me to bear it and live.

With a growl, Fel shook his head. His eyes focused on Malek, with the same blend of malice and respect Malek had seen countless times in countless opponents. The gauntleted hand struck out at Malek, catching him in one leg, the tips of the claws biting deep.

Blood poured from the wound. Blistering heat seared it as Fel's claws, tipped with the same energy as his club, scorched the torn flesh. Now it was Malek's turn to stagger, struggling to hold himself upright.

This ends, he thought again, blood swimming in his vision. He lifted the axe high, smiling as he swept it down toward his opponent's neck.

You see it, and you choose to fight. Well done.

Then everything was heat, heat and blood, as the energized blade of the axe cleaved skin and meat and bone and Fel's braid-bedecked head rose into the air and fell again, leaving a red trail behind it.

It thudded to the sand at Malek's feet, the grisly, determined scowl still frozen on its features.

The pain he'd been holding firm against returned, bursting into his consciousness all at once, and he fell to one knee.

Gritting his teeth, he thought of the generals in his histories. How would they have fallen, knowing the eyes of an entire people were watching? He stared ahead, resolute, willing away his pain and unsteadiness.

Holding the axe one-handed, he lifted the head by its hair and held it up. The crowd answered, a rolling cry, the thunder before some great storm. They rose from their seats, chanting Malek's name like a promise, like a benediction.

Soon. Malek's eyes scanned the stands for a tall figure, crowned with a blaze of red-brown hair. *Soon you will know everything, my people, my Prince of the Air.*

And everything will burn.

They pressed around him as they always did, crowding around him as he walked out of the pit. Fingers dipped themselves in the gore on his arms, traced over his hands, felt the roughness of the sand against his arms and legs. A few pressed against his leg, sending a flare of pain through his wound.

He let them do it. He was their Destroyer, after all. He reached for the more insistent hands and clasped them in a bruising grip, staining them with Fel's blood.

His eyes widened as he caught sight of a man so tall he towered over all the others. He leaned against the railing and favored Malek with a grin. Mischief sparkled in his bluer-than-blue eyes.

Malek blinked to hide his surprise. It wouldn't do to be caught off guard. Not here.

He settled for smirking at the man's clothes. Brighter red than his hair, tight-fitting enough to leave little to the imagination. Curls of black fabric wove around his upper arms, reminding Malek of his scar.

And the dagger he'd taken, and hadn't used today. He glanced at it. Soran's gaze followed his. *So sorry to disappoint you.*

He wondered how Soran had managed this. He had told Kenn to be sure the Skyknight got what he wanted, yes, but after he'd flat-out refused a luxury box *and* insisted on claiming to be someone unimportant—

"Do you have any words for us?" someone called. The man's hair was dark, dark and long, and beside anyone but Soran he would have been tall.

Jolted out of his reverie, Malek pulled off his helmet and looked quickly over the crowd. They stared, all too readily convinced his smile was for them.

"Oh, if you do, I would love to hear them," said Soran. "I'd love to have something to tell the other Skyknights back home."

Malek frowned. He'd meant to make Soran come to him.

"It's easy enough to hear the things I have to say," Malek answered.

"Nothing, then, for me to bring back to my towers in the sky? The Seraph sent me all this way to see you, after all."

The crowd hushed. They leaned toward Malek, expectant.

Damn him.

"Very well," Malek snarled.

Soran leaned forward. He opened one hand and then closed it, as though grasping for a prize.

Malek laughed. "For all of you. Four words."

They pressed forward to hear, whispering. Malek held up a bloodied hand, and they fell silent.

"Remember what you are."

He turned back toward the door, sparing them no more attention. The sounds of the throng followed him. Cheers for his victory. And for his little pearl of wisdom, from those who thought they understood it. Growls from those who'd wanted a speech and gotten a sentence. Quizzical noises from those trying to puzzle out its meaning.

And overlaying them all, Soran's indignant huff. He'd hoped he could trick Malek into saying more, no doubt. Or something more personal.

But that was for you, Prince of the Air. The heavy doors leading out of the pit thudded open for him. He stepped through them, leaving Soran and the crowd behind.

CHAPTER SIX

"YOU KEPT it," Soran marveled. He slid his fingers along the scar on Malek's arm.

He'd noticed it as soon as Malek walked into the arena, the red-pink slash starting at his right shoulder and ending just before the elbow.

Soran didn't know the histories, but the mark fit somehow. Those ancient brutes from the Old Empire would have had scars. Especially before alterations let them look like anything they wanted.

Malek didn't turn his head. Soran scowled. Malek had gone to ridiculous amounts of trouble to give him a luxurious, private room. The least the damned fool could do was respond to his touch.

Then again, it was a freshly healed wound. Maybe he was just too used to hiding pain.

"Yes," Malek answered. "I kept it."

Soran moved his fingers again. This time, he was rewarded with a ragged gasp. "I'm flattered. You told me that anyone who scarred you is dead." He pouted in a parody of shock. "Unless that means you want to kill me."

"I won't harm you. Unless you're here to toy with me."

I'm already doing that. You're letting me. Soran pressed his fingers to the scar again. Then he lowered them and turned away.

The room was big, all sharp angles and dark walls. Rows of seats circled the table, rising in tiers. *How many people fit in here?*

The datapad tucked into his pocket pressed against his skin. Senator Derell's list of victors hadn't been complete, but this room looked big enough to hold a full council of war. Had Malek hidden that many victors?

Soran thought of the woman in the bar. Vareth had been there, too. What happened, exactly, when Malek and his hand-picked fighters gathered around this table?

"I'm not toying with you," Soran pouted, his gaze moving to the hologram in the center of the room. It spread out on the table in front of them, a scintillating mirage of red light. "I never thought Dis could be so pretty."

The buildings ringing the Grand Arena were feeble imitations of towers, misshapen things half shackled to the ground. Or so he'd thought yesterday. But rendered in pure light, they rose above the pit like mountains, sharp sentinels guarding a treasure at their center.

Soran had a sudden vision of this room, packed with people, their bodies thick with muscle, their eyes bright. And yet he would be spared their wrath, as long as he didn't set himself against them.

He had to admit that was tempting, in its way: to see doom and destruction pouring from the Molten Belt as it finally boiled over, and know its eruption wouldn't touch him.

"Pretty," Malek repeated. "You're more right than you know, Seraph." He walked over to the console, tapping at it. "If it's beauty you want, I have something better to show you."

With a flash of light, the hologram shifted. For a brief moment, Soran caught sight of the spires of his home, rising golden and delicate above the table. He leaned forward, intrigued.

A map for Aerix's defense? Or will he besiege it, too, if I spurn him? Soran shivered, the tablet with Derell's information hot against the lining of his pocket. If Malek did suspect him—

Then the image shifted again. The new hologram was a fiery orange, halfway between the amber of the Aerix hologram and the bold crimson of the one Malek used to represent Dis. It sprawled over the entire table, a panorama of sharp towers and broad pyramids unlike anything he'd seen before.

It glittered, dense and opulent. The buildings were built simply, all angles and bold, unadorned planes. But that simplicity only served to highlight the grace of the shapes. Soran didn't know what the buildings were made of, and the orange hologram didn't help him guess, but he imagined mirror-smooth metal and polished, dark stone.

He'd never guessed he would find something so spartan beautiful.

And that city looked as dense as Delen. After the Old Empire splintered, very few cities remained anywhere near this large. The Senate had brought peace to the territories decimated by war, but it had come at a great price. Cities like this were a thing of the past.

Even Aerix was smaller now than it had once been. Only the

Senate's capitol was anywhere near as large as the fiery panorama stretched out across Malek's table.

But for all its splendor, something about the forgotten city looked familiar. He'd seen that arrangement of buildings before. And those roads, a network of thoroughfares lfeeding into the circle in the center of town. Fiery veins leading to the city's heart.

A pyramid rose behind the circle. That surprised Soran, given what he felt sure it represented. He wouldn't have expected Malek to build anything that would diminish the seat of his power.

But its resemblance to the first hologram left Soran with no doubt. "This is the Dis you want to build. Once you win your little war."

A wall surrounded the great city, the hologram's version of it shining like fire. Towers rose along its length, as tall as the ones inside the city. *They would pierce the sky*. Soran shivered again.

He pressed his fingers to the iridescent barrier. The hologram shimmered, disturbed. The projection felt warm. For a wild moment Soran imagined that it really was made of flame and he would draw his fingers back blistered.

"The Dis I want to build? You could say that." Soran could hear the smile. "But if you did, you'd be missing the point. And woefully ignorant of history."

Soran frowned. "History?"

"This isn't the Dis I want to build, Seraph. This is the Dis I want to rebuild."

Soran laughed, high and loud. "That again? Don't get me wrong, I've seen for myself that your city needs its heroes. And what better hero for Dis than a gladiator with big dreams? Bloody heads and promises."

"Soran," Malek growled.

"It's brilliant. But do you really think anyone will believe it? Dis, the crown jewel of an empire?"

Malek turned. The orange light of the hologram lit his eyes.

"Really, Malek," Soran pressed. A warm heat shivered through him. "You're too smart for wishful thinking."

Malek roared and lunged. Soran stepped aside, his blade already in his hand. "Calm down. I didn't come here to fight. Unless you want more scars."

Malek froze, his hands still tightened into fists. "We were scholars, Seraph. We were warriors. We were trained as your Skyknights are trained."

Soran's eyes flicked to the hologram again. He stared at the fiery pyramids, the rising towers, the bright wall surrounding it all. At the latticework of the streets. What might a parade of soldiers look like, pulled from Malek's pits and given real weapons and armor, trained to march as one?

"And now you chop each other's heads off in the pits," Soran sneered. He slid into a fighting stance of his own. "Quite a step down, if what you say is true."

Malek didn't lunge at him again. He only laughed. "What would you think, Seraph of Aerix, if I said that you are right?"

"That I'm right? The pits are your dominion. The pits made you what you are." His gaze moved to Malek's arm, taking in not only the scar he'd left there but the many older scars crisscrossing Malek's flesh. "What would you be without them?"

"Nothing."

"Then how can you say the things you're saying now?"

"You don't need to ask that question. The answer is right in front of you."

Soran hissed. "You think I am a fool."

"I think you don't see what I'm offering you."

Soran smiled. He'd felt sure Malek would attack him for that little barb. Instead, Malek was still talking. *You should keep to your fights, Destroyer. You make it entirely too obvious when someone else has the upper hand.*

He edged closer to the table and the hologram glowing on top of it. "So this is what you're going to do with the world if you win it. You and your little winner's circle."

Malek's jaw slackened in stunned surprise. The look lasted only a moment, his features smoothing into their usual stern glare.

Soran pulled the tablet from his pocket and tossed it onto the table. The hologram rippled as the small, thin object skidded across the surface of the table, the stately buildings dissolving in a flame-red mist and reforming as it skidded to a stop in the center of the table.

Malek dove for it. He snatched it up and held it out in front of him. His hand shook and he tapped the screen, scrolling through the names. "How long have you known?"

"Since I got back from my visit. It made some people curious."

Malek's hand tightened around the tablet. The thin metal buckled and Soran winced. He remembered Malek's arms wrapping around him, the grip tightening, inexorable. "Don't do that!" he howled. "You'll damage it!"

Soran barely had time to hear the clang as it fell to the floor before Malek barrelled into him. He felt himself swept up in impossibly strong arms. Then a shock of pain flared through his back and his vision flared with searing orange light. The dagger fell from nerveless hands as he closed his eyes against the light.

Something solid lay beneath his back, sturdy and metallic. He felt heat, a prickling warmth overlaying the pain.

He hissed, showing teeth. A figure loomed above him, pinpricks of fiery light glowing in its eyes. He scrambled to move his arms, but broad hands held them pinned. His legs were no help either. Malek had already stepped too close for him to kick.

"If you're going to keep me here," he snarled, "turn the hologram off. You're blinding me."

"And risk you worming your way free? I think not."

"You already know who gave that to me. You can guess what they offered."

Malek leaned closer, his chest hovering just above Soran's, his lips close enough to brush Soran's ear. "And what I offer isn't enough for you?"

"I have a city."

"One city. Why settle for that? I'm offering a planet."

"To me?" Soran snickered. "Do you plan to present it to me as a gift once you've won it, then?"

The lips against his ear went still.

"That's what I thought. Don't be so quick to betray your intent, warrior."

"Warrior, is it?" Malek's lips slid down to Soran's neck. "Not 'savage' or 'brute?'"

Soran thrashed in his grip, half wanting to break free of it, half wanting to wrap his arms around Malek's back and draw him closer still. "Brutes don't try to save the world."

Malek laughed against his neck. "Save the world? Only from itself."

"By setting yourself up as its new emperor." Soran's lips twisted into a grin. "And they call me arrogant."

"I do this for my people. If that means leading them, so be it. But it's not control I want."

Soran twisted his arms. The big hands locked tighter around his wrists. "No?"

Malek's lips moved against his neck, their movement feather-light. "What I want, Seraph of Aerix, is to restore my people to their rightful place. And yours. If that means—taking control—"

The deep voice faltered. Soran could hear Malek's ragged breath. He smirked.

"—so be it. But if someone rises to surpass me—"

"Surpass you?" Soran wrenched his body hard to one side. One arm broke free of the hand that held it. He wrapped his arm around Malek's back. "Don't make what you want so obvious. Someone might take you up on it."

Malek straightened, one hand still tight around Soran's other wrist. The light of the hologram wreathed him in flame. "Clever. But you've lost your weapon. And handed over whatever advantage secrecy might have given you."

He let go, stepping free of Soran's half-embrace. "If you're not careful, Seraph of Aerix, I might think you want to lose."

Soran sat up and slid to the edge of the table. His wrists stung from Malek's bruising grip, and he massaged them with his hands, glaring at his host. "Is that why you think I came here?"

He slid off the table in a swift motion and jabbed his fingers at Malek's chest. "Is that what that room is for? For you to swoop in and claim me in a fancy little bed you designed yourself? I am no pawn, Lord of the Pits."

Malek's hand wrapped around Soran's wrist. Without warning, he twisted hard. Soran shrieked. His wail of pain echoed, piercing in the empty room. The hall had been built to hold a whole council of war, and built to ensure every word spoken would be heard.

His lesson taught, Malek let go. Soran crouched, still growling, more wary than submissive. *You'll pay for that, King of the Barbarians. And for everything else, too.*

Malek was speaking again, as slowly as Soran had. "I want an alliance, Seraph. I offer you a place at my side, and you repay me with insults and betrayal."

Soran only glared and slid a foot out toward the spot where his blade lay on the floor.

Malek's hand swept over the table. The hologram made way for it. Orange light curled around his arm like a phoenix's fire. Soran gasped into the silence, his breath heavy from pain.

Malek's hand rose from the maelstrom, the tablet clutched in his thick fingers. "Which vulture in the Senate gave you this? Did whoever it was offer you a place of honor too? Or did you settle for a promise that they'd withdraw from Corian?"

Soran reached out to pluck the tablet from Malek's palm. He might not have been as strong as Malek, but he was fast. "I don't owe you anything."

Malek spread his arms wide and gave another cold laugh. "No. You don't. But my people were like your people once. Where they passed, death and destruction followed."

"And now they're—"

"Thugs and savages."

Soran blinked. He could still hear the storm in Malek's deep voice. But was Malek agreeing with him? "Then you realize you're not soldiers."

"We're nothing. My people are debased, degraded, set against themselves until they have become less than shadows. You're right: they're beasts. And so am I."

"You admit it? Before, you were calling yourself an emperor. Offering me the planet like a toy."

"Admit it? Is that what you want? For me to confess? Fine. In the pits, I was a beast like anyone else. Clawing and tearing as it fought for its life. There is only one difference between me and the others."

Soran leaned forward. His lips parted.

"I am the beast that opened its eyes."

Soran stared at the lines of Malek's face, carved there by battle and sorrow and this burden he carried, whatever it was. Soran shook off a sudden chill and spoke. "Pretty words for a barbarian. Are you planning a war or writing poetry?"

"Make no mistake, Seraph of Aerix: what my people have become, yours will become. When the Senate has its way with you and your city, you will do what I am doing now. Scramble for the brightest and the best. Vow they will be enough. That if they are not, you'll make them enough." The booming voice was quiet now. "Because if they are not, no one ever will be."

Soran shook his injured wrist. "Oh, I don't think s—"

He stopped. Malek lowered his hands and bowed his head.

"Maybe they break their word," Malek said. "Maybe your towers fall to some great siege. Or maybe nothing happens at all. Maybe they wait, and your glory fades and dims on its own."

"I won't let that happen."

"Then you understand what I meant offering you that pretty little room. And you know what will happen once you finally admit it."

CHAPTER SEVEN

VARETH SLAMMED her fist down on the table. The hologram shimmied with the blow, became a golden mist, and reformed into the spires of a faraway city. "We have no friends in Aerix."

The tablet lay in front of Malek, half-hidden by the hologram. His grip had dented its frame, but it still worked. The names scrolled past, bright red beacons. An endlessly repeating list of the people gathered in this very room.

Murmurs answered Vareth's accusation. Malek waited. The first thing he'd learned studying the strategies of the ancients was how, and when, to wait.

He'd tried to teach the others that patience. Some, like Kenn, remained silent, but most hadn't taken the lesson to heart. They only grew louder, their overlapping voices spitting harsh, guttural words in the language of the pits. The sounds rolled through the room, a thunder of mounting rage.

"Perhaps Vareth is right," Kenn said finally. His voice was quiet in the packed war room, but a hush fell over the assembled victors. If anyone had missed his words in the din, no one let on. "Or perhaps we need an alliance, no matter what else has happened."

One corner of Malek's mouth quirked up. Kenn had always understood him.

Vareth's eyes met Kenn's visor with stubborn evenness. "He went straight to the Senate."

"That's true." Tena stepped closer to Vareth.

"But then he went straight to Malek," said her twin.

Heads turned. The frowns on the faces of the assembly deepened.

"Is that what you two think? Or is that what the City Council told you to tell us?"

"Dia," Vareth began.

Malek's eyes flicked over to Dia. She'd joined the victors eagerly. She had a gift for finding like-minded others. But it was risky to admit anyone into his inner circle that he had neither groomed nor chosen. Vareth had vouched for her. But sometimes she got into trouble of her own. Like that evening in the bar, where she'd run into Soran. Or Soran had run into her.

"The Council doesn't tell us to do anything," Tena answered.

"Besides," Tor said, "they don't like him much either. They just think he might be useful."

"To us or to them?" Vareth put in. "I've got no problem with someone keeping an eye on them, but this?"

Malek stepped toward them. "Easy."

His victors knew conflict. They'd lived with it all their lives. It had honed them into the fighters they were now, the best of the best. But they were used to doing things their own way. And killing anyone who didn't like it.

"It's me the Seraph serves at the moment," he said.

Dia and Vareth both frowned. Dia's mouth opened once and closed again.

It was Kenn who broke the tension. "We know what they know. Unless they were lying to him." The dusky lips did not smile. "And the line of communication the Senator provided has already been tapped."

Malek had expected nothing less. "Excellent."

"It's a risky way to give you what you want."

The speaker was thinner than Fel but taller, his body hidden by plates of armor, his face framed by a helmet. His hands were heat-burnt and gnarled. Scars and lines pitted his face, and he blinked owl-yellow eyes at the crowd. In such an ugly face, the alteration looked too odd to be beautiful.

"Risky? Of course. But it's as good as a confession," Malek countered, his eyes bright. "Whether the man who said it realizes that or not."

Which he does. Malek moved his right arm and relished the tight feeling in his scar. *But he might not know that I do.*

He thought of the video Kenn had shown him. Soran, standing in front of the mirror in his room, his delicate fingers sliding down his own body. *Will you invite me in? Or do you still intend to make me wait?*

"Well, I have something for you myself," said the newcomer. "No tricks. No lies." He stepped forward, reached out his arms, and turned to give them all a good look.

It wasn't impressive. Not at first glance, at least. Its plates, colored a dull brownish-purple, bore no device. And the armor was light, with none of the intimidating thickness favored by the strongest or jagged edges favored by especially cruel or flashy gladiators. The armor didn't have lights to dazzle audiences, or shining lines of energy that promised force fields or weapons.

"You build that for us, Zarel?" someone scoffed. "Looks like standard issue to me. Ugly standard issue."

"His shop's been full of junk for years," said someone else.

Of course it has.

Zarel smiled, a lopsided grin that made the victors look closer.

The unassuming plates curved with the muscles beneath them, carefully molded to the wearer's anatomy. They fit tight to one another, the seams between them thin and exact. He flexed, a dancer's twist, and the armor moved with him. Only the barest hints of the mesh layer beneath showed as he squatted, lunged, punched and kicked at the air.

Malek saw the flash of a blaster in his hand. A big one, from the look of it. Where had it come from? And how had he drawn it so quickly?

The victors had only an instant to recognize the blaster before bolts of white heat streaked toward the far wall. Two victors flung themselves out of the way by long-honed instinct.

The bolts of energy thudded into the wall with a deep, percussive sound. A nova of light burst from the impacts.

The two victors peeled themselves back out of the corners they'd tucked themselves into. They cursed, their hushed voices the only sound in the room. The blaster had torn a circle through the wall, the metal surrounding the hole warped and rippling outward from the place of impact, a black hole at their center opening out into the smoky night.

The room filled with the click of weapons, drawn and readied as quickly as Zarel had drawn his.

Someone snarled. "You can't do that here!"

"This place is ours," said someone else, steel in his rough voice. "It's not yours to destroy."

Kenn's voice dispelled the storm. He had the luxury of lowering his voice, and knew it. "If he weren't one of us, he'd never have made it in the door."

The victors lowered their weapons. Their hands dropped halfway to their sides, their bodies still coiled and ready. No one moved. But Malek saw their eyes slide in their sockets, drawn to the damaged wall.

"When the war begins, we'll lose more than a wall," Malek said.

"But coming here—here!–"

"—claiming to be one of us, and then—"

Nothing happens by accident. Not here. You should know that by now.

"Our war will raze the planet," Malek said. "Do you understand that?"

A reckless laugh answered him. "Yeah. We set the world on fire," said a thin man, tall and lanky, his grin too wide for his narrow face. He glanced at the hologram. "We burn everything to the ground." He glared back at Malek. "That's why we follow you. That's why we're here."

"There will be plenty for you to destroy. But you're misunderstanding me."

Someone gasped. Malek turned. She muttered something and fell silent. The thin man squirmed.

"When I say that war will raze the planet, I mean every part of it. No part of our world will be spared. Not even the places that belong to us."

"They won't reach us here," said someone. "We'll crush them if they try it."

Zarel laughed, a mirthless, hollow sound. Most of the victors whirled to face him, weapons readied, teeth bared. A small minority remained still. Among them were Kenn, his face inscrutable under his golden visor, and Vareth, her jaw set.

Malek nodded once, the gesture a solemn salute. "Reach us here? No, they won't. But the places that are sacred to us will not last forever."

Zarel bowed his head.

"You call me Destroyer. I tell you to destroy in my name. And you wail over the loss of one wall?"

"It—" Dia tried. Vareth shook her head.

Anger flared in Dia's eyes and her fists clenched tight. For a moment, Malek thought she might rebuke her mentor. But instead, she only looked down.

"Zarel did nothing," Malek went on. "Have you forgotten what will happen to this city, to the heart of it, by our own hands?"

The victors quieted. The angry murmurs subsided, the only sound the hum of the lights and the hologram projector and the ragged breaths of the assembly.

"Thank you for that defense of my character," Zarel said, his mouth still curled in that lopsided smile. He pressed a hand to one of the plates covering his chest. Light flared there, white beneath his fingers. He lifted his hands away and it dimmed to a smoky gray, the design coalescing into the straight lines of Malek's spearhead mark.

Then he looked up. His gaze swept over Malek's gathered followers, his unnatural eyes wide and unblinking.

Some fought to stare back at him. Their resolute gazes wavered, and all of them blinked and looked away. In the end, all eyes were drawn to the hole torn in their sanctum. They stared at the wall for a long, silent moment. Someone whistled, a long, low sound.

"That blaster could be useful," Vareth rumbled. "The armor could be, too." She laughed, her rough voice as contemptuous as Zarel's smile had been. "Or would be if it fit."

"Don't worry. This is just the standard prototype. It's for the pack of brawlers the rest of you plan to lead." A smirk curled one edge of his mouth. "The rest of you get customs."

"Nice," said Tena.

"I don't suppose you have specs to show us?" asked Tor.

"To take back to the City Council?" someone behind him muttered. Tena turned and fixed the speaker with an icy stare.

"Oh, I have them," Zarel answered. His armor-sheathed hand reached out for the edge of the table, ran over its surface as though caressing something prized. "With me, in fact. And I'm sure this projector of Malek's could show them all to you easily enough."

Dia grinned. "Then why don't you?"

"I thought you might like to come and see what I've built in person. That is, if you can stand all the 'ugly junk' you'd have to walk past to get to them."

"I have some names for you, Senator Derell," purred a familiar voice, broadcast over a speaker. "They're transmitting now."

Malek tensed at those words. His hands clenched into fists, even though there was no Seraph here to attack.

By our own hands, he reminded himself. He sat back, trying to relax. The chair he sat in was high-backed and wide, a fitting seat for the Lord of the Pits.

He didn't need it. Not really. The room was dark and small, the light strips on the wall clouded by grime. They flickered periodically. Malek's chair, however, had been carefully polished, and the terminal nearby shone clean and bright.

Kenn sat in front of it, his visor retracted. In the light of the terminal, his face glowed a cold, bloodless brown. His eyes were fixed on the readouts before him, looking for any sign that the Senator might detect his surveillance.

Or doing all he could to keep himself from focusing too much on what he was hearing. Malek chuckled softly, closing his eyes to listen more fully.

"Then the barbarians trust you for now," came another voice, in the rich, cultured accent of the capitol. "Excellent."

Malek could hear the laughter in Soran's voice. "I wouldn't go that far."

"We're glad to have any information, Seraph. I'm honored to provide Aerix as much protection as I can."

"As much as you can? I thought we had a deal."

"It wasn't about lists, Seraph. It was about why Malek is collecting people. Not who he's collecting."

"But I've only just gotten here, Senator. And I don't think you can separate the two. I suspect his little clique is spreading."

Kenn's voice cut through the recording. "My Lord."

Malek opened his eyes and saw Kenn frown. He waved a hand. "There is nothing you can do about it now." He frowned. *How much do you think you can give away, Prince of the Air?* "Even if you ought to."

"What do you mean?" Derell asked, his voice clipped and eager.

"I don't know. Not yet. Maybe nothing. But I did run into a crowd of people watching a videofeed of one of Malek's speeches. Some people seem to like them quite a bit. Others, not so much."

"That's nothing."

"No, but I did see someone in the crowd who the others identified as a 'quitter.'"

"Then you know where some of them gather?"

"After the speech, she said a few things. Things about people like you. I'm afraid they weren't complementary."

"They insulted us? Openly?"

Soran chuckled and nodded. "And afterward, someone wanted to talk to her about it. Don't you think it's worth asking why?"

"Then they aren't just an honor guard."

"No, I don't think so." Soran laughed. The sound danced through the dark room, filling its corners. "But neither do you."

Malek growled. For Soran to lay it out like this, so clearly—

He heard a sharp intake of breath. He thought it might have been Derell. Then he realized it had been Kenn.

Kenn's long fingers trembled against the console. "My Lord—he can't—"

Malek felt it too, a hot coiling rage at the center of him. What did Soran think he was doing? Still, acting against Soran would risk the wrath of his Skyknights. It would give the Senate the perfect excuse to move against Dis.

Whether Malek's faith in Soran would prove justified or not, for the moment listening was their only option.

"But I already told you what you want to know, Senator," Soran went on. He laughed. "'He fancies himself a warlord.' Where do you think he got that idea?"

"Seraph." The word was crisp and cold. "What does he intend?"

"I don't know what he intends," Soran snapped, his tone a perfect facsimile of impatient irritation. Malek snickered at the smoothness of the lie. "I spent the week exploring the city. Taking in the local color."

"Taking in the local color?" Derell's eyes widened. "When you were supposed to be finding out what he was doing?"

"I said I think he's getting this from somewhere. I didn't say I knew what he's going to do. Not yet."

"Soran, if you think this is some kind of game—"

"Everything is a game," Soran purred. "You're the one who asked me to play it."

Malek smirked. Kenn's hand twitched again.

"We asked for your aid. In return for it, we promised to work for a withdrawal from Corian. Against the advice of a very influential segment."

Soran laughed again. "Why, Senator! Whatever happened to all those things you said about Aerix deserving to be protected?"

"I can't do anything for you if you're going to play coy."

Don't worry yourself unnecessarily, Senator. It appears he does that with everyone.

"I wish I had more to tell," Soran answered, all innocence. "Half of what he says is drivel about the glory of the Old Empire. Did you know that people scrawl his little symbol in alleys, like they expect him to appear and rescue them from their miserable little lives?"

"He's making promises to them," Derell said. "But what is it he's offering them? Why are they so taken in?"

"That depends on his audience. I'm sure what he's offering them isn't what he offered me."

Malek heard the growl, a low, thunderous rumble, before realizing he himself had made the sound.

"My Lord?" Kenn asked.

"Hold," Malek snarled, half at Kenn and half at himself.

"Promises he's made to you?" Derell's voice sounded as indignant as his own.

"If you don't get your goons out of Corian, I might have to ask someone else for protection."

Derell cried out. Kenn gasped. Malek bit his lip to keep from laughing out loud.

"I have my people to think of, Senator. He wants something from me, remember?"

"Then you've set yourself against us."

A peal of laughter answered him. "Would I be sending you their names and pictures if I had?"

If he intended to betray me, why would he let me hear this? Whose side are you on, Prince of the Air?

"Then—"

"Then I want to be sure that you have something better to offer, Senator. Other than an agenda and a pointless waste of time."

"Understood."

"Good," Soran chuckled again. "I'm glad we understand one

another."

"You're staying there, then?"

"For the time being. I have some business to finish."

You do. I'll have your answer before you leave. Or you will find yourself with an enemy.

CHAPTER EIGHT

ALL SORAN heard was a soft click, followed by the hiss of his door sliding open. No alarm or bell rang to tell him that someone had come in.

You could at least have knocked.

He was standing at his mirror, spreading a mist of silvery glitter across his cheek. Skyknights didn't usually paint their faces, and those who did kept it subtle: a ring of dark color close to the eyes, a hint to deepen the lips. Obvious makeup was for those who couldn't afford or earn the alterations to perfect themselves for real.

It certainly wasn't something a Seraph would do. But Soran had never cared much for others' expectations.

He didn't turn to face his visitor. He just tracked Malek with his eyes, watching in the mirror as Malek moved to step behind him. He pouted. "You might have told me you were coming." He'd only managed to apply the silver shine to half of his face.

Malek stepped closer, his thick brows knotted. Soran shivered, looking at the reflection close behind him. Apparently, he wasn't the only one who intended to look tempting; Malek wore sleek black pants and a matching vest with no garment beneath it. His chest and arms were bare, save for the dagger strapped to one arm.

"You knew I was coming, Seraph. Why else would you wear that?"

Soran smirked. He liked what he saw. Especially if Malek had sculpted most of that without alterations. Scars crossed his skin, every jagged streak and raised mark testifying to a mistake he'd made in the ring.

And then there's the scar that didn't come from the pits. His gaze moved to the reflection of Malek's arm.

He turned to give Malek a good look at the bodysuit he wore. It matched his skin tone almost perfectly. The thin fabric accentuated his shape but hid his skin away. It made him look nude but unsexed, like a sculpture rather than a living man. It was plainer than most of the things Soran had brought with him, but that was just part of the illusion.

Besides, he had his makeup to compensate for the plainness. Or would have, if Malek hadn't interrupted him.

He studied Malek's face in the mirror. *Does it feed your desire to see me like this? Does it frustrate you to see everything but what you most want to see? How does it feel, knowing I'm still hiding from you?*

He opened his hand and let the makeup brush fall from his fingers. It landed at his feet amid its own silvery dust. "I knew you were coming? I thought you wanted something from me first."

"I did."

"Then I had no reason to expect you tonight." Soran whirled to face him, leaned just close enough to be intimate. "You've broken the rules."

Malek smiled back at Soran, a tight-lipped grin. His eyes gleamed with a cold light. "Broken the rules?"

"We both know what you want. You want me to admit you're right. And offer Aerix up to your little war." He reached out like he meant to touch Malek's face. But instead, his hand shot toward Malek's arm and pulled the dagger from the straps that held it there. "But I haven't agreed." He brought the blade up toward Malek's neck.

The grip on his arm was bruising, immediate, and inexorable. He watched his own hand lower and fought down another laugh. *You're stronger than I am, King of the Barbarians. But if I'd meant to strike, you'd be too late to stop me.*

"That's mine," Malek growled, twisting hard. "Drop it."

Hot pain blossomed through Soran's arm. His hand opened. The blade fell to the floor.

The grip on Soran's wrist loosened enough to let him draw his hand away. "Very well then," he said. "It's yours."

He slid closer, reaching out to touch the empty band where the blade had been. "But you've lost a bigger prize than I have." He slid his fingertips over Malek's arm and up to his neck. His hand wrapped around the back of Malek's head. "Do you always lose control when you find something you want?"

Not waiting for an answer, he pulled Malek's head down and pressed Malek's mouth to his.

A low growl came from Malek, wordless and deep. Soran opened his mouth to deepen the kiss. Maybe Malek would see that he was gloating. Either way, it served his ends well enough. Malek's arms rose to encircle his slim body, clutching tight at the prize they'd finally won.

Soran tilted his head, presenting his neck to Malek's lips and teeth. Malek's hand shot up to grab at Soran's hair, and pulled his head back with just enough force to sting. He lowered his head to lick and bite at the sensitive skin of Soran's neck.

Soran's free hand clutched at Malek's back as he slid closer, pressing his counterfeit skin against Malek's body. Its heat sent a flush of desire through his hidden flesh, and he moaned again, no longer bothering with pretense.

Malek growled once and pushed Soran away.

Soran's body twisted automatically. He hit the floor as gracefully as he could. "Still playing games? And here I thought you'd finally make these visits worth my while."

Malek stared down at Soran. "I intend to."

"But—"

"But first I want to make one thing clear. You say I'm here because I've lost control?"

Soran hissed but said nothing. If Malek would rather shove him than admit to the blatantly obvious, fine.

Malek drew the tablet from a pocket in his pants. He tossed it at Soran, who caught it and cradled it in one hand.

Malek snickered. "That little trinket in your hand says otherwise."

"You think that means—"

"It means, Seraph of Aerix, that you gave in first."

Soran stared at the tablet in his hand in sudden revulsion. With a cry, he threw it aside.

"I have your answer already," Malek said. "I wouldn't come here otherwise."

Soran scrambled to his feet. Better to look as awkward as one of Malek's barbarians than to take his hand after that. "Suppose you're right, Lord of the Pits. Suppose I want nothing more than to present Aerix to you on a platter."

He tossed his painted head, feeling his confidence return. The flush of desire he'd felt earlier returned with it, a pleasant sting goading him on. He stepped backward, just enough to encourage Malek to follow. "What then? Do you really think I can just fly back to Aerix and tell my Skyknights to prepare for someone else's war?"

"It's their war too. The Senate will not stop until they've—"

"—destroyed every remnant of the Old Empire. So you say."

Malek followed. "I am through with your stalling, Seraph."

"I'm not stalling. Not this time."

"Then what is this?"

"Strategy." Soran cast a quick glance around the room. Another few steps and he would back into the bed. *You're still following my lead. And you still don't know it.*

He stepped close. Too close. As close as he had when they'd kissed. "And a petty desire for some...reciprocation."

"Reciprocation?"

"I've come here twice now. I've heard your claims, your demands, your speeches. I've heard what you've had to say. But my Skyknights haven't." He reached out a hand to touch Malek's chest and traced the raised contour of a scar. "You're so sure you have me. But I'm not my people. Why not make your case to them in person?"

Malek smirked, stepping forward. In answer, Soran stepped back until he felt the edge of the bed against the back of his leg. He fought down a laugh.

"Then you're done pretending," Malek murmured. "Or you're trying to lead me into a trap."

Soran slid his hand over Malek's chest. Malek's breath hitched, and Soran bit back a chuckle. "Not unless you're doing the same. I've come to your city every time you've asked me to, and you've done nothing to me."

"Because I want you for an ally," Malek growled and reached out to push Soran down. Soran fell back onto the bed with a fey laugh.

He wrapped his hands around Malek's back, felt the texture of the vest. "You can't harm me, warrior. You'd be starting the wrong war."

"And you'd be starting the wrong war if you invited me to Aerix to trap me. My victors would lead this city against you. And the Molten Belt would follow."

"Beasts they may be, but they're loyal ones." Soran tilted his head up to brush his lips against Malek's. "And if you did open their eyes—"

Malek pressed his mouth against Soran's before he could say anything more.

Soran opened his own mouth and squirmed, too hot now under the tight bodysuit, cursing it for separating them.

Malek broke the kiss, apparently animated by the same thought. He grabbed for the fastener and yanked it down in one brusque motion. The fabric parted, opening like an old skin ready to be shed.

Soran arched his back, pressed his exposed skin against the calloused fingertips moving on it. Malek laughed and drew away. He looked down at his own fingertips as though amused by their power.

"Fine. I'll visit your city. This alliance is, after all, about more than the two of us."

Soran reached out and drew the bedcovers down. He slid his boots off and reached for the half-opened fastener of his bodysuit. Malek's hand wrapped tight around his.

"Do it yourself, then," Soran teased.

Malek peeled the cloth off of him. He left it on the floor, priceless and forgotten. Then his hands reached up again to slide Soran's undergarments off, tossing them to the floor as well.

"No more hiding," Malek rumbled, his voice a dark, thunderous purr that made Soran squirm again. The roughness of the sheets reminded him of Malek's hands on him earlier, and he moved again, wanting to feel more.

Malek stepped toward him and slid out of the vest. "No more stalling. No more games."

"No more," Soran agreed. "Not here." *Do you realize how much power you've given me? You need this as much as you hope I do.*

Soran watched Malek strip off his clothes, his motions studied and slow. He laid each garment aside with such absurd fastidiousness Soran muttered in irritation.

His eyes swept over Malek's body: the brown, weathered skin, the muscles beneath, the scars twisting across it. He found himself staring at a pale mark on one leg, transfixed by its contours. He felt a stab of jealousy, a swirl of possessiveness that sent a new spike of heat through his flesh. *You had no right to mark him. None of you lived to be worthy of this.*

His lips twisted into a smile as he looked Malek over again, seeing the obvious proof of his desire.

Malek stepped forward. He wrapped his legs around Soran's body, clutching him tightly. Soran slid a hand over to the nightstand and drew out a container of lubricant he'd found in one of the closets, hidden just well enough that he would surely find it.

Had it always been there, or had some poor lackey tucked it away after their meeting in the war room? Sneering at the thought, he tossed it up at Malek.

Malek caught it with the practiced reflexes of a warrior. But not the trained grace of a Skyknight. Soran snickered, watching Malek twist it open. He dipped his fingers in, then took himself in hand, dark eyes narrowing in pleasure as he coated his flesh with the oil.

Soran hissed a vulgar phrase in the dialect of the pits. He grinned at Malek and licked his lips.

Malek's eyes widened. Black-stained irises glittered as he stared down at Soran. Then he snickered and positioned himself. Soran laughed, a mad, wild sound that became a moan as Malek pierced him at last.

Malek growled and drove in deeper, one hand gripping tight to Soran's hip. Soran gasped and bucked his hips to meet his partner's thrusts. Malek stared down at him, the dark eyes bright with concentration. His mouth twisted into a snarl and he pulled back to push in even harder.

Soran trembled and he shifted his legs again, opening his body wider. He reached down to touch himself because even this wasn't enough, would never be enough, and no matter what Malek offered him he would want more.

"Deeper!" he cried. His other hand groped in front of him, found the scars on Malek's chest and curled over them.

Malek's hands wrapped around Soran's hips, pressing their bodies together. Soran yelped, then hissed. He opened his eyes to stare at Malek's face, at curled lips and bright eyes, hard and gleaming as obsidian.

That little trinket in your hand says otherwise.

Soran thrashed, sending new waves of desire through his body. He snarled and Malek answered with a snarl of his own, rearing back and pressing in. Soran heard his own cry of defiance fade into a wail of need.

It means, Seraph of Aerix, that you gave in first.

Malek growled something in the dialect of the pits, an insult or an endearment Soran's mind had lost all power to translate. He wrapped one hand around Malek's back, dug his nails into the skin beneath them.

He canted his hips again and drove himself back onto Malek. His other hand moved frantically over his own flesh, stoking the heat within it until he shuddered and cried out. His release spattered his chest as his body spasmed over its invader. Malek flooded him a moment later, letting go with a rumbling roar.

Soran smirked through the haze of pleasure. *You have me, Lord of the Pits. For the moment. But don't forget how much you wanted this.*

Don't forget what I've taken from you.

CHAPTER NINE

MALEK DREAMED.

He dreamed of himself, wreathed by the black clouds of his city and flanked by the lights of its factories. Then the blackness and light shifted. Vareth and Kenn stood at his sides, the rest of his victors behind them. They formed the vanguard of a vast army, pouring from the Molten Belt. Above him he heard the scream of starcraft, swooping down from the skies to rain death on his enemies.

He smiled in his sleep, turning in the bed as the image changed again, the flames thinning as they twisted skyward, becoming a delicate metallic filigree. He'd never seen them in person, not yet. But he recognized the towers suddenly rising around him, the ships zooming through a black sky.

But he wasn't dreaming about Aerix. The strands of metal shot up from the ground like shimmering roots. They twined around monoliths of stone and metal and curled over the smooth surface of pyramids. Figures appeared amid his armies, their bright blue eyes staring into the sky.

He didn't need to look at the man behind him to know who he was. He smiled as the figure streaked past him, dark red hair like blood streaming behind. He reached out a hand, but Soran stepped away from him.

The ground beneath them rose, lifting them through smoke and clouds alike. He stepped toward the platform's edge and Soran followed. When he looked down again, the flames of war burned, climbing up to the skies just as the gleaming towers had.

Then the platform shifted again. A throne appeared in the center of the dais, built of sturdy plates of metal, as in Dis. Its back rose in a chevron shape, reminding him of his own spearhead symbol.

But as he watched, the metal tendrils sprouted from the floor around it, winding over the arms and back of the throne in elaborate patterns and finally freezing there. *Symbiosis? Or do those vines wait to choke it?* He growled and turned to look at his companion. But Soran only laughed, a giddy half-mad giggle, and bowed to let him pass.

He took his seat on the throne, wary, not wanting the filigree to come alive and trap him. But it lay still. Soran smirked again and stepped toward him, reaching down for a kiss. As their lips met, he caught sight of a flash of metal. *Another gleam from the decorations? A reflection from Soran's clothing?*

Or the knife, catching him off-guard at last?

He twisted to one side and reached for Soran's wrist. But no sooner had his hand closed around it than the dream faded around him.

He'd thrown an arm around Soran in his sleep. But Soran, too, was sleeping. He murmured, an amused little purr. *Are you dreaming of me also?* He brushed his lips against the nape of Soran's neck. The skin felt soft, not yet weathered by the harsh atmosphere of the city. He pressed a kiss to it, suddenly aware that his own lips were chapped and dry.

Soran whirled around, snapped awake by the sensation. Trapped by Malek's arms, he could turn but not move away, and his thin hands curled into claws against Malek's chest.

Malek felt him tremble and waited. Soran's fingernails dug into his chest, but the mild prick of it was nothing. He watched the bright blue eyes narrow, the thick lips curl into a mocking smile.

"So," Soran relaxed his hands and pressed them against Malek's chest, "you're awake."

"So are you, apparently." Malek looked down at Soran's hands. "I see you've decided I'm not a threat."

Soran wrapped one arm around Malek's back. "Have I?" His other arm curled around the back of Malek's head, drew it down into a kiss.

Malek chuckled and kept his mouth closed. Soran opened his mouth wide and locked his arms tight around Malek's back.

Still snickering, Malek opened his mouth and let Soran's greedy lips swallow his laughter.

Malek chuckled, remembering the rumors about the Skyknights' alterations. He'd never paid much attention to such stories. Giving in to desire on occasion was pleasant enough, but to let to let lust drive him would impede his plans. He had attractive enough people among his chosen elite, should he want them.

He'd noticed Soran's interest immediately. And planned to make use of it from the beginning. But he had never imagined he'd be lying here now.

He tilted his head up, breaking the kiss. "So much for playing coy. Are you always this eager when you finally give in?"

Soran's mouth twisted into a scowl. Then he arched against Malek again, pressing their bodies together. "And if I am?" he answered, his lips moving to Malek's neck, ghosting over the skin and the muscle it covered. "Then what?"

Malek let Soran have his moment. It wasn't often Soran labored for his pleasure, after all. But if he wanted an answer to that—

Malek pulled away, and Soran looked up, his brows knitting in irritation. Malek took advantage of the moment to grab Soran's chin and hold it still. "Then we have a world to conquer, Seraph of Aerix."

Soran grinned and licked his lips.

Malek looked out on a sea of faces. His great hands gripped the sides of a podium carved not with the arena's circular mark, but with his spearhead symbol. The symbol itself was dark, but pipes of light encircled it, illuminating it from behind. While the podium itself was plain yet sturdy, the design had been fashioned with thoughtful care.

Black banners ringed the arena stands, adorned with the same mark, like the crowd had come to the pits to watch a bout, just like they might on any other day. But the monitors focused only on Malek's podium now. Only on him.

They filled the stands of the arena, but the sands today were empty. There was only the podium, and the man standing behind it. Screens projected an image for those too far away to see. But today they all focused on the same thing. Their faces were dirty with soot and red or tanned with the heat of the factories. Most were citizens of Dis, but Kenn and his spies had told Malek that some of them had come from across the Molten Belt.

Most didn't know what had brought them here. They couldn't know, not when Malek's negotiations with Soran had begun in a room none of them had ever seen and concluded in a bed none of them had ever known existed.

And yet they had all come at his call, as obedient as his elite. He smiled at that.

But all this had happened so quickly. He'd planned to wait. But then Soran had visited, and left, and come again.

And given Senator Derell information.

It was about why Malek is collecting people, Senator Derell had said. And Soran hadn't given him the answer, but he would find out soon enough. Which meant his people had to know first. Had to know now.

Ready or not.

His victors were all here, dispersed in an exacting mimicry of randomness that only Kenn could make convincing.

A handful of others wore hoods or cloaks to cover their features. One bore a series of unique tattoos. Another had dyed her skin. A third had reshaped his face to resemble a beast. So far, most of the crowd hadn't noticed. They were too focused on Malek, waiting for what he had to say, the silence crackling with their anticipation.

But every now and then, Malek saw someone's gaze flit away from him. He watched one woman stare too long at the person standing next to her, saw a man squint to focus on someone far away, blinking as though he'd seen a ghost.

Perhaps you have. The victor he stared at, a broad-framed man with graying hair, had supposedly died years ago, his reflexes dulled just enough by age that he'd met an untimely end in a brawl after his last match.

And of course, there was Soran, his head and shoulders rising above all but a few who had seen fit to modify themselves to be taller. At Kenn's suggestion and Vareth's insistence, he'd worn a hood as well.

Which made it less obvious what he was. But few had the telltale physique of one of Aerix's aristocrats. Anyone with sharp enough eyes could guess that a Skyknight had come to see this. Anyone with a sharp mind could wonder why.

And he was close enough for Malek to see him smirk.

Still, you've earned the right to it, my Prince of the Air. How is it that every time you give me what I want, you also manage to force my hand? Malek didn't let himself smile too broadly. He swept an arm in front of him in the manner of an experienced showman.

"I meant to give a message to the people of Dis," he began, "but there are too many of you here for that. You've come from the Molten Belt and the provinces that surround it, more pouring into the city than even my pits can hold. Why is that?

"Usually, you come to this arena to watch the fights. To see what the Senate and the Councils and all the other forces claiming to civilize our society forbid you: battle, as those born to battle fight it."

A few voices and fists rose in the crowd. Others stared ahead quietly. Malek ignored them. They'd be his soon enough. Or remain irrelevant. "The Senate bids you build for them. You built their world with your own hands. Think of Delen. How much of its metal comes from Dis and the Belt?"

"Almost all of it!" someone shouted.

"They decide your purpose and your rank and dictate the very course of your life. But how much of what they have came from you?" He lowered his voice. "This world is yours. You created it."

They did not cheer. It was too much for them. They were not ready. Not now. Not yet.

He'd known they wouldn't be. This was too soon. But the Senate knew of his elite already, and Soran had made his promise.

They would come to him, ready or not.

They had to.

He swallowed and went on. "Here you destroy. Here your shame becomes your strength. Here you see yourselves."

This time the crowd did answer, a low rumble of approval. Malek held up a hand. "But today I am not bringing you bloodsports."

Soran laughed. Malek couldn't hear it, not over the noise of the barely-restrained crowd, but he saw the movement, and a moment's gleam of blue from the eyes winking under the fabric.

"I have proven myself the greatest of the fighters. You've dubbed me the Destroyer. I hear what you whisper: that I am unstoppable." He lifted a hand and swept it in front of him..

A cheer rose. He cut it off with a violent gesture. "But tell me, any of you, all of you: What does that mean?"

He fell silent. They stared at one another, bewildered, some still growling in remembered approval. Most simply waited, each no doubt hoping that his neighbor could unravel Malek's riddle.

"You're stronger than anyone else," someone called from the front rows. He thumped a meaty hand against his chest. "You're the best we've ever seen. You could kill anyone in the Belt without blinking. Seems to me you don't need anythin' else."

Malek chuckled. He saw the white flash of grins spread from face to face—greedy, predatory little smiles on the faces of those who'd gathered to hear him, knowing little smirks on the faces of his victors.

And on the face of his new ally.

"I don't need anything else. Not Malek, the man who stands before you. Not the Destroyer, the legend he made of himself. But think. I fight. I kill. Why?"

"Power!" someone called.

"For power? That woman there said I have more power than I could ever need. But even if I wanted more, what would that matter to you? Why listen to me?"

"They tell us we're scum," said someone else. "You just said the world belongs to us."

"It does belong to you. I've spent years collecting the stories you've never heard—myths and legends, yes, but also history. This city's history. The Belt's history. Our history—as our people taught it. You've been told they never wrote it down. That they were too stupid, too brutish, too violent to write. Do you like hearing me say that isn't true?"

"Yes!" called several voices.

"Then all you have to do is record my speeches and listen to them carefully enough to reason out the truth. Why make the trek out here to see me speak?"

"Something's happening," the woman answered, flint-gray eyes focused on Malek. "We all know it."

Malek nodded, his face grave. "Then look around you."

On cue, the victors stepped forward, just far enough to make themselves visible. The few who had worn hoods removed them. They made no further moves, neither stepping toward Malek, nor nodding, nor speaking. The monitors' focus shifted from one victor to the next, displaying close-ups of faces the crowd had long since stopped expecting to see.

As one, the audience gasped. Whispers and cries followed, names shouted like discoveries, epithets whispered like prayers.

"I thought Alar the Silent was dead," Malek heard, a tiny snatch of wonder carried to his ears on the wind.

"I thought—"

"But I thought—"

"But she—"

"Everyone knows he—"

"It's not my prowess in the pits that makes you admire me," Malek said when the noise began to die. "It's that I have a purpose. Without that purpose, I am no more than anyone else here. A fighter like any other.

"The men and women who run this planet robbed you of your heritage, because your heritage is dangerous. I'm bringing it back to you."

The gasps and whispers became a cheer, ringing painfully in Malek's ears.

They have to. He smiled.

And Soran frowned. Malek thought again of the Skyknights' famed sensitivity and fought down a snicker. "But these victors are not coming back to the pits."

Another gasp. A rumble of discontent.

Malek felt it too, deep within himself. *Not coming back.*

Even here, even giving his people back their heroes, it settled like a lead weight in his chest. *They are not coming back.*

I am not coming back.

"Why should they?" he forced himself to say. "They're the best of the best. If they come back to the pits, sooner or later they will fight one another. Is that really what you want—your heroes brought back to you, only to die for you in a blaze of glory and a pretty spray of blood?"

He could hear their confusion. Some growled in anger. He welcomed it, closing his eyes and letting it wash over him. After all, he was angry too.

They could attack him, he realized. Security was tight, aided by hidden contraptions Kenn and Zarel had invented, should they need to activate them. And his elite would rush to his aid, should the mob turn its rage on him. But the crowd was large, and large crowds had their own kind of power.

Still, he didn't fear them. They belonged to him. This speech would make sure of it.

"It would be a waste!" he roared. "These people you've spent your lives admiring, killing one another for a moment of entertainment. Turning on one another. Why? You've named me your Destroyer, your favorite bringer of death. But I say you admire me because you know I'm more than that.

"And it's not just me. Look at yourselves. Look at these victors who've come back to you. You think you're seeing dead men and women coming to life. But they abandoned the pits. They became warriors. Then they vanished, leaving that behind. And now they've come back. You welcomed them. But why welcome them when they abandoned you?"

He watched the victors close to him; he saw their faces harden. He saw the telltale slide of hands as they reached for hidden weapons. He saw Soran smile, a glitter of blue peeking from under the only hood anyone still wore. Then Soran drew it back, shaking out his hair. A few people in the audience gasped.

Good. Let's see if they're ready to face the truth. Or whether they choose to tear their world to pieces to preserve the lie.

"I'll tell you why. Because you admire them. For the same reason you admire me. In the pits, they learned to be warriors. The people who rule this world said they deserved nothing, but they found a great destiny through blood and fire. Just as I did. Just as you will."

Faces turned to him, rapt, attentive. Adoring. Too adoring for what he meant to tell them, and some deep uneasiness stirred in him.

They weren't ready.

"I asked you why you were here," he said. "I know why already. Do you?"

They went on staring.

"Only a few of you gathered here fought in the arena. But all of you watched. You saw what they had become, and your spirits answered. You were once warriors, too.

"The ancient records prove it. We will broadcast those records. If our channels are cut, we will broadcast them again. So will you. You will record them, and watch them, and give them to those who have not seen."

Someone roared, perhaps inspired by Malek's words, perhaps

enraged by the implication that he might not have it. Others took it up, the sound echoing through the crowd.

Malek couldn't help but glance at Soran. But Soran wasn't so inspired, or didn't want to look like it. Instead, he threw back his head and laughed. He swept an arm in front of him in a sarcastic gesture, no doubt wanting Malek to see it.

Malek ignored him. Better to save his attention for the crowd. "They are warriors. You hope to be. They have something to fight for. I ask you now: do you?"

Thousands of eyes fixed on him. Thousands of faces hardened. They would turn on him, or his words would forge a new purpose for them. Either way, they would be more than they had been.

"Will you accept the lives the Senate has bestowed upon you?"

A chorus of "No!"

"Then how will you find your freedom? By doing nothing more than watching pit fights, staring from the stands or gathering around a videoscreen?"

"No!"

"Will you exult in what you are for only a moment? Or will you carry that freedom with you when the fights are over?"

They watched, and listened, and waited.

"My victors are free. They came back to show you how to free yourselves."

They leaned forward, rapt and attentive. Malek slashed a hand diagonally in front of his body in a forceful gesture of refusal.

"I can say no more for now. Speaking to you here is risky enough. But you will learn the truth soon enough."

Some blinked. Some shook their heads. Others nodded, and pumped fists in the air, and cried out. He silenced them again with another sharp gesture, and spoke his next words lower than the rest, to be sure they would lean in and listen.

"When I do, you will be ready. When I do, you will know the truth. I will tell you why your lives were stolen, and I will show you what you really are." He waited. The hands that had clutched the podium curled into fists at his sides.

He heard the trill of Soran laughing.

He spoke clearly and slowly, each word a javelin hurled at his enemies, a goad to prick the hearts of those he sought to lead.

"When I do, you will take back what is yours."

He raised a hand and roared, the bellow of the Destroyer as his opponent fell.

They answered, their hands rising into the air.

I am the beast that opened its eyes. Malek closed his screaming mouth and smiled.

And now they choose to open theirs.

CHAPTER TEN

SORAN PACED through a hall of monitors, their displays a riot of light and movement. But not sound; he'd turned down the volume so he could watch them all at once. That left only a low, steady buzz as they competed with one another. Glyphs scrolled across the bottom of the screens, a dizzy whirl of information.

He'd thought of drawing drapes over the windows, long panels of black glass that would ensure no overly curious member of his army could peek in at the wrong moment. But he was a Skyknight of Aerix, and Skyknights didn't block out the sky unless they had to.

Besides, Kenn and his little minions were broadcasting all over the planet. There was nothing playing on these monitors that wasn't available for anyone to just access for themselves.

One flickered. Vareth and Dia appeared, sparring, the smaller woman's movement a flurry of punches and kicks. Soran pursed his lips and turned away.

Behind him, he heard footsteps. High-caste people, their movements almost silent under the buzz of the monitors. But Soran was the Seraph, his alterations the best Aerix's doctors could provide. And alterations or no, a sovereign had to hear his enemies coming.

These weren't enemies. He could tell that from the quiet. But one of them was standing far too close.

He whirled to face the offender, a woman with pale skin and two long black braids. Gold ribbons wove through them, glinting in the light from the windows. Her eyes were almond-shaped. They might once have been dark, but now they were blue, richer than Soran's but less bright.

"Skycaptain Ania," he snapped. "Won't you at least stand back?"

The young woman bowed her head, as decorum required. She stepped backward with the smooth, easy grace of a high-caste Skyknight. But when she lifted her head again, a grin flitted across her face. "My apologies, Sor—Seraph. It's just that I—I can't believe there's so much of it."

"Ania," her companion put in from a sensible distance, turning away from a monitor.

He had dusky skin and dark brown hair. His eyes, a slightly brighter blue than Ania's, shone above a slender nose and thin mouth. His blue-gray clothing was as precisely pressed as his hair was styled. On his left breast shone a silver insignia, proclaiming his rank.

"Tanth, don't—" she began. Then she frowned and inclined her head again. "First Skycaptain Tanth. Please do not—"

Soran waved a hand. "That's all right, Skycaptain. I know perfectly well how close you two are." He chuckled, seeing Ania blush. Tanth scowled and said nothing.

Soran shrugged and turned to another monitor, studying the lined face of an older victor for signs of anger, determination, interest, or boredom.

He would have expected boredom. This "programming" had run for hours. And each program had been precisely captioned, as though Malek's little army had nothing better to do than record an endless series of propaganda films.

But the victors didn't look bored. Some grinned, fierce and feral. Others looked determined, their mouths as grimly set as Tanth's. Others stared directly into the cameras, standing tall, their muscular bodies radiating pride.

Soran had expected that Malek's team would air something like this on the arena's channels. They hadn't. If anything, the programs showing the bouts had grown tamer. Malek rarely gave comments afterward, beyond a scant few sentences in praise of the winner.

How terribly dull.

He spread the real message on an ever-shifting array of little-used frequencies broadcast throughout the Molten Belt. Some ran all day and into the night. Others played one little show and went dead, only re-emerging hours later.

"Well?" Soran turned around to face his Skycaptains. "What do you think?"

He shouldn't have been so irritated. He'd told them about Malek from the beginning. Still, he'd made the two flights to Dis by himself. Somehow, now that it came down to it, he wasn't sure he liked the idea of sharing.

The broadcasts, the plans, the coming war. Malek had offered all of it like a secret. Like a gift. And now Ania was staring at a monitor, a faint blush reddening her cheeks. Soran scowled and pursed his lips.

Tanth shook his head.

Ania didn't turn to look at Soran, but she did talk. "I think it's fascinating. That one—that's Vareth the Crusher. I never thought we'd see her again." Her hands moved to mimic one of the attacks Dia was demonstrating.

Soran blinked. *See her again? We?*

Some Skyknights followed the fights, of course. Watching barbarians fight and die was, sometimes, just too intriguing to pass up. But—

"Why, Skycaptain Ania," he said, smirking. "I never figured you for a fan."

Tanth snorted. "Then you don't pay much attention. I can't go a week without hearing about some bout or other."

Tanth's voice wasn't deep. Not compared to someone like Malek's. The regimen of alterations left very few Skyknights with low voices. Still, for a Skyknight, the smooth, deep pitch of his voice was an anomaly.

It made him something of a curiosity, and even made him popular in some circles. The younger Skyknights liked to hear him recite from histories, or recount legends from the old times of war, just because they liked his voice.

Ania turned. "We learn techniques. We're trained to defend the City. But when has any of us even had to step out of a starfighter in recorded memory? These men and women are warriors. Real ones."

Tanth shook his head. "These men and women pummel one another for sport until one of them dies. That's a barroom brawl under lights. Not a battle between warriors."

"Oh, I'm with you," Soran stepped closer to Tanth, purring with laughter. "But I did invite him here."

Ania glared. "Just—just look at that. What does it look like? That's the block from the Third Form." She raised her hands, slicing through the air. "That doesn't look like a barroom brawl to me."

She smiled, gliding through a sequence of steps with the grace and smoothness of a well-trained Skyknight. Then she stopped and looked at Tanth and Soran. "Did you two ever figure they'd know something like that?"

"No," Tanth answered, his voice flat. "And whatever I think, it's already been decided."

Soran grinned. "Yes, it has. And why should I be surprised? I've been to the Grand Arena. Though whatever that is—" he nodded to the monitor—"it's much more interesting than big brutes running at one another with axes and clubs.

"I saw one myself on my last visit. And yes, they're impressive. If you like watching an unwashed brute chop a man's head off and wave it around." His mouth twisted in an exaggerated expression of distaste.

"You saw Malek fight!" Ania grinned.

The image of Vareth and Dia flickered out with a crackle of static. Soran chuckled. That happened sometimes, the hidden broadcasts found and stopped. Sometimes it reappeared right away. Sometimes it replayed hours later. Sometimes Soran never saw it again. Soran chuckled. Kenn was probably behind all this. If the Senate hacking annoyed him, that was all to the good.

But no one else in the room was thinking about Kenn. And Ania was still looking at him with that lopsided, eager grin. He huffed in annoyance. "I watched Malek? How would you know who I went to see?"

"Easy," Ania answered. "If you'd seen anybody else, you would either have complained less or sounded more like you meant it."

Tanth stood resolutely silent.

Which probably means he agrees with her. Soran's cheeks flushed. "What exactly are you implying?"

"My deepest apologies, Seraph." Ania glided over to another monitor, her almond eyes still sparkling with mirth.

She paused, a little too long. Soran's head snapped up, his eyes narrowing as he stared at Ania. Her hand cleaved the air, mimicking a deadly strike. Her eyes were bright, the skin of her cheeks flushed with pink.

Tanth glowered right along with him. That was good, at least. The last thing Soran needed was one of his Skycaptains fawning over savages.

"Just listen to him!" Ania said. "He sounds almost like Tanth."

Tanth growled. Soran sighed and looked over at the monitor. Malek stood at a podium bearing his symbol, probably the same one he'd used for his recent speech. As before, the spearhead design slashed across its front, pipes of light glowing cold white behind it.

Malek's eyes, black as his symbol, stared ahead. He spoke in clear, clipped tones, his voice moderated and precise.

That's a bit much. Even for a showman like you.

He used the pits' dialect, the usual low, guttural growl even and clear. As clear as one could make those noises, anyway.

"Do you know what he's saying, Seraph?" Ania asked.

Soran had picked up a few words, including the phrase he'd startled Malek with in that fancy little room. He snickered, his flesh tingling at the memory.

But picking up a few vulgarities wasn't the same as understanding a whole dialect. Frowning in concentration, he gave the command to turn up the volume, and listened for long moments.

He scowled. "Not all of it. I understand enough to know it's his usual blather about the Old Empire. Battle and glory and history and such. Beyond that, I couldn't tell you." He shook his head. Why did it bother him so much? "It's a language for beasts. Even Malek himself agreed." He grinned. "I called them thugs and savages, and he didn't argue the point. Maybe he decided to snarl one of his speeches in their native language."

"That's not a speech."

Soran turned to face Tanth, his grin widening. *I'm sure you wouldn't think so.*

But Tanth didn't say something derisive. He lifted his head high, staring at one of the windows, light sparkling in his eyes. He opened his mouth and began to recite.

What are you doing?

Soran recognized the words immediately. Every Skyknight learned the ceremonial language from young childhood. Their teachers demanded they take it as seriously as practicing their first fighting forms. Only people like Tanth took it that seriously. But they learned them, all the same.

Soran's lips moved silently as Tanth's voice rang through the hall. He could see Ania's doing the same. The old stories were a sacred tradition. When one Skyknight began to recount them, it was natural to join in. A reflex, almost.

Another monitor flickered on with a crackle of angry sound. Jolted out of his reverie, Soran stared at Tanth. "What exactly was that about?"

"The program, my Seraph. Malek isn't giving a speech. He's reciting."

"Reciting?"

Tanth closed his eyes, his lips moving in synch with the words coming from Malek's projection. After a moment, he spoke again. "Listen to the rhythm. It's metered." He hummed, ticking out the stresses in the words. "That's not a speech, Soran. That's poetry."

"Poetry?" Soran threw back his head and laughed, too loudly. "You mean to tell me that in his little forays through stolen records, the Destroyer found poetry?"

"Poetry." Ania shook her head. "I never would have thought...but it makes sense. They stole this stuff—" she swept a hand in front of her, indicating the flickering monitors—"from the Library."

"So?" Soran snapped. A queasy feeling twisted through his gut.

"So they keep talking about the Empire. The stuff Malek found in the records he stole."

"Ania," Tanth said, his voice even sterner than usual. "Don't tell me you actually believe Dis was the capitol."

The capitol? There were conspiracy theories, and then there were conspiracy theories. Malek had always claimed Dis was a great city once, but surely he didn't think that a factory town had once been the capitol of the Empire!

Ania put her hands on her hips in an exaggerated gesture. "Of course I don't believe it! But—" She stood straighter, her posture as rigid and formal as Tanth's—"if they found records of ceremonial fighting styles, why not poetry too?"

We were scholars, Seraph.

Soran shook his head. He heard a small sound from Tanth, a gasp of surprise the deep-voiced Skycaptain couldn't quite suppress.

We were warriors. We were trained as your Skyknights are trained.

Soran coughed to compose himself. "Well, if he did find art from the Empire, it's a pity he ruins it by growling in that dialect."

Tanth blinked, his scowl deepening. "Not if that's the language the poem was written in."

"Language? It's nothing but gutter-talk, for a brawl or a fight. Or a bed."

Tanth's face twisted into a mask of distaste.

"Maybe it isn't," said Ania.

"I don't like it," said Tanth. "I suspect I like it less than you do, my Seraph. I think you'd be done mocking it if you didn't like it."

Soran grimaced. That Malek had risen to lead a city of thugs and hooligans, he could handle. That he'd made warriors of a few of them, he could respect. That the wisest and the strongest wanted war against a Senate his city had always hated, he could honor.

But—

This isn't the Dis I want to build, Seraph. This is the Dis I want to rebuild.

Soran had said it himself, hadn't he? *Dis, the crown jewel of an empire.*

Damn it.

Soran leaned toward the monitor. He remembered the bar where he'd watched Malek speak and heard the patrons cheer and argue. He remembered the cadence of their words, Malek's precise pronunciation. "You're right. These aren't the noises they make in the pits. This is clearer. Crisper."

As if on cue, the screen flared once, a searing white that stung the gathered Skyknights' vision. Then the broadcast died.

"Not again!" muttered Ania.

Soran stared at the dead screen. "So there was an older version of their speech, then. Lost to time and history. And Malek wants to recreate it, like the obsessive he is."

"Unless the language of the pits was the formal language spoken in the Belt centuries ago," Tanth said.

"When the capitol of the Empire was there," Ania finished.

Soran's hand moved to his belt so quickly that even his two best Skyknights couldn't catch him. But both saw the bright silver of the blade in his hand, the fey glint in his eye.

Ania's eyes widened. "Uh, that is, if you...if you actually believe what these propaganda videos say about it." She held up a hand. "Which we don't. So calm down."

Soran lowered the blade. He leaned against the dead monitor and pressed his free hand to the still-warm metal. "Oh, you're brilliant, King of the Barbarians! Gutter curses and maledictions. Growls fit for beasts. Until you come along, and prove that the snarls of a pack of dogs were once the language of high art."

The other Skyknights didn't answer. They just waited. They knew Soran and he knew them.

But they didn't know Malek.

"I don't see why Malek would learn a dead dialect," Ania said. "He's a fighter. Not a poet. Why go to all the trouble to learn a language?"

"Pride," Soran answered. Another monitor went black with a screech of feedback. *Perhaps you're nobler than I thought, King of the Barbarians. But I have my towers, my starships, my Skyknights. And like any beast, you have scraps.* "The Senate thinks of the gladiators as throwaways. Brutes, fit for lives of hard labor and pointless brawling." He nodded to Ania. "Even their speech is crude. And then along comes Malek. Their hero. Their Destroyer."

"Speaking the people's dialect," Tanth said.

"Oh, he always did that. His accent is terrible. But now he's speaking their dialect like a Senator giving a speech."

Ania opened her mouth. Soran shook his head. She bowed and fell silent.

Soran laughed again, the last trilling note of the fit of laughter that had seized him. "All over Dis. Across the Belt. And anywhere else on the planet intrigued enough to receive the transmission." He pulled his fingers off the monitor, tossed his dagger into the air with his other hand, and caught it.

Tanth looked up, the mirthless blue eyes staring straight at Soran now. "You invited him here. You promised him our aid. I hope that's enough."

"I didn't promise him anything," Soran purred. "I told him that if he wanted an alliance, he could try to convince us. Even I can't waltz out there and tell the Skyknights we're flying to someone else's war."

Tanth nodded. "He's set something in motion. Something that will set the flames of the Belt ablaze in the hearts and minds of everyone in it. Or so he hopes."

"Well, it's not my fault he's convincing," Soran said, thinking of rough hands on his body and the pressure of a fighter's bruising grip.

"He convinced you," Ania retorted, her voice sharp.

Soran threw his dagger up again. "Just because he's up to something doesn't mean we play by his rules." His hand flicked out to catch it. "You should know me better than that."

"That's exactly why I don't like it," Tanth answered.

"He set something up and so did you," Ania agreed. She wasn't smiling now.

His eyes still locked on Soran's, Tanth inclined his head, exactly as formality required. Then he turned on his heel and walked toward the door at the end of the hall with measured, purposeful strides.

Ania shot a look at Soran. Scowling, he waved her away.

CHAPTER ELEVEN

"WE CAN'T allow it," the woman said, hands crossed in front of her. Like so many in Dis, her skin bore a scar: a jagged, pale streak across the skin of one brown forearm.

Others sat arrayed around her. One crossed his arms, echoing her gesture. Another glared from under knotted brows. In the harsh light of the hall, Malek could see perspiration gleam on his bald head. Another had a metallic forearm, a replacement for a lost limb, tipped with a blade. It flicked in and out of its mounting as its owner's gaze flicked from Malek to Kenn to Vareth and back again. Only one seemed unaffected, staring at Malek and his companions with wide, unblinking eyes.

Clearly, they were nervous. That was something, at least. But Malek scowled at them anyway. *The Hall you stand in is too good for you.*

It was nothing compared to the Great Hall in his records, of course. Still, it was clearly the same place, or rebuilt to look something like it.

The City Council sat on a raised dais at the center of an octagonal room. A ring of metallic steps circled the platform. They sat in plain chairs, but the high backs of their seats rose above them in chevron shapes like the throne from his dream. Light strips cut across the walls at bold diagonals that hinted at movement and life.

What had it looked like then? The loss was a physical pain.

And now these fools were in his way.

The ancients, his records said, had built their Hall out of alloys long lost. The metal hadn't just reflected the glow of the lights, but cast it all around the room in prisms, bathing the room in patterns of light. Patterns meant to calm and soothe in peacetime and to stir the blood in war. Malek had imagined them many times, poring over the descriptions.

And in the days of Dis's glory, only one throne had stood in the center of the dais.

Malek clenched a fist. He had plans, of course. Plans to rebuild it all. But how much of the ancient glory could he recapture, even once he'd finally won his glorious victory?

He blinked and forced his attention on the twins. They stood one on each side of the hall, their expressions unreadable.

Like the council members, they bore blades and guns in plain sight on their belts, a sign of the Council's favor and trust. Dis had always been a city of fighters. Most of the people seated on the dais in front of him had a history in the pits themselves.

The twins, for their part, carried blasters on one hip and blades on the other. When drawn, the blade would electrify, like most of the pit fighters' weapons. The other victors went nowhere unarmed, but they'd had to sneak what they carried past the sensors. Malek had left even Soran's dagger behind.

He'd worn it too often. People would be looking for it.

Instead, he carried two small blades and a few other devices, fashioned by Zarel out of materials chosen by Kenn. Most would ignite when thrown or explode on impact.

At his side, Vareth's fists clenched, mirroring his own.

Kenn, for his part, said nothing, his posture stiff and his visor concealing his face. He wore his crimson Arena insignia on the band at his shoulder, not the symbol of Malek's elite.

That was probably wise. But he didn't have to hide his true allegiance. Hiding was no longer an option, not when Soran had forced their hands. Not when the victors had come back, too early.

Vareth knew it. She wore Malek's symbol openly, a defiant slash of black against a plate of metal at her breast. Malek had considered ordering her not to. But now, he had to admit he appreciated her boldness.

"You can't allow it?" Malek said, echoing the words of the woman on the dais. "How can you say that, High Councilwoman Xin?"

"That is our judgment."

"Judgment? We are citizens of Dis, like any others. And any citizen may come and go as he likes. The City Council has no control over that. Unless you've made new rules I haven't heard yet. Or unless new rules have come down from higher places."

"Higher places?" said the quiet one from the shadows. He was new; Ilen was his name. Only the twins knew him well.

"We don't like the Senate's meddling any more than you do," he was saying. Malek watched him, cautious. Was that a confession of similar feelings? Or just an attempt to soften the blow?

"Someone has to stick it to those bastards now and again," a deep-voiced woman growled, rising to her feet. "Why not someone who's actually frightening?"

Xin laughed and rose to her feet. "I agree with that. I think we all do."

"I don't," put in the one-armed man, grizzled and gray-haired. Malek didn't know him personally. That was probably by design.

He'd been a fighter in the pits, years before Malek's rise to power. The prosthesis on his arm was his signature weapon. The audience had long since forgotten his name, and called him the Blade after it. He'd won a championship just a few short years before Malek went from a promising new fighter in the arena to a force in its administration. Soon after that, however, he'd retired from fighting.

Malek suspected it wasn't a coincidence.

Why shouldn't you resent me? Soon after my ascension, those you would have respected most began to disappear.

But does that make you so afraid of being in my pocket that you prefer being in the Senate's?

Xin stood tall, her expression harsh. "We can't let you go now. Not with these broadcasts going out all over the Belt."

"None of them are coming from official channels, High Councilwoman," Kenn said. "The arena channel is broadcasting nothing but the matches. Even the speeches Malek made after them are gone now."

"That doesn't mean anything," snarled the bald man, his voice sour. "We've seen the videos and you're all in them."

"It's too much," another woman put in. "Too much, too fast. We've looked the other way because the pits brought us prosperity. But we're not going to be a home base for whatever revolt you're planning."

Xin nodded. "We've sent your two liasons back to you for months, telling you to keep whatever it is you're doing under the radar."

"We have," Malek answered. "But now we must go."

"We don't like the Senate's nonsense either," Xin said. "That's why we've let you get away with all of this."

Vareth scoffed. "Let? You haven't let anyone do anything."

A flash of fear skipped from one Councilmember's face to the next. The Blade's weapon twitched, its point flicking in and out again.

Malek fought down a laugh. "Vareth is right. Tena and Tor have come back every time. Telling you our answer is no."

"Your answer." The Blade chuckled, cold and malicious. "You think your answer is the City's answer? You think we're gonna stand for you and some poncy Skyknight telling us what to do?"

"Besides," added the shifty-eyed one, "you said nothing in that speech about stirring up a city halfway across the planet to help you build a revolution."

Vareth's hands tightened into fists. "Wouldn't need to do that if you weren't getting in our way, old man."

Malek hissed and gestured for silence. He had no problem with Vareth tearing the fool apart. But letting her do that now would kill his movement at its birth.

And this still might. He bit his lip to keep from snarling. He needed them, all of them.

Xin shook her head. "We owe you. Everyone knows that. We'd be nothing without the pits." Her arm slashed at the air, the reddish light shining on it as it moved. "We're the Senate's refuse bin, and the pits are the only reason the rest of the world gives a damn about us."

"Then let us go," Kenn said.

"We've spent years staying out of your way, and years keeping your secrets." Xin cast a glance at the twins. Malek saw Tor twitch and blink.

Is that distaste for the Council or for us? The twins always had chafed under Kenn. They'd liked working as liaisons between the victors and the city, and always hoped the Council would stand behind them in the end.

"We don't all like it. One-arm here can't stand it. Don't tell us now that we've made a mistake."

"We're just here to pass messages, High Councilwoman." Tena said.

Tor laughed and nodded. "We're not here to take sides."

Xin looked like she might say more, her face glowing livid orange in the light of the hall. But she only closed her mouth and shook her head. "You may run the arena, but it belongs to Dis. This history you've unearthed isn't just yours. It's ours."

"This unrest is ours?" Malek strode toward the dais. "This bitterness is ours?"

"You're the one stirring it up." The Blade's weapon flicked in and out of its mount. "Seems to me that makes it yours."

"I'm giving Dis back its history. The people know who stole it."

"Everyone's got plans," growled the Blade. "The Senate has 'em. You've got 'em. Dis may be the planet's trash bin, but everyone wants a piece of it."

"Because of the pits," Vareth raised her fists. "Because of us."

"The pits aren't you," the Blade retorted, and lunged for Vareth. She froze, a pillar of muscled weight. Malek smiled. Even if the damn fool ran down the stairs to get at her, she wouldn't be going anywhere.

Ilen scrambled to his feet, twin blasters in his hands. Slender but well-muscled, he threw himself between the two. "This is a Council meeting. Not a ring in the arena, either of you."

"There is one other city that belongs to itself," Malek said. "Is it so surprising I want to visit it?"

"We're not here to help you start a riot," spat the Blade. "Or a war."

"If a riot happens, it will happen. If war comes, there are far worse allies than the Skyknights of Aerix."

"Maybe so," offered the deep-voiced woman, "but the City Guard are already blocking your way."

Malek laughed. "You're misunderstanding me. Anyone who tries to bar my way—or stop any of my victors—will be forced out of it."

"You bastards would kill your own people," the Blade growled, his eyes trained on the blaster still pointed at him.

"The people are with us," said Kenn, raising his visor and giving the Council his best earnest expression.

"Are they?" The bald man drew his own weapon.

Malek heard the sharp sound of daggers being freed from sheaths, the hum of blasters readying. The twins stood fully armed, facing them, blue electricity crackling over their swords, their blasters glowing standard-issue turquoise as they charged.

The quiet one still stood with one blaster aimed at Vareth, but the other aimed at the Blade.

If we do fight, whose side will you take?

If he did choose the victors' side—and they got out of this—he would have to make a point of contacting him.

"Even your liaisons brought you here to tell you you'd gone too far this time, Destroyer," said Xin, a coil at her hip unraveling into a spined whip.

Malek watched the twins carefully. Tena's blaster was trained on his head, Tor's at Vareth's. But neither had aimed at Kenn, and Kenn was the one who had taken the twins under his wing.

Kenn stepped up to his place beside Malek. Metal glimmered in his grip. A good throw with some of Zarel's incendiaries could break through the light fixtures, and probably set one of them ablaze. That would give them some time, at least.

But what would it mean for them when they got back? When the rest of Dis found out that the very man who'd promised them a great destiny had set their Council hall on fire? Malek's head throbbed. He wished he were home, at his desk. Studying, and thinking, and planning.

This war must happen, he reminded himself. *If the Council has to burn for that, so be it.*

"We're not here to fight your battles for you," Tor said finally, turning on his heel. Tena followed suit a moment later.

"But you are here to fight his?" the Councilwoman said, her voice flinty with rage. "To turn this council hall into a battleground?"

"It seems to me," Tena said slowly, "that you're the one doing that."

"We're leaving," Kenn said, his fist still wrapped tightly around whatever he held.

The quiet man lowered the blaster pointed at Vareth. "I see no reason why we should prevent a fight out there by starting one in here."

Xin snarled, staring at the orange-streaked faces on both sides of her hall.

"Aerix doesn't give a damn about the city," the Blade growled. "They only care about themselves. And I say we're better off following their example than sucking up to some flyboy prince so they can get the glory." He scoffed. "If there's any glory to be had in whatever the hell he's planning anyway."

"You already know what that is," Tor answered, blue flame licking brightly along the surface of his blade as he turned. "If you've been paying attention."

"And getting a pack of fragile little brats, to do what you want is going to make that happen?" The Blade sliced at the air. "Skyknights fly starfighters because they're too delicate to fight on the ground."

"Understood," Malek answered. "But I am only leaving the city. There is no guarantee I will achieve anything. Those of you who worry my aims are the wrong ones may well be proven right by my own failure."

"Let's hope so," the Blade spat.

Malek swept his arm in front of him in another mock bow. Then he straightened. "So do you plan to make an issue of this? Or will you let me go and wait before setting yourselves against me?"

The council members murmured. Some glared at Malek, cursing to themselves in the dialect of the pits. None raised their voices.

After a moment, Ilen spoke. "If we bar Malek from leaving the city, we're no better than the Senate. If we bar our own people from resisting them, we become what they want us to be."

Malek nodded. "We are going, no matter what you say."

"You can't do that!"

"Don't waste lives throwing bodies in our way. You'll need them, when the time comes. So will I."

Grimacing, Xin nodded. "Go. Do whatever it is you plan to do. But I won't sacrifice this city to you. I won't let you bulldoze your way through our people."

"Don't think we're yours," snarled the Blade. "If you've done anything today, you've made sure we're not."

Malek raised his head. "I would expect nothing less."

CHAPTER TWELVE

"MALEK THE Destroyer," Soran murmured. "Drawn out of his little nest at last."

Senator Derell paced. He didn't even look out the windows. "Absolutely not, Seraph."

"My apologies. But I already promised him the chance to come here. In exchange for more information."

That wasn't what had happened at all. But it made perfect sense to pretend it. Especially when he had no more information to offer, not really.

He'd found out a few more things about a few more victors, most of them personal. Like that Tena was Tor's identical twin, her body feminized by hormones and alterations paid for with the twins' winnings in those few team fights they'd reminisced about in the bar.

Maybe gossip, to the Senate. But Soran was used to people with altered bodies and had no reason to care. It might explain why the twins had started their career in the pits, but it didn't explain where their loyalties lay now.

And Derell was here for politics, not secrets only fools would care about anyway.

Seeing Derell turn away, Soran allowed himself to grin. His guest wouldn't see the flush rising to his cheeks as he remembered the promise he'd made to Malek—and the things that had followed it.

Malek had played coy in the beginning, but once Soran had made his little promise, the King of the Barbarians had made up for lost time. He'd come back to Soran's fancy little room again and again. Soran reached up to touch his own cheek, remembered the scrape of calloused fingertips against his skin.

With that memory came others, ghosts of sensations flickering in his flesh. A mouth pressed too fiercely to his, the lips chapped and rough. His neck arched hard as they slid downward, kissing hard enough to leave the purple imprints of bruises on the smooth skin. Thick-muscled arms embracing his slender body too tightly, heedless of his fragility or deadly aware of it. A broad hand gripping at his flesh, moving over it as though compelled. The cold gleam in dark eyes as they watched and waited for him to give himself over.

You wanted to make me need you. Soran let his hand fall. *But you've made yourself need me.*

"You promised him?" Derell's voice snapped Soran out of his reverie.

Soran shifted his voice into his best conspiratorial purr. "I have something to show you."

"If you're playing more games with me, Seraph—"

"All you need to do is look down, Senator." Soran walked to the window, the memory of Malek's touch warming his blood.

Derell rushed up to stand beside Soran and frowned at the sight below.

The Square of the Sun stood several stories below the tower, a raised platform built of golden metal. Its massive span linked a ring of towers. The space between them served as a gathering place.

Or once had, anyway.

The craftsmen who had built it had inlaid a massive sun design into the floor. When the plaza was empty, those lucky enough to look down could see the intricate outline. Those walking below would only see a twisting mosaic of metal and stone.

In the long-ago days before Aerix's isolation, it had been a waypoint. Half market and half park, where traders, diplomats, and others came to deal with the denizens of the City in the Sky. But the Square was empty now. The only thing of note were the black banners ringing it, Malek's spearhead symbol winking silver as the flags flapped in the wind.

"It's already happening, Senator." Soran smiled. "He gave me his word he would come, in fact."

"All this for information?" Derell bared his teeth. "Or have you made up your mind?"

Predictable. "We're already planning his arrival. He will be welcomed with a festival."

"And you meant to tell us about this when exactly?"

"I'm telling you now."

"I should have this city leveled," Derell growled. The color in his iridescent eyes swirled, an echo of his rage.

"We can't do anything to him while he keeps himself holed up in Dis," Soran retorted, serenely calm. "The pits might as well be a citadel. If anyone you sent managed to get that far, his victors would tear him to pieces in minutes." He chuckled. "And that's if you get that far."

"Your point?"

"But here in Aerix, surrounded by trained warriors..."

"You're offering him to us."

"I'm offering him a chance to spread his message. That's what he wants. That's why he agreed to come."

Among other things. Soran fought down another shiver at the memory. His mouth twisted into a mocking grin. "Though it seems his communications team has proven quite capable of getting past you, Senator."

"Who are they?" Derell's voice was tight, his eyebrows creased in irritation. Light flickered on his badges as he moved.

"Is that a test? Fine." Soran spread his arms wide, the perfect picture of generosity. "That would be Kenn. And whoever Malek has working under him. Possibly the twins, though I don't think so."

"Kenn. The slim one with the helmet. I suppose that makes sense."

"He may be coming. I get the impression he's close to Malek." Soran held up a fist and clenched it. "Two birds, one stone, perhaps?" It was an enjoyable thought. As much as he didn't like Derell, he'd appreciate someone getting Kenn out of the way.

And Vareth, if Malek had the bad taste to bring her, too.

"The last time we spoke, you said you wanted Malek's protection more than ours," Derell persisted. "Now you want him dead?"

Soran took a step back. "Dead?"

Derell smiled placidly. "Isn't that what you were offering, Seraph?"

"I...I merely wasn't aware of your intentions. I thought you meant to capture him. I haven't heard of an execution in decades."

"Who said anything about an execution?"

Soran blinked. "You?"

"That would be barbaric."

"You're the one who mentioned killing him."

"Am I? I'd just as soon wash my hands of this whole business."

"Then why talk about him dying?"

"Sometimes, when a wild beast has grown too dangerous, it must be put down."

"Put down," Soran repeated. "But not executed."

King of the Barbarians. A beast to be hunted. He nearly broke out in laughter again. "Grown too dangerous? A city makes deathmatch fights its official sport for generations, and now they're too dangerous?"

Derell's mouth twisted into a scowl. He stared down at the brightly-lit sunburst. His body shook, as though he were forcing himself not to speak.

Soran stepped behind him, reaching for one of the blades in his boots. The hilt's warmth against his fingers reassured him. Powerful as Derell was, Malek was right. He was no warrior. But just as Soran took his moment to gloat, Derell whirled around. Soran slipped his hand behind his back.

"I have no quarrel with you, Senator," Soran said at last. "You want Malek out of the way. I'm giving you a chance to make that happen."

Derell stared at Soran's arm. He breathed deeply for several long moments and then spoke, pronouncing every word, slow and precise. "It's peace we want. It's peace the Old Empire could never settle for. It's peace that our system ensures."

Soran slid his hand to his side, revealing the blade but making no threatening moves. Derell's eyes flicked to the weapon. Soran smiled. "Peace?"

Derell laughed, a mirth so easy it made Soran glad he held a weapon. "Your city is a marvel, Seraph. But you've lived too long shut in it."

"If you mean to kill Malek, why now?"

"Those broadcasts—"

"Don't insult me. You knew what he took from Delen's library. He was a celebrity even then. I'm sure his broadcasts help him spread whatever he found in those books. But he doesn't need them."

Derell's eyes narrowed. "Malek is a dangerous man. When his aggression isn't properly directed."

"Properly directed?" Soran licked his lips again and laughed. He thought of Malek, holding a bloodied head by its hair. "You think you can direct him?"

"We think he should keep to his little cesspool. As long as he stays in his pits, everything else is irrelevant."

"Keep to his cesspool?" Soran chuckled and stepped toward the window again. He looked out at the banners' dance. "And here I thought you wanted the pits shut down."

"Shut down?" Derell's mouth curled in a smile, but his eyes glinted hard and cold. "Personally, yes."

"Personally?"

"I told you once before, Seraph, I don't always agree with my colleagues."

"They want the pits open?"

"Peace isn't a matter of treaties, Soran. It has to be cultivated."

Soran frowned. That was the opposite of an answer. "Then you prefer him lording it over his gang of thugs." They'd known about the victors from the beginning. But why ask Soran to gather information for them if they didn't care?

"It's the Senate's job to keep brutishness from spreading. Not every city is as...orderly as yours."

"Social order? What about the ancient Empire our friend is so fond of?"

"What are you—?"

"If I didn't know better, Senator, I'd say Malek agrees with you."

"Agrees? With us?"

"Look at the broadcasts. Watch the lessons he's giving them. Martial arts, yes. But the kind that happen in a tournament hall, not in a sand pit. History. Language. Poetry." Soran's lips curled into a grin. "A pack of barbarians. And yet you call Malek their king."

"The men and women at their head were dictators. Brutes keeping whatever hold they could on other beasts' leashes."

Soran looked down at the banners. The cloth curled and twisted in the sunlight, the symbol winking as it moved. "Were they, Senator? Were they, if the things Malek found in Delen are what he says they are?"

His lip curled in distaste. Aerix had barely avoided the Senate's social order. The accord a long-ago forebear had signed had made sure of that...at the price of the city's isolation from the rest of the world on which it rested.

Then again, if men like Derell are the best the rest of the planet has to offer, that deal was a bargain.

"You said it yourself, Seraph. You told me that Malek's men were calling him 'Lord.' Our world is a world with no lords and no masters. Just a place for everyone, and everyone in his place."

And what would my place be, Senator Derell?

Soran's eyes flicked toward the window. A glint of silver shone on one of the black banners. It flashed as the light hit it and vanished again, a crackle of lightning against a dark sky. "And you think that your system brought peace."

"You say Malek knows his history, Seraph of Aerix. Don't pretend you don't know yours."

Oh, I know how the Empire fell, Senator. Soran was glad that Derell wouldn't see his snarl. He closed his eyes and breathed in, shifting his face into an impassive mask. He dropped his blade on the ground. It hit the floor with a sharp tinkle. Derell stared down at it.

"I understand, Senator," Soran said. "And I stand by my offer. You'll have your chance at Malek. If you want it."

Derell kept looking at the blade. "If I want it?"

"There's no other way you can reach him," Soran soothed. "And isn't it better for you to act than to let him broadcast his propaganda all over the planet?"

"Very well. But don't give me cause to regret this, Seraph. As marvelous as your city is, if you force my hand—"

"I understand, Senator. You've done a great deal to protect my city." Soran's lips quirked in an easy smile. "I can't promise you that your agents will succeed. But I can give you your chance."

"Understood," Derell held out his hand to shake. Soran took it. Derell's hand locked around his in a squeezing grip.

It was nothing Soran couldn't handle, especially not after Malek's embraces. But Derell must have known Skyknights' modifications left their extremities delicate. Soran's eyes narrowed. "Then we are agreed. Farewell, Senator."

"Farewell, Seraph. Don't make me regret letting you get away with this."

I hope Malek doesn't force me to let your minions succeed. Soran's hands clenched. *I'd hate to get in the way of Malek killing you someday.*

CHAPTER THIRTEEN

"YOU ARE late."

Malek blinked at the voice, deep for a Skyknight's. Surely an envoy sent by the Seraph to welcome him and his entourage should have something better to say than that. Vareth muttered beside him in the dialect of the pits. Kenn kept his face hidden behind his visor.

Then again, this was Aerix. And Soran had sent these people. Maybe a snub was only to be expected.

Their hosts had the otherworldly bodies of all Skyknights. They towered over the victors. The one who had addressed Malek stood ramrod-straight, his posture perfect. His clothing was plain, but his breast bore a silver insignia, no doubt the mark of some high rank.

His companion stood tall and still enough, the sunlight glinting off golden threads braided into her hair. She held her hands at her sides, as carefully positioned as the other's. But Malek saw her fingers twitch. He looked up to see Skyknight-blue eyes twinkle above her still mouth, as if she were fighting the impulse to smile.

At our expense? Malek wondered, remembering Soran's smirking contempt.

The woman smiled. "Forgive the First Skycaptain's manners. On behalf of our Seraph, we welcome you." Her graceful body dipped in an elaborate bow. "And on behalf of our City."

Malek looked. Just beyond the two Skyknights stood a ring of elfin sentinels, their blasters at the ready, humming with energy. But he could barely pay attention to them, because behind the Skyknights flared the bright sun of Aerix's skies.

Malek had never seen anything like it.

He knew, of course, that the sky over the rest of the planet was paler than the haze over Dis. And he'd seen skies that weren't black or gray. Sometimes the smoke and the lights of the factories made the daytime sky a fiery brown, or covered the city in a midnight-blue fog.

But Malek had only seen this fierce azure in holograms or on monitor screen. Or white clouds, pure and pristine color, nothing like the black smoke billowing from the factories or the slate-gray brume that foretold rain. And the sun, rising behind the Skyknights, stung his eyes.

All around him towers rose, polished mirror-bright, burnished by sunlight. The glinting metal hurt his eyes, too. But they looked almost as if his holograms had taken form, willed into being by the power of his vision. He blinked in pain, then opened his eyes, unable to resist.

This is happening too fast. But it is happening as it should, nonetheless.

As it must.

He closed his eyes again, afterimages burning on the backs of his eyelids, and gave an answering bow. "Thank you for the welcome, Skyknights of Aerix. And I must offer you my apologies. We were...delayed."

He didn't need to say it. Blaster fire and blades alike had torn deep, dirtied gouges in Vareth's armor. Black scorch marks dotted Kenn's. Dark dried blood stained the dents and scratches in Malek's, and a knife-slash tore across one of his cheeks.

Still, they were the first guests welcomed into the city in months. Politeness was not only prudent but necessary.

"Not Skyknight," the woman said. "Skycaptain." The smile she'd been suppressing curled the corners of her lips. "His rank is First Skycaptain, in fact."

"First Skycaptain Tanth," Kenn said, inclining his head. "The Seraph's right hand."

The ghost of a grin flitted across Tanth's face. "Indeed. As Skycaptain Ania is mine."

"You honor us," Malek said, doing his best to shift the burr of the pits' dialect into an elegant sound. "Your city—"

He stopped, his voice stolen by the purring thunder of a starfighter. The craft, no doubt some lesser Skyknight on patrol, was a streak of quicksilver against the sky.

Aerix is the one thing on this planet worth preserving.

"You honor us as well," Skycaptain Ania said. Her hands twitched at her sides. "You and your entourage. Vareth the Crusher, who hasn't been seen in the ring in years. Kenn the Silent. Who should be dead."

"You know about us," Vareth rumbled.

Tanth's smile became a frown. "Of course."

"We knew the Destroyer was coming. And we've seen you on the broadcasts. But the two of you have been—" Ania shot a glance at Tanth. "I never thought I'd see you in person."

Vareth laughed. "There's no shame in following the matches."

"We're pleased to see that a Skycaptain follows the arena bouts," Malek said. "But there's no time to talk about that now. Not if the event is going to go on."

Tanth scowled. "It will. You're in time for that, at least. Now tell us what happened."

"Some trouble with the City Council." Vareth's eyes narrowed. "Our business, not yours."

Tanth's frown deepened.

"Some of them didn't want us to leave Dis," Malek said. "And put themselves in our way."

"That didn't last long," Ania said. She looked over at Vareth's damaged armor. Her fingers danced at her side again. "I wish I could've seen it."

Vareth smiled back. Tanth shook his head. "You're here because my Seraph sent for you. Nothing more, nothing less."

Now it was Malek's turn to glare. "You're his right-hand man. You don't know why we're here?"

Tanth took a step toward the victors. "We know exactly why you're here. But I'm not the Seraph of this city. I have no love for the Senate, but that doesn't mean I want my City involved."

"Tanth—First Skycaptain," Ania cut in. "We're wasting time."

"There is time," Kenn put in. "Two days until the festivities."

"Wait." Malek held up a hand. "I tried to tell you what I see in your city. I didn't finish. Those of us in Dis and in the Molten Belt have never seen light like the sun on these spires. Most of us never will." His mouth curled. "We're covered in dirt and blood. We fought our own people to get here. And if you've been paying attention to the broadcasts, you know that even our voices are broken."

Ania frowned. "You're guests of the Seraph. You don't need to talk about yourselves like—"

Malek snarled, a rumbling threat. Ania stepped back.

"You think we're here to drag you down," Malek said. "We're here because we know the threat stationed at your borders. We fell to it ourselves, ages ago."

Tanth stared ahead, impassive.

"You've made patrols," Malek went on. "In Feris. In Corian."

"They left."

"Soran told me they would. We both know why."

Ania chewed her lip. Tanth said nothing.

"How long do you think they will stay gone?"

Tanth turned on his heel. "Come on. Like Ania said, we're wasting time."

Malek walked across a room painted deep purplish-red. A royal color, for an emperor visiting generations too late. Or something more prosaic: the color of blood dripping dark from veins, poured out to greet a gladiator guest.

Either was a black joke coming from Soran. Malek smirked.

The light of Aerix's midday sky streamed in from a massive window. Hints of purple and blue shimmered in the red. But the color was too dark next to a window large enough to take up a whole wall. Or at least, it looked dark now, with the curtains drawn back to reveal the sky and the craft gliding through it.

Malek had opened them as soon as he'd come in, even though the blaze of blue had stung his eyes. He couldn't look at it directly, but he couldn't close them again either. His hand clenched, still dark with Dis's grime.

Soran must have wanted Malek to notice that too. Laid out with painstaking precision atop the crimson comforter, where Malek had to see it, was a two-piece set of clothing, the fabric bleached a brilliant white. The pale color made him think of Soran's skin, what he might look like splayed out on the plum sheets.

Strange how deep he's wormed into my blood.

Malek had known from the beginning that Soran wanted him. And he'd had no qualms about playing to those desires. His designers and builders had outdone themselves decorating that little room in Dis. And Soran's desire had stirred his from the beginning. A Skyknight was a rare gem, perfection winking from the dirt and rubble of a crumbling world.

And Soran reigned over them. The last of the old nobility.

A fitting consort for a would-be emperor. *But desire never drove me. Not like it drives him.*

Before Soran, he'd gone to one of his victors, a woman even a Skyknight might find striking. Kiara had worked the streets of Dis before her time in the pits. Her body still bore a twining pattern of tattoos, black shapes that curled over the curves and muscles of her flesh. Even after she'd left that work behind, she'd spent her winnings in the pits on alterations that kept all eyes on her. Her alterations let her shift the tattoos' designs at will. Let her offer her fans—and her former clients—a new, sensuous pattern every time they saw her in the ring.

She made sure her audience could see it. Instead of the armor most fighters favored, she relied on force fields and fought her bouts nearly nude. Her past, and her little gimmick, had drawn crowds.

It hadn't drawn Malek. Instead, she'd visited him, reminded him of a need he'd barely noticed. He'd gone to her gladly, pleased with her frankness and impressed with her skill. He'd grown fond of her over the months, but it had never flowered into passion. Instead it became a routine, well-worn and comforting. A routine that fed an appetite like any other, to be sated and enjoyed and forgotten.

And yet now here he was, staring down at clothes intended for him, thinking about Soran's body twisting into obscene gestures of welcome.

Malek's hands clenched. How many times during Soran's short visit had he found himself returning to that fancy little room, the need a red-hot thorn in his flesh? He shook his head to clear it and reached down to touch the cloth. It was softer than the coarse fabrics favored in Dis, but he recognized it. A martial arts uniform, of the Skyknights' tradition, made comfortable and simple.

And whoever had made it had clearly customized it not only to suit the style of the gladiators, but had tailored it to Malek's shape and size.

Where exactly had Soran found those measurements? Not everyone in Aerix was Skyknight-tall and thin, but few were Malek's size.

He let the fabric fall from his fingers. Then his eyes widened and he stared at the spot he'd touched.

He'd cleaned himself after the fight, but there were gray marks on the fabric. Fingerprints, half-smeared. Apparently the soot in Dis didn't come off so easily.

So that's why you chose this color. No one from Dis could wear it without getting it dirty.

He moved to the window again, closed the curtains and drapes. He touched a switch and lights flickered to life in the walls.

He wondered whether Soran would come to him, as he had come to the room he'd given the lord of the Skyknights. Or was Soran still playing coy, an echo of Malek's own refusal to meet him when he'd arrived in Dis? In any case, if he was planning a visit, it wouldn't happen until he'd stripped himself of dirt and blood.

He sighed and peeled off his armor. He closed his eyes, remembering the angry roars of the group converging on the victors as they had made their way to the city limits. One fool had leapt at Vareth. She'd tossed him aside as easily as a child tossing a doll. The next had been luckier. He'd managed to dent her armor.

Kenn's attacker had been wiser as well. He'd wielded an electrified whip. Its radiant lightning had caught Kenn as he tried to dart away. Malek frowned at the thought of it. It had looked almost like Kenn's attacker knew. Like he'd expected the slight drag of Kenn's feet, the moment of delay.

Malek had drawn his blade and dispatched the man in a violent spray of blood. Another had fallen to Kenn himself.

Malek had whirled around to face two more. They'd snarled

something about the difference between an arena and a real fight, but they'd fallen just as easily as any other enemy.

But no sooner had he finished with them than he'd found himself face-to-face with the Blade, the weapon tipping his arm gleaming under the streetlights.

"The Council made its decision," Malek had said.

"Ilen made a decision. Xin went along with it. Doesn't make it the right one."

He'd lunged at Malek, who had dropped to the ground and twisted away just in time for his blade to open a cut in his cheek rather than slice open his neck. They'd grappled. Malek had freed one of his blades and scored a deep gash in the arm that ended in the weapon. Driven by rage, his assailant had barely felt the cuts.

He'd heard the crackle of the whip, an electric snapping echo of its sound as Kenn fired his own weapon, the crunching thuds as Vareth's fists made contact with flesh.

"This is madness," Malek had said. "Sending our own people after me knowing they will die."

"You kill them every day in the pits," the Blade had snarled back.

He'd almost answered. Pinned by a man who'd long ago decided they were enemies, he'd almost let slip the purpose he'd hidden for so long.

But circumstance had stopped him.

It had come in the form of blaster fire, blue bolts of light shocking the night sky to brightness. The Blade's face had twisted into a snarl and Malek had managed to kick him away.

"Yes, I made a decision," Malek had heard the gunman say. He'd stood up to see Ilen waving toward the city gates with one of his blasters. Behind him stood the pale, lean-muscled figures of the twins. "And you three should get gone."

Vareth had wanted to chase down the gang's leader. Kenn had stopped her. "Better that we get on our way," he'd said. The twins hadn't bothered to reply, already turning back to their grim work.

Malek shook his head and looked down at his armor. In the unsoiled room, the gear only looked dirtier. Then he peeled off the undergarments beneath, discolored from the same smoke that stained his fingers.

He slipped into the bathroom. Lights brightened as he walked in. They gave a harsher, whiter light than the warm orange of the bedroom, no doubt to show every ashen smear of the dirt he'd carried with him. The tile of the floor was vivid white.

He turned on the shower. The water warmed immediately, a comfortable and soothing heat. For all that, the spray was surprisingly forceful. His wound stung as the water hit it. *Is it always like this, or do you just want to be sure it cleans me well enough?*

The soap was gritty too, abrasives molded into the crimson bar. *I gave you one like this when you visited Dis.* He watched bubbles rise as he passed the soap over his body and rinse away as the water hit it. *Did you copy its design for me?*

He looked down at his feet. A pool of gray water had formed around them and was slipping down the drain.

Seeing it, he scrubbed more vigorously. The rough surface scratched away a layer of gray he hadn't known was there. The abraded skin stung, tender and new. He passed his fingers over it and thought of how Soran's touch would feel.

He opened a small packet of shampoo. It was red and translucent. Soran had thought of everything. Malek lathered it into his short-cropped hair, his fingertips digging in hard to remove as much of the grime as he could.

He shook his head under the water and closed his eyes as the soap rinsed away. *How will I look to you, Seraph of Aerix, with this purification done?*

How will I look to your city? Like a savior or an interloper?

He touched a panel in the wall, and the pressurized rain died. He stepped out of the shower and wrapped himself in towels softer than anything he'd felt before. For a moment, he just stood there, closed his eyes, and savored the feeling.

Then, unwinding the cocoon of softness, he opened his eyes again.

CHAPTER FOURTEEN

"EVERYTHING IS prepared for tomorrow, then?"

Malek's brisk pace might have been too fast for someone in Dis, but Soran found it easy to match his strides. He smirked. He didn't think he'd ever seen Malek nervous before. Or was he just excited?

"Of course. Everything is ready," Soran answered. "Provided, of course, that your little entourage makes itself presentable."

Then again, you clean up nicely.

The steely hint of stubble around Malek's mouth was gone. So was the grayish cast that Dis's soot had given his skin. In the sunlight flooding in through the windows, the olive tone looked warm and vibrant. Soran's fingers twitched to touch Malek's cheek, to move over its newfound smoothness.

Or over the line of a fresh wound scoring one cheek.

The jagged pink cut had been cleaned and tended. Soran couldn't tell if it would scar or not. But if it did leave a permanent mark, it would leave less of one than it would have in Dis. Only the most vain or insecure gladiator would bother with the creams and salves that kept Skyknights' skin unblemished.

"You want to make sure we look presentable?" Malek said. "You're providing the clothes we'll wear."

Soran snickered. As nice as this clean, groomed Malek looked, he still wore his hair severe and close-cropped. A style for the ring, but not for a festival.

And Soran had given him fancy clothes to wear tomorrow, but he had on plain clothes now. A shirt and pants he'd brought with him, dyed a rich black that matched his hair and eyes. They were clean and neat, but Soran could see signs of fraying at the elbows and the knees.

And Soran wasn't the only one who'd noticed. As Skyknights and other high-caste workers dashed through the halls, paces slowed and heads turned.

They should have known better. They'd have their chance to gawk at him later.

Including the surprisingly short woman Soran saw pass by, her eyes narrowed.

She couldn't have pretended to be a Skyknight. Wisely, she didn't try.

Her eyes were a lustrous green, a popular shade with high-caste civilians. She moved with a fluid grace that even Soran had to admire. It wasn't a Skyknight's gait, but it didn't have to be.

Are you really going to try something now? Soran turned his body toward Malek, trying his best to keep it inconspicuous.

He'd expected Derell's assassins to make their move during the festivities. That way, they could melt into the crowd. Soran could deny any involvement and so could the Senate. An unfortunate encounter with extremists, the kind you unfortunately courted when you made friends with barbarians.

But Malek's message had already begun to spread. What better way to stop it than to make sure the last of the great cities never heard it at all? Soran put one hand on his hip, as if ready to retort. But he kept his gaze focused on the woman watching Malek.

"Oh," he purred, sidling up to Malek. "It's not you I'm worried about. It's not even that pet machine of yours decked out in a helmet. It's that ugly brute the two of you brought with you." He hissed in irritation he didn't have to feign. He'd disliked Vareth from the moment they'd met. "Really, Malek. I thought you meant to help your little pack of barbarians leave their crass roots behind."

A frown curled the edges of Malek's mouth. *Good.*

Soran turned a corner, and Malek moved with him, automatic.

The crowd thinned as they went. That was only to be expected. Malek had come to make plans for tomorrow. Plans that no one else needed to see.

Soran kept talking. "I understand how precious your victors are to you. But you're here for a festival, not for a fight."

"Vareth is no more a fool than I am, Soran. You should know that. And you also knew who I was bringing from the beginning."

"Of course." Soran stepped closer and fluttered his eyelids. He heard no footfalls, whether hasty or measured.

The corridor was empty.

Soran bit back a curse. He couldn't turn away from Malek now.

Where did you disappear to?

"You asked me to come here, Soran," Malek was saying. "Now you talk as if I've made some false move, when I gave you exactly what you want."

"You know I'd never say that," Soran murmured, leaning in. If anyone saw them now, it would prove disastrous.

But no one would, except the woman waiting to make her move.

"Soran. What precisely are you doing?" Malek's eyes flicked from Soran's face to the hall around him.

Damn it. "You know I want you here." Soran wrapped a hand around Malek's back. "I just don't understand why you'd bring that mockery with you."

Malek growled and pushed him away.

Soran stumbled and caught himself. He cursed under his breath, but at least Malek was looking at him again. He walked back to Malek and reached out, as if he hadn't noticed Malek's anger. "You of all people shouldn't need a bodyguard."

Malek grabbed Soran's arm and twisted. Soran hissed at him to let go. He didn't. The discomfort became a slow spread of pain, blossoming through the joint.

"Vareth has stood at my side from the very beginning. She is as wise an adviser as she was fierce in the ring."

Soran fought to ignore the ache in his arm. Their shadow had finally reappeared. Her footfalls were inaudible now, covered by the sound of Malek's voice and his own snarls of pain.

"And far more worthy of trust than you have proven to be," Malek finished.

Damn you both. But agonizing as it was, Malek manhandling him was useful. It made it all the more believable that he would grab for his weapon.

"Let go, you brute!" He curled his hand around the hidden blade and thrashed in Malek's grasp.

"We've been over this before. Do you think that just because I've come to your city, you can start your endless stream of insults and recrimina—?" He bit off the word.

His eyes narrowed and his grip loosened. Soran flexed his shoulder and sighed with relief.

"You don't mean a word of this, do you?" Malek whispered. He didn't move, but his hands clenched and his weight shifted.

"I mean every word of it," Soran hissed back. He turned and pushed Malek as he moved, a friendly signal to their shadow. "But that isn't the point."

The would-be assassin dashed toward Malek.

But, free of Malek's crushing grip, Soran was already prepared.

His blade flashed once in his hand. Then it was a streak of silver speeding through the hall.

He saw the woman's eyes widen, bright spheres of shocked, unnatural green.

To her credit, she didn't try to move. There was no dodging a blade hurled by a Skyknight. She simply matched his throw with one of her own.

Instinct made him twist away before he realized she'd aimed it not at him, but at her intended target.

He watched her fall to the floor. *You're dedicated, at least.*

He felt rather than saw Malek slam into the wall. The woman's mouth was open as if to cry out, but she made only a choked little gasp.

Her eyes were still fixed on Soran. She slid forward on her knees and crawled toward them. Soran ran for her, his long strides closing the distance between them.

Malek was a step behind him. He could snap her in half, and no doubt he planned to. But Soran was quicker, which meant he was closer. And his enhanced reflexes made it easy to wrap a slender hand around the hilt of his blade. He yanked it out and plunged it in again.

Blood spurted over his hand. The assassin's hand and mouth opened, her weapon falling from nerveless fingers. Soran glanced down at it. A small dart, smeared with a colorless oil.

Poison, then.

He moved to pick it up, but it fell apart even as his hand closed around it.

Startled, he opened his hand. A small trail of powder fell to the floor. A shimmering puddle lay where the oil had been.

"It's made to dissolve," he murmured.

That wouldn't hide the puncture wound. But Malek was a gladiator. Even cleaned up, his body was still full of old marks and tears and scars. Who would notice one tiny scratch?

But before he could look back atMalek, he felt himself lifted.

His exclamation of surprise died, forced out of him with his breath as Malek slammed him into the wall.

Pain flared through his back. He shook his head, dazed. He heard a voice, sharp and harsh, the sound resolving into words as his head cleared.

"How many others?"

Winded though Soran was, his arms wrapped tight around Malek's bulk. His hands curled into claws and dug into the layer of rough cloth covering Malek's back.

"There were five," Soran gasped. "Five total. Five, and now one of them is dead."

"One of them."

Soran wriggled in Malek's grasp, wanting any advantage he could get. But Malek didn't fall for it. "Before I had any chance to question her about the others. How convenient."

"Five, and I killed one for you," Soran ground out, his arms still wrapped around Malek's back in a violent parody of an embrace.

Malek only growled. Soran hissed in impatient anger. "Those darts were poisoned, you brutish fool!"

Malek's grip relaxed.

"She threw another one," Soran said. "Don't bother with revenge until you know you're all right."

Malek's eyes widened. Then they narrowed again, cold and calculating. Finally, he loosened his grip, twisting just long enough to let Soran see a jagged line in the dark fabric of one sleeve, and the brighter color of the skin beneath.

Which was whole.

Soran sighed in relief and sagged against the wall. If his little stunt got both Malek and his would-be assassin killed, he'd have no allies left. And at least two powerful enemies.

But his moment of relaxation was short-lived. Malek shoved him again. A second shock of pain lanced through his body.

"Poison like that would take effect immediately," Malek said. "There would be no point if it didn't."

"Forgive me my concern."

"You knew she was here. She expected you to help her."

"And got my blade in her heart instead. If that doesn't prove my loyalty, what does?"

The pressure around him lessened. He breathed raggedly, the sound of it filling the empty hallway. Every movement hurt.

But Malek was still unsatisfied. "You knew she was here. You taunted me so I wouldn't notice."

"So I could attack her!"

No answer.

That was good, under the circumstances. Soran kept talking, anger and pain goading him into it. "You say you're as intelligent as anyone in Delen or Aerix. So think!"

Another growl—but Malek let go.

Without Malek's weight to support him, Soran slid to the ground, collapsing against the wall in an undignified heap. Malek loomed over him.

Defiant, Soran stared up at him. "What would have happened if I hadn't convinced her that I was on her side?"

Still looking directly at Malek, Soran reached out for the wall behind him and rose to his feet. He held the other hand out, careful not to smear anything with the blood staining it.

Malek laughed, a harsh, bitter bark. "Point taken. But how did she get in here in the first place if you didn't invite her in?"

"There's an army just outside my gates. How exactly did you expect me to let you and your little minions past it unless I promised none of you would come back out again?"

Malek didn't answer. Which meant he was thinking. Or so Soran hoped.

He put out his bloody hand, reaching for Malek's chin. Malek flinched. Soran ignored it and held on. "I asked you to come here. I promised you I'd give you what you wanted. Do you really think I intended not to?"

"You're toying with me and them. Do you really think I intend to let that go?"

Soran pressed his bloody fingertips against Malek's lips. "I made a promise. Now I've killed for you."

Malek's eyes shifted in their sockets. They stared down at his bloodstained hand.

Finally.

"Now they tried to kill you. Now you can stand in front of my City and tell them what they tried to do. Is this really how you want to repay me for that?"

Malek smirked. "There is blood on your hands, Seraph of Aerix. And yet all of this is still a game to you."

Soran's smile matched Malek's. He slid his finger back down to Malek's chin. The red smear on Malek's lips suited him. An echo ofeverything he'd scrubbed away. Except that this time, the blood hadn't come from one of his opponents.

This time, Soran himself had left it there.

A hungry warmth spread through his flesh. "A game, Malek? Maybe you're right. Maybe it is all a game to me. But there is one important difference now."

"And what is that?"

Soran's free arm reached out to wrap around Malek's back as he leaned in, his lips hovering almost close enough to touch Malek's.

"I've finally chosen a side."

CHAPTER FIFTEEN

WHETHER TRUE or false, those words were all Malek needed to hear.

He crushed his lips to Soran's, not wanting to give him a chance to take the words back. Soran murmured into his mouth, a gasp of surprise or a purr of triumph. His bloodied hand slid to encircle Malek's head. His other arm moved along Malek's back. His fingers clutched blindly, as though they could tear through the rough fabric of Malek's shirt and dig into the skin beneath.

They slid lower, circling Malek's waist. Malek closed his eyes and lost himself to the moment. He had paid enough for it, after all.

No.

"Not here," Malek forced himself to say. If he had missed one assassin's presence thanks to Soran's taunts, how much more might he ignore for the bliss of his touch?

Soran snarled.

"Not here," Malek repeated. He tilted his head toward the nearest doorway. "Inside."

"There's no one here to see us, you fool." Soran glared down at the body on the floor. "And if anyone did, they'd guess what happened anyway."

Malek growled. Soran looked at him. His blue eyes glittered, hard and cold.

All right. Malek stepped out of his embrace. He walked toward the door and pushed it open. Soran let out a sharp trill of laughter and closed the door behind them. "As you wish, Lord of the Pits."

Malek moved to the window and pressed its mechanism. The glass clouded, darkening until it became an opaque white. Satisfied, he turned his attention to the ceiling's filigree. This was Aerix. There had to be a camera somewhere.

He frowned. Even with his sharpened vision, he couldn't make out anything amid the elaborate design.

Soran scoffed. "Give me your knife."

Malek proffered it, and Soran snatched it up and climbed onto one of the chairs. The blade flashed briefly in his hand. Malek watched, pleased, as a small metallic sphere came loose in his hand. A lens winked at Malek from between Soran's slender fingers, bright as a gem.

"There." He dropped it in front of Malek. It hit the floor with a forlorn tinkle.

Malek lifted his foot and brought it down on the tiny camera. The metal dented and splintered under the weight. Not taking any chances, he ground it into the metal of the floor. Then, finally satisfied, he stepped away.

Soran leapt down from the chair. "If anyone asks, the clean blade is mine."

Malek looked at the scraps of metal on the floor. "That was the only camera?"

"Of course." Soran stepped closer, his smile widening, and lowered himself to his knees in front of Malek. "Trust me," he whispered.

Malek didn't answer. How could he?

Soran reached for the fastener of Malek's pants.

How fitting, my Seraph, that you touch me with bloodied hands.

But when the red-smeared fingers touched the cloth, a thought cut through his anticipation. This wasn't his home in the pits, where everyone expected to see him spattered with an enemy's gore. He could rinse away red handprints on his face or his shirt, and let whatever mark remained speak for itself. But a bloodstain in an intimate place? He grabbed at Soran's wrist and twisted hard.

Soran yelped. His pretty face twisted into a mask of rage. "You—!"

Malek growled a warning and raised Soran's hand to his face. Soran blinked, startled enough to lapse into silence.

Malek smiled and opened his mouth. He lapped at the blood running down Soran's slim wrist and licked his way up the back of his hand.

Soran laughed, a tinkling twitter that faded into a moan. Malek chuckled in answer and turned Soran's hand around.

The coppery smell of the blood filled his nostrils as he laved the creases in the palm. Blood meant his arena, his pits, his domain, and now here it was, waiting for him in the pristine halls of the City in the Sky. He pressed his lips to the skin, letting it swallow a snicker. Then he took Soran's fingers in his mouth, one by one, and sucked the sticky red off of them.

Soran murmured in answer, and Malek couldn't tell if it meant pleasure or scorn. It didn't matter. He opened his mouth, pulled the last delicate finger free, and lowered Soran's hand to his waist.

"Now you may do as you will," he said.

Soran gave a trilling laugh and did not move. He clutched at Malek's hips and nuzzled the fabric covering his thighs.

Half of it was probably just pleasure at Malek's ministrations. Still, if anyone saw them now, it would look like a sign of devotion.

Malek murmured in answer. Soran wasted no more time, his deft hands working at the fastener. Malek reached down to twist his hand in Soran's hair. *You've pledged yourself to me.* He grabbed at Soran's hair and forced his head back.

Soran hissed at the sting, but looked up at Malek and licked his lips. His hands moved, busy as ever, pulling Malek's undergarment aside without bothering to look and wrapping the hand Malek had licked clean around the base of his flesh.

Malek moaned, low and deep, at the feeling of Soran's hand on him. A hand that had killed, and killed for him.

He felt Soran's lips on him, a parody of a shy kiss. Then Soran opened his mouth, the dainty jaw stretching wide to take him in. The smooth slide made Malek smirk even as his hands clenched in Soran's hair.

They'd done this before, during their first frenzied nights in Dis. Malek had shoved Soran to the floor in a room full of glittering lights and laughed at his protests. And then silenced them.

But this was different. This was the Seraph of Aerix, monarch of a fabled city, moving with a practiced grace his tattooed victor might have envied.

Well then. He let Soran work at him a while longer, savoring the heat building up in his flesh and the sight of Soran on his knees in front of him.

He canted his hips, a moment of warning, and began to move. Soran made a choked sound and he pushed deep. Thin fingers scrabbled at Malek's waist, curled under the fabric of his clothes, the nails digging red lines in his skin.

Through a mist of pleasure Malek felt Soran's other hand pull away. He watched Soran reach to unfasten his own garment.

For a moment Malek wanted it. Wanted the evidence of Soran's own desire laid bare in front of him, the frenzied movements proving his need.

For a moment he wanted even more than that. He'd seen Soran's skin before, pale and smooth, untouched by the elements that aged everyone in Dis before their time. But how would Soran's exposed body look here, in an ornate room in a city as pristine as he was?

But this was a promise of fealty, not a game for Soran's pleasure.

"No," Malek said.

Soran froze, staring up at Malek with sharp, glittering eyes. Malek met his gaze and waited for him to blink. Finally he did, lowering his gaze with a whine of surrender.

That was all Malek needed. His hands clenched around Soran's head and pushed it down, finesse forgotten as he pulled it back and down again, the heat in his flesh building.

Soran gave another strangled gasp. His whole body shuddered, wracked by a violent tremor, as if Malek were tearing it in two.

As if he'd stolen the pleasure for himself.

The feeling undid Malek at last. His hips rocked of their own will, pushing him even deeper. He growled out his release and flooded Soran's raw, open throat.

When sense returned, Soran was staring up at him, his lips curled.

The news of the attack spread fast, despite their little dalliance. Soran made sure of it.

Malek hid how much it amused him. Their story was unbelievable, a bloody blade in a spotless hand. Anyone who knew anything about Malek would only have more questions.

But Soran was their Seraph, and that was all that mattered. Malek had seen their too-colorful eyes track his movements when he walked by. But Malek wasn't the one who had needed to explain, and both he and Soran knew it. Soran had been ready with his message as soon as they walked out of the empty hallway.

"We chose to welcome three illustrious guests," he'd said. "But someone took it upon herself to follow them here." He'd paused there, his mouth puckering. Malek had thought of what had passed between them just before and fought not to laugh.

Soran had welcomed him and his closest advisors into a hidden city. And almost as soon as they had landed, death had slipped in behind.

Malek the Destroyer. His own mouth had twisted in a bitter smile.

He'd opened the curtains in the room again. The sky still seared him. Even after a few days, he couldn't believe anything so vivid existed. He looked out at it, the last vestige of a world that had fallen and been consumed.

People of Aerix. Do you realize my victors fight for you, not just for themselves?

They would learn it soon enough. Were learning it, if they paid enough attention to understand what had happened this morning.

"We know she wasn't one of us," Soran had said. "She didn't have the alterations to be from Aerix. And yet somehow, she came here. And slipped unnoticed into one of the towers. And made an attempt on Malek's life."

Slipped into one of the towers. Unnoticed, Soran claimed. A high tower, meant for the high castes and dedicated to their business. Everyone in Aerix would wonder how she'd made it in. What would they think, knowing that an assassination attempt had happened so high in the skies over the city?

Soran hadn't seemed bothered by it. Malek had seen his feathery eyebrow rise, the corner of his mouth quirking into a secret smile. Amusement at his own lie, perhaps.

"But of course, a man famed for going undefeated in the deathmatch arena doesn't die so easily." Soran had looked over at him then, swept his eyes over Malek's body. His citizens wouldn't see it, of course. They'd see concern, or admiration. Or the same curiosity that would drive them to the Square of the Suns tomorrow to watch the beasts perform.

Malek had stared directly back at Soran. Soran hadn't flinched, but Malek had seen his fingers twitch at his side. He'd fought not to smile.

Then Soran's expression had shifted. When he spoke again, he'd purred. "Fortunately, the gladiator was unharmed. Of course, the same can't be said for his attacker. As I'm sure you can easily imagine, her wounds proved fatal."

Malek had growled, half in amusement and half in annoyance. Then his eyes had widened in realization.

If anyone asks, the clean blade is mine. Was that how Soran planned to sell this to his people? The angry gladiator fresh from the death pits, destroying anyone who got in his way?

Malek shook his head and looked at the purple-red walls. Blood for a fighter, a would-be warlord. Blood for a Destroyer. Blood for a beast.

He remembered the coppery taste of it on Soran's hand, the shape of slender fingers in his mouth. He laughed and licked his lips. Soran was clean, as long as his lies held.

He'd said he'd finally made his choice. He'd cemented it by falling to his knees in front of him—

—and given his people a reason to fear Malek, at the same time.

That could be a problem.

This wasn't how Malek had meant for this to happen. He'd meant for the City to celebrate him, gawk at him, find him just dangerous enough to envy. But what would the people expect tomorrow, now that Soran said he'd killed someone? A grunting villain, barely containing his bloodlust? It might thrill them. A famous gladiator killing a meddler who wasn't welcome in the City anyway. But would it win them to his side?

And would it keep them there, once they began to doubt? Dis would be his, when he needed it. The histories told him that. But Aerix belonged to someone else.

Someone who'd made a promise. Could he trust it?

He walked over to the closet. The garment for tomorrow's festivities hung on the door, luminous in the light from the window. Except for a tiny spot where his dirtied hands had touched it, hidden somewhere in its folds.

Very well. I'll play your barbarian. But whether Aerix knows it or not, I didn't kill for you.

You killed for me.

CHAPTER SIXTEEN

MALEK WASN'T the only one who cleaned up nicely. His victors stood just behind him, Vareth to his left and Kenn to his right. Both wore white uniforms to match Malek's.

Dressed in proper clothing, they looked almost like real warriors.

Soran fought not to scowl, even as he admired the way the garments hid their scars and imperfections behind flowing white. Kenn's slender build made him look almost like a Skyknight. His hands were balled in fists at his sides. It looked almost natural, just as his stance looked almost even.

The uniform even flattered Vareth. The bright white of the uniform made a sharp contrast against her deep brown skin. It couldn't hide the contours of her reshaped bulk entirely, but it fell loosely over them, making her look elegant as well as broad and strong. Maybe in Dis, she wasn't so ugly after all. Maybe in Dis, she could even be beautiful.

Kenn had retracted his visor, apparently trying to look less forbidding. He should have left it down. Everyone could see him squint in the sunlight. Malek and Vareth squinted too, and Soran noticed with satisfaction that Malek couldn't stop blinking. Which made him look less noble than he wanted to.

Still, if not for that... Soran looked back at Malek again. Dressed formally, he almost could have been one of those generals his broadcasts talked about.

I had no idea you believed cheap conspiracy theories, Soran had told him at that first meeting. And now the conspiracy theories stood before him in the flesh. He closed his eyes, savoring the tremor that ran up his back again.

He couldn't help but wonder. What had the symbol of the Old Empire looked like, all those ages ago? The Senate had been so careful about erasing it. Had the victors found it again? Had they shown it in some broadcast he'd missed in the middle of some long and empty night? What would it look like, stitched into the fabric of a finely made martial arts uniform or molded into the armor of generals?

Like a black spearhead glyph, drawn with a bold and forceful hand?

He opened his eyes. The stand on his other side held weapons, long staves made of fine, polished wood. No two were exactly alike. He'd used the data on the tablet to guess the victors' height, weight, and style, and refined the weapons from there.

He could have required the combatants to use metal ones, could have fitted sensors to the staves' tips, lights that flashed when they hit. But this was a special occasion, and special occasions called for ceremony. The ends of each staff were wrapped in cloth stained with red, dry pigment, too vibrant a red to quite match blood.

No one would die, of course. Even if this hadn't been ceremonial. He'd had enough death for one week. But you didn't just bring Dis's most famous victors into your city and not show them off.

He tugged at his shirt to even it out. Like his visitors' uniforms, it was brilliant, blinding white. Front and center, it bore the symbol of the city, embroidered in a pale silvery thread that made the emblem invisible until the light hit it.

Most Skyknights wore a simpler symbol, a bird's wing, flared out as if in flight. But Soran was the Seraph. His device bore two, the full wingspan of the bird. A sword blade lay between the wings, pointed down, representing its body.

Soran's clothes were plain and tight-fitting, with a smattering of gems spangled over the fabric. They winked in the light as he moved. Even his hair bore a few tiny jewels.

He'd painted a faint mist of silver over his cheeks as well, a reminder of that first night with Malek and the glittery brush Malek had knocked to the floor. The ghost of a smile flickered over his mouth. He'd allowed himself a bit more freedom outlining his eyes and frosting his lips with a layer of opalescent white.

All of Aerix would be watching this on camera. Better to show off than to hide.

Tanth and Ania stood behind him, mirroring Malek's entourage. They wore the same loose-fitting uniforms that the victors wore, in brighter colors, with the Skyknights' symbol printed on them and the marks of their high rank. A few gems glinted from the folds of the fabric, faint nods to Soran's attire.

Tanth wore a paler shade of his usual blue; Ania wore a bright yellow that echoed the gold ribbons in her hair. She'd put it up for the occasion, her braids twisted into an elaborate scalloped curl fastened at the back of her head.

"Citizens of Aerix!" Soran held up a gloved hand. "We are gathered here today to welcome honored guests."

He looked out over the crowd. Some people smiled, taking in the spectacle. Others stared, expressionless, waiting.

Some faces scowled. They'd come only because it was their duty.

Right.

"It is not often we welcome anyone, especially not in this day and age. Our affairs are our own, and we've always taken pride in that, as a city and as a people."

Scattered cheers. Well, that was something.

"If anyone wants to be permitted into our city, they must prove worthy of the privilege."

More cheers.

He waved a hand toward the victors. "You all know our guests are famous for their victories in the arena of Dis. And you've all seen the broadcasts that fill dead channels at all hours—and sometimes take the place of live ones."

He cast a significant glance at Malek. "You might say that isn't our business. That you're here to see celebrities, not involve yourself in their politics. But apparently their enemies have no qualms about involving us."

The crowd hushed. Malek smiled.

So far, so good. But you won't like what I'm about to say.

"I don't blame the recent attack on the Senate. I point no fingers. Whatever our guests might say about it."

Just as he thought, the words earned him glares from Malek and Kenn alike. Vareth growled and clenched a fist, but kept her arms at her sides.

"But whatever happened, someone out there didn't want them to speak to you today."

Murmurs of discontent answered him.

"Someone who snuck into the City behind them."

"No one sneaks into the City in the Sky!" snarled someone from the audience.

"Whatever problem they have they dragged here with them," growled another.

Soran's lips twisted in distaste. He was supposed to be convincing these people. "You heard it yesterday. Someone wanted so badly to keep them from speaking to you that a woman was sent to keep them silent. By killing Malek."

Scattered muttering answered him. But they'd heard about this before.

"As you all know, that particular—issue—has been handled already. Not surprising, considering who these visitors are."

Or better said, who I am. Soran allowed himself the luxury of glancing in Malek's direction. To his credit, Malek didn't react.

Soran stepped toward the crowd. "But this is Aerix. We choose who we welcome. No one else, Senator or soldier or warrior from Dis, decides what we want to hear."

Scattered cheers rose from the audience. The angry comments became a rumble of dismay beneath it. *Finally.* Soran smiled. Malek stepped closer and moved to his side.

For a moment, all was silent. Malek raised a hand, and his lips curled in a showman's smile. Someone close by called his name, and others took it up.

Like Malek had stepped right out of the pits for a match.

Well, the victors would give them a show. After Malek said his piece.

"People of Aerix!" Malek called. The crowd hushed.

Soran fought down a chuckle. Malek was still trying to hide his accent. And still failing.

"We know how rare it is to be invited into your great City," Malek went on. "You—and your Seraph—honor us by granting us the privilege."

His eyes shifted to fix on Soran. Soran ignored him.

"But gathered here, you honor us far more. Soran is right. We're here to impress you, yes, but we are also here to ask you to listen to us." Malek tilted his head and looked up. Soran saw him squint and chuckled.

"We're here to show you our skills, in the fighting ring and out of it. But we are not invaders. We have no interest in looting your home for its secrets." His arm moved again in a sweep of white. "But we're not here to impress you. We're here to show you that we are kin."

No one applauded. The crowd whispered, restless, unsure whether to question, cheer, or curse.

"Bold words," Soran said, his voice silken. "And the Destroyer will have his chance to prove them. But first"—he waved toward the rack of weapons—"let's see what he and his victors can do."

That earned cheers, at least. Soran smirked.

He gestured first to Kenn. "Kenn the Silent. His career began in the pits, and a fateful match ended it. But, of course, he won."

Am I talking him up enough, Malek? "Most people thought that match killed him. It didn't. But he still works in the arena, designing traps to snare the unwary."

And broadcasting the victors' message across the planet. But it wouldn't do to let our friend Derell hear that.

Kenn didn't wave. The only acknowledgment he offered the crowd was a slight smile. His visor slid down to cover his eyes.

That was enough, it seemed. The crowd roared. Kenn twisted his body into a pose. But Soran's keen eyes noticed an awkward pivot to the ankle he crouched on. And Soran wasn't the only trained warrior watching.

Kenn straightened. "My days in the arena are over. If I take up one of those"—he nodded to the weapons on the rack "—you will only see me fall."

"Maybe we want to," called someone. "We didn't invite you in here. Or the stragglers you dragged in."

"But perhaps I can offer you something," Kenn finished, his voice smooth.

Beams of light streaked from the visor and projected golden holograms: small circles in the air around him, concentric rings of ever brighter light.

"Keep back," he said. "These are toys. But even toys can be dangerous."

He opened his tight fist and dropped something silver and metallic into his empty, outstretched palm. It expanded as he held it, glinting with energy. It locked into its new shape, a flat, bladelike leaf.

Soran's eyes widened. *I never said your minion could bring his knives in here.*

Kenn threw. The leaf whizzed through the center of the projected target. The crowd gasped and shrank back.

It found its mark and burst apart. The metal flickered with energy again and fell to the ground as a rain of glittering metallic dust.

If those are your toys, what are your real blades capable of?

Kenn twisted to aim at another projection; as before, Soran could see a quirk in the movement. Kenn threw again, just as easily. Again, his leaf-blade vanished in a cloud of light and sparks. More followed, as quickly as Kenn could move. The crowd oohed and ahhed. That was a Skyknight's aim.

Or almost was. One or two of his throws missed the center of his rings. Soran didn't bother to keep from gloating. His grin would look like pleasure anyway.

But every throw came close enough. The projectiles passed through Kenn's holograms and they winked out.

"He's cheating!" someone called out. "He projected the targets himself. Of course he's hitting them! How could he not?"

"The same technology that lets me project the targets tells me where they are," Kenn answered. "But the throws are mine."

He turned, visor facing the heckler, and shifted another of his blades. Soran tensed.

The knife sped toward the crowd, aimed unerringly at the heckler. Around it, people scrambled back, shoving each other.

The blade burst harmlessly into a rain of glittering ash, too far from the crowd to singe anyone.

"How dare you!"

"I would not have harmed you."

"Kenn is right. If we meant to harm anyone here, they'd be dead," Vareth rumbled from her place at Malek's side.

"Enough!" Malek roared. "This is a demonstration, not a battle."

"Understood, my Lord." Vareth lowered her head. "But if they want to watch someone they're sure isn't cheating, I'll be glad to oblige them."

Soran sighed and swept his arm out again. "Vareth the Crusher, a favorite for years. Despite her strange appearance," he couldn't resist adding.

Vareth lifted her arms to let the loose-fitting sleeves slide down and flexed her massive muscles. The audience clapped and gasped.

Malek glared. Apparently he wasn't happy with the veiled insult. Soran fought down a snicker and addressed the crowd again. "She built her body victory by victory, if the rumors about her alterations are true."

"Of course I did," Vareth growled the words, not even trying to smooth away her accent. "In my city, we earn what we become."

Gasps rose from the crowd.

"We have Skyknights," someone called out. "Not brutes like you."

"Altered from the time they're small. I earned this body piece by piece. Whatever your Seraph has to say about it."

Soran's eyes narrowed. He opened his frosted mouth to speak, but someone standing near the heckler snarled before he had the chance.

"This is a farce," the man spat. "First they attack us, then they insult us?"

The crowd cried out in agreement. Vareth grimaced and showed her teeth.

Too exaggerated, too obvious. You're playing this to the hilt, aren't you? The barbarian who doesn't want to hide it. She lumbered over to the rack of weapons and picked up the heaviest staff.

Maybe the Crusher was more intelligent than he'd given her credit for. "Very well, warrior." Soran waved a hand and gestured to his companions.

Tanth stepped forward. A frown crossed Ania's face, but she smoothed it away. Soran rolled his eyes. *You'll get your turn soon enough. Even if the Crusher is your favorite.*

"As First Skycaptain, Tanth will have the honor of sparring with Vareth."

Tanth picked up one of the lighter staves and turned to face his opponent, inclining his head. He twirled the staff in his hands, showing off for the crowd. They cheered.

Vareth shifted in her stance and growled, for all the world like the beast Malek had claimed to be.

"The rules are simple," Soran called out as the fighters took their places. "The first fighter to score three hits to a vital target on the body wins. The pigment will rub off to mark them. If one of the combatants is knocked out, or knocked down long enough to be marked three times, that counts as well."

And try not to kill each other, if you can help it. We mean to forge an alliance, not make an alliance impossible.

He lifted his hand and lowered it. "Begin."

CHAPTER SEVENTEEN

THE TWO fighters circled each other as soon as Soran closed his mouth.

Malek would have expected nothing less from either of them.

Tanth had his augmented reflexes. But Vareth had been built like a mountain even before her first victories. If Tanth got close enough, she'd shatter his delicate frame like a bundle of dry sticks.

Or at least, she would in the arena. But this was a game, not a fight to the death. With wooden sticks standing in for blades and too-orange paint in lieu of blood. And it wouldn't do to break the First Skycaptain.

Malek's lip curled. A deathmatch would be pointless, pointless and wasteful. Even the ones back home in Dis—

He shook his head to clear it. This wasn't the time to think about that. This wasn't a deathmatch. Those issues were for Dis. For when he came back home. For when he finally came clean with his people.

If they welcomed him back home. He thought of the High Council and frowned. Would his war begin at the gates of his own city?

But he wasn't here to worry about that. Not while his best champion fought. He blinked again and turned his attention back to the match playing out in front of him.

Vareth whirled her staff in warning. Tanth got the message and danced around her. The edge of his long staff swished through the air close by one massive arm. Then he tensed, ready to spring. She growled, the heavy weight of the staff crashing down in front of her.

He jumped back, his expression unwavering. She spun to match him, and Malek heard a few impressed gasps from the crowd. They were used to their bird-boned Skyknights, startled that Vareth could move so quickly. Malek grinned.

But skill and training didn't make her Skyknight-quick. By the time she turned around Tanth was gone again, sidestepping so nimbly that he might as well have disappeared.

Malek's lip curled. He remembered things like this from his own bouts with Skyknights in the arena. They had been few and far between, fortunately for him. A good fight made his blood sing with anticipation, but fighting a vanishing opponent was just an exercise in frustration. And made a pit fighter look foolish, even if he won.

Malek saw Vareth's brows knit. The crowd knew better than to laugh, but some of the spectators encircling the makeshift ring grinned. Malek looked over toward Kenn. *At least in the pits, someone who moves like that might just land in a trap.*

Not that Skyknights usually fell into traps. The few Skyknights Malek had fought had been as clever as their First Skycaptain was now. They'd skipped past Kenn's best-laid traps as easily as they'd slipped away from him.

He'd only seen a trap catch one once, in one of his fights. His foe had stepped on a hidden panel and a volley of sharpened projectiles had come flying at her. She'd twisted aside just soon enough for them to pierce her arm and side, not her chest. He'd tracked her by the blood from her injury.

But Vareth couldn't do that here. She bided her time, watching and waiting for some misstep from her opponent. He made none.

Malek studied his moves, the precision movements of his lean body. He slipped past Vareth again, just as he had before. Of course.

He's using the same set of steps, over and over.

As if in confirmation, he slid to the side with the same shift of his feet and pivoted to face Vareth again, twisting his body again exactly as he had before.

Vareth had already noticed.

Slow as she was in comparison to her much lighter opponent, she matched him move for move. The heavy staff thudded against the mosaic on the floor and left a smear of orange-red pigment in its wake.

Malek looked over at Soran. The glossed lips curled into a moue of distaste and annoyance.

You see it too, don't you?

Still, as readily as Vareth read her opponent's movements, she couldn't get close enough to counterattack. Her counterstrikes slashed at empty air. And Skyknights, however formal their fighting style was now, had once been warriors. Even with his alterations, Tanth moved like a ghost.

He'd seen Skyknights' agility before, in the ring and out of it. And his chasing after Soran had involved a few fights of its own. But Soran had always wanted to be caught. He grinned, glancing down to the scar Soran had left.

When he looked up again, Tanth was attacking, lowering his staff for a downward strike. But when Vareth lifted her arms to counter, he struck out at her abdomen instead. The movement of the staff left a line of bright red pigment over the pale fabric.

"Tanth, one!" Soran called out.

First blood. Or what passed for it here in this makeshift arena.

Point for you, Prince of the Air.

The crowd, quiet as most of them had been, reacted just like spectators in Dis, watching real blood pour from a wound. They roared so loudly the sound rang in Malek's ears.

And the people of Aerix consider themselves so much more civilized than the brutish killers of Dis.

Vareth growled and swept out her staff in a brutal arc. As before, she missed her opponent by inches. Tanth spun away, twisted back into his fighting stance. When he whirled around to face Vareth again, Malek saw the corner of that solemn mouth quirk up into a little grin.

The expression mimicked Soran's so well that Malek felt a twinge of heat. He turned to Soran again, a steady thrum in his flesh, and watched the gleam of the tiny gems on Soran's clothes and in his hair.

But it wasn't Soran he should be staring at.

To Vareth's credit, she didn't rush her foe. Malek could see the anger in the way she stood, the twitch of her coiled muscle, her bared teeth and squared jaw. But she was the best of his victors, and that meant she was no fool.

She bided her time. Once or twice, she darted in with a rough, rumbling cry. But she knew he would expect her feints. And she knew enough now, despite the streak of bright orange-red staining her torso, to counter him as well.

Malek looked out at the people who'd laughed earlier. Some still scowled or chuckled, but many watched intently, studying both fighters' movements. Good. That was exactly what Malek wanted from them.

But the watching and waiting couldn't last forever. Vareth bellowed and lunged, throwing all her formidable force into the attack.

Perhaps even Skyknights could tire. Perhaps the sound unnerved Tanth, who was used to ceremonial bouts with opponents almost as formal as himself. Perhaps he was gloating. Either way, the smooth gait faltered.

His staff was up and ready before she reached him. Hers clashed down against it with a mighty crack, and Tanth's body shivered as he struggled to hold his own against the big woman's strength. Vareth grinned, bearing down.

A look of panic crossed Tanth's face. He shivered again, his arms inexorably lowering.

In Dis there would have been cheers. Here there was only silence, breathless and hushed, as even those who favored Vareth watched and waited.

Tanth panted, a thin sound of pain coming from him as he fought.

Then he bowed to the inevitable, dropping his weapon and twisting away.

It hit the mosaic-patterned ground with a clatter. The crowd stared at it. Then the whispering began.

Soran gasped, the strangled sound of someone choking down a scream. His brilliant eyes were wide with shock.

But he didn't speak. Instead, the people in the crowd cried out their disbelief.

"Can he do that?"

"Is that allowed?"

"Remind me of the rules."

Malek could barely hold back a laugh. *Survival is the only rule. Especially when winning and surviving are the same thing.*

Vareth roared and moved to stand over the discarded weapon. She waved the staff again, her message clear: *Make a move and pay the price.*

A very steep price. One direct blow from Vareth would bring him down.

And yet he needs three hits to win this.

But, weaponless or not, Tanth hadn't given up. He crouched down, his fists raised. Vareth growled out a taunt in the dialect of the pits.

Malek smirked. He knew full well what she was doing, of course. Gladiators were showmen as much as they were warriors. In Dis, Vareth was stoic. Lumbering and quiet, trusting to the power in her altered frame and the striking sight it offered to win people over. But here, she was glad to play the savage.

The citizens of Aerix might come to trust Malek, knowing his accomplishments and reputation. They might accept Kenn, who looked and fought almost like them. But Vareth was too different, too alien, too strange.

And watching Tanth, the First Skycaptain, dance around her, fleet footsteps on a mosaic of bright gold, she seemed glad to play the villain.

Malek hoped she wasn't pulling it off too well. He snapped to attention as Tanth lunged, rushing straight at Vareth as though his slender, altered frame were powerful enough to force her massive bulk aside by the power of momentum alone.

Vareth roared, springing up, and the thick bulk of the staff moved. Malek saw a flash of blue as Tanth spun—

—and then his ears filled with the crack of the staff against flesh.

"Idiot," Soran snarled, loud enough for his outburst to be broadcast to all of the City. His champion landed in a heap of blue fabric and contorted limbs.

"Vareth, one!" Soran corrected himself a moment later, hurling the word as though spitting out some bitter mouthful.

Vareth's bulk cast a dark shadow over her fallen foe. Tanth twitched, thin limbs shifting as he struggled to right himself. A bright slash of orange-red stained his side, and he groaned. But even that spoke to his skill. If he had moved any slower, he would have taken that blow full force in the chest. That would have left him stunned, not writhing on the floor of the Square.

"This ends in two blows, not three," Vareth said and raised the staff. "I'm not supposed to kill you."

Hisses and boos rose from the crowd. But most were half-hearted. When Vareth moved to strike, they had already lapsed into silence. They watched her movement, not her face, but Malek saw the exaggerated grin fall, a grim, grave smile replacing it.

The twitching heap on the ground moved.

The contorted limbs shifted, sliding into a perfect fighting stance so quickly that Malek almost didn't see a thin leg sweep out. It struck Vareth's ankle with far more force than Malek would have thought possible from someone who had just been thrashing around.

But that was the point, wasn't it? He watched Vareth crash to the ground. *Speed until speed could do nothing more. And wits for the rest.*

Tanth was on his feet when Vareth hit the floor. He reached down for his staff, the movement slowed by his injury. But slow for a Skyknight was still faster than anyone else.

Vareth reached out for his legs, driven by a fierce instinct Malek had seen many times in the pits. The moment a gladiator knew she was losing, and that losing would mean death.

He had no doubt, rules or no rules, alliance or no alliance, that if those dark hands closed around flesh it would splinter, shattered by the blind force in their enhanced grip.

But they grabbed nothing but the silk of the uniform. Tanth moved again, and a red-orange smear of pigment shone bright against the flesh of Vareth's neck.

He held his staff there, poised against the hollow of her throat.

"I do not know if this counts as the third hit or the second," he said. "One strike to the ankle is not a vital blow, after all."

"The rules don't matter now," Soran whispered, his voice harsh.

No, Seraph. No, they don't.

Then Tanth spoke again. "But if this were Dis, you would be dead."

Vareth glared, her face a mask of rage. Then she relaxed. Her frame rumbled in a deep laugh.

"I would," she said at last.

"Then do you yield?"

"I yield."

The Square erupted in cheers.

CHAPTER EIGHTEEN

SORAN WATCHED Tanth struggle to his feet and grinned.

Vareth scooped Tanth up and set him down, as easily as a child with a toy. He stood, but stared past her into the crowd, his mouth drawn with the pain he must be hiding. She bowed to him and then to the audience, but a frown tugged at her lips.

The barbarian from the pits. Trying to be gracious after her first defeat.

The crowd roared again. Some even called Vareth's name. Pleased by her gesture, Soran guessed.

"People of Aerix!" he called out, grabbing at Tanth's hand and raising it high. "Your winner!"

The cheers only grew louder.

He'd heard the thunder of the crowds in Dis, the growling eagerness of a pack of beasts. His own people drowned it out.

He smirked. Aerix had stood alone forever, rising high above the world around it. Now the greatest of Aerix's champions had come in challenge, and the First Skycaptain had bested one of them.

It had come with a price. Tanth sagged against him. He slid behind Tanth and steadied him, still holding their linked hands high. Out of the corner of his eye he saw Malek smirk. It didn't matter. No one expected a speech from Tanth after that.

The medics had already rushed in, waiting for Soran to let go. He gave the crowd another moment and then let them whisk him away to tend whatever Vareth's blow had shattered in his delicate body.

He would need the repair. He had another show to do.

Malek stepped up to Soran and bowed low, the same formal

gesture a defeated Skyknight would give after a match in the sparring ring. Soran gave him his best indulgent smile.

Malek straightened. His black jewel eyes looked over the crowd, and he swept a hand in front of him. "City in the Sky! Your warrior has proven himself today."

The crowd cheered. Malek let them, then cut them off with a sharp gesture. "I say warrior for a reason. My people were once warriors. Now they scrape together weapons and armor, meet in an arena, and batter one another until one of them dies."

Soran blinked. Malek had come here to show off. Why talk that way about his own victors? Was Malek that disappointed in his champion's defeat?

"But you know this already," Malek went on. "By your lights, I am as much a barbarian as any of them. A barbarian standing on a pile of corpses."

Gasps rose from the audience. Malek only waved his hand again. "Are you surprised to hear me say it? It's the truth. Some of you are here for a show and nothing more. If there were shame in that, we wouldn't have come here and given you one today. But this is about more than a show. You've all heard that someone didn't want me here today."

And now she's dead. Thanks to me.

"Someone who wasn't a Skyknight. Someone who snuck into your city to get to me."

"That's impossible!" someone cried.

"Your own news reports confirmed it," Malek returned. Soran couldn't help but chuckle.

A sea of faces turned to Soran. "Yes," he said, smoothing his voice into something even. Solemn. Concerned. "What the Destroyer says is true."

The audience whispered. Malek let them.

After a moment, Malek spoke again. "She used poisonous darts that dissolved on impact. I would have died, and no one would have been the wiser." He grinned, a wide wolfish smile not at all like the usual small curl of his lips. "But I am a far less subtle killer."

The whispers died. *Malek the Destroyer, ever the showman.* And claiming responsibility like that meant he wasn't just going along with Soran's little lie, but embracing it. *If anyone asks, the clean blade is mine.*

"We victors are not what we once were. Instead of mighty commanders or decorated generals, we are entertainers. Those of us who also work in the factories are builders too, but that's all. Entertainers and builders. Nothing more than that, for generations now.

"But you've seen us kill, so you know that we are dangerous. You've seen us fight, and you've seen Kenn's demonstration. You know someone tried to kill me and died in the attempt, which confirms it."

Warming to the lie, indeed.

"By testing himself against us, your First Skycaptain proves that he too is a warrior."

The faces of the crowd still looked puzzled. But they knew a compliment when they heard one. And Tanth's win had made them giddy. So, of course, they cheered.

"Your Skyknights are falcons, keeping watch from the air. You know it and you love them for it. You know that they're trained in war. That they spend years studying both how to pilot their starfighters and how to fight. But to you, war is an ancient art."

A few Skyknights looked attentive. Other people blinked, especially the high-caste guests. Everyone knew Aerix's history, of course, but war wasn't their purpose.

"You've heard of the Old Empire. Of the world that ruled it. The shining jewel of the galaxy. That was our planet. Our people. Now all we have are your Skyknights, keeping alive traditions that the rest of us forgot.

"And we have the Senate." His lip curled around the words. "A pack of fools hiding and cringing in the capitol they've made for themselves. Thieves who stole a world out from under us when we weren't looking, and keep it only because they always have."

A few scattered cheers, a handful of polite boos. That was politics. Just because they'd surely come expecting it didn't mean they had to like it.

"Your Seraphs are the greatest of your Skyknights. The skies over this world should belong to them. Not to scum."

A warm heat curled through Soran's flesh. Someone in the crowd cheered.

"And yet your Seraphs have made peace with scum for generations."

How dare you! The warmth in Soran rose to a bright anger. His hands clenched.

"The last of our planet's nobility, forced to negotiate with trash. Don't you think that is a shame?"

"Made peace with them?" called one of the hecklers. "You fell to them."

Malek's eyes narrowed. Vareth growled. Even Kenn turned his head.

But only Vareth took the bait.

"The Empire fought and fell," she said. "While Aerix negotiated with the people who destroyed it."

Soran whirled around to face her. "Aerix made peace. We have a city. You have the pits."

He swept an arm in front of himself in a gesture of grudging respect. "You're prestigious there. And you know how to fight, like Malek said. And you speak very well for people who have lost their history. Maybe Malek is right. Maybe even my Skyknights and I have something to learn from you. But you're talking politics, not fighting."

He tilted his head toward the crowd. "And they came for a show, not a lecture."

"For a show?" Malek growled. "You could come to Dis for that."

"You chose to come here."

"We could give you a show anywhere. But we came here. Because war isn't as far away as you think it is. Look to Feris. Look to Corian."

Malek clenched a fist and pressed it to his chest. "If I were the conspiracy theorist some people say I am, why would the Senate sneak someone into an autonomous city to kill me? What danger could I be if I have nothing to say? Here in Aerix, you are the envy of the planet. The rest of our world stares at your spires and wants what you have. Why should you rule the skies while they squat on the ground?"

"You envy us too," someone called from the crowd.

Malek laughed and bowed his head, a fighter acknowledging a hit. "I do." He looked up at the towers rising around them. "But I would never take what belongs to you."

Wouldn't you? You promised me a planet if I would give myself to you. And offer all my people up to your little war.

Malek clenched his fist, as though crushing something in his grip. "I'm not the one who wants to tear the spires of Aerix down."

Eyes widened in the crowd. People frowned and shifted, restless. A murmur began, low and quiet.

"That's what you're afraid of, isn't it?" Malek lowered his voice to match the hushed whispers of the crowd. "That after all your Seraph did so many centuries ago, the world will come for you anyway."

A voice rang out from the gathered throng. "We'll outlast them! We always have."

"Your enemies surround you. Is the Senate stopping them?"

"We don't need any aid from the Senate," Soran said. "And if they did offer it, you'd tell us not to take it."

Malek smiled. "Am I your adviser now?"

Soran hissed. "Speak your piece."

"Your treaty doesn't stop them. What that means is up to you."

"What would you have us do?" a woman called from the front rows. Her eyes shone a pale purple. Not a Skyknight. Soran frowned.

"I would have you rediscover what the Skyknights have always known: that your people are not cowards."

A growl rose from the crowd. Soran made sure Malek wasn't looking and added his own soft sound.

"Easy." Malek held up a hand. "I do not say that as a matter of policy. What you do is up to your Seraph."

Eyes shifted from Malek to Soran. Soran's scowl deepened. *You already know that what the city does is up to me, barbarian.*

"But that is a matter for your sovereign and not for you. I am not here for him." He smirked. "Not today."

Why you–! Soran held his head high and shook out his hair, to show the crowd he felt as indignant as they did.

Malek chuckled. "Your people are closer kin to mine than you think. You never lost your traditions. If the Senate hadn't forced us to abandon ours, we would be just like you. Your spires rise high into the air, untouched by the corruption that claimed the rest of our planet. Why? Because you never lost sight of what you are. But now you hide from a world that doesn't deserve you anyway."

He chuckled and shook his head. "I don't blame you. I have its blood on me. But it's worse than that. Even in the pits, I've served its ends."

Soran's eyes widened. *Served its ends?*

"Does that surprise you?" Malek asked. Who was he talking to? To the people, or to Soran himself?

"I didn't learn the things in my broadcasts in an arena. And your Skyknights are not beasts, pitted against one another in battles to the death."

"Very well," Soran returned. "But Aerix is no toy."

Malek looked out over the crowd. "I could ask for your aid. For your City to ally with me. I could tell you to abandon your flimsy alliance with a power that keeps us all in its thrall. I've already told your Seraph what I hope he will do. And I will call on you, soon enough. To remember our kinship. To think of the broadcasts. To understand that what was taken from us by force and what was given to your Seraphs are two sides of the same coin. I hope you will remember that when you think of what you saw today."

Soran gave Malek an indulgent smile. "Is that all?"

"Just one more thing," Malek returned, his own smile just as mocking. "The same thing I said to a crowd of fans once after a fight. To your own Seraph, who came all the way to Dis to see me."

Soran could feel the crowd stare.

"I did," he said, looking only at Malek. "I went to Dis and watched you fight."

"And you talked to me afterward. You wanted me to say something. Something you could take back home with you."

"Yes."

"Do you remember what I said?"

Soran nodded, determined not to make this easy.

Malek's gaze swept over the crowd. Bright, altered eyes looked back at him, unblinking.

They waited. Malek's smile deepened. Then, at last, he spoke.

"Remember what you are."

CHAPTER NINETEEN

A SEA of faces stared back at Malek. They looked almost exactly the same, their frowns eerie echoes of one another, their furrowed brows wrinkled in the same ways. Slender hands clapped, a polite little shimmer of sound.

Malek looked over at Vareth, who glared at the crowd. Kenn's visor hid his eyes, but his lips were drawn. It didn't matter. He hadn't expected them to understand yet. Not the way people in Dis did.

But they would come to understand. Soran had, and so would they.

Amid the confusion, heads lifted. Brows uncurled. The audience applauded faster, louder, longer. One young man, dark-skinned and dark-haired, cried out and raised a fist. He turned to the crowd behind him and yelled something in the old, formal language of Aerix. Malek didn't know it well enough to catch the words. But he knew the tone well enough. He clenched a fist in triumph.

Soran favored Malek with an elaborate bow. He swept an arm in front of himself, indicating the crowd.

Perhaps it was a signal. Perhaps it offered them permission. Their reserved applause became a roar, loud as anything Malek had heard after a bout in the pits back home.

Malek waved again. The crowd parted and Tanth re-emerged. He carried his staff in his hands, the bright paint still smeared. He held his head high and moved with even strides. But his thin lips were drawn.

Malek wasn't sure whether that should surprise him. The City in the Sky would have easier access to supplies, yes. But the medics in Dis were used to reassembling men and women just barely clinging to life. And who needed to fight the next match in their tournaments. Sometimes as soon as an evening later.

Tanth would move with his usual grace, spin through techniques almost as well as if Vareth had never hit him. Not well enough to win, but he didn't need to win again.

Not for this.

Malek offered a bow of his own. "First Skycaptain."

Tanth bowed back, his movements stiff. A new surge of sound swelled up from the crowd.

Soran cut it off with a wave of his hand. Ania stepped forward. The ribbons in her hair and the gems on her clothes glinted. She walked toward the rack of weapons with sprightly, bouncing steps.

"All congratulations to our victor," Soran purred. "But you didn't come here just to see the Crusher lose."

He gestured toward the staves on the rack. "You came to see Malek the Destroyer."

The crowd roared again, expectant.

"To see him fight."

Malek walked over to the rack. He could have swaggered. Could have done what Vareth did: drawn his lips back like a beast. But this mattered too much. He wrapped his hands around a staff almost as thick as Vareth's. He lifted it and felt its weight and the grain of the wood under his palms and fingers.

He did not wave to the audience. He did not smile. He would show off when he fought, and not before.

His gaze passed over them and fixed on Tanth and then on Ania. Tanth pressed his lips together and stared back. Ania smiled. Light glinted on the ribbons in her hair. They stepped closer, closing in already. Malek dropped into a fighting stance.

"The rules are the same," Soran said. "Three hits and a fighter is out of the contest. Regardless of who they come from."

Some people in the audience laughed. Others hissed. Did they worry Malek would lose too soon, or not want to see him best two Skyknights?

"Begin," Soran said.

Streaks of bright fabric flashed before Malek's eyes. Their long-limbed dance would have been beautiful if he'd had the time to watch them. Even now, with the Square of the Sun below his feet and the crowd gathered around him, it might mesmerize. He blinked his dazzled eyes.

His body knew what his mind did not. He moved with them before he realized he had done it. He twisted and turned to keep from exposing his back to either of them, striking out with his staff at the blurs of color that weaved in front of him.

He couldn't get close to them. They wouldn't let him, not until he learned the steps of their little dance. Tanth had moved too predictably before. So Malek focused his enhanced eyes until the blue blur of movement resolved into something clear. Tanth's legs moved, fast and nimble, but his back stayed straight and tense.

Malek smiled. Outside of a sparring ring, Tanth might have passed those wooden movements off as formality. Here, they testified to his injury.

But wound or no, he ran at Malek, swinging his staff.

Clever. I would have expected you to hang back. Malek blocked the blow. The impact sent a familiar, warm jolt through him.

This was too clean, a gilded, overglorified sparring ring. But the old hunger answered, deep and bright. And unreasoning, as it always had been.

So much is different now, he told it.

A blur of yellow caught his eye. He hadn't had time to study Ania, not while he watched Tanth. And she hadn't fought a bout yet, which meant he hadn't seen her movements. Hadn't had a chance to learn their choreography.

That could cost him.

He whirled around and lunged. The Skyknights could keep him dancing around the Square of the Sun forever. Patient endurance might win him a bout against one of them, but not both.

She raised her arms to strike. He swept his staff low, aiming for her stomach. She twisted away, but the staff glanced against her side. An orange streak appeared on the yellow fabric of her uniform.

A peal of laughter echoed in his ears. He pivoted on his heels in search of the sound.

You're eager to fight me. So eager you laugh, even when the first hit is mine.

First blood, his mind wanted to say. But just like before, it wasn't blood. Just an orange shock of paint. Malek snarled his disappointment. He'd sparred a thousand times, but this felt false. A match against worthy opponents, made into a child's game.

And yet Fel's death had been a waste. Fel's death, and so many others. Ania and Tanth were the best of Soran's Skyknights. And Ania liked this enough to laugh at the first blow. How much worse would it be to lose her?

"Malek, one!" Soran called. Malek allowed himself a chuckle, hearing the irritation in his voice.

Half of the crowd hissed, but the other half cheered.

Good enough.

He mirrored Ania's movements, refused to blink. He'd said his piece, and he'd won Soran's loyalty. But if the High Council in Dis hadn't listened to words, would these people, from a faraway city, who fancied themselves his betters already?

He needed their respect. More than that, he needed their awe.

Ania skipped around him, bursts of energy driving her on. She used the same steps and pivots and strikes as Tanth, but she had no use for his ceremonial style. She favored lunges and turns as sudden as a small child's dance. He parried a strike and she dashed away again, shifting through her movements with a Skyknight's grace. He caught sight of Tanth out of the corner of his eye: slower, stiffer.

Understandable, given his injury. But this wasn't about his wound.

He spun to face Ania, whirled his staff, knew by now how she would move to guard against his blow.

She didn't. She mirrored what he had done just before.

You're learning. Malek gave her a laugh of his own, short and quiet and filled with the same respect her laugh had given him. He feinted again, as if he'd become too fascinated by her movements to remember he had two enemies now.

He rushed at Tanth instead.

But Tanth had already shown he was no fool. Malek's staff crashed against his.

It wasn't a point, but the crowd roared for it all the same. Malek spared them a smile. Let them have their pride. They would need it in the coming days, whether they warmed to Soran's decision or not.

Ania's laugh pealed in his ears again. He spun to face her, twisted to block a blow he'd come to expect.

But this time, she was too fast for him. Her staff caught him in the chest, hard enough for the shock of pain to surprise him. The blow stained his loose garment with a red-orange blaze of pigment.

"Skyknights, one! Malek, one!" Soran called, a little thrill in his voice. Malek smiled and growled in challenge. He understood Ania's laugh better now.

You would've fit in well in the pits. Before I realized we'd be fools to invite you to fight in them.

Tanth approached, raising his staff high. Malek knew what was coming and ran at Tanth himself. He might not have a Skyknight's speed, but if he could close the distance between them, the First Skycaptain's long limbs would never reach him.

His staff thudded hard into Tanth's belly. Tanth crumpled under the impact, a fragile thing already cracked.

The blood sang in Malek's veins and he dropped into a deeper crouch.

Tanth did not fall or falter. He caught his breath and turned and ran, apparently eager for the protection of distance. Malek saw the bright red blur on blue cloth as he dashed away.

"Skyknights, one! Malek, one and one!" spat Soran.

Come now, Prince of the Air. Don't you want to see me win?

A wild blur of yellow streaked toward Malek. Only the smear of color told him it was coming. He couldn't have moved out of its way if he'd wanted to. Not without a long cycle of altered reflexes he didn't have.

He whirled his staff, too blindly for a legend. But it blocked the blow, and that was good enough.

The impact jarred him more than he expected. That was speed, speed and skill, and the kind of training even the pits couldn't give someone.

Tanth danced toward him again. He'd lapsed back into his too-precise movements, dashing toward Malek and then hastening away when Malek moved to counterattack.

Pain, perhaps. Or weariness from fighting too long. No man was invincible. Not even the one who'd bested his best victor. Malek darted in again, and again Tanth backed up. A bright flare of yellow caught Malek's eye, the flap of the fabric a movement like flickering flame.

He couldn't feint again. He'd already tried that. He answered Ania's challenge with a full-throated roar.

Unlike her teammate, she didn't dance away. She twirled the staff in front of her, daring him to come closer.

But it was time to use guile of his own. At the last moment, he turned and dashed past. His staff caught her long legs hard, and she fell to the gleaming ground.

Vital targets only. Malek crouched down to strike at her exposed belly even before he saw the orange-red that stained her calves.

"Skyknights, one! Malek, two and one!" Soran's voice was venomous.

Ania glared up at him for a moment, so brief he only caught the blue flash of altered eyes before she leapt back to her feet.

Not so happy when you're losing.

Or is it because you couldn't protect him?

Malek had already turned back to Tanth. Tanth's face was pale, his lips pressed together. The orange stain on his garment echoed a wound even if it wasn't one. But he squared his legs and crouched low.

Malek had seen it before in the pits. Fighters who should have fallen, determined to last long enough to fell their foes. Once they did—if they did—they would have a chance at restoration, thanks to the arena's medics.

Kenn had done it, long years ago. And Tanth would take two hits to fell.

Malek spared the First Skycaptain a respectful nod.

He was not surprised when Tanth returned it.

Tanth darted in with the last of his dancer's grace. But his strikes had grown slow. Malek parried easily. He twisted to the side and gave himself only an instant to crouch down into his stance again.

A Skyknight at full speed would have been gone before Malek could counterattack. But Tanth was weary. Malek's staff flashed out and scored a reddish slash in his side.

"Skyknights, one! Malek, two and two!" Soran spat.

The crowd cheered in spite of itself. They had come out here to see Malek the Destroyer. And now he'd almost felled two of their greatest champions.

The thing inside him stirred again. He gripped the staff tight, eager to swing again, to finish what they'd begun, to shatter the bird-bones of his enemy.

You are not here for that.

In the pits, there was no shame in going after a weakened opponent. Audiences came to the arena to see death. And sometimes those deaths happened thanks to traps and snares. A hunt for an enemy wounded in some hidden trap could be a show, too.

But this wasn't Dis. Tanth had earned their pride, proved himself their champion. To go after him now would make Malek look like a bully and a coward. Prove to them all he was the barbarian the Senate claimed.

He had to win if he wanted to win them over. But he had to do it on their terms.

He turned to Ania and smirked in blatant challenge. She grinned and advanced.

She wove around him, twisting through the patterns he'd studied. He mirrored them, feinting with his staff when she struck from too far away.

You know better than that.

Tanth had done that, baited Vareth by letting himself fall and knocking her down when he did. What did Ania want?

A glimpse of blue from the corner of one eye answered his question. A glance at the crowd's expectant faces confirmed that answer.

Pretending not to notice, he played his game with Ania. He darted forward as if trying to get close enough to strike. Ania laughed again and skipped back.

He did not give himself another moment to play up the suspense. Not when Skyknights were so fast. If he landed the blow he intended, so be it. He was giving Tanth more chance than he ever would give an opponent in the pits. He growled and lunged.

As before, Tanth's reaction came slow. Malek raised his staff, aiming high—

—and the blow hit him hard in the belly, a near-perfect mirror of the one he'd struck against Tanth.

The crowd roared so loudly it almost drowned out Soran's cry. "Skyknights, two! Malek, two and two!"

Malek's grimace shifted into the same smirk he'd given Ania. He'd seen Tanth use his weakness to bluff once already.

Now Aerix's champions had nearly bested him. And now the battle was truly joined.

A gleam of sunlight caught his eye. He blinked and dropped into a low, balanced stance, not wanting its dazzle to weaken him. Sunlight—bright sunlight he wasn't used to, glinting off something tall enough to catch his eye—

The ribbons in Ania's hair.

Tanth's answering nod was even more subtle, a tiny gesture Malek would never have caught if he hadn't seen her first. They rushed at him from opposite sides.

He hastened backward. They converged on the spot where he'd just been standing.

Still two against one, but it kept them both in front of him, where he could fight them off one by one. If he let them come at him from the sides—or worse, from the back—he would never have time to finish one before the next landed the final blow.

Ania yelled and ran toward him. Was that frustration or eagerness? He crouched low and swept his staff in front of him.

But Ania had learned from the strike that felled her just before. She leapt high and Malek's staff sliced at empty air.

But Malek was the Destroyer, greatest fighter of Dis's arena, and Skyknights weren't the only ones who could move fast.

He knew he had to be ready when she landed. Against an opponent altered and trained all her life for speed and agility, he had only his instinct and his strength.

His eyes caught only a sunlit blazing blur. He growled, a roar of challenge and defiance. His weapon moved before his voice died. He couldn't think, only trust his hands and arms and the training years of fighting to the death had given them.

He heard a crack as his weapon connected. The yellow blur crumpled at his feet, a wrinkle of fabric, a tangle of impossibly slender limbs. Dark blue eyes caught his and closed. A groan rose from her twisted frame.

Elation pulsed through Malek's blood. Through its haze, he barely noticed that Soran hadn't called the point.

Tanth circled him, clockwork movements cold and slow.

Malek recognized their smooth glide. He'd seen it before in the pits, the steady, unhurried movement of an opponent who'd lost all hope of glory, all dreams of gilded victory.

Malek grinned. Out of the corner of his eye he could see Soran, leaning forward to watch.

Don't you want to see me win? Malek allowed himself a long, low laugh.

Tanth twirled his staff. Malek didn't answer it. Tanth didn't strike.

Malek didn't see the staff rise. He darted to the side when his body told him to, raced past just as the staff swept downward. The bright blue of Tanth's back might as well have been a target, laid out vibrant and still in front of Malek.

Malek's muscles tensed with their own greed. The elfin body in front of him had broken once already. It would take only one blow to shatter it completely.

Something old and hungry rose up in him. Long years ago, he had become the Destroyer, his body a lattice of scars, his eyes black empty holes.

No. I need him. I need all of them. He snarled and tensed his hands around the staff, tight with the effort of holding himself back.

Then he moved. A diagonal smear of pigment appeared on the blue fabric draped over Tanth's back.

Malek blinked, startled by the gentleness of his own movements.

Tanth pitched forward with a faint grunt of pain. But he did not fall.

The crowd made no sound for a moment. Then it erupted into cheers.

Malek smiled. *I too know how to dance, when it is required.*

"Malek, three and three," said Soran, his voice low.

Malek dropped his staff and raced to Ania's side. The medics had already swarmed around Tanth again and borne him away.

Malek reached out for Ania. Slender fingers grabbed at his and tugged tight. He caught a flash of gold from the ribbons in her hair, the impossible white of her smile.

With a bow of respect, he hoisted her up.

The crowd shrieked its approval.

"Our winner," Soran called, "is Malek the Destroyer." He waved a hand in Malek's direction with a flourish of glittering gems.

Ania lifted their joined hands and laughed, full and wild.

Malek smiled. Let Vareth play the barbarian. He would play the visiting prince, gracious in his victory. He looked over the crowd, held the gazes of the ones who cheered the longest.

A twist at his wrist brought him back to reality.

Ania ducked. He followed suit.

Something silver whizzed past the space where his head had just been.

Five of them, Soran had said. Five, and he killed one.

Someone turned, too broad and short to be a high-caste citizen. And too eager to disappear into the crowd.

Manners forgotten, Malek lunged at the retreating shape.

CHAPTER TWENTY

SORAN'S HAND gripped the hilt of a hidden blade. He drew it, hoping the chaos would hide it from too many eyes. But the city would see all of this eventually anyway. And Malek had just been talking about warriors. Seeing the Seraph fight might even make the people happy.

He might have thrown his knife, crowd or no crowd. But for once, Malek was quicker. He leapt at a dark shape, trapping it under him. Too small to be a victor and too broad to be a Skyknight, it thrashed beneath Malek's weight.

Soran saw another flash of metal in the corner of his eye. He cursed and pivoted out of the way. Did the assassins know what he'd said to Malek? Or had all this made them doubt him?

The blade caught a too-short woman in the shoulder. Light flared in his vision. He blinked before he realized why he should.

When he opened his eyes again, the woman had fallen, a jagged red hole all that remained of her left shoulder. Soran shuddered. He'd killed countless times. No Seraph held his rule by being squeamish. But the bloody spray and raw gape of the wound shocked him. Her arm hung down below it, lifeless meat.

A knife couldn't do that. Had that blade—exploded?

Kenn threw it. One of the little toys he brought to show off with.

But this was no pretty little pyrotechnic show, no smear of too-orange paint to mark a hit. This was muscle and flesh. The bright gold of the Square's mosaic ran with blood, a spreading stain.

Soran ran toward the security guards swarming over her. Did they think they could do anything? Or did they only want to hide the grisly sight?

Had Derell's little party all attacked? Sounds of scuffle rose from the audience.

One of the security officers froze. She collapsed a moment later. Soran's enhanced eyes caught sight of pale skin, a blue pallor, half-closed eyes. Medics left Tanth's side to rush toward her. *There's no use. She's already dead.*

A cold spike of anger curled through him. *One of my Skyknights is dead. And the Senate's pawns killed her.*

Shrieks of dismay rose from the crowd. And growls of rage. A crush of people converged on a short, slender figure and forced it to the ground.

"They have poison darts!" Soran yelled. "They dissolve!"

"They use an oil!" Malek cried, his voice rough from grappling with the assassin. "Requires a puncture wound." Soran heard the thud of a blow.

More gasps. People stared down at the ground, spread backward, pushed at others behind them.

The Skyknight security officers were already in motion. They herded willing people off the platform into shops and buildings. But others' panic wasn't so easily quelled. Soran tapped at his microphone. More security was already winging in, the starfighters' engines roaring above them.

"Search for others," he whispered into his microphone. "Short and broad-framed. Thinner than our visitors. If you find anyone, capture them. Don't kill unless you have to."

"Understood, Seraph."

"Stay calm!" called a familiar, low voice.

Tanth stepped into the crowd, his movements labored and mechanical. The last member of the medical team tagged along behind him. She reached out, trying to draw him back. He pushed her away and winced at the effort.

Soran sighed. *Damned fool.*

But foolish or not, it worked. People turned toward their First Skycaptain turned victor. Screaming mouths closed and fell silent. Men and women who had fallen to their knees stood, looked to the Skyknights, followed them into the nearby buildings, and let themselves be sealed in.

Soran didn't leave. He'd rather fight than hide. And he'd made a show of promising Malek his loyalty. *There were five of them. I killed one. But we've caught only three.*

He heard the purring roar of the Skyknights' craft winging in from above and glanced over at Malek.

There were cameras everywhere. He couldn't say anything aloud.

But he needed to make sure Malek understood. He kept his hand down, but fanned out his fingers and tucked in his thumb. *Four.* He closed his hand again.

Malek blinked. So he'd seen it, at least.

That would have to do.

Skyknights poured out of their fighters and shouted commands at the crowd. Most obeyed, but others, too panicked or angry to understand, pushed forward or froze in fear. Vareth pushed through the crowd, her dark, scarred face a mask of anger. People leapt aside to let her pass.

She stepped toward the assassin the crowd had felled. The dead Skyknight, pale skin tinged veiny blue and lips purpled by the poison, lay nearby.

Only three people stayed. The two who held the assassin down, and a serious-looking Skyknight. The two civilians stared up at Vareth with even, unblinking gazes of their own.

"It's us he attacked," Vareth said. "He's ours."

"In our city," one of the civilians answered. "Our city, our business."

"He belongs to us."

The two looked at each other, then at the Skyknight.

"We'll handle—" the Skyknight began.

Vareth clenched a fist. "You handle your business. We handle ours."

Soran frowned, but shook his head at the Skyknight. The assassins were after Malek. Better to let Malek's victors handle them.

This one, it seemed, still had fight in him. He twisted his head to glare up at Vareth. "Nothing belongs to you."

"Bold talk from a man who's already dead."

"I don't matter. Our planet matters. Peace matters."

"Peace?" Vareth scoffed.

Malek shook his head, swift and violent.

"Your peace is falling apart," Vareth said. She opened her mouth like she wanted to say more. But she only hissed and snapped her mouth shut, her eyes on Malek.

The assassin spat.

That was, apparently, too much for Vareth's vow of silence. "Death will pour out of the Belt and take the ones who sent you."

"Never!"

"And I won't wait for it to come for you."

She slammed her foot down hard into his chest. Soran heard the crack of splintering bone, saw the man's face twist into an impossible rictus. Vareth growled and twisted her foot for good measure, grinding her heel against his shattered ribs.

He did not scream. A wet, ruined gurgle came from his mouth. His head tilted like he meant to protest what she'd done to him. But there wasn't life enough left in him to finish the gesture.

Vareth lifted her foot. It left a low depression where his ribs had shattered, a physical mark of her power. *So you are as strong as they say.* A fey smile curled Soran's painted lips.

Some watchers drew away, their faces green with disgust or gray with horror. Others leaned in, craning their necks to stare at the body. A hint of a smile curled the lips of one of the citizens who'd caught the assassin. Just as quickly, his face smoothed into a cold mask again.

And I thought you were trying to keep him away from her.

The other's face was stony, his eyes too wide. Shock, or anger at losing his prize. But he said nothing and turned away. Vareth, for her part, had already noticed the people watching her. One by one, she turned and favored them with white-toothed smiles.

Soran thought of the younger victor, the one he'd seen in the bar, with braided hair and a quick temper. *Recruitment*, he realized. *Through killing.*

He couldn't say he was surprised.

"You shouldn't have done that," Kenn said. "It gives us one less to question."

Malek hefted the man he'd been grappling with to his feet. Soran noticed with satisfaction that he didn't move quite like Vareth had. But that didn't make Malek gentle. The man winced as Malek set him down and hissed in pain.

"Who sent you?" Malek demanded.

The man laughed and glanced at Soran. "You already know." He looked as if he might spit, but settled for twisting his lips in disgust.

Not to be outdone, Soran grinned back at him.

"How many of you are there?" Kenn asked.

The assassin's eyes never left Soran. "You know that, too." A hand twitched at his side.

Vareth laughed and raised a fist. "Then tell us something we don't know. Where is the other one?"

"That's the one thing you will never know." His hand moved again. Malek tensed and slipped backward, obviously expecting a strike.

It never came. The dark brown hand rose, a tiny pinprick blade held aloft in it.

Soran tensed, ready to move. It would mean saving Malek—again—but he'd be faster.

Still, trying to stab a warrior like Malek with what was essentially the tip of a needle—well. It might work if he moved fast enough. But it would take luck.

But the man didn't lunge at Malek. Instead he swung his arm

down, toward the brown meat of his leg, and pierced the exposed skin there. A red drop welled up from the wound. A sheen of oil glistened around it. The wound blackened, a sped-up picture of decay.

The man's eyes rolled back in his head, a hint of brown showing above an expanse of unseeing white. Foam flecked his mouth. The sound he made was quiet and wet, like his compatriot's. He fell to the ground, empty weight. Vareth cursed, sharp and loud.

Soran turned away, all business.

"There was another?" he said. For the benefit of the cameras, the people, the assassin still at large. Behind his back, for all he knew. What had those fliers found? Surely something, by now. It couldn't be that easy to lose a stumpy, hideous outsider.

Malek glared at Soran. *Yes, yes, I know, I'm the one who told you in the first place. Now hurry up and play along, or we both look like fools.*

"There was," Malek said.

Finally.

The voice in Soran's ear crackled to life again. "We don't see—we found something before—she eluded us."

"Where is she now? In the Square?"

"No."

"Well then," Soran looked back at Malek. "At least your teams drove her out."

"No, Seraph. We...we didn't do anything. She was gone by the time her companions attacked."

Soran looked at the black banners, still waving in the wind. A glorious visit from the outside.

What now?

The City had delighted in the victors' performance. Cheered Malek's speech. But now everything was chaos. Now starfighters hovered above. Looking for something that had already happened, for something else that still might.

Soran hissed. There were still cameras everywhere. Derell would see all of this.

"Gone," he repeated, smoothing his voice to empty impartiality.

Kenn's visored head glittered. Vareth clenched a fist.

"She wasn't part of the attack," the voice said.

"She wasn't supposed to be," Soran realized.

Malek looked at him. "One of them is still at large?"

"So it would seem."

"Seraph?" said the voice in Soran's ear.

Soran ignored Malek and answered his Skyknight. "You're tracking anyone of an unusual size and shape already."

"It's not that, Seraph. It's not where she's headed. We know where she's headed already. It's why she's headed there."

Soran pursed his lips. "Where is she going, then?"

"She's leaving the City."

"Leaving the City? But she was here to kill Malek, like the others. Or the other victors. Why leave, if her intended victims are still here?"

"Fear maybe. Since the victors made such quick work of her compan—" The man's voice trailed off. "Wait."

His next word was an explosive curse, shouted so loudly it made Soran wince.

"What is it? Have you found her?"

"No. We found everyone else."

"Everyone else?"

"The soldiers that the Senate had stationed in Feris. There's a Senator with them."

Soran snarled. "Derell." At least Feris was far enough away that it would take time to reach Aerix.

Vareth grimaced, showing teeth. "Derell."

How did she know about him?

The voice in Soran's ear spoke again. "Yes, and—"

"And?"

"They have others with them. Too many to come from Feris alone."

"Corian. The ones they sent away."

Vareth laughed. Malek's frown deepened.

"They're coming," Malek said. "You knew they would. Now what will you do?"

CHAPTER TWENTY-ONE

"HE PROMISED me they'd leave!" Soran's mouth curled in rage.

"Don't tell me you expected Derell to keep his promises," Malek returned. "Don't tell me you haven't been making plans." He'd just gotten used to the sunlight. Now its beauty mocked him. He couldn't let it beguile him. Not when it was time to prepare for war.

He'd sent word out already, and his allies had heard him. But Dis was far away, and the Belt had little more than a handful of broadcasts to ready it.

There should have been more. Should have been so much more.

"Of course I've made plans," Soran snapped.

"Then you knew this day would come."

"I gave Derell what he wanted. As far as he knows, you killed the first assassin and that big brute killed the other one."

"Gave him what he wanted, Soran? I'm still alive."

Soran snarled in disgust and glared at a pair of ornate doors like his stare could open them. They obliged him and slid open with a soft hiss.

Beyond lay the Seraph's war room, wide and open as Malek's. A massive hologram filled the middle of the room, just as Malek's did in Dis. Like Malek's, the room was dark. Its designer had tinted the tall windows black. Probably so the sun's light didn't flood the room and wash out the details of the hologram.

Its light cast the people arrayed around it in an eerie glow. Some people sat, and others stood. The space was vast, but they crammed into it, compelled by the sudden threat.

This hologram rose up from the floor. It had to. In order to show the height of the towers, the projection stretched almost to the ceiling.

The lowest parts of the city sprawled purple-blue near the assembly's feet. The color shifted to a cool blue near the first ring of platforms, a brighter green at the next. The spires shone orange and yellow, the Skyknights' towers gilded with blazes of light.

Above them all rose the Seraph's tower, diamond-white.

Malek looked past the hologram at Tanth, his ramrod-straight posture covering what must have been pain or exhaustion or both. Still, his blue-tinted eyes were wide and alert.

"First Skycaptain," Soran ordered, his face studiously blank. "Show us what you know about the force gathered in Corian."

Tanth pressed a finger to a console on the wall. The hologram rose to eye level and shrank, then expanded to reveal the territory around the city. Corian shone an angry red, the army gathered at its gates a seething mass of crimson. The broader shapes of tanks and the curves of starfighters' wings shone in their midst.

The doors slid open again a moment later. Vareth rushed in, her countenance dark. Kenn stood near the wall, calm and composed as ever.

He was thinking, no doubt. He always was. But he only asked, "How many are there?"

Flawless faces turned to glare at him. Malek smirked. *This may be your war room, Skyknights of Aerix, but this battle isn't yours alone.*

Tanth answered. "We cannot be certain. We know only what our few patrols were able to discover. And that was some time ago. We...sent fewer, after the Seraph's visit to Dis."

Vareth growled. Soran scowled back at her.

"We have starfighters," Ania said. "If they come here looking for a fight, we blow them away before they get near the inner towers." She grinned and pointed to the hologram. "They'll attack the Below. From the ground. What air support could they have? All we'll need to do is shoot them down."

"Yes, if we're talking about one garrison from Corian," another of the Skyknights put in, the patterns of the hologram gleaming against her dark brown skin. "But we're not."

Another nodded. "The Accord is the only thing that protected us. Without that, we're just one city."

Tanth nodded. "They have a planet's worth of soldiers. We may be trained warriors—" he shot a glance at Malek—"but if they want Aerix gone—"

"Never!" Soran cried.

"They come for Aerix, we save it," Vareth rumbled.

"You save it?" snapped a Skyknight.

"There are only so many Skyknights. If it comes to that, you'll need us."

Kenn turned to look at Vareth. Malek could guess why. *And only so many victors.*

Too soon. This was all happening too soon. If they'd been able to leave Aerix, Dis would be swollen right now with converts. With recruits, men and women from the factories and the pits alike, ready to swarm out of the Belt, elated at the news of a possible alliance with the City in the Sky.

And now Malek was stuck there.

He'd expected the assassins to try something, ever since Soran had told him there was more than one. But this? There was no guarantee the people of the Belt would come. The victors would, of course. As always, they awaited his command. But he couldn't be certain about the rest. Not when Dia had convinced some and angered others.

Not when he hadn't revealed the last truth to them, the one that would make them truly his.

"Are we sure we want that?" another Skyknight interrupted. Blue eyes darted from Vareth to Kenn and finally to Malek. Malek held the man's gaze.

I am here for a purpose. Whether you approve of it or not.

The Skyknight cast his eyes downward. "I...I mean no disrespect to our guests. Our city could withstand one assault—" he glanced up at Tanth, who nodded—"but they can always come back, and back, and back."

"But."

He shivered again and looked away. "But the Senate doesn't want them here. They've left us alone for generations. They'll leave again if the victors go back to their homes."

A murmur spread through the crowd. Heads turned toward the victors. Brows furrowed, some in anger, some in what looked to Malek like barely-checked despair.

"We are not leaving," Malek said.

Soran's head snapped up. "What?"

"If you want us to leave, you're too late for that," Kenn said.

"What?" Soran said again.

"The victors already know what happened here."

Malek's lip quirked into a smile. Of course they did.

"They know about the attacks, the assassins, the Senate's army. Why do you think we arrived after my lord Malek? I told them what happened before we even left the Square."

Soran moved toward him. Malek saw his hand shift to his side. Probably drawing a weapon. "What did you tell them, and what happens now?"

Malek stepped in front of Kenn. The last thing Malek needed right now was a fight. If the Skyknights and the victors couldn't unite against this threat, even the Belt emptying itself for war would mean nothing.

"Then the victors are on their way," Malek said.

"They'll bring others with them, too," Vareth added. "Do you think the Belt watched Malek's broadcasts for nothing?"

Malek nodded. "Yes. They're coming. And bringing weapons."

He closed his eyes, remembered Zarel's modified blaster, the smoldering, melted hole it had left in the wall of the victors' headquarters.

Ania looked down at the hologram. When she looked up again, she was the only one of the Skyknights still smiling.

"Rescuers?" she said. "Our City doesn't need those. But it might need reinforcements." Her grin widened. "And I want a look at those weapons."

The assassin, it turned out, was lean, light-skinned and dark-haired, with dyed orange eyes. Her cheeks slanted at a sharp angle, an angle even a Skyknight might find eerie.

Behind her stood an army.

Armored soldiers lined up in ranks, dark blue visors covering their eyes. They looked to Malek like a parody of Kenn's, soulless and empty. Their armor gleamed, a cool winter-gray.

They reminded him of the armor Zarel made for him and his victors. Had the factories of Dis built the armor their enemies wore? More importantly, what did the Senate think it was doing? These soldiers could swarm the Below easily enough, but they couldn't hide from a Skyknight in the air.

He stared at the woman, the odd shape of her cheeks, her thin lips. Was that a style in her home city? Where had she come from, and how had she become what the Senate wanted her to be?

"Seraph of Aerix," she said. "I am Halcyon."

"Halcyon," Soran returned. "Is that a name, or just what the Senate calls you?"

"It is all the name you need."

Soran smirked. "I assume you're contacting me on their behalf?"

"You harbor one of their enemies. Which violates an agreement that has lasted for generations."

"Enemies?" Soran asked. His eyes widened and his voice was silken-smooth. Malek cracked a smile. "The Senate has no enemies."

"You invited Malek the Destroyer to speak against the Senate. In front of your entire—"

"Malek and two of his victors came to Aerix as guests."

"Guests. Who played at war for your amusement."

Malek's brows knitted. He'd heard Kenn speak like this. Clipped, quiet, measured. But this woman hardly sounded human. Was that by design?

"Play?" Vareth snarled from behind him. "Are you saying you want us to do more than that?"

Kenn waved a hand and she quieted, but Malek heard her mutter in the dialect of the pits.

I agree with you, old friend.

"We let our visitors show off their skills in sparring matches with our Skyknights," Soran said. "If you watched them, you watched the First Skycaptain win."

"Aerix hasn't invited guests in a generation. And you decide to start with war games."

"With sparring matches. Skyknights do that too, young and old. Surely the Senate can't find fault with a sporting event." He chuckled. "Especially when no one dies."

Halcyon's altered eyes narrowed. "Malek the Destroyer came to your city to preach war. We've all seen it. You broadcasted it to the whole city."

Malek stepped forward. "All this talk of war. I'm not the one bringing an army."

"The army is a precaution," Halcyon said. "And an incentive. Nothing more."

"An incentive?"

Halcyon ignored him and turned to Soran. "You made a promise to the Senate. One that they still hope you will keep."

"Your friends are all dead, Halcyon," said Malek. He stared at her altered face, at the strange orange of her irises. The color of flame, of burning, of a place where armies passed.

"We are warriors," he said. "We are—"

"You are butchers."

"Even the Senate can't blame us for answering a threat with violence." He glanced over at Soran. "And don't blame the Seraph for my words. They are mine, and mine alone."

"Indeed," Soran said. "Malek the Destroyer is entitled to his opinions. Just like anyone else in the City. He is entitled to talk about them. That doesn't mean the City shares them."

"Aerix should never have opened its gates to him."

"Aerix." Soran laughed again. "You talk like you don't know who opened them."

"We know exactly who opened them."

"Then you know I welcome whoever I will." He chuckled, short and sharp.

Malek smiled. *So you have made your choice.*

Halcyon's face betrayed no emotion. "Our forces will reach the City in two weeks' time. You have until then to turn Malek over to us."

"To turn over Lord Malek," Kenn said. "What about the rest of us?"

"Lord?" She didn't look at him, not even to chastise. "The others may return to Dis and to their...sport. So long as they confine themselves to it alone."

"I'd rather—" Vareth began.

A glare from Soran quelled her. Malek raised an eyebrow, impressed.

Soran turned back to the videoscreen. "The Accord—"

"Was meant to ensure neutrality. Not to give your city free rein to harbor dissidents. You have fourteen days, Seraph of Aerix."

Soran didn't answer. He only stared, dyed eyes and painted face glittering, lips curled in barely-checked rage.

"Fourteen days," he said at last. "Fourteen days for a free city to do as it wills, without interference from those who promised to leave it to live and thrive. And after that—what?"

He laughed again, high and wild. "The very thing the Senate swore never to do for generations?"

"Seraph," Halcyon said, her voice cold. "You broke your vow first."

CHAPTER TWENTY-TWO

"FOURTEEN DAYS," Soran murmured. He lounged on the bed in Malek's suite and peered at him through half-lidded eyes. "Thirteen if they left right after Halcyon hailed us."

He'd worn orange-red, ablaze against the blood-plum of the sheets underneath him. His shirt, a gauzy mesh, already lay open. Gold-threaded fabric wound around his legs.

He'd painted his lips to match, a rich red-brown no Skyknight would wear, and dusted his eyelids with a faint hint of the same. Rubies glistened at his ears. War lurked at the corners of his city now, and he wanted to borrow its flame.

He remembered his visit to Dis, Malek's hologram wreathing them in fire. The avenues of a remade Dis, gilded and gleaming. All roads leading to the pits at the center of the city. And Malek holding its promise out to him like a prize.

"Thirteen days." Malek leaned down toward Soran, a smile twisting one corner of his mouth. "Then you fight for us. For me." His mouth hovered just above Soran's. Soran thought Malek might kiss him, but he made no move.

Neither did Soran. Part of him wanted this. To close the distance between them, seal away the things unspoken. He'd told Malek he'd made his choice, after all. But now his city itself might burn.

"Don't look so pleased," Soran snarled instead. His hands twitched. His arms wanted to wrap around Malek's broad back, to glide along the scars they found there.

He wouldn't let them. Not yet.

"Pleased, Soran? I want them gone. I want this city untouched. I don't want it stained by their—"

"You want war, Malek." He spat the words. "You're a beast, like you said."

His eyes flicked to the dagger he'd given Malek so long ago, strapped around his arm again. The muscle beneath it bulged, and the slender blade looked too thin against it. Too delicate. Soran thought of Tanth and shuddered.

Malek's gaze followed Soran's. His lip quirked, and his hand moved to his blade. "I want war, yes," he said, and pulled it free. "That doesn't mean I want this."

Soran scowled.

"But this is how war begins," Malek admitted.

"With my city!"

"They were already coming for your city, Soran." Malek held up the knife. It shone as bright as the day Soran had lost it, so many months ago. Apparently Malek had finally had a chance to clean it properly.

He'd told his people that Malek had killed the assassin. Of course his blade would be clean now.

Soran snarled. "And I'm supposed to have faith in you. In your tiny band of victors."

"Not just my victors. Men and women from Dis and the Belt who are tired of the Senate and its lies."

"Fans who carve your initial into their skin and rub it with ash and ink because they can't afford tattoos or alterations."

"Soran—"

"And you think that will save Aerix. A pack of wolves, following the wolf who bays the loudest. Maybe Senator Derell was more right than he knew."

"Senator Derell." Malek's expression hardened. He turned the blade over in his hand and laughed. "Your friend. Where is he now?"

He looked at the dagger for a moment longer. Then he lowered it to Soran's chest.

Soran exhaled a ragged sigh. He expected the knife to prick him, but it didn't. The tip of the blade touched his skin and he froze. Malek held it against his flesh, his movements all leashed force.

"Fans who cut my initial into their skin?" He chuckled. "You come to my rooms and lay yourself out like a gift. Then you call me names and hope they sting. Tell me, Prince of the Air." The blade bit deeper now. A drop of blood welled up around its tip. "Is that an insult, or a request?"

Soran laughed, high and wild.

"You made your choice," Malek said, and drew the knife down.

It tore a line of fire through Soran's skin. He sucked in a breath and watched the blood well up where it had passed. Parted his lips in a moan or a cry or a curse that died before it left his throat.

Malek watched with avid eyes. Soran stared back and licked his lips.

The blade moved again. Slow, deliberate, cruel. It carved the point of the spearhead design into his skin, a jagged blaze that fed the heat inside him.

"How dare you?" he teased, trying not to laugh again.

Malek set the blade down. Soran looked over at the smear of red on it. Free to move now that Malek had put it down, he writhed.

Strong hands seized his wrists, no longer gentle. Soran cried out, half in surprise, half in wry shock. Why should he notice pain like that, with a fresh wound cut into his chest? But it came from Malek, so of course he did.

"Be still," Malek growled. Soran spat in his face.

Malek blinked, placid as a beast of burden. He made no move to wipe his cheek. Only the sharp angle of his brows showed any sign of anger. One lip twitched and curled into a smile. Soran stilled under his hands.

"That's better," Malek said. His grip loosened, and he lowered his face to Soran's wound.

Soran slid his wrists free and reached up to touch Malek's back. His fingers ran over the lines of muscles, the dip of his spine, the rough lines of old scars. One hand slipped to Malek's arm, the scar he himself had left there.

Malek's tongue slid over the red line of the cut. The movement soothed and stung, and Soran twitched under it. He arched his neck and hissed.

Malek's other hand moved lower, slid under the waist of Soran's pants, curled over the curve of his hip. Soran shifted again and snickered and Malek raised his head to look at him. Blood smeared his lips and chin, a vivid red smear.

Of Soran's own blood. He blinked, not sure whether he wanted to close his eyes and block out the sight or stare.

Malek's lip curled. Soran gave Malek a red-painted scowl of his own.

With a violent motion, Malek yanked down Soran's pants. He pulled them off and threw them down onto the floor. Soran squirmed in anticipation. He reached down to pull aside his undergarment, silken fabric finer even than everything else he'd worn.

Malek licked his lips. Not the same way Soran would, all tease and show. Like he knew Soran would stare, no matter what he did.

Or like he just wanted to taste Soran's blood.

Stung by the sight, Soran curled away. "You need to get—" he began, and waved toward the nightstand. Malek wasn't the only one who could hide supplies.

Rough hands stopped him, their grip tight enough to bruise. They pushed him down, held him there. He stared into a red-stained face and was still.

A hand wrapped around his flesh, moved on it fast enough to make him tremble. A gleam lit Malek's eyes, and the hand withdrew. Soran's hips followed it, beyond shame.

He heard a zipper opening, cloth falling, a cabinet opening, a container twisting open. He didn't look. He looked down at himself, instead. At his smooth, altered chest with a red tear ripped through it, blood bright as rubies against his skin.

When he lifted his head Malek stood naked at the foot of the bed. Soran tried to look at him: at his muscular chest, his scars, his straining, waiting flesh. But his eyes returned, again and again, to the bright red smear on Malek's lips and chin.

"Soran," Malek prompted.

Soran slid to the edge of the bed, pushed his legs obscenely open. Malek positioned himself, a frozen suspended moment, and pushed in deep.

Something burned, bright flame in the cut on his chest as Malek's thrust pushed him open. Its stretch stung and he yelped. Malek curled a stained lip and began to move.

The friction lit his insides, an effervescent heat. He opened his mouth, gasped again, let it shiver through him. His cut stung and he remembered the blood again, warm and wet on his chest. He shiftedwanting Malek to drive deeper inside him, to shiver him open. He rocked backward, slammed himself over the flesh invading him.

Malek pulled back and held himself there. He looked down at Soran's wound, his darkened eyes wide and unblinking. He smirked.

Soran called him a wretch, a beast, a barbarian, hissing the words in the pits' dialect just to make them harsher. Malek laughed and plunged in again.

His hands clutched at Soran's hips. Soran glanced over at the knife on the nightstand, wished his blood stained it, too. Wanted Malek's fingers to smear red prints on his flesh.

Soran writhed. He closed his eyes to block out the sight of Malek glaring down at him, but it remained in his mind, imprinted on the backs of his eyelids, wanted and terrible and too much, too much.

You made your choice.

Remember what you are.

He wrapped a hand around himself, half for the pleasure of it and half to end this sooner. To let the heat scour him, blaze so hot and fierce and bright it drowned out that face and the sting in his open flesh.

He thought Malek might stop him and tensed, waiting for the grip that could crush his wrist like glass. It never came. Only another laugh, sharp and derisive.

His eyes opened before he could stop himself. He saw the mark on his skin, the smear of his blood, Malek's reddened mouth twisting into a white-toothed grimace of pleasure.

So you think you've made me yours. He snickered.

Malek's grip tightened. Soran opened his legs wider, threw back his head and opened his mouth in a cry of welcome and surrender and defiance.

Malek froze for a long unbearable moment. He growled a word of his own, some curse or benediction. He pulled back, the movement slow, all trembling, desperate control.

Soran pushed out his chest, an obscene demonstration. *Look. If you want to see it, have your fill.*

Malek battered into him again, all force and speed.

Everything became heat and light. His hand froze forgotten around his own flesh. His release came anyway, came as Malek's own release flooded him, claiming him as surely as the mark on his chest had.

He hadn't been far wrong.

Dia answered their call. Her smile twisted into a scowl when she saw Soran. He glared back for a moment, then grinned at her instead.

"My Lord." She nodded to Malek. Then she turned to Soran. "Seraph of Aerix."

She wore the same braids Soran remembered, but now she held a weapon in her hands. Well-made, of uncertain design, clearly new. A blaster of some kind, large but sleek. Light, from the way she held it.

Her armor looked new too, light like the armor he'd seen on Malek's opponent in the ring. But it fit her frame well. Malek's spearhead sigil was a gash torn across her chest, filled with some black ink or dye.

Around her gathered a band of people so mismatched Soran could hardly have called them an army. Some he'd seen before: the twins and a tattooed, tall woman he'd never had a chance to speak to, but whose striking proportions had caught even his eye. But he didn't know most of the crowd.

That, at least, was a good sign.

They looked strong, broad-muscled in the way of the pits or of the Belt. Some were thin, their bodies badly proportioned shapes halfway between a victor's bulk and the slim grace of a Skyknight.

Ugly. But anyone from outside Aerix—or from the slums of the Below—was ugly. His lip twisted.

Most of the victors' companions wore armor like Dia's. All of them carried weapons, from pikes glowing with bright energy to blasters to massive handheld cannons. And all bore Malek's mark. On their armor, if they had it. The ones that didn't wore it dyed into their clothes. Or painted on their foreheads or cheeks. A few wore the glyph as tattoos, inked into bare shoulders or chests. One or two bore scars, just as Soran had predicted.

His wound stung. He'd coated it with a salve to promote healing, and to numb the itch as it healed. He'd felt nothing but a cool chill in his chest ever since. He'd liked that, a soothing counterpoint to what Malek had done to him. But now it twinged in sympathy.

How long have you been training them, Malek? Do they have any idea what they're getting into? You fed them on tales. Do you realize how many of them will die?

He hissed at the itch in his chest and forced himself to greet them. "Victors. People of Dis and of the Belt. The City of Aerix appreciates your aid."

It was an insult wrapped in a compliment. The crowd didn't know it. Or if they did, they didn't care. They pumped their fists in the air, waved their weapons, readied them and made them glow bright with energy. Bright with thirst for war and blood.

Soran looked over at Malek. The dark, dyed eyes gleamed.

The cobbled-together army turned to him, as one.

"People of Dis and the Belt," Malek said. Soran snickered, pleased to hear Malek's words echo his own. "I had hoped, if things came to violence—"

If. Of course. They could be watching.

"—that I would call on you to defend our own cities. To fight for Dis, lest they raze once again what they already stole from us." He clenched a fist. "And I had hoped to show you why this fight is needed. I had hoped that I would not call on you—that I would not need to call on you—until I could make sure you understood."

Soran snickered too, a mirthless sound. He let himself giggle once, with Malek's noise to cover it.

"But those who oppose us have forced my hand. Make no mistake: they want me dead. They want this movement dead before it is born. And they will destroy a city to make sure that it dies. A city they vowed to spare. They accuse us of barbarity. Of spitting on their sacred peace. And yet an army marches on Aerix."

"They're afraid," scoffed Vareth.

Malek nodded and turned back to the crowd. "Yes. But what is it they're afraid of?"

"All of us."

Soran recognized the voice, low and steely. Tena. She held a massive spear, her pose almost ceremonial. Her fingers pressed at something on its shaft and it glowed with energy, a lightning-storm curling so bright around it he saw some of the others close their eyes.

Tor held a similar weapon. It flickered and flared once. "More have come since last night. Thousands."

Malek nodded. But he was too busy making a speech to celebrate strategy. "They hope you won't come for a city that isn't yours. They think you are mine, and nothing more."

"We belong to ourselves!" called a ragged man next to Dia.

Malek nodded again. "You wear my symbol. You cheer me in the ring. You see me kill. And they think you'll kill for me. That you're a pack of wolves, following their snarling leader."

Well said, King of the Barbarians. But that wasn't Derell's line. That was mine.

The band of fighters hissed and booed and waved their weapons. Some cursed, a snarled roil of invective in the dialect of the pits.

"I say if you follow me, you follow me because I tell you you don't have to follow them. I say if you belong to me, then you belong to me for one reason alone: because you don't belong to them."

The roars of rage became an eager shout. Soran understood his cue well enough. He waved a hand and waited for them to quiet down.

"And neither do we," he said at last. "We told them that generations ago. They say we negotiated a treaty, promised them we wouldn't interfere. We say we wanted to be left alone."

Scattered cheers answered him.

"We invited your leader. Now they order us to turn him over." He reached down, too quickly for the crowds to see, and held up his own knife. Not as flashy as this little army's new toys, but it would do. "But there's one problem with giving us orders."

He waited. Malek wasn't the only one who understood timing. When the crowd stopped blinking and breathed ragged and expectant, he spoke again.

"We are not theirs either!"

The roar of the crowd drowned out his voice.

CHAPTER TWENTY-THREE

"WELL." SORAN'S thick lips curled. He waved a hand. "This is the Below. I suppose I should welcome you."

Tanth looked almost as displeased. But at least he knew how to be less obvious about it. He didn't bother to speak. He just trudged onward, a tight frown betraying his discomfort. His movements were still stiff, but hints of his grace had returned. He slipped past curling twists of metal without trouble, injured back or no.

Malek wondered at it. Was that just Skyknight agility? Or was he familiar with this place? Skyknights weren't supposed to spend their time on the ground, if they could help it.

A lattice of metal twisted around them. But not in the delicate, ornate patterns of the filigree above. The tunnels here were cobbled together out of metal—apparently, any metal the builders could find. Thin plates formed walls, and wires twisted around them. Thick pipes extended down from the platforms high above. Malek wondered if they carried water down from the high City to the people here, or if they were filled with its refuse.

The spires and the platforms above gleamed, polished with impeccable care, but grime smudged the walls here. Glyphs were sprayed on the walls or, more commonly, cut into them, crude markers of location or distance.

The sunlight didn't reach down here. The people had no chance of seeing the blue sky above. Lamps lit the way instead, peeking out like gems from the ruin of the walls. But this was clearly Aerix. Even down here, there was beauty. Even down on the ground, in the slums of a city where the worthy lived and soared among the clouds.

Malek reached out and ran his fingers over one of the glyphs cut into the walls. Dirt had never bothered him.

It made him wish his victors were here.

He willed himself to focus and looked up at Ania, who followed Tanth through the maze of corridors with her usual eagerness. Soran walked just ahead of her, his lips curled in contempt. Tanth led them, glancing occasionally at the glyphs on the walls.

"Vanguard should be here any moment," he announced.

Something metallic emerged from the shadows, the tip of a slender rod. It swept out in an arc in front of the person who held it. It tapped against one of the pipes with a distinct, exaggerated click.

Malek's eyes widened. He'd heard of tools like these, but never seen one. He'd never met anyone who needed them. Most imperfections could be repaired with simple alterations. But then, not everyone could afford them. Not in Dis and the Belt, and perhaps not in the slums below the City in the Sky.

And some things, even alteration couldn't fix. Malek glanced at Kenn, then back at the man stepping out of the shadows.

He wore plain gray clothes cut of rough cloth. The only hint of color was a blue shawl over his shoulders. It had frayed, and stains mottled the faded fabric. Still, tattered and dirty as it was, he wore it like a mark of office, slung over his shoulders.

He had light skin like Soran and sculpted features, delicate and slender. His long hair was a rich, brown-streaked gold. Perhaps an alteration like his height.

But if he had been altered, it must have happened long ago. Wrinkles lined his face, even though Malek guessed he was only a few years older than Tanth. His frame was slender too, taller than the victors. Malek might have wondered how well he ate, but he moved with a grace Malek had already come to find familiar.

But no Skyknight would make his home on the ground.

Malek looked at his eyes.

They were blue, Skyknight-altered. The dye bled out from his irises, as it did even with the most expertly dyed eyes. But this was no side effect. The dye leeched out into the whites of his eyes, marbling them with blue. What had happened to him?

He wore a small device clipped over one ear. It glowed with blue light. A communication device? Another tool to orient himself? Malek wasn't sure.

The man—Vanguard, was it?—flicked his hand once. The cane folded in on itself and drew up into his hand, nothing more than a trinket now. He dropped his hand to his side. Only the slight gleam of metal where its edges stuck out revealed that he held anything at all. With a smooth, practiced gesture, he tucked it into a loop at his belt.

"Seraph of Aerix and victors of Dis," he said, with a precise bow. "I welcome you."

"Vanguard of the Below," Soran said. "We are grateful to your people. But it's the victors you should welcome."

Tanth glowered at him.

"They are the ones who will be coming here," Soran finished, his voice smooth.

"Vanguard." Ania stepped between Soran and Tanth. "We're here too."

Vanguard's lined face burst into a smile. "Skycaptain Ania. But if you are here, then—"

"Hello, Vanguard," Tanth said, his voice stiff.

Vanguard's smile deepened. He bowed his head in another formal gesture, borne out of obvious respect. "First Skycaptain! I'm glad to— that is—you honor us with your presence."

Soran snickered. A smile curved the corner of Tanth's mouth, but he said nothing more, and only bowed his head in acknowledgment.

Vanguard didn't respond, so Malek stepped forward. "I am Malek the Destroyer. Vareth the Crusher and Kenn the Silent are with me."

Vanguard nodded. "Thank you." He waved a hand. "As I said, welcome."

"You are the leader here?" Kenn asked. His visor was retracted for the moment, and Malek saw his eyes dart to the collapsed metal cane at Vanguard's belt and the device tucked over his ear.

"One of them," he said. "We have no single ruler. Not when our numbers always grow."

"That doesn't surprise me," Vareth said, looking around. "We've seen it before."

The faces turned to her. Some hopeful, some appraising. Many closed off entirely, a hard look Malek knew well.

A woman stepped forward, glaring at Malek, her lined mouth puckered in a weary scowl. "You're a celebrity."

Malek nodded.

"Your city loves you."

"Some people in my city do, yes," Malek said, thinking of the Blade and his little mob. He moved a hand to his cheek and traced the jagged line their fight had left there. "Not everyone."

"Go show off to your own people! Leave Aerix alone."

"They aren't leaving."

That was Soran, his altered eyes stern.

"Seraph." The woman's gaze met his. "These people don't belong here."

"But they are here now. And you are all a part of this City. And whether we like it or not, we above or you here below, we all must defend it."

They passed buildings made from any material imaginable: concrete, metal, stone, things Malek couldn't recognize. Some rose as high as their construction would allow, stretching up and up toward the skies these people had been denied. Some of the metal had even been polished. Dull and dirty compared to the glittering City above, but cleaned as best these people could.

Small hovercraft zoomed past, most just large enough to accommodate one pilot. A rare few had room for a passenger. The craft bore signs of age as well: dents, scratches, dirt, flickering lights, thick welds from crude repairs. Malek decided he liked it.

Soran didn't. His too-blue eyes glittered with disdain, and he muttered about the dirt, the mismatched buildings, the vehicles that couldn't fly. Malek chuckled. Soran had liked Dis well enough.

He walked behind Vanguard, slowing his movements to an easy lope. Vanguard swept the cane out in an arch. A light blinked blue at its tip, and matching lights flared to life on the little device at his ear. A signal, perhaps? A description of the buildings around them?

He lifted his hand to a wall beside them and slid his fingers over a glyph cut into it. Malek had done the same thing before. Now he realized why the glyphs hadn't just been painted.

People followed them, slipping out of the corridors. After days with Soran and his court, they looked small. Stunted.

But they were no shorter than the victors. Smaller, perhaps, without the muscular bodies of fighters in the pits. And not nourished as well. Dis was no great city, but the victors were its favored sons and daughters. But these motley bodies, wrapped in a cacophony of coarse cloth, had their own wiry grace. Their version of Aerix's dialect made him think of his own.

Ancient words ground down by toil. Here, as there.

He could understand some of it. Awed whispers from people who had never expected to see Skyknights, much less the Seraph himself. A breathless retelling of Malek's feats in the pits. A mention of Kenn. A murmur about Vareth's size and strength. A comment on his speech. Quieter whispers. Words he couldn't quite decipher, but their meaning clear: *The Seraph said he needs us.*

The corridors grew wider as they moved, the space between the curling walls of metal growing larger. There were more buildings too, more buildings and more people.

And more light. The glittering lamps grew larger here, vast globes filled with smaller lights that cast a cold white glow over the buildings, the people, the victors. It might have flattered the Skyknights. But it revealed these people's every scar, every wrinkle, every blemish. Every smear of dirt on mottled cheeks and hands.

They came forward as he watched: young, old, tall, short, dark-skinned and pale. Some stared bright-eyed under the light. Others scowled, clearly wary. Some stared at Soran and the Skyknights, some at the victors.

A woman with dark skin and a shock of wiry curls stepped toward them. Darker moles pocked her face, and a scar curled over her chin. Like Vanguard, she wore a colored shawl laid over her shoulders. Others stepped forward with her, all wearing the same scarves, in shades of yellow, blue, green, and red. Malek looked back at Vanguard. Perhaps it was a mark of office after all.

Vanguard nodded to the assembly. "Soran, the Seraph of Aerix, and two of his Skycaptains. Skycaptain Ania and—" his smile widened "—First Skycaptain Tanth."

He waved a hand in the direction of the victors. Perhaps he knew where they had been standing. Or perhaps he had vision enough to know they were there. "Malek the Destroyer," Vanguard said, "and his companions—"

"We know them already," said a pale man beside the curly-haired woman.

"We saw your little show," said another, dressed in green. "And what happened after."

"Then you know what's coming," Soran said.

The shawl-clad elders—or so Malek thought of them, even though only the dark-skinned woman and one other had streaks of gray in their hair—nodded in ragged unison.

"An army of my victors is on their way now," Malek said. "But we don't have starfighters."

"They'll be fighting from the ground," Soran said.

"Which means here," Vareth said. She looked out at the crowd. Kenn lowered his visor and did the same. Malek saw his head turn. Studying the terrain, probably. He'd built traps in the pits, hiding places for ambushes.

These tunnels would be a perfect place to build them for real. Malek smiled.

"We'll fight with you," Vanguard said. "The Seraph is right. If they come for Aerix, they come for all of us."

"If the high towers fall, it's our homes they crash down on," said a young woman, barely more than a girl, her voice soft but strong.

The crowd poured after them like a procession.

"There are plenty of places in the Below where you can disappear."

Vanguard tapped at a piece of metal with his cane. The gesture looked almost affectionate. "Whether you want to ambush an enemy or just want to elude him."

"Strategy." Soran smirked. Malek wondered if he was impressed, or mocking him.

Ania looked at Soran. "He would know."

Tanth, as before, said nothing.

"You know how to fight," Vareth said.

Vanguard nodded. "I used to."

"You were a Skyknight," Malek said, looking at Vanguard's blue-stained eyes.

"I was supposed to be," Vanguard answered.

"Your eyesight," Kenn said.

"We all have alterations. Most of us have good vision without them."

"But Skyknights need more than that," Malek said.

Vanguard nodded. "The enhancements begin early. If something happens to the navigation systems in our starcraft, we have to be able to see for ourselves."

"Alterations from youth ought to repair whatever is wrong," Kenn said. He looked down at his own legs. "But sometimes they're not enough."

"No," Soran said with a scowl at Kenn. "Sometimes they're not."

Malek's eyes widened. *All those alterations. That regimen of training, years long, to mold a Skyknight into a raptor of the air. How often does it go wrong?*

"I had my first correction early," Vanguard said. "Earlier than other children. They hoped that by the time I was prepared for the enhancements, my eyes would be ready for them."

"But it didn't work," Malek finished for him.

How often do those who should live in the City above find themselves down here instead?

"It did. At first."

"At first?"

"I trained with the others for most of my childhood. Alterations made me taller, slimmer, quicker." He flicked the cane in his hand several times, retracted it and then twirled it as it extended again.

"Van," Tanth said, his voice pained.

Vanguard turned his head toward Tanth's voice. "My defect—only a few of us have it. Most of the time, imperfections are weeded out. By our breeding. By our alterations."

"But yours..." Malek prompted.

"I can see light. See your shape, your movement. My cane shows me what is around me, and the earpiece feeds me what it senses if I need more than that." He shook his head. "But beyond that, nothing. Not any more."

Malek nodded. "So you ended up here."

"Malek!" Soran warned. His electric eyes glittered, hard and cold.

Vanguard held up a hand. "Some would say that it's better to be born low than to be born a Skyknight and not measure up."

"Would you?" Kenn asked.

Vanguard shook his head. "No."

Soran said nothing. Instead, Tanth spoke. "No?"

"I found my place among these people. I taught them things. Things I had learned in the academy. I showed them how to watch, and wait, and listen. How to move with grace and speed, whether they could see or not. I lost the ability to fight when my vision went bad, but I could still teach them what I knew."

That, apparently, was too much for Soran. "And you think that makes you worthy of—?"

Vanguard cut him off. Malek's smile deepened.

"They want a Skyknight to lead them, my Seraph. Even if that Skyknight isn't one."

CHAPTER TWENTY-FOUR

"IT'S ALREADY begun."

Soran didn't like Tanth's glower. Or his pronouncement. But like it or not, it was true.

He stared at the videoscreen. The victors, their would-be reinforcements, filled the image. Looking like they'd been in a fight already.

Just like Malek and Kenn and Vareth had after battling the assassins. Apparently this was going to be a pattern. Soran looked over at the three of them and curled his lip in distaste. How would they look after battle? He turned back to the gang of victors on the screen.

Whatever had happened to them, it must have been more than a minor skirmish. Scorch marks from blaster fire or energy weapons blackened their armor. Deep scratches and dents from blades or axes or clubs marred the plates. Rain drenched their gear, their skin, and their hair, but hadn't quite washed away all the bloodstains from their bodies. Their weapons glowed with energy, their bearers too wary or too proud of their toys to power them down. Lightning crackled over the tips of spears and arced over the blades of edged weapons.

If that was some city council's doing, Soran would turn in his starfighter.

Only a few people had emerged from their fight unscathed. Here and there, a few stood out, their bodies clean of cuts or bruises. One stood near Dia, the tattooed woman from before. Her ink wound around her arms and shoulders and twined over her cheeks and forehead. She wasn't even wearing armor. In fact, Soran could see a surprising amount of tattooed skin.

If she'd been a Skyknight, he would've chalked it up to agility, well-used. But no one in Malek's gang of brutes could move like Soran's elite. And where the other victors' rain-drenched hair clung to their foreheads, the tattooed woman's red curls were dry.

Like she hadn't even gone out into the rain. *Maybe she hadn't.* But more likely it was—

Force fields. Derell's tablet had mentioned some fighters using that trick in the ring.

She wasn't beautiful. Not to Soran. But he'd been to Dis long enough to know people from the Belt would think she was. And she carried herself like she knew they found her attractive. She was here for war, and her muscular body and cold stare showed it. But she revealed herself like someone who'd forgotten shame.

How many victors had force fields? How many of their followers did? Almost none of them, from the singed and tattered look of them. But they clutched their weapons in tight, proud hands.

Clearly, they'd put a lot of faith into whoever had designed them. Soran looked from one warrior to the next. Some held blades, some guns, some both. The gear they wore to protect themselves was equally mismatched. Some wore full armor, some chestplates, some gauntlets that looked like they'd been designed more to frighten a foe than to protect their wearer.

Zarel, the victors had called the man who designed it all. *I hope, for your sakes, that he's as clever as you claim he is.*

He was ugly, Soran remembered. Even uglier than the rest of them, his skin a mottled brown, loose and lined with wrinkles. Only golden-altered eyes made looking at him bearable. But he knew what we were doing, so they said.

And they were from Dis and the Belt. Half of them probably made armor and weapons for a living anyway. Soran chuckled. What about Halcyon's soldiers? Were they wearing armor forged there, too? His lip curled in a familiar, comfortable amusement. Malek wanted war for the glory of it. Very well. Soran could want war for the irony.

The members of the makeshift army smiled too. Even the ones without armor or fancy weapons, their bodies too small and slight. Some gave him wry looks, others wolfish. One or two looked him over, their gazes all appraisal.

Wondering whether I'm worth fighting for? I could say the same about you.

Dia's image looked back at Tanth. Some unlucky enemy's blood had baptized her armor in a spray of red. The braids at one side of her head had been lopped off, and a long cut crisscrossed that cheek. She'd smeared healing ointment over the wound.

"It has begun," she said, echoing Tanth. "But we fought them off easily enough."

Vareth smiled.

Malek's face stayed stony. "Who attacked you?"

"Senate soldiers. They ambushed us in Ember City."

"They meant to stop you," Ania said. "You weren't supposed to get here."

Tena scoffed. "Maybe they thought so."

Tor looked at her. "They weren't after us. Not really."

"They meant to cut off our tail," agreed the tattooed victor, with a laugh.

Vareth nodded. Soran shot her a frustrated glare and then turned his gaze on Malek.

What exactly are you and your little band of killers talking about?

"They meant to stop the others from following," said Kenn. "To keep the people from the city and the Belt from coming with them."

A young man stepped forward. He wore a patchwork of leather over his chest, shoulders, and thighs. His chestplate bore Malek's symbol, sprayed onto it in silver paint by a crude but eager hand. For someone from the Belt he was lean, muscles just beginning to curve at his shoulders and arms. Long-fingered brown hands clutched at a pike, far better made than his makeshift armor. One of Zarel's creations, probably.

Its tip glowed bright with energy. The heat seared away the bloodstains on the point, but the water on his hands glistened rust-red.

He barked a harsh little laugh of his own. "They tried to stop us. We followed anyway." He bowed his head to Malek. "My Lord."

The corner of Malek's mouth quirked up, but his voice stayed crisp and cold. "How many did they manage to cut off?"

The tattooed victor smiled. "It might not matter, my Lord."

"They claimed they'd come only for us, and would leave Ember City be," Tor said.

"But when the people made it clear that we were welcome—" Tena began.

"They leveled half the city," finished a woman in the the crowd.

Soran whistled low. Apparently the Senate was no longer playing around.

"The districts further in still stand, but where we were, everything was fire." She clenched a brown, weathered fist and her lips drew back in a snarl like Vareth's.

"Some of us came because we wanted to," said the young pikeman. "Some of us came because we had no other choice."

Vareth smiled, her grin hard and cold.

Malek was relentless. "How many victors have we lost?"

"Five, my Lord," Dia said.

Five assassins dead. Five victors dead. Soran would have laughed, if they hadn't been coming for his city.

Dia pressed a hand to her chest in a salute to the fallen. She rattled off a list of names. All but one meant nothing to Soran. A young man who'd disappeared from the arena rosters shortly before Soran visited Dis.

No great loss. Not when Malek's victors were all living legends. But Malek's hand balled into a fist at his side, and the growl Soran heard came from him, not Vareth. *And I thought you were willing to give anything for this.* "And your tail?" Soran asked, his voice smooth.

Dia shook her head. "They killed two thousand, at least. People who knew your speeches, my Lord. Who'd seen your broadcasts. Who knew what united us in Dis."

"Who'd practiced fighting, most of them," Tor added.

Tena nodded. "Maybe not ready for the pits. Definitely not ready for this. But they wanted to fight. So we taught them."

"They learned fast." The tattooed victor flashed a grin.

The pikeman stabbed at the air above him. "I killed three."

Soran fought down a chuckle. Little band of killers, indeed.

"The people in the Below are learning, too," he said, not to be outdone. He had no love for them. But they were his, just like these people were Malek's.

"But more are coming," Kenn prompted.

The pikeman nodded. "Every city we pass, some come with us."

"But they delayed us," Tena said.

"We're half a day behind as it is." Tor's face was calm, but Soran saw him blink, and one hand twitched at his side. "And we still have this rain to deal with."

Tanth looked no happier. "You're certain you drove them off?"

Dia smiled. "Everyone who came for us is dead."

"No doubt." Soran chuckled. He glanced at the overeager pikeman and the glow of his still-readied weapon. "But you're not the only ones they've managed to hold up. Malek and his team arrived late as well."

"The city council stopped us," Vareth rumbled. "Not the Senate's goons."

"My dear Crusher," Soran purred, "do you really think there's a difference?"

"You're thinking they're behind both?" Kenn asked.

"I think if they delayed you once, they can do it again."

"Then you should hope your little birds are ready," Dia said with another scowl.

"The Skyknights of Aerix are always ready. Let's hope the same stays true for you."

Vanguard—aided by Ania, Tanth, and the victors—had done a surprising job of rallying the people down in the Below in just a few short days. They'd made a training regimen out of the lessons from the victors' broadcasts and the Skyknights' training.

Soran had helped them too, on occasion. Put together a little broadcast for them with a few basic tips. He'd left most of it to the victors and to Ania, who'd thrown herself into the project. He scowled in distaste. Teaching them was useful, but did she have to be excited about it?

Like the people of Ember City, they learned fast. That was probably Vanguard's doing. He'd shown promise once. Soran supposed this was the last of it, a gleam in the depths of a cesspool.

And Malek and his little honor guard had made the Below and its desperation useful. *If you can't be a Skyknight, be a barbarian instead?*

They'd put together a little show for him, to demonstrate their progress. He was their Seraph, and they took inordinate pride in showing off their skills to the Seraph himself.

At least here it wasn't raining.

They inched their way up the sides of buildings, clutched at pipes, leapt from one to another. Most used ropes they carried with them. Friends and comrades watched for them, steadied them, helped to catch and right them when they made false moves.

He looked at one of them, a dark-skinned girl. She looked back at him, blinked, allowed herself the indulgence of shaking her head once.

He could guess why. The Seraph of the City was looking at her. She'd likely never seen a Skyknight in her life before this.

She leapt from one roof to another, a length of rope streaming from her back. She landed heavy on her feet, and Soran's enhanced eyes caught a brief wince. But she straightened up as quickly. Her head snapped to attention and she stared out at the rooftops like they hid a real enemy.

He pursed his lips. They looked like insects, crawling through the broken places at the bottom of the City. Moving with an insect's desperate grace. He had no use for such creatures. He was the Seraph, and ruled from the skies. But Malek was right. Aerix would need them.

He heard the sound of footsteps behind him. Of course he did. His sharpened ears would have caught the movement even yards away. But he waited until he felt the bulk of Malek's body pressed up against his back.

"Well," said a familiar voice into his ear, low and pleased. "What do you think?"

"I think they'll do well enough against the Senate's fools," Soran answered, as quietly. He felt a twinge of pain in his new scar, sudden and intimate, and his eyes flicked to Malek's arm. "I think you—"

But even the scar he'd left on Malek couldn't hold his attention. Not when he caught sight of the blue blur in the corner of his eye. He had a Skyknight's vision with a prince's practice, but whoever it was moved Skyknight-fast.

That told him enough to turn.

"Tanth," he said.

"Seraph." His First Skycaptain stood in front of him, the usual frown plastered on his face. But at his side his fingers twitched. That was something Ania did, not Tanth. Soran frowned. He hated this place, low and strange, and hated the people crawling around in it. His eyes darted to Malek again, a bitter, angry glance. "What is it?"

"Our scouts report that Halcyon is closer than we expected."

"How close?" That was Malek, but the words might as well have been his own.

"They're just outside the outskirts of the City," Tanth said.

"And Dia's squadron isn't," rumbled Vareth, with a curse.

CHAPTER TWENTY-FIVE

STARFIGHTERS FILLED the sky above him.

Malek had seen them streak past, gleams of polished silver that sliced through the sky. He'd watched their flight from the window in his room or overhead when he'd walked the platformed streets. He'd seen them above him on his way to the festival, hovering in the air for security. He'd watched them fly down, fast as thought, in the pandemonium after his sparring match. He'd seen their white trails crisscross the skies.

But he'd only seen a few of them at a time. A patrol of two or three, at most. He'd never seen them ready to fight. Now hundreds of them fanned out above the high spires of the city, sleek and deadly.

They weren't his. And his people weren't ready. They'd poured out of the Belt, out of Ember City, but he hadn't had a chance to train them himself. And what waited in Dis, when he and Kenn and Vareth marched home after the first battle in what would surely be a war?

But it didn't matter. He would have to win this battle.

And he would win this war. That he knew, as surely as his name.

He wore old and dented armor, his symbol a jagged scar carved into the breastplate and dyed black with Dis's soot. Vareth and Kenn had drawn it on theirs. Vareth in a proud, defiant hand, and Kenn with a careful, studied stroke. He'd made his choice long ago.

Or Malek had made it for him.

They were the only ones from Dis with him now. But he had Soran, too, risking his City and perhaps his life. Heat stirred in Malek's breast. But he felt more than desire now. Something old, and fierce, and familiar as an old friend. He closed his eyes and lost himself in it. It whispered that when he opened them again, he would stand on familiar sands, and the enemy he'd face would be his and his alone.

He opened his eyes. He had no time for illusions.

But how long ago had he lost that feeling? How long had it been since he'd last stood on the arena sands and felt only elation? He'd seen what his people had lost. And he'd realized, once and for all, that his pride came with a price. He'd stepped onto those sands and thought only *What a waste.*

But this wasn't a waste. This was the contest he'd wanted. He wrapped his hands around the hilt of his blade.

It wasn't the best weapon. Not for this. But Zarel and his toys were miles away, and he wanted to feel its weight against his palm.

Aerix was more beautiful than he had ever imagined. And now it was arrayed for war, in its full power and splendor. The Skyknights around him were a phalanx of spears, polished and gleaming. At Soran's word they would speed toward his enemy.

The people of the Below waited as well, deep in their hidden city. They, too, would come when Soran called. And Soran wore his mark now, carved into his skin.

The old hunger surged through him. The eagerness to test himself, to prove his worth by might and strength and cunning, and by mastery over his fear.

He watched and waited from a platform high above his enemies. He was on the lowest level, a place of shame and humiliation to the people of the City.

But Aerix was the one place on the planet that had never fallen. *Let them come.*

Below him the tanks rolled in, painted the same gray as the soldiers' armor. The soldiers arrayed themselves behind Halcyon, their guns trained on the columns that supported the high platforms of the city. There were starfighters with them, bigger and blockier than Skyknights' craft.

There weren't many. But they were massive. The best chance the Senate's army had against death from above.

Malek could smell the electricity feeding their weapons. He'd smelled it a thousand times in the pits. But now the air seemed made of it, a storm with war machines for lightning clouds, its heat and light impossible to outrun.

And with them came Halcyon's soldiers in perfect rank on rank. There were thousands, their faces hidden behind visors, their weapons held in patient hands. Their dark blue visors resembled Kenn's, enough that Malek's lip curled. *What makes you think you have the right?*

Only Halcyon kept her face uncovered, the dyed eyes bright, the exaggerated, sculpted cheekbones unmistakable. A display, Malek guessed. His victors were a band of warriors in cobbled together armor, weapons and bodies altered to their whim.

Not an army.

It was a snub and a threat, meant for them.

Malek slipped his hand from the sword's hilt. This was no arena. This was war, and guns and machines would decide it.

Halcyon stepped forward. Ignored the starfighters above her, their lasers all trained on her body. She would die in an instant if Soran made the first move.

Which he won't.

"Seraph of Aerix." A microphone in her suit magnified her ringing voice, and glyphs projected in the air around her, in time with her words.

Let no one say the Senate's bureaucrats don't make themselves clear. Malek favored Halcyon with a little half-smile.

And Soran answered.

Malek had never seen Soran in a starfighter before. The closest he'd come was a projection. Kenn's hologram, back when Soran had visited Dis in an unmarked ship. He'd hidden then. He wasn't hiding now. Sunlight gleamed against the polished silver of his craft.

Malek wanted to watch it. To see his Prince of the Air speed to war in a lance of quicksilver. But it would sear his eyes, and he couldn't allow himself that luxury. He forced himself to look at Halcyon and her phalanx of the nameless and listened to the purr of the starfighter's engines instead.

It slid down to hover just above them. Malek let himself look. The iridescent egg of its cockpit cracked open.

A faceless phalanx waited. So did Halcyon, her expression schooled to stillness.

Soran leapt down to the platform with a prince's grace. And too little formality. But that was good. It showed his contempt.

He wore no gems and jewels. Not today. Today he was ready for battle, and for flight. His suit clung to his body, as always, a light mesh built for movement and agility.

The weapons he'd always hidden hung at his belt and back: blasters, blades, slim knives for throwing, polished bright as Halcyon's soldiers' armor. He held one of the blasters, a lightning-crackle of energy revealing that it was already charged.

He didn't point it at her. Not yet.

"Commander Halcyon," he said. "If that's what I should call you."

Halcyon's lips twitched. "I'd hoped you wouldn't have to."

"Then you shouldn't have come at the head of an army."

"I had no wish to. But two weeks have passed, and Malek the

Destroyer is still in your city."

Vareth snorted. "No wish to? That's right. You wanted to kill him from the shadows and go home."

The orange eyes moved from Soran's face to Malek's. "Is a barbarian's safety worth throwing away a truce that has lasted generations?"

Soran looked at him too. Arched an eyebrow, as if Halcyon and all her warriors weren't even here. As if this were just another move in their months-long little game.

Malek nodded.

Soran, for once in his life, said nothing.

"Is protecting a beast worth throwing away your City?"

"Am I? Those tanks and fighters are yours. And if my guest is a beast, why are you so afraid of him?"

Halcyon looked up at the sky, at the starfighters aimed like lances at her and her army. "The Senate doesn't fear Malek. Or the wolves baying at his heels. However eager for blood and slaughter they might be."

She looked at Vareth. Vareth grinned back. It was a shame she didn't have the cannons Zarel had made for her. They would have looked good now, mounted on her shoulders and aimed at this overglorified assassin.

"Senator Derell has already told you. He wants peace. Peace the Senate has preserved for generations. Will you let Malek destroy it?"

Malek smiled, a hard and bitter grin. *You know exactly why I'm here, don't you?* He stepped over to Soran's side. "Peace is a fragile thing, Halcyon. If you must tear down a city to preserve it, it's become too fragile to protect."

Halcyon ignored him. "We don't want your city, Seraph. We want only Malek."

"Only Malek." Vareth growled. "I don't think so."

"You're already killing," Kenn agreed.

"Already killing?" Her sculpted face was all smooth innocence.

"Ember City," Malek said, his voice cold.

"Ember City," Soran echoed, his voice so intimate a purr that hot jealous anger flared through Malek's veins. "What could possibly have happened there, if all you want is Malek?"

"A brawl." She didn't smile. Nor did she hesitate. "An incident of minor unrest that was put down."

"Unrest?" Soran asked, his tone clipped and careful. "Once that begins, it's not easy to end."

"One ends a disturbance by removing its source. Don't you see what you risk by protecting it? Malek's band of victors hoped to bring friends with them. Criminals and thugs who look to the people who kill in the ring as heroes."

"You came as an assassin, Halcyon," Malek reminded her.

"I came to remove a threat. I had no desire to kill." She glared at Malek. "I am not like you."

"Do you still think this is about me? The people of Ember City heard my words. But they make their own decisions. I did not demand they come here."

Halcyon turned to Soran. "You choose the wrong symbol, Seraph of Aerix, if you choose this man. You give your city over to him—to his barbarians and to their purpose."

"He asked for the people's ears. I let him speak. You ask for our freedom."

"We ask for one man. Whose protectors have been routed. Whose reinforcements aren't coming."

"I wouldn't be too sure. Dis's victors don't die easy."

"But the innocents they sway do."

"Innocents?" Vareth spat the word. "A minute ago, you called them thugs and criminals. Keep your lies straight, lap-dog."

Halcyon's lip twitched. "Seraph. The people these victors recruit are no one. They are desperate, starving, lost—"

"Whose fault is that, Commander?" Kenn asked, his clipped voice cold.

"Enough!" Malek waved a hand. He glanced at Soran. All eyes followed.

"You want the right to come here and make demands," Soran said. "Tell us to give you what the Senate wants, just because they want it. We're not a city of slaves."

The laugh bubbled up in Malek again, from somewhere deep. He remembered Soran's challenge, on that first day they met. *Suppose I call you and your barbarians. Suppose you rush to my aid.*

For the first time in generations, Aerix is in debt. To you.

Soran had known what that debt would mean from the beginning. Whatever fires of war spread across the world would catch Aerix up in them. And the City that now rose above the world would be only a part of it.

His Skyknights would wear Malek's mark, and he would too. Perhaps he'd even known a victor like Malek would demand a scar for a scar.

Malek had teased him with it then. Had held out the promise of defying him. Of overthrowing him, even, as one more seduction. And it had worked, as he'd known it would.

But Soran had held off that fate for as long as he could. The Prince of the Air belonged to no one. *We're not a city of slaves.*

Malek's smile deepened. *You finally understand. What they are. What they demand. What they will do.*

Better to be mine than theirs.

Halcyon had heard it too, apparently. "Slaves? The Senate has never believed in—"

"Then tell me, Halcyon. What happens next?"

"That depends on you."

"I turn over Malek. I give you one man, as you say. The others go home to Dis, directionless and broken." He shot a glance at Malek, his sky-bright eyes all aglow with derision. "Ember City goes silent. The Belt follows. The restless heat roiling it cools."

"That is all we want."

"Then what, Halcyon? What happens when the next angry victor from Dis makes her way here? When she asks if anyone remembers the festival? Or how it ended?"

Halcyon blinked. "We ask for Malek as a sign of your good faith, Seraph."

"That's exactly what I mean. You hope that we will return to isolation—"

"That was the City's policy. Until this barbarian caught your ear."

"It was. And now you hope. You recommend. What would you do if I refused to follow your recommendations? What would you do if one of my Skyknights remembered this visit? If some of my people offered aid to Malek and his people?"

"You rule Aerix. That wouldn't happen without your permission."

"And who would decide whether I give it?"

Halcyon blinked again, owlish and innocent. "I fail to take your meaning."

Soran laughed again, high and wild and defiant. "I'm not yours, Halcyon. Neither are the people of this City."

"Then you will see your city fall to prove a point?"

"Then I will refuse to give you what you want."

The shout rang in Malek's ears. *And I thought this was a game to you, Seraph of Aerix.*

He saw only the silver blur of Soran's body, the darker red streak of his hair. It whirled and spun, and blaster fire arced from the swirl of Soran's movement. Malek hadn't even seen him aim.

The bolt of energy caught Halcyon in the chest and flared against her armor. Malek saw her wince, the sculpted face twisting in pain.

Not much more than that. But it didn't matter.

Soran leapt back into his fighter, another silver streak in Malek's vision. The cockpit of the starfighter closed over him.

Malek heard its engines rev, but had no time to watch its rise. He took aim at the nearest cluster of faceless, visored gray and fired. Beside him, he heard the low thrum of Vareth's cannon. Far smaller than the one the victors would bring, but deadly nonetheless. A high-pitched buzz meant Kenn, firing off a shot of his own before rushing away to meet Vanguard and his fighters.

The silver shapes above him streaked through the air, and flame rained from the sky.

CHAPTER TWENTY-SIX

SORAN ROSE above a world that had already begun to burn.

His Skycaptains slid into formation beside him. Together they dove for the gray mass of men and women who marched toward the City. Their laser fire left streaks of flame where they swept down to strafe the enemy.

Tanth separated from him first. His squad broke off to engage one of the starfighters, their movements crisp and sharp, their purpose clear. As a unit, they swooped down, raining blast after blast at the craft until it blazed, a dark mass of fire hurling down toward the earth.

He let himself look for a moment, then peeled away. Tanth was precise. Soran was fast. The fastest of the Skyknights, who not even his best could catch. And it felt so good to be in the air.

He'd had to meet Halcyon on the lowest platforms in the City. Almost on the ground. His lip curled, and he would have spat if he hadn't been in his fighter. He was the Seraph of Aerix, and he wasn't meant to stand on the ground.

Meeting Malek in Dis was one thing; everyone in Dis was grounded. Even meeting the people of the Below had its purpose. But Halcyon and her phalanxes had marched through the dirt. If he flew down close enough, he could see its stain on their boots. All to get to his city. To try and tear it down.

His toes curled in visceral, phantom disgust. He could almost feel the grit of dirt between them, coarse and rough.

A group of Halcyon's men raised up a launcher. It hummed as it charged, a low, deep rumble, and orange heat roiled in its depths. Soran swerved out of the way just as a flaming bolt streaked out of it.

Heat on his wing, but nothing more. *Idiots.*

But not all of his Skyknights could fly as fast as he did. One darted down toward the soldiers, trying to copy Soran's move. Their launcher shot caught her directly in the wing. There was a flare of light and heat, and smoke billowed from the wing, a circular hole blasted right through it. The starfighter spiraled to earth.

Soran shrieked in rage and challenge. The sky was his home, and the home of his people. And he was their Seraph, and the highest towers belonged to him.

Any Skyknight who couldn't keep his place in the sky wasn't worthy of it. So the training taught. And so Soran believed. Malek the Destroyer was right about that, at least. But any fool who shot a Skyknight down would die today.

"Wings One and Two, with me!" he called, and raced toward one of the tanks. The Skyknight it aimed at rolled to avoid a projectile wreathed in crackling light and sped away.

The tank abandoned its more elusive prey. It fired again, this time at the column supporting the platform. The impact left a crater, dark and round, and lightning curled out from the point of impact.

Soran sped down to meet the tank. In the corner of his eye, the silver of the companions flying beside him flickered. He called out the command to fire and orange flame hurtled down to sear the weapon that had desecrated his tower.

He snickered at himself. *Is this how it feels, King of the Barbarians? Or is this just what made you want a war?*

He'd killed before, of course. He'd seen blood, and death, and the stunned despair of men and women who'd just realized one of his knives had buried itself in their flesh. But this was different. *Perhaps, King of the Barbarians, there is a reason for your savagery.*

He turned his gaze to the platforms, looking for Malek. He found Vareth first, a dark tower of muscle, standing at her lord's side as always. He snickered. Maybe he'd misjudged her, but she was still Malek's sycophant.

She fired into the masses of soldiers, a heavy pulse of heat and light. It hit one man full in the chest, a charred hole blasted through his armor, and the two companions beside him fell as well, thrown to the ground by the blast's percussive force.

He couldn't look for long. The tank couldn't get to him now, but the launchers could. Bolts of orange flame whizzed toward him. He turned, hard and sharp, and dodged the next. *They're trying to draw me away.*

He'd lost one of the Skyknights at his side. He scowled and flew in again, dodging two bolts that crossed just above him and made the sky flare orange in his vision. The tank below was scorched black with Skyknights' laser fire.

Just one more shot.

The gun swiveled around to track him. Apparently whoever manned it had realized where the real threat came from. Soran snarled in frustration and made ready to evade.

A bolt of blue light struck the soldier manning the gun. It wreathed his helmeted head in lightning. His body jerked, the electricity overwhelming it, and he fell.

Soran and his Skyknight fired. The tank's hull flared with flame, consumed at last. Soran sped away from the explosion, its smoke on his heels.

He looked over to see Kenn, tucked away on a high platform above Malek and the others. He moved with slow precision, tracking the tanks' gunners, the soldiers manning the launchers, the men and women who fired up at the platforms from the ground.

Malek wasn't far below. He didn't have an energy-blaster like Kenn, or a pulse weapon like Vareth. He had only his gun. Soran had seen it before the battle, heavy and blocky, clearly made by the crafters in Dis. Well-used too, its paint worn, its metal scuffed.

That surprised him more than it should've. Malek had always been a pit fighter. Who was he killing with that gun? But he used it well, firing again and again into the crowd. The soldiers dropped, one by one, almost like dancers playing a role.

Malek the Destroyer, indeed. Warmth spread through him again and he fought not to squirm.

The noise of the tanks' fire brought him back to himself. Projectiles wreathed in incandescent white lanced toward the platforms' base. The platform rocked, and a mass of men and women standing on it lost their footing. Soran watched one woman go down, shot in the back by errant friendly fire.

Other people slipped off the platform entirely. The lucky ones tumbled to the ground. Blaster fire speared the unlucky. They died as they fell.

The fighters came on too, slow and heavy as they were, stars of energy and thick projectiles alike fanning out from their weapons, gouging holes into the twisted metal and crumbling stone of the platforms.

One platform tilted downward. People fell to the the ground below. Some fired even as they plummeted. Others clung to the column that supported the platform and climbed, trying to reach the next platform by the strength of their limbs alone. But climbing meant turning their backs to their enemies. A metal lance, wreathed in flame-bright light, caught one of them. It buried itself in armor and in flesh.

The soldier it had hitthrew back his head and screamed.

Soran had seen death. But he'd never seen the City damaged, the pillars that held it up blackened and charred, holes torn in its surface as though by titans' hands.

And only the people of the Below climbed. It was madness, desperation, a futile attempt to rise. Only the lowest of the low tried. Only those so broken that their only hope was to climb, and hope whatever level they crawled to would take them in.

But the man Soran had just seen die wasn't one of the mad ones. Just someone who didn't want to die.

"The starfighter," he called over his communication line. "We take it down. Now."

He didn't bother to wait for their acknowledgment. He gunned the throttle and raced toward it, his fury driving him onward.

The starfighter was heavy. Bulky. Far larger than the Skyknights' sleek craft. It lumbered onward and spat another barrage of energy and projectiles at the already damaged tower holding up the platforms.

"You don't deserve to share the City's air," Soran snarled, and loosed his own barrage of laser fire.

That caught the enemy's attention. The guns along the side of the craft shifted to aim at him. He twisted to the side, hard, just quickly enough for the thick pulses of energy to miss his craft's slender, polished wing.

Hah.

They moved again. He wove to avoid them. It felt good. His body tensed, just the same as he might have in hand-to-hand combat, and he shifted in his seat even as his craft swerved to avoid the enemy fire.

There was no separation between him and his ship. It was him, a part of his body, a pair of wings, light and sleek, crafted to match his own altered limbs. The starfighter moved with him, as him, an extension of himself. *Let's see the Lord of the Pits do that.*

He fired at the side of the enemy ship. The barrage of energy tore blackened, jagged holes in its side, and a fierce joy raced through him at the damage.

Another bolt of energy lanced toward him. He swooped down under it, fired down at Halcyon's troops for good measure. A few men fell, their featureless brothers marching past them. Some stopped, frozen by grief or surprise or shock.

Those died. Some by Soran's gunfire, some by the fire of the other Skyknights. Ania and her squad sped after one of the tanks, weaving around it. Firing, then speeding away, then diving in again.

She's toying with them.

But he'd done the same thing himself. Why let those mockeries of fighters just fall from the sky when you could rip them open piece by piece?

He chased a few more of Halcyon's soldiers, let out a high laugh watching them scatter. The skies were his, and these intruders were fit only for the death he rained down on them. In front of him, the tank Ania danced around burst into flame.

Well then.

He swooped back toward the starfighter again, intent on widening the black wound his lasers had already torn in its side. It twisted to evade him.

No you don't.

He sped after it, the rush of throttle making him giddy. He raced through the sky—his sky—and lined himself up with the streak of angry black. His laser fire caught the already-damaged hull and tore the holes open wider.

The craft listed, pitching to one side, and Soran crowed in triumph.

But that was still a game. And this was a battle, not a sparring match. Or even a fight in Malek's pits, death and blood for a cheering crowd.

This was his city, and the Senate would tear it down if they could.

If they could.

He turned again and aimed his next barrage at the thing's engine. Light and heat flared from the point of impact, and Soran swerved to evade smoke and heat and something that had blown off in the blast.

The craft had swayed before. Now it fell, its nose peeking up and thrusters roaring with its pilots' last desperate attempt to keep it in the air.

We'll see about that. Soran fired again. Another flare of heat and smoke—black and choking, like the stuff Soran remembered from Dis— and the thing finally went down. It flailed, listed, spun like a dying bird falling to earth.

The soldiers below rushed to get away from it, colliding with one another in their haste to flee from the falling starfighter.

Soran couldn't savor it, not really. He couldn't hear their cries. But savoring such music was for Malek and his ilk anyway, greedy for death. Soran was happy enough seeing the enemy craft mangled and lifeless on the ground where it belonged, a torn wreck mirroring the black holes its weapons had torn in the column supporting the platform. There would be more holes like that, if the Skyknights didn't stop Halcyon. More platforms toppled, more people spilled out onto the ground below.

More Skyknights downed.

He couldn't allow that. He wouldn't.

He zoomed down toward the nearest pack of soldiers and their launcher.

"Seraph, don't," came Tanth's voice over his communications link. "Not even you can get out of the way in time."

"Is that so?" Soran cut the link and fired, straight down at the energy cells that charged the weapon. He slammed the accelerator as far as it would go and turned upward, hard and sharp.

Thunder roared below him, the herald of the storm.

Then the energy cells exploded.

The blast tossed his craft high into the sky. He could control nothing. White fire flared before his eyes, and for a moment he didn't remember to care. The floor beneath his feet scorched them with its heat, and even in the protection of his cockpit he could hear only the noise of the blast.

That's not all I have for you.

His own thought returned him to himself. He turned, sharp as he dared, and sped away from the blast.

That was only the beginning.

CHAPTER TWENTY-SEVEN

THE PLATFORM Malek stood on rocked under his feet.

He ignored it and took aim. Two soldiers fell, shot through the chest. Another twisted away just in time, and lost only his arm and not his life. The pale gray shell of his armor shattered, a stump of meat and blood beneath.

The silver trails of Skyknights caught Malek's eye, but he had no time to admire them now. Only fools would stop and stare.

Or look for the Seraph's craft somewhere in the blazing sky.

And Malek was the enemy's target. The prize, the objective, the thing to be won. The corner of his lip twisted in a wry smile. He'd always been exactly that, from the moment he fought his first tournament in the pits. But now the real enemy was coming for him.

He saw it in a young soldier's eyes, her visor long since blasted away. He ducked to avoid her shot and saw light sizzle at his shoulder. A blossom of heat in his breastplate, a sting that told him some of the energy had slipped between the cracks.

The platform listed again, and he fell to the ground, rolling to take the impact through his back. He hissed a curse, saw her next shot speed over his head in a flare of white light. He covered his face against the flurry of metallic dust it threw up.

Golden light flared in front of him. He hastened to his feet, fixed his eyes on his enemy just long enough to see the flames char her flesh and armor black. A gleam of polished metal darted past. *It seems I owe one of your warriors, Seraph. Or was that you?*

He fired a spray of energy at the soldiers and used the time it bought him to drag his companions on the platform to their feet. At least the people of Aerix kept their bodies slim and light. They glared at him with too-bright, altered eyes, stared at him from beneath sooty brows.

One glowered down at him, the sculpted face bruised and smeared with dust and dirt, the long, pale hair disheveled and tangled. The man curled bleeding lips and spat on Malek's foot.

"I don't begrudge you your anger," Malek said. "But take it out on your enemies. Not on me."

The man turned away, snarling something that was lost in the whine of the Skyknights' engines, the loud, low thuds of the tanks' blasts.

And the crackle of the tower supporting them as pieces chipped off and fell to the platform below them. The City was beginning to shatter.

The shape of a starfighter rose above him. Skyknights circled it, leaving flame and smoke in their wake.

But it stayed in the air long enough to disgorge another crowd of soldiers. Some leapt to the platforms and charged into the defenders, guns and weapons drawn. Others climbed down on ladders. Some carried small launchers or pieces of bigger ones: energy cells, the telescoping barrels of weapons.

Vareth vaporized one, blasting away both the ladder and a pair of unfortunate souls climbing down it. She roared in triumph and kept shooting.

A grin tugged at the corners of Malek's mouth. He'd saved his victors for exactly this. Now, at last, they could deal death to the deserving.

Halcyon's men rushed at the defenders. Malek drew his blade. They were too close now to shoot down. Lightning energy flared along his blade's length, and in the light it gave off Malek saw fear and awe in his enemies' eyes. He wondered if any of them had been fans of his fights.

It couldn't matter now. He cried out and lunged at one. His blade might not pierce the armor. Senate stuff might be too good for that. But he could catch one of them in the shoulder. Crack open their perfect little shell.

The one he caught wasn't mesmerized long. Aerix's defenders weren't the only ones who had realized that every hesitation invited death. He twisted to evade Malek's blow.

But that moment of awe had given him long enough. Malek's blade caught him in the hip, and the strength Malek had built up in the pits let him drive it down hard. It took more force than anyone had to shatter a pelvis, except maybe Vareth.

But the pain would be enough.

The man stumbled. Malek brought his weapon up again and aimed for the collarbone he'd missed, and the man dropped like a stone. Malek crouched in his fighter's stance and gave the crowd his best showman's glare.

Some avoided him, lunging at anyone else, cutting down tall, sculpted men and women with blade and laser and bullet alike. Others ran for him, a wild mania in their battle cries.

He cut two more down with his blade. Strength sang through his arm. But just beyond him, a squad of Skyknights fell, spinning to earth, a flock of dying birds all killed by the same plague.

Vareth fired again and inclined her head to him. It wasn't a question. The grim set of her mouth, the eyebrows slanting down over her eyes, told Malek everything.

She roared, a summons and a battle cry and a promise all together.

The people of the Below swarmed out of their hiding places in a vast wave of mismatched color. The wave burst fierce and frothing upon the outer ranks of Halcyon's soldiers. A cacophony of light flared from their weapons.

Malek watched one man fall. The man screamed, a cry of pain that became a battle cry, and shot his attacker's knees. She collapsed, and others in the bright rags of the Below cut her down. The man died a moment later, shot by someone else.

His companions did not slow. Malek knew the sight, knew the people, knew its meaning. He'd seen the rage of the forsaken before.

Malek cried out in challenge and raced toward the fray. Where he passed, men and women fell, the ground of the platform littered with winter-gray bodies, their limbs jutting out at unnatural angles.

Many of them would die. Most, if the victors didn't make it here soon. The unmodified, the mangled, the twisted, offering their lives for a City that had room only for the perfect. But death in battle was better than death in their hovels. And if they lived, they wouldn't be urchins any more, eking out a desperate life far from the skies where the worthy belonged.

They would be warriors, and even Skyknights would know it.

A cascade of dust and metal wrenched his attention away from his new protégés.

Debris, charred gray and brittle, dropped down onto the platform. Gray ash filled their vision and stained their bodies. Smoke billowed into the blue skies, a cruel reminder of the smog that darkened Dis.

Smoke, with flame below it. Malek cast a quick glance around. Everywhere, the gleaming city showed its corrosion. A barrage of missiles from one of the tanks hit the column to the right of him.

He abandoned his sword for his gun. "To the next tower!" he cried in a ringing voice. "On the left! Quickly!"

Faces turned to him, dyed eyes bright with suspicion.

He didn't turn to look at them. He fired down into the swarm of Halcyon's minions, tilted his head toward the platform. "You're modified. Jump."

One of the women from the Below, pale-skinned, curly hair loose and wild, snarled up at the platform. She waved a knife, already dripping with blood. "You do what he says."

Armored hands clutched at her. She turned only long enough to slash her blade across their owner's throat. "Or I climb up and tear you apart."

Malek grinned.

"No!" someone began. "Who's to say they won't just—?"

"They're after me," Malek said. "The next shot comes for us."

The woman laughed. "The next shots bring your tower down. Then you fight with us. Down here."

The man beside Malekshook his head in a violent gesture.

"Towers can fall," the woman said, grinning. "Just like anything else."

"Aerix's towers will never fall," someone else murmured, so low Malek almost didn't hear it. "They can't. They can't. They—"

Malek looked at the grinning woman. *Forgotten people know the things others forget.* "This one is about to."

"The Skyknights will save us," the quiet-voiced one protested.

"Then climb."

The platform to the right of them fell.

They watched, horror and fascination twisting their perfected faces.

The platform twisted and warped like a live thing. Some of the defenders tumbled to the ground. Others clung to the column, slender limbs finding purchase anywhere they could. The platform swayed as if given momentary life by the energy bursts that crashed over it. Then it came loose from its mounts, and fell.

The Skyknights took their vengeance, swift and bright.

That stirred them to action. They raced to the edge of the platform and dove. Malek would have gone with them, but he was no high-caste citizen of the City in the Sky. He'd built the body he had now through practice and exercise, not through reshaping himself for lightness and speed.

He might make the jump. But he couldn't be sure of it. And if he didn't make it, he would need them.

A tank's gun swiveled toward him and the platform beneath him alike.

Come and get me, then.

He watched three of the defenders land.

"I'm coming across," he called, and leapt.

A projectile wreathed in flame hit the column just behind him. The sky was smoke, and fire, and the platform in front of him gleamed. Long slender figures stood on the other side, their bodies tall and sculpted as creatures from dreams.

But the vision before him wasn't enough. His fingers brushed the platform's edge and he clutched at it with a gladiator's strength. The strength of a man who'd been at the brink before and known one moment could mean the difference between victory and death.

Laser fire singed his close-cropped hair. The defenders stared down at him. One lifted a foot—sculpted and slim, but dangerous enough if she brought it down on Malek's fingers. "You're the reason this happened!"

"I just saved your lives. Your tower is falling."

The foot lowered—onto the platform in front of him. Bright-dyed eyes stared, first at Malek's uninjured fingers, then at the woman's foot.

A long moment passed. Malek held on, ignoring the strain.

Then slender arms—he didn't know whose—surrounded him, reached out for him, lifted him up.

He smiled.

"Lord Malek!"

The voice didn't come from his companions. It came from his communications link. Accented with a familiar, rough burr. The sound of home.

"Dia," he said, the corner of his mouth twisting into a smile.

"We're just outside the City," she said. "We're on our way."

He couldn't exult for long. Where the platform had been, now only a black and yawning mouth remained, torn jagged across the column he'd jumped from. Even as the defenders watched, the tower tilted, the wound too great for the column to bear.

Below, the tanks cleared a path. Gray-shelled insects slipped away where they could, leaving the bodies of their fellows in their wake. The people of the Below leapt at the soldiers manning the launchers. And onto the tanks, their guns blazing, intent on ripping their way inside.

What a waste.

One tank's gun swiveled and froze, aimed away from the tower. Another tank stilled, right in the path the spire would take when it fell. Malek frowned. He'd trained these people to defend the city, not to throw themselves at the enemy.

Still, war has its cost. For Soran's people, as for mine.

The spire swayed. It glittered, catching the light of the energy blasts consuming the sky.

The defenders awoke, as one, and shrieked in desperate horror. They fired at the tanks, the people manning the launchers, the soldiers on the ground, a wild chaos of rage.

Malek swept his gaze over the battlefield and found Halcyon standing on top of one of the tanks, her visor retracted. She stood posed atop it, fist raised, and shouted a battle cry.

Malek took aim and fired. His shot sped toward the spot where she stood. She leapt down to avoid it, too fast.

Alterations. That only made sense for an assassin, and he'd seen her fancy eyes and cheeks already. What more could she do that he didn't know about?

The Skyknights sped in, their gleam blocking his vision. Their engines roared, a banshee's whine. The sky lit with their fury, poured out in a mass of laser fire so bright it burned Malek's eyes.

Soran must have led them, from the speed. But Malek couldn't see. He saw fire, and light, and one of the tanks blasted in front of him in another blinding eruption. Flames rose from others, a mirage-mist in which he could distinguish nothing.

He shot into the space where he'd seen Halcyon vanish. He felt sure he'd missed, an afterimage still dancing in front of his eyes. The rest fired into the charred hole at its base. Dust and smoke rose from the point of impact, a gray-black cloud. The top of the spire wobbled again.

The men and women of the Below moved at last, a wild mass, pushing to *get out, get away—*

The spire pitched to one side, a dead golden skeleton of filigree, and crashed to the ground.

CHAPTER TWENTY-EIGHT

SORAN STARED down at the wreck of the tower.

Malek had abandoned the platform, and the others had followed him. Only a shell of the spire remained, the once-polished platforms jutting out like stunted limbs, the filigree dulled to lifeless yellow.

Its fall had crushed a tank. That made Soran feel better at least, a bright little tendril of vindication twisting up amid empty, dull horror. People died in the City all the time. Even Skyknights weren't immortal. But the City was. Polished and pristine and untouchable, spared the fate of the hapless world.

There was no one in the dead spire. Hadn't been from the beginning. They'd evacuated the towers near the City gates long before the battle. They'd prepared themselves, crammed into homes not meant for them. They'd ushered a few people down to the ground, tucked them away in hiding places in the Below. Vanguard himself had welcomed some of them.

They'd forced themselves to live with that. A man who'd once been a Skyknight was at least someone worthy of honor. Or someone who might have been, once.

But he couldn't stop staring at the fallen spire.

Aerix had been spared the fate of the world. For generations. And now it had come for them.

He swerved out of the path of a launcher's fire. *Perhaps I understand you at last, Lord of the Pits.*

He fed more power to his weapons. Their energy hummed all around him. He breathed in and out again, let their hunger comfort him, and swooped down toward another one of the tanks. It looked like the thing the tower had crushed. Only it was still standing, still functioning, still firing. It would pull down another tower if he let it.

He did not remember giving the command, though he must have. He only knew he shrieked in challenge, and the Skyknights' engines answered him, a long, low whine of lament. They fell on the tanks, lasers blazing. Soran's own shots left one inert, wreathed in smoke from flaming wounds.

It wasn't enough. It would never be enough.

"Hunt down the rest," he called over his link. As if the tanks were living things, prey hiding out between the towers, fleeing their predators in the sky. "The tanks and the starfighters."

"Seraph. The launchers," Ania said. "They've shot down three of my best."

"The rest don't matter. Vanguard's squads on the ground will take care of them. And Malek's, from the platforms."

But Malek himself spoke next. The careful, cultured tones he'd used at the festival were gone now, replaced by the accent of the pits. "There are few platforms left. The starfighters are bringing more enemies with each pass."

"You're—"

"Those that aren't overrunning the platforms are climbing. Finding holes the tanks and starfighters' bombs are leaving. Slipping bombs into the breaches."

"Slipping bombs into the breaches?" To shoot at the towers was bad enough. To sneak into them, to blast them from within? That was desecration.

"More of your towers will fall. Soon."

He had no answer for that. He was too busy swerving out of the way of a ball of orange fire.

That first tank—he had the people of the Below to thank for it. They'd rushed in and swarmed it. No doubt killed those who manned it, knowing they'd die themselves when the tower fell.

He had to admit he hadn't expected that. To him they'd been a crowd of unearthed insects, creeping from their nests at Vareth's call. He'd expected them to vanish back into their hidden places—on the ground!—when the real danger came. But they hadn't.

How many had died? If he dove he could look at their bodies below, piled high on the ground. At their stunted bodies and their heavy, thick limbs. Their too-natural faces. Their ugliness.

But he had a battle to fight. And something to avenge, now.

He roared after one of the tanks, scorched the thing's hull, turned the Senate's device painted on its side into a black and twisted mass.

He had just let himself exult in it and twisted around for another pass when Tanth's voice came over his comm.

"Seraph. Leave the tanks alone. They're not the real threat."

"First Skycaptain," Soran snapped back, intent on his prize. "What are you—?"

Tanth interrupted him. That caught his attention.

"Look to the starfighters," Tanth said.

Soran pulled up and looked around. The starfighters were lining up, and aiming for the outer towers. They lumbered over to the city's outskirts, patient and enormous, the fanned weapons on their hulls crackling with white heat.

Soran looked down. The people of the Below, still pouring from their hiding places, had overrun the soldiers with the launchers. Just as he had predicted before.

They'd apparently commandeered one. He watched it spit a flaming projectile at one of the tanks. The tank stopped in its tracks, the hole torn in its hull trailing black smoke. Skyknights peeled off toward the tank to finish the job, and Soran saw more orange flames light the sky.

He'd have to commend Vanguard later.

"And the starfighters are flying in to take their place," answered Tanth. As if to confirm his words, a blaze of white poured from the ring of starfighters. It flared against another spire.

Another wound torn in the City's body. Another black hole belching scrap metal and smoke and dust. The smoke wreathed the tower, hiding the filigree in a cloud of sick, polluted gray. Above it, Soran could only see the top of the spire. It rose above fire and smoke and dirt and dust, a careful twist crafted by some long-ago artisan. Shaped and perfected long ago, probably by altered hands.

Hands like his own.

He sped toward the nearest, heedless of how much energy and fuel it might waste. His shots blasted a hole in the rear of the craft. Another burst of laser fire caught it, the Skyknights flanking him adding their own shots to his.

The starfighter tumbled and fell, still spraying flame. Wild shots flared out from its dying hull, burning the people below, Vanguard's men and Halcyon's troops alike.

It wasn't enough. He sped away, his engines screaming. The top of the spire broke off and crashed to the ground below. Broken filaments of metal jutted into the sky.

And just ahead of him another flare of weapons fire lit the base of a third spire.

There were too many. Too many here, too many everywhere.

Gray-armored men and women stretched out gloved fingers to trigger the mechanisms on their launchers even as the unaltered, misshapen people of the Below ripped them from the controls and bashed at energy cells that had already emptied.

Soran had known it from the beginning. Known it from those first patrols over Corian and Feris. Known it from the ashen color of Tanth's face when he'd first come to report, in those months before he came to Dis.

They'll make it in.

"Bring their starfighters down!" he cried. "Bring them down!"

The Skyknights answered. They streaked past him, a volley of silver blades hurled toward the hearts of the enemy.

And Soran flew fastest of all.

He chose one whose weapons were already pulsing with energy, ready to be unleashed on a nearby tower.

He darted in, intent on doing the same thing he had to the launcher before and shorting out the energy cells that fed the weapons. At his command, two other Skyknights flew in after him. But either they'd seen his stunt before or learned from it. The fanned guns aimed at him. He swerved away, just in time for one to singe his wing.

Light filled the sky around him. Everything flared white and scorched his vision, and for a moment he thought of Malek, the sky too much for him to take.

His starfighter spun. The battle flared in front of him, a cacophony of whirling light and black smoke. He pulled up, hands tight on the controls, lips drawn back in a grimace as he fought to right himself. *Come on, come on!*

Finally, the spinning world resolved itself. The starfighter's weapons glowed white with recharged energy. It burned in his vision.

The metallic glimmer of a Skyknight's fighter brought him back to himself. It sped past him, blasted at the starfighter's engines. Two more streaks of metallic silver followed, their guns blazing as well.

The starfighter listed, its barrage of energy discharging, harmless and bright, into the sky above him.

He righted himself just in time to snicker at the display. And for his augmented vision to make out the symbol of a Skycaptain painted on the craft's side. Ania.

"Seraph," she said, her voice all exaggerated formality. "You said to bring them down." She laughed. "Besides, you needed saving."

Soran almost snickered, but the laugh died in his throat.

A long, low rumble filled their ears, a sound Soran almost didn't recognize at first. Then he saw the explosions, one after another after another, the rolling growl like the noise of an oncoming storm. The kind that could keep even Skyknights out of the air.

Smoke rose up next, a choking black cloud that made Soran squint. He could hardly see Ania in front of him through the gray that filled his vision.

"What is it?" he demanded.

He heard cracking metal and chipping stone.

"No!" he shrieked, and dove down to the ground. Laser fire sprayed from his guns, indiscriminate and searing. Everything below him burned.

"Seraph!" Tanth called over the comm, urgency in the normally-clipped voice. "Don't! You'll kill your own people!"

Ania's voice followed his, high and frantic, all protocol gone. "Soran!"

He didn't hear the rest. The rest didn't matter. Not when the spires were cracking, useless husks of dead metal with chipping stone at their cores.

He flew to one, his craft curling around it like his weaving dance could lend it strength. Smoke rose up all around him and a cascade of dust fell over him and blanketed him in gray. He ground his teeth and hissed and fired into the smoke-blanketed dark.

But the next one to speak over his communication line wasn't a Skycaptain.

"Soran," said Malek's rough-accented voice. "The victors are coming."

The spire swayed. Debris pelted the cover of his cockpit, and one sharpened bit of metal scored a deep line in the glass.

"Soran," Malek said again.

The scar on Soran's chest itched, and he chuckled at the pain. He remembered the point of his own knife digging into his skin, red blood welling up from his cuts. *Your mark on me.*

"Where are you now?" he spat back. "Your platforms—"

"We're not on the platforms." Soran heard the sounds of a scuffle. A clash of blades, a deep, wet gurgle, the sound of something heavy falling.

"You're on the ground."

And your enemies are dying. He could imagine it easily enough: a ring of corpses for the Destroyer, a bloody crown of laurels laid at his feet.

The cracks in the spire deepened. Soran swerved out of its way, still circling.

He heard the thud as it crashed to the ground. Its fall raising up clouds of dust that billowed out around him. He curled his lip and forced himself to look ahead, ahead, only ahead.

The outer ring of spires had fallen. Only one or two remained, their tips rising above flame and smoke, the amber light of the fires playing on the twining metal. His chest tightened, seeing them alone and surrounded by devastation.

And yet they still rose. And beyond them, so did the heart of the true City.

Soran looked down. The broken tops of the dead spires littered the ground below, bleached bones of silver and gold. Flame licked at them, consuming what remained.

And Halcyon's people flooded into the City.

He saw them rushing in, their guns spraying fire. He could see them all now that the dust had cleared. His ears filled with their battle cries. The people of the Below fought back, but not for long. Not easily. Not now.

It seemed the loss of the spires—the places they could never hope to call their homes—disheartened even them. Soran curled his lip. He'd rarely thought of Vanguard before this, of his life and of his fate. Now he almost felt pity for him.

He swooped down over them, raining fire down where they passed. Anything to stop the wave of them, flooding into the streets of a City they had no right to enter. Skyknights followed moments after, made the sky rain fire over them.

And still they came on. *How many were you and your cronies hiding, Derell?*

He opened the communications link again.

He should have reached out to Tanth, or even to Ania. Given them orders. Reassured them that his little moment of madness had passed.

Instead, he called Malek.

"You say that your victors are finally coming, brute?"

"Turn your craft around, Seraph of Aerix," Malek answered. "They're already here."

Chapter Twenty-Nine

SORAN DIDN'T turn around, of course. Malek didn't mind. He'd see them soon enough, their weapons glowing with the same bright lights as the starfighters' weapons. Lightning wreathed their pikes and blades and guns.

Malek wasn't far from the wreck of a platform. Only a few of the platforms still stood. Most of them were mangled, crushed under their towers when they fell. Kenn and some of the snipers from Aerix's army fought from whatever was left. Some people from the Below fought with them. But the towers weren't safe anymore.

The rest had taken refuge in the tunnels. He'd been in one himself, led there by a group of people from the Below. One of the Senate's loyalists had gotten close enough to hook a blade under his armor, tear part of his breastplate loose, and sear the flesh of his chest beneath. She'd paid for it with her life, and Vanguard's people had ushered him into their secret places and treated his wound.

There were more places to hide now, but it only filled him with rage. To see the spires torn down, the filigree that had pierced the sky, now torn and twisted and splayed out on the ground.

This is exactly what they want. This is what our world has become. This is what they make of it. Everything that should be exalted, cut down.

And forgotten, as though it had never been.

He'd seen it coming. He'd heard it whispered in the halls of the pits, after the bouts were done and the audiences had gone home. He'd seen it in the books he'd stolen from Delen. He'd raised up his victors to fight it. To stop it. To repay the destroyers with their own destruction.

And now his victors were here.

Now the thunder of their battle cry rumbled so long and loud Malek wasn't sure who had started it. Maybe Dia. Or the twins. Maybe even Zarel, the man who'd designed the weapons they used.

Now those weapons gleamed, fresh and new, and glowed with energy and hunger. Their glow lit the ground just as the Skyknights' laser fire lit the sky. It flickered on the faces of the victors themselves, blue and green, orange and purple. *This weapon is mine, made for me, and now you see how you will die.*

Some were blasters, altered to be lighter, to fire faster, to recharge more quickly. Some fired complex blasts, halos of energy that caught two or three soldiers at a time, branching energy that caught and scorched anyone nearby. Some were swords like Malek's, or long spears and pikes wreathed with lightning and heat.

Malek couldn't help but smile. *This is what they stole from us. This is what we once were. What we were always meant to be.*

A battle cry swelled in his breast. His fingers tightened on the hilt of his sword, and the old hunger rose in him. Lightning crackled over the blade, and the sound thundered in his blood. Just like it had in the pits, for all those years when he'd been innocent.

He'd have to tell them all, eventually. When he returned to Dis, after this battle. He'd have to make it past the city council, whatever they thought of this battle. But he would manage that easily enough if he came back a victor, as always. His people would flock to his banner.

He wouldn't have hopeful words for them. Not then. He'd have to tell them what they'd lost, so long ago when the old Empire fell. What they never could regain, no matter how much information Kenn released or how much they trained in old techniques long lost.

Malek had lost his innocence, so long ago, reading those stolen documents from Delen. And he'd rip away theirs, just the same.

It was necessary.

He frowned. Even here, that loomed. Even now, he knew what he'd have to take from them. Just like he'd stolen away their favorite victors and hidden them away for revolt.

But for now, he had his revolution. The twins, standing just beyond him, lightning crackling on the tips of their spears. A halo of light flaring up around his tattooed onetime partner, her force field deflecting the bullets and laser fire of the foolish.

The people of Ember City, pouring forth from the Belt, painted in his colors and fighting in his name at last. *This is the beginning of our vengeance, and we will scour this world clean.* He roared, his whole broad frame reverberating with the sound, and ran out to join them.

Every movement of his arm meant death. Everywhere he went, they fell before him, sprays of red cascading from them. He felt the blade's heat, the lightning crackling over it, bright with his own hunger. But he didn't feel its weight. It was his, a part of him, and its thirst was its own.

The enemy scattered. He didn't wonder at it. He'd taken great care to hide his victors away, and now they emerged, bringing death to those who had dared defile the last worthy place in this world. Ghosts they'd forgotten, men and women they'd thought dead, who rose up on the long road from the Belt to Aerix, and came to strike them down.

Some fled, leaping over the crumbling ruins of the towers with grace born of their panic. He cut one down who raced past him, terror or foolishness bringing him just close enough to swing at Malek's exposed side and miss.

But even those who managed to avoid the victors racing in only met death in the alleys. The people of the Below knew them better than anyone.

Vareth had already reached the others. She wielded a massive mace now, and even as Malek watched, two of her enemies fell. They looked like toys next to her, lifeless dolls in suits of armor. She swung her mace at one, punched another with an armored fist. His visor cracked from the impact.

People flocked to her. The victors, eager to see their commander, and the recruits, thrilled to meet a woman they'd admired who'd vanished and reappeared. And now stood before them in the flesh, with the blood of real enemies painting her armor.

Fire flared in his vision. Skyknights swooped down, apparently not trusting their new allies. Or perhaps, Malek realized, taking advantage of their arrival. They rained fire on the tanks, wove around the starfighters in a dance of death, blasted at the wave of soldiers rushing in to fight the victors.

Malek yanked his blade free from the body of a fallen enemy to see Tanth and Ania speed past him in the sky. He smiled at them and growled a welcome in the dialect of the pits.

The people on the ground converged around Vareth. Two victors, broad-muscled and strong, carried something over to Vareth. Malek caught a glimpse of black-painted metal.

He laughed, low and deep. An irrational desire surged up in him to rush over to her himself. To fight at her side. To hear her voice, not over the vastness of the battlefield or through a device but with his own ears.

To watch her take up her real weapon.

But that was foolish. Vareth had her own people to command. And besides—

"Lord Malek!" called a cacophony of ragged voices.

Everywhere around him he saw his own glyph. Painted on faces.

Carved into armor. Tattooed or scarred onto skin of every shade. Some had even painted it onto the handles of their weapons, and he saw hints of it on one man's bloody axe-blade.

They will learn what they have lost. But for now, they are mine.

He gave them his best showman's smile and raised his blade into the smoky air. There was no time for a speech. Not here. Not now. Not with the battle already raging around them. But they answered him just as they would if he'd made one, roaring his name.

"This City is the last place of beauty in our world!" he cried. Eagerness sang in his nerves. Everything fed it. His anger at the desecration. The roar of the crowd. The blood of his enemies, spattered on his half-shattered armor. The sight of the Seraph above him, raining cleansing flame on those who dared to profane Aerix—and had for so long profaned their world.

"They have torn down the outer towers!" Malek went on. "They have no right to them. They must not reach the inner City!"

"Wait!" called a voice, gravelly and strained.

He knew that voice.

And only the best of his victors—the handpicked elite that he had chosen—would dare to stop him now. He looked into a face familiar for its ugliness. And for the bright yellow eyes that stared out of the deep sockets.

"Zarel."

Zarel held out something in his hands. A wolf's grin curled the edge of his mouth. "Your blaster, my Lord."

Malek curled his hands around it. He recognized it as the same gun Zarel had shown off in the victors' war room so long ago. He lifted it, surprised that something so big felt so light. His wound ached, but only barely.

His smile deepened. He'd seen this gun shoot a hole through a wall.

"And the armor we brought for you is—"

A low, percussive roar cut off the rest of what Zarel was saying. The sky above them flared with light.

He thought it must have been the Skyknights, or a volley from the stolen launchers, fired toward the still-advancing starfighters. Then he heard the victors' cheers, the rev of some young Skyknight's engine like a rumble of applause.

Vareth stood, twin launchers mounted on her massive shoulders. She held a trigger in one hand, squeezed it, and the sky lit again. Rockets burst from the launchers and streaked toward a starfighter's engines. One clipped the edge of a wing. A black plume of smoke rose from it, and the tip of the wing glowed molten orange-red.

The other hit the engine.

The crowds around Vareth cheered again. The blast brightened the sky, and Malek raised a hand to shield his eyes.

When the light dimmed again, he saw the starfighter plummet. Flame and smoke poured from the shattered energy cell.

A slim craft sped in to take advantage. From the speed and the smooth movement, it could only be Soran's. A pair of Skyknights followed behind, all gleam and grace. Malek clutched the blaster tighter, heat stirring in his flesh.

Laser fire streaked toward the damaged cell, precise and deadly. The flame Vareth's rockets had started flared outward, consuming the cell and wreathing the starfighter. It hung in the sky, a blazing flower.

Then, the strain too great, it burst apart, the explosion a red blaze that filled the sky.

Vareth and Soran. Malek laughed. *Apparently you work well together.*

Vareth growled a battle cry, but the victors and allies gathered around Malek needed no further encouragement. Some raced to Vareth's side, some to the next ring of towers to defend them. Others gave weapons to the defenders. Or armor they'd carried with them, the plates tucked in on themselves in compact shapes so the victors could carry them. People dressed in torn, burnt cloth slipped into the tunnels and emerged in armor, his symbol emblazoned on the breast.

An ache in his wound reminded him that they would have his weapons with them, as well. The twins, their own silvery armor already smeared with blood, raced over to him, carrying something between them.

He glanced one last time at Vareth, at the machine her commands set in motion, at the Skyknights careening overhead, and followed.

He looked down at the gun in his hands, felt the hum of heat gathering in its energy cells. It wasn't fully charged, not yet, but it would be soon enough.

The blaster was black, and bore his spearhead sigil in silver on the side. He ran a finger over it and smirked.

The armor matched the weapon. Plates of black, fitted tight to his broad frame. They'd slipped as easily over his muscles as they had slipped out of the cylinder they came in. A fine metallic mesh protected the spaces between them. A black helmet covered the back and sides of his head.

He tapped at the breastplate. A line of white light flickered under his fingers. He moved his hand away and watched it grow, the top edge twisting into a point. The point glowed and brightened. Then the light died, leaving a silver symbol behind.

It looked as if he'd drawn it there.

So this is what has become of my name.

The people gathered around him—the twins, would-be warriors from the Belt and the Below, a few tall stragglers from Aerix—watched in solemn silence. They lowered their heads to him. Tena and Tor pressed their fists to their chests in a gesture of respect.

"Lord Malek," a voice said, high and reedy.

Malek's eyes widened. That was neither Tor's nor Tena's voice.

He looked over at one of the defenders. The man, Skyknight-slim and pale-skinned like the twins, mimicked the twins' gesture.

"You belong to your Seraph," Malek said, his voice soft.

"I do."

"The spires of your city are shattered. Your enemies say I am the reason why."

The man looked up. His eyes were green, the green of leaves long lost and forgotten. Very little was green in the world any more, unless it was tucked away in some rich hobbyist's greenhouse. "The City stood on borrowed time. We all knew it."

"No!" The woman beside him lunged, a blur of delicate limbs. The man dodged her blow, but it was Tor who held her back.

Malek favored the pale young man with a little half smile. "We have no time for such arguments," he said. "The outer City is breached."

"Because of you," the woman hissed.

"Enough," Tena said. "We're all fighting the same enemy."

Malek nodded. The blaster hummed in his hands, hot with energy, hot with his own anger, hot with his need to avenge his Seraph's city.

"Follow me," he said.

Chapter Thirty

Soran swerved to evade a barrage of fire from a low-hovering starfighter.

And, if he was honest with himself, to get a better look at Malek.

He looked like the warrior he'd claimed to be, his blasted armor replaced with slick black, his logo a flash of silver on his breast. He held a soldier's gun, hefty and substantial.

Probably more than just hefty and substantial, since it was one of Zarel's toys.

The bolts of flame that pulsed from it confirmed that. A heat-shimmer of displaced air surrounded them. Where they passed, people fell, tossed aside like armored toys.

Those caught in their beams were less lucky. Their flesh mangled and tore under their armor, skin and muscle seared away, melted armor clinging to what meat was left.

And when the bolts finally hit something more solid than mere human bodies—a wall, a launcher, the side of a tank—light burst outward from the impact, a personal, handheld explosion. Soran's eyes widened. Was this impressive or horrific?

He'd liked watching flame burst from Vareth's shoulder-mounted launchers. But those were just big weapons for a big body to wield. This was something else entirely. Soran dove down to riddle the underside of a starfighter with laser fire just so he could look closer.

Vareth stood below, her launchers still belching fire. She shouted commands to the people manning the stolen launchers. A starfighter fell, aflame from the blasts. Perhaps in the days of the Old Empire,

Vareth could have been a real general.

Just like Malek had been saying all along.

Soran scowled and fired again. His own target finally went down. It spiraled to earth, its weapons crackling uselessly, too damaged to aim at the craft that had sped so nimbly away.

But through the smoke of its slow death Soran could see two of his own Skyknights fall, their craft gleaming, lifeless birds that plummeted down and down. Their pilots ejected, but Soran couldn't see more through the smoke.

Malek's blasts of energy lit the sky again, but this time it didn't lift Soran's mood. He imagined the pilots parachuting to earth only to face the enemy's soldiers and his lip curled again. Worse still, another tower cracked, split at the base, the inside dark like a rotten tree's heartwood.

That isn't one of the outer towers. Rage rose in Soran again, hot and hard and blind.

The victors' arrival had excited him. Their weapons' fire had dazzled him. He'd delighted in it. Let it heat his blood even as it rallied his people.

Enemy starfighters had fallen. His Skyknights had made sure of that. And the victors had halted their advance on the ground. Brutes and savages they might have been, but they'd made ready for war, when no follower of the Senate had dreamed of it until they'd threatened Aerix.

It's peace we want, Derell had said. *It's peace the Old Empire could never settle for. It's peace the Senate arose to preserve, and peace that our system ensures.*

Soran had scoffed. Scoffed, and exulted in the warriors he led and the ones the Lord of the Pits had brought with him. And he'd stared, like a damned fool, at Malek and his new toy. While the other starfighters ignored the carnage, lined up, and aimed at the inner towers anyway.

Hadn't that been their plan all along? To overwhelm Aerix with sheer numbers?

His engines roared, giving vent to his anger. His craft sped through the smoke and spewed laser fire at the nearest starfighter's heavy bulk.

Most of his shots went wide. He bit his lips on another scream.

He'd trained all his life as a fighter. Learned from the time he was small how to fight in the sky. Shaped his body and mind for war, for this, just as much as the victors had. And now he was so angry he was missing.

Below him, another nova of energy flared from Malek's gun. But it wasn't the ground he needed to worry about. Not even if Halcyon was down there. Not even if Malek's absurd weapon had torn her to scrap metal and bloody meat. Only the City mattered. Only the skies. Only the towers that had risen to pierce them for generations. Only the shudder and shiver of the spires, and the bolts of white heat rending them.

This wasn't like the fall of the first tower. This wasn't everyone, ally and enemy alike, gathered around a gleaming needle of golden filigree, watching it split, and tear, and topple, and fall at last to earth. This was two, three, five, his vision full of winking gold and the smoke that shrouded it. The creak of metal filled his ears, above him and beside him and below him, and fire flared up from wounded metal, everywhere.

And these towers weren't empty. Figures leapt from them. Some onto platforms that caught and held them. Some onto whatever bits of ornament would hold them, for some desperate climb—to a platform? To the ground?

This can't be real.

And yet it was. A hole torn in the fabric of his world that let smoke and fire in, and him falling with it, into something wide and gray and cold.

He gritted his teeth and closed his eyes. A roil of energy fed his lasers. His chest itched, the steady burn of a wound healing, and heat curled through the places in his body where Malek had driven in and in and in—

He opened his eyes.

"Skyknights!" he shrieked over the link. "Bring the starfighters down!"

Another blaze of flame from the ground hit one of the fighters. Vareth, perhaps, or one of her little minions below.

They got the first shot in.

The scream of Skyknights' engines was a whine of music in his ears. He raced ahead of them, his own engine shrieking higher and louder than the others. *We can't let our visitors have all the glory.*

He tore off after another, whole and unscarred and even more of an affront for being undamaged. He didn't bother with its weapons. That little trick was too cute. Amusing as it might be to watch its own energy choke itself, he didn't want that.

He wanted it, and all its ugly, unwieldy siblings, ripped from the sky.

"This sky belongs to me," he whispered, not knowing or caring whether he'd left the link on. It didn't matter.

"I'm going in," he heard over the link. A steady voice, an even voice. A low voice that might have calmed him.

He barely noticed it. His enhanced eyes caught the glitter of another craft beside him. He didn't look at it. He didn't care.

Skyknights knew speed from their beginning, and Soran was the fastest of them all. He moved with it, his rage a blaze of fire. It poured from his lasers and burst from his screaming mouth, a war cry that might have brought any fighter from Malek's pits to his knees.

A blossom of fire began in the starfighter's engine and flared outward. Soran let himself stare, let the yellow and white fill his eyes.

The voice called over his link again. He paid it no heed. Sounds of triumph and distress mingled in his ears.

He wanted only the heat of his enemy's destruction. The heat washed over him, pure and clear, and he gave himself up to his hunger.

A Skyknight tumbled from the air beside him. The craft trailed smoke and flame.

Who is that?

Soran wrenched his eyes from the dying starfighter and peeled away.

The destruction echoed everywhere around him.

Everywhere around him, Skyknights danced, and everywhere they passed flames rose in their wake. Ania whooped over the link. "Got one!" She called out orders to her wing, and Soran caught sight of one of them, a glimmer in the corner of his eye. It zoomed off after another starfighter, its engines and weapons glowing with energy.

Soran smirked. Maybe her eagerness was good for something after all.

And yet the Skyknight he'd seen fall wasn't the only one their enemies had shot down.

"I've lost the others!" said someone. "They—"

Soran couldn't make out the words. They crackled and faded in and out. But he could hear the tone, even and crisp despite its message. And the voice.

A low voice.

Tanth?

"First Skycaptain!" he called. "Are you—?"

"I'm fine, Seraph. But they shot down the wing I led. All but one of us. And they—"

The shriek of an engine and the roar of some projectile—one of the launchers?—cut him short.

Soran snarled. Below he could see another white circle of heat and light. Malek, again, probably. And his followers, cleaning up whatever was left.

His instincts screamed to go after Tanth. Tanth was his First Skycaptain, and these fools of Halcyon's had already taken too much. And now they were after the best of his people. The man whose wing of Skyknights flew at his right hand.

But he was the Seraph of Aerix, and around him his City was

falling.

And if he didn't want to see it crumble, he would have to bring down the fighters destroying it.

And Tanth was the best of his pilots. And the only person to defeat Vareth the Crusher in single combat. If anyone could hold his own, Tanth could.

Still—

"Wings Five and Six, are you close to the First Skycaptain?"

"Yes, Seraph," answered two voices in succession.

"Go after him," Soran answered. "The rest of you—with me. If these fools want into our city, they'll pay for the privilege. Malek the Destroyer isn't the only one who can bring death to his enemies."

Engines shrieking, he peeled away, his lasers hot with energy before he even aimed them. The other Skyknights' fire flared out in a brilliant blaze of light. He added his own to their glowing chorus with a shriek of rage or eagerness or both. A shower of sparks poured from the closest starfighter. It pitched to one side and one of the wings who'd followed him roared after it to blast the wound open wider.

A fierce, greedy heat curled through his chest, but he tore himself away and left it to them to finish. There were many, too many, and he was here to kill them all. Just like Malek below him. He saw a bright circle of light somewhere below him and gave a wild laugh.

The enemy fighters tried to moved aside, slow and ponderous, their thrusters flickering in a vain fight for enough speed to avoid him.

Oh, I don't think so.

He didn't know how many starfighters he downed. His vision filled with light gleaming on delicate metal that twisted and blackened and splintered and fell. He didn't know how many towers he saved. Malek and his victors and Vanguard and his men were a roil of movement below him. The sight of the chaos soothed him.

Everything burned, and right now, that was all he wanted.

Up ahead, the gleam of a Skyknight's fighter caught his eye. It sped straight for an enemy ship, others following. They danced around it, worried it, shot at vulnerable spots and danced away. Soran smirked.

But the Skyknight in the middle wasn't teasing. That craft's weapons charged, slow and steady, trained on one spot even as the enemy starfighter pitched and rolled to aim at the others darting in and out.

"Hello, First Skycaptain," Soran said, and snickered.

A laser blast caught the underside of one of Tanth's companions. It plummeted to the ground, spiraling down and down.

Tanth's second savior swooped in, but the starfighter was ready. Another blaze of light arced toward the second Skyknight, and Soran snarled all the louder and raced in, his weapons blazing.

The enemy craft lolled, tossed off balance by Soran's blast of laser fire. But it wasn't enough. A beam of white light trapped the hapless Skyknight, and the craft exploded, so forcefully Soran had to twist away.

Only Tanth remained. He flew straight for the very weapons array that had felled the others. It glowed, gathering new charge. So did Tanth's lasers. But he didn't fire, not yet. He waited, lined up his craft to take the shot.

Soran yelled and darted in again. *Someone has to distract them.*

A bolt of energy blasted out from Tanth's fighter. An answering white bolt shot out from the starfighter.

It wasn't aimed at Soran.

He whipped around, gnashed his teeth, and raced in to look.

Smoke poured from Tanth's craft's wing. It twisted and spun, struggled to right itself.

And kept falling.

"No!"

Soran's weapons blazed. The charge cell glowed with the damage Tanth had already done. It flared white in his vision when his own blasts hit it.

Somewhere in the shock of white, Tanth leapt from his doomed craft. The silhouette of his opening parachute blossomed against the bright haze and fell.

CHAPTER THIRTY-ONE

THE SLENDER form fell to earth, drifting through smoke.

It looked perfect, too perfect. Thin and delicate and fragile.

Is that Soran? The thought came before Malek could stop it, and his heart hammered hard in his chest.

He nearly forgot himself and ran toward the fallen one. Even here. Even in the middle of battle, the first battle in a war he'd spent years preparing for. Even now that his dreams were finally playing out in front of him, in smoke and blood and flame.

He'd expected sacrifice. He'd trained his victors for it. He'd seen it every night in the pits since his awakening. He'd known the price of victory, and accepted it long ago. Anyone could suffer, anyone could die, any stronghold or city could fall, if victory waited on the other side.

He'd known it from the beginning. And yet now his eyes fixed on the sky and refused to blink. His limbs twitched with the need to run to the downed Skyknight, so hard he could barely restrain them. He laughed at himself, coarse and rough.

Voices yelled over the communications link, a cacophony of fear and dismay. He could have listened to them, but the roil of emotions within him had its own demands. It called for destruction. For death. For revenge.

Was this how Soran felt? He loosed another bolt at his enemies. The brilliant white leaving no trace of where they'd been.

It calmed him. He looked out at ash and carnage and allowed himself a smile.

And with it, his head cleared.

That can't be Soran.

The figure stepped out of the smoke, tall and slim. It walked with purposeful strides, too stiff to be the Seraph's. And there was something odd in its step. Not just a rigid gait, but something fixed, something frozen—

His back. He's injured.

That happened before this battle.

That happened—

Malek's mind made the connection an instant before someone howled Tanth's name over the link. The wails Malek expected followed it, a flood of anguished sound.

—during the festival.

"Protect Skycaptain Tanth!" cried Soran over their din. But the people of the Below had started already, a swarm converging on a priceless treasure. Perhaps Soran's comparison to insects hadn't been so insulting after all.

Another shot from his weapon blasted a hole through the enemy line. Someone shouted to the victors. Not Vareth's low rumble, but Dia's higher, sharper cry. The brown blur of her body streaked across Malek's vision, and her weapon, a spear, shorter and broader than the twins', glowed against the smoking darkness.

Malek's mouth twitched, caught between a frown and a smile. She moved with deadly speed, and anyone in the way didn't stand for long. *Don't forget to watch your back.*

She had a line of victors to do it for her now. They flooded into the space Malek's blast had left and closed in on any of Halcyon's fighters brave enough to fill the gap.

A pike flashed, an awkward mimicry of Dia's movement. Malek remembered the young man who'd bragged about his kills. The boy might get himself killed copying Dia's recklessness. And that would be a loss. Such spirit, properly directed, had promise.

But with enough men like him willing to die to retake the planet, the Senate didn't stand a chance.

Soran's voice snarled into his ear. "You say so much about your warriors, Malek. My First Skycaptain is the best of mine."

"Understood."

"I won't lose him for your war."

"You want me to go after him." Malek looked up. Skyknights hovered in the clouds. They massed around the space where Tanth had disappeared, a lost flock, watching and waiting. Their weapons lit with energy. But they'd lost their direction.

"Your Skyknights—" Malek began. Debris cascaded down from another of the towers. "You need them to—"

"My city is crumbling to protect you, Lord of the Pits!" Soran snarled. There was no affection in that voice. Only cold, slithering threat, the kind that would cut down friend and foe alike. "You're not going to let him die."

This isn't about what you want, Prince of the Air. But Malek couldn't bring himself to say the thought aloud. Not when Aerix had lost so much already.

And it wasn't a terrible idea. Halcyon was out there, somewhere, hunting him. But he wasn't going to find her now anyway. Not with bolts of lightning-death that charred anyone to ash who tried to even get near him.

Malek chuckled. *If you want to find me, you'll have to face me. Assuming Soran hasn't already shot you dead from the sky.*

Not that Halcyon was a worthy opponent. She was a lackey, doing the bidding of lackeys. And in such close quarters, Malek would have to forsake his big gun. But Malek had won his title and his rule on the sands of the arena. He'd seen men and women rise by their own strength, and fall by their own weakness.

Halcyon was as good as dead already. But maybe when she died, she would see the truth.

"Get Tanth into the tunnels!" Malek cried. The hum of his weapon filled the air. "I will cover you!"

Soran screeched an order to the Skyknights. Some hesitated, unsure whether to let an outsider protect their own. But to their credit, most dispersed. Their engines shrieked and the smoke-clouded sky lit with their laser fire.

A group of victors came too. Vareth was busy, still leading the groups that had stolen the launchers. But Dia streaked toward him. Her pikeman came after, a faithful pet with blood-spattered armor.

"My Lord," Dia said, panting with exertion. "You're going to hide?"

Malek turned away from her. He followed a slim youth, clad in the rough rags of the Below. His guide slipped through the rubble left by a fallen tower with the grace of someone who'd always disappeared to survive.

Dia sighed, but followed. Malek looked back at her. "I'm going to protect a man who could easily have died to protect us."

"The Skyknights can do that."

"The Skyknights need to save their city. We need the towers of Aerix standing."

Dia stopped in her tracks. Her fierce, wounded face turned to him. "Do we?"

Malek's eyes widened. He remembered his own words, in his war room in Dis, so long ago. *Have you forgotten what will happen to this city, to the heart of it, by our own hands?*

He'd meant Dis, when he'd said it. But was Aerix so different? His lip curled, and he favored Dia with a wry smile. "They do. Or this falls apart." He tilted his head toward the falling spires. "This alliance. This battle. This promise."

Dia blinked and shook her head. Then she nodded.

"They're looking for me." Malek stared down into the dark of a passageway. His guide slipped inside and waved to him. "Let them come and find me."

"We'll come with you."

Malek recognized the voice. And the glow of the pike, crackling with electricity. Blood smeared it now, thick red shadows that its heat burned away. Beside him stood others, all bearing his symbol. One wore it painted on her brown cheek with ash.

A chance to stand beside their legend. Malek snickered, a mirthless sound. "With that weapon? Down in the tunnels?"

"So I don't go down into the tunnels, then." His hands tightened around his weapon. "Zarel made this. Now you're telling me to abandon it for a sword? Why not just stay here and stick the fools who come after us before they get close to the Skyknight?"

Malek's lip quirked. "Wise enough. Take what you need to fight. You others"—he pointed—"come along. But the rest of you stay here. This is no arena bout. This is the beginning of a revolution."

They wound their way through wreckage. The pikeman stayed behind, his weapon a gleam behind them.

Tanth towered over the press of bodies. More than once, he ducked down to crawl into some narrow passage between the mounds of debris. But as before, he needed no guidance.

Malek had used his gun one last time, turning and firing a parting shot before following his guide down into it. He could still feel the last of its heat against his skin, a fading promise of ferocity. Now he had his sword. He'd made sure to keep even it at low power. The surface here was meant to be a place to hide, and he didn't need to make a beacon of his blade.

In the pits, it would have been. Even outside, it might have been. A bright flash and dazzle, showing Halcyon where to find him. Not here. Here they picked their way through remnants that had already been shattered.

Malek's free hand reached out for a remnant of filigree. He picked it up and ran his thumb over the metal, its once-bright surface clouded by dust and grime. Dark eyes stared back at him from under heavy brows.

They could hear war above. The sizzle and crackle of energy bolts. The low roar of explosions. The crash of towers as they fell.

He let the piece of metal drop. There would be time, later, to think about what all this meant. For now—

He hastened over to Tanth. "Can you fight?"

"If I have to." Steel flashed in Tanth's hand, and Malek looked down to see a smooth, sculpted blade like the one he'd taken from Soran, all those months ago. His other hand rested near a blaster at his hip.

But the only others around them now came from the Below. They poured from the tunnels, whispering in urgent voices. The elder Malek had seen before, with a pale yellow shawl and a cloud of wiry black hair surrounding her head, pointed down a tunnel. Others in the same shawls of office came after her.

"Follow," they said. They read the glyphs he'd seen Vanguard read with his fingers before, saw the questions in his eyes and whispered what they meant. "Hall of meeting, to the left." "Dead end." "Long tunnel ahead." He listened and learned with his own hands and eyes. He saw Tanth do it too, bird-delicate fingers ghosting over grooves in the metal.

"Not that way," someone said. Malek looked down the tunnel. It looked innocuous enough.

But this was a city of hidden people. And they had just brought Kenn down here, who laid the arena's best traps. He smirked and followed his new companions.

The bones of the City rose above them, a skeleton of twining pipes and filigree. It had stopped raining dust. Malek heard another crash somewhere above, another tower's death. Here it sounded like thunder. Just a storm, somewhere far away. His lip quirked and he stared upward.

It would have to be protection enough.

"This is the safest place we have," said a familiar voice.

One of Malek's young followers scowled. *It's not safety you're after, is it?*

Malek caught sight of the silvery sweep of the cane just as Tanth looked up. "Vanguard? You shouldn't—"

"Protect you? You protected me."

"I did. But this is war."

"All my life, you protected me."

"Van, if they come for you, you can't fight them. Even Kenn left the pits. And he's not blind."

"The sky is falling, First Skycaptain. Your craft is gone and you're grounded. For once, let me help you."

Tanth leaned against a rusted length of pipe, his face gray and drawn. Had the bout at the festival injured him worse than they'd realized, or was he feeling the loss of his wings? How many generations had it been since some enemy had shot the First Skycaptain himself out of the air?

Malek stepped forward. The ground rattled, and the pipes

overhead shook. The globes stayed lit, their light cold and unwelcoming.

"They'll find us," someone whispered, looking up.

"They can't find us here," said someone else. "They won't."

Malek turned his head. "They can and they will. They're looking for me."

The elder in the yellow shawl answered. "But if they're looking for you, then you haven't protected him. You've brought them after him."

Malek didn't look at her. He watched Vanguard instead, who was leading Tanth down some private corridor. A small crowd of people followed. One by one, they slipped down the corridor and vanished.

Malek growled. "They'll find me long before they find him." He turned to the men and women wearing his symbol. "Come on."

One of them smiled, the same wolfish grin he'd seen on the young pikeman. Apparently it was infectious. "We're going back up?"

"Not quite." Malek's grip tightened around the hilt of his sword. "But now that Tanth has reached the heart of the city, we can make sure they meet us halfway down."

CHAPTER THIRTY-TWO

THE CITY was a ruin.

Soran didn't want to believe it. Many enemy starfighters had fallen. Of those that remained, many hovered blackened and burnt, the corners blasted off their rectangular hulls, the metal beneath a tangle of torn membranes. Only a few remained unscathed now, and the Skyknights would reach those soon enough.

But diminished as the enemy fleet was now, they'd made sure to take the towers with them. For every one that stood, three had fallen around it. The survivors pierced an empty and lonely sky.

He flew toward one of the hovering craft, weapons hot, but a wing of other Skyknights wove death around it before he could get there.

And over the wreckage, the greatest tower rose. His tower, the Seraph's Tower, untouched and untouchable. A beacon, pure and bright, shining above something that had already broken. Was that what Malek had meant when he'd said *Aerix is the one thing on this planet worth preserving?*

Malek was down there somewhere. With Tanth. His First Skycaptain. His best flier.

Who the enemy had chased to ground and into hiding, like a beast.

A new spark of rage kindled in Soran. He let it grow, found a new starfighter to target, raced after it with speed even Ania couldn't match. Others took up the war-scream coming from his throat and engine. He heard them speed after him, but he reached his quarry first.

It didn't even try to evade him. It didn't have the chance.

He poured his fury out in bright bolts of heat. But this time his dance of death had a purpose. Holes in the enemy hull widened, bright molten wounds dripping metallic blood.

The best of his Skyknights downed. One more desecration, one more violation. But Soran had signed up for this game. He gritted his teeth and forced himself to think of the advantage. With Tanth hidden down in the Below, and Malek down there to protect him, Halcyon had someone to go after.

And if she found him, she'd have to go through Malek to get to him. Soran's lip curled in a grin in spite of himself. He could stay up here and handle the starfighters, at least for now.

Soran had no illusions about the starfighters. They were here to do just what they did now. To bring the towers down. To teach Aerix, and its Seraph, what it meant to defy the Senate. But his cold rage did not abate.

You thought we wouldn't be a problem for you. Malek was right. We are.

His smile deepened, sharp as a blade. There was no ending this, no turning back. Not now. The Senate had made itself his enemy from the first shot it had fired at his towers.

But even if Malek and the ragged little army General Crusher had cobbled together out of pit fighters and street urchins did fall, enough of his city would still stand for something to be salvaged.

His ancestors had made a promise. So could he.

And he could break a promise, too.

Fiery bolts sped past, from Vareth's launchers. But they didn't launch into the air. They hit the mass of grounded soldiers pouring into some tunnel or other.

So you're with him, in the end. Of course.

To their credit, the people who'd stolen the launchers kept shooting at the starfighters. Even the hooligans from Dis, painted or tattooed or scarred with Malek's symbol, understood where the real enemy was.

You should be careful, Crusher. His spite burned slow and deep, a half-cooled ember of fierce pleasure. *You'll give away where your lord is.*

Another starfighter burst apart, its smoldering body a bright flower of sparks.

"How many of the starfighters are left?" Soran asked over the communications link. He turned his eyes away from Halcyon's little procession of insects and tried not to snicker.

"There are six here," came Ania's voice. "And a few others further away. If we can't go down there and—"

Go down there? Soran knew full well how attached Ania was to Tanth, but following the ground troops was foolish. "Don't."

The line went quiet for a long moment. No other Skyknight finished for her. None of them dared.

When she spoke again, her voice was eager as always, but with a strained note Soran wondered if the others could hear. "If we can't go after those ground rats, I say we take care of these fools in our skies. Starting with these six near us. Then if the soldiers are still poking around the tunnels..." Her voice became a snarl.

"Indeed."

"We can't let them tear down any more of our City," said a man's voice, higher than Tanth's. Wrong. Off. A replacement, a substitute.

They were in a war now. How many more substitutes would there be by the end?

But he couldn't let himself think of that now. The six starfighters, ragged though they were, were moving. Converging.

Choosing a target, and sending a message.

"No!" Soran cried. Then, realizing his people were waiting for a command: "We can't let them reach the Seraph's tower. Shoot them down, at any cost!"

A chorus of Skyknight engines screamed. They raced toward the tower with all speed.

With one last look at the tunnels, he roared ahead to join them.

The starfighters converged in a ragged hexagon around the center of the city. One listed as Ania's craft worried it. Her usual loops and flourishes were gone now. Every twist and roll reflected one thing now: desperation.

He fired at its flailing bulk himself. Ania could down it, but the sooner it fell, the sooner they could bring down the others.

She peeled away from it as it fell. The silver streak of her fighter sped downward, racing toward—

"Skycaptain Ania!" he called over the link. "Come back! We have a job to do."

"Seraph. They're everywhere. They're getting in—"

They're already in. "The highest tower must not fall."

"One tower doesn't matter." Her voice was thin and cold. "Not more than the others."

A shock of white light made Soran wince. A spray of debris followed. He clenched his teeth on a curse and swerved.

This one, he reached first. He seared a bright red line of flame across its hull. More shots joined him, and it fell, still firing, as though its crew hadn't even noticed they were dying.

They probably haven't. They probably can't. I betrayed the Senate, and now my City is a symbol.

Now it falls to shame the others. To frighten Malek's little revolution away.

He followed the dying starcraft until its gunners gave up or its targeting systems failed. Energy still poured from it in a glitter-white spray. But the burst was aimed at nothing now, the last clench of a deadly muscle no longer in a mind's control.

He wove out of the way of it, its heat searing one of his wings. It fell to the ground, its malfunctioning weapon scorching its own allies below.

He let himself laugh, but only for a moment. He had to find Ania. If she was angry enough to defy him, to go against all her training, then how were Skyknights any better than the rabble Malek tried to make Aerix's saviors?

With another curse, he followed the streak her craft had left in the clouds of smoke.

A golden-orange flicker caught his eye. He focused his enhanced eyes on it. A line of flame on the ground, like a river of heat. Halcyon's soldiers fled from its source, or died.

He had no doubt who that was coming from. He wrenched his gaze away. He couldn't let himself notice that the blaze was beautiful.

"Skycaptain Ania," he said, his voice curt. "You are needed up here."

"I understand, Seraph, but I—"

"Join the other Skyknights. That's an order."

"No." Another rain of laser fire; another line of flame, bright like a vein of gold through rock.

"Malek is down there," he forced himself to say.

"I know."

"Then what are you going to do? Blast the tunnels open trying to kill the soldiers running into them?"

Her voice was a beast's growl. "What good is the Seraph's tower if it stands above a gutted city? What does it stand for then?"

The low hum of an enemy engine filled his ears, and the sharper vibration of its lasers powering up. *Damn it.*

"It means the same thing it has always meant, Skycaptain," he said, not bothering to listen for a response. Instead he rocketed away, back toward his tower and the things that threatened it.

Another ship burst apart before his eyes. A prize that should have been his.

He sped toward an enemy fighter. Its weapons crackled with gathered energy. He loosed laser fire at the glowing, pulsing cores.

Around him, he heard the high whine of other Skyknights' weapons. The air became a blaze of light, and the fighter's energy cell overflowed with it. He heard the thunder of its impending explosion, the plaint of a dying beast.

The burst shook his craft, a heavy vibration, but this time he was ready for it, above the blast.

And above the fray, his tower. Gleaming for the moment.

But even here he looked down, through clouds of dust, looking for Ania's rivers of fire.

CHAPTER THIRTY-THREE

"THEY'RE IN," said the elder. She ran toward Malek and the others, her hair a dark halo around her head, a sheen of sweat making her brown skin gleam.

She wasn't injured, and there was no blood on her garments. That was good; it meant she hadn't faced them herself. Which meant that the men and women his victors had trained could deal with it, for now.

Malek thought of the young pikeman, blood sizzling on his weapon. He remembered the young man's grin, wide and eager and toothy.

I told Soran I was a beast. A beast with open eyes. Was the young pikeman? Had he learned from the broadcasts, or did he want only to fight?

He got that wish now. If he hadn't died already.

That thought made Malek's lip curl, the first grim shadow of a frown. And yet, if he was still alive, still killing, still stemming the tide of soldiers that streamed in—

His mouth quirked again. He shouldn't have liked it. But some part of him did, an old, deep fire in his blood. His old companion, kindling to the sound of his name and the feel of the arena sands under his feet. Failure meant death, but victory meant power. Meant earning the glory he won through sweat and blood.

Would the young pikeman have been a victor, if he'd found his way to Dis before this fight? Or would his eagerness have proven his undoing? Would he have been cut down in his first fight by a slower and more careful opponent, who'd learned better than to rush in all fierceness and heat?

A rattle from above brought him back to himself. The dust and the shaking had only grown more frequent.

"Tanth?" he asked, looking at the elder.

"He's with Vanguard. If anyone can keep him safe, he can."

Malek nodded. It would have to be enough.

"It is time," he said. The light that wreathed his sword brightened. "We take the fight to them."

His followers tightened their grips on their weapons. Some glared. Some grinned. The air crackled with energy as blades and guns powered to life.

It felt good, sharp, electric. He allowed himself to revel in it.

And over it all, the sound of screaming engines and laser fire, too long and loud for handheld guns.

Skyknights? But why would they come here?

Gray-carapaced soldiers flooded into the corridor with a crackling hail of blaster fire. The warriors with him roared and leapt to the attack.

The ground in front of their enemy opened, and a pack of Vanguard's people rushed up out of a hidden place beneath. Malek grinned as the wave met their foes together. *Did Kenn teach you that one?*

It felt more like the pits than his gun had. But he was looking for one quarry, and one quarry alone. *You all look the same.* Sudden irritation drew his brows down over his eyes. *Do you want this, Halcyon? To fight and die in a city not your own? For what? So things can go back to the way they've always been for you?*

His sword sliced through a neck. He watched the body fall with something almost like regret.

But something caught his eye—a quick, lithe movement from one of the gray-clad soldiers, who darted away from a crowd lunging toward it.

He couldn't chase it now. He and his followers had their own troubles. He stopped to tear a burly-framed man away from a rangy girl. She turned to glared at Malek, bereft of her prize. Then her eyes widened with recognition and she bowed her head. He inclined his head to her and looked up.

"Come out, Halcyon!" he called. "I know you're there. No need to hide behind your minions now."

One of the armored shapes moved, far more graceful than its fellows but otherwise identical to them, a blue visor over its eyes. It might have reminded him of a Skyknight, if he hadn't learned the difference.

"I have no need to hide," she said.

The walls of the tunnel rocked, spraying debris. Malek planted his feet, and he saw Halcyon stumble. She caught herself and twisted upright.

"The Skyknights!" someone called out. "They'll bring the tunnel down around us all!"

Malek looked only at Halcyon. If the Skyknights were coming, it meant they'd managed to keep the starfighters off their towers. "No need to hide, Halcyon? Ironic words from an assassin."

She raised her weapons, a small blaster held in one hand, a thin blade in the other. Energy lit it with a soft, cold glow. It didn't look deadly, just eerie.

That made Malek trust it even less.

"My team and I came here for one life, pit fighter." Halcyon's voice broke into his thoughts. "One life."

"No!"

A slim woman lurched up from the ground, clearly injured. She'd smeared Malek's symbol on her cheeks in dark grease, and blood spattered the glyph. She stretched out a hand toward Halcyon's ankle, a grasping claw.

Brave, perhaps, but foolish. Halcyon barely even turned to face her. A bolt of energy shot out from the blaster, and caught her in the chest. She fell, and stilled.

Malek did not let himself blink. He'd known the price of war from the beginning. So had the girl. If she'd been paying attention.

"One life, Halcyon?" he sneered, circling. He would have to get that blaster out of Halcyon's hands. And to do that, he'd have to distract her.

The ground shook under Malek's feet again. Whatever the Skyknights wanted, they would break through soon.

He saw a flash of gray as Halcyon caught herself, and a burst of energy from her weapon. The roiling ground saved him from the blast.

"Only once you made it necessary." She watched him struggle to his feet, lips curled, expression cold.

Now you're toying with me. That is a mistake. "One living, one dying. If you wanted that, you should have met me in the pits."

The sound wasn't loud. It wasn't a cry, or a growl, or a snarl of indignation. But Malek heard it all the same. Halcyon canted her helmeted head toward the field of bodies. "How many have died today?"

She swept out with the blade. A white arc of energy flared out from it. Malek twisted away. It glanced off his side, and he braced for the pain of a burn.

But where he had expected heat, he felt only cold, a pricking numbness in his muscles. He growled with pain and anger and twisted his body into its stance again.

Paralysis. That can't be all your weapons do.

"You know my reputation, Halcyon," he shot back. "Did you think taking my life would be easy?"

She lunged. Malek smirked and met the blow. Even that instant of contact chilled the wrist that held his blade.

"Easier than this," she said.

"You meant to kill only me. But what did you expect to happen once you managed that? Look around you."

She didn't. She planted her feet and gripped her blade's hilt tighter.

"They wear my mark, in paint, in ash, in scars. Did the Senate really think destroying me would destroy all of this?"

But it wasn't Halcyon who answered. Two of her fighters rushed at him, one from each side.

He stepped back. They lunged for each other, missing him. He saw the fuel cell of one's blaster brighten, didn't dare to let himself hope the fool would shoot his friend.

He didn't. But they did land in a heap in front of him, tangled up together. *Fools. You'll fall to your own mistakes.*

"What power you have, you built on death," Halcyon intoned, her voice colder than Kenn's.

But her little minions' stunt had shocked the others following Malek awake, it seemed. Where they had moved away, giving Malek and Halcyon room like they'd expected a pit fight, now they remembered. This wasn't a one on one fight. This was a battle to be won.

Malek's allies caught his eye and circled. Very well. He'd give them their moment, if they could use it. "You've said that already, Halcyon. Is that the only thing the Senate lets its stooges say?"

"Is this what you want? The towers of Aerix crumbling over streets piled with the dead?"

One man, a wiry victor freshly recruited by Dia, growled an old battle cry dredged up from the old histories, and leapt at Halcyon.

Dia had been glad to pull him from the rolls of the last tournament. Malek had been glad too. The tournament would take his life. The war probably would too. But at least it would offer him something to fight for.

He stood no better chance than the woman before him had. The white sword flashed again, and a half-moon of pure light caught him in his leap. The light didn't sear him, burn him, or scorch him like lightning. It simply caught him, and his limbs froze, and he fell.

Malek bit his lip to keep from roaring. He'd known the price from the beginning. But paying it...

He squared his shoulders and gripped his blade tighter. Blue lightning crackled over his blade, and the old hunger flared up in him again, a bright heat that seared away Halcyon's chill.

The rumble of engines filled his ears. And this time, it came with fire.

Laser blasts tore through the walls of the tunnel, a scorching rain that seared them open.

"The Skyknights!"

The voice quavered. Had it come from one of Halcyon's minions, or from one of his own followers? Was that sound hope or fear?

His allies converged on Halcyon, not waiting for a sign from him. Their cry was no shriek of challenge but a rumble of grief and pain, dredged up from the core of the Molten Belt and given life here, in answer to death.

Halcyon went down under them, people of all shapes and sizes, some in armor, some in thick leathers, some in little more than cloth.

The soldiers converged on them in turn. Even as Malek's blade flashed and cut them down, a few of his allies fell, bullets in their backs.

Laser blasts rained from the sky. They tore through the soldiers' ranks. And through some of Malek's allies as well.

"What are they doing?" cried a quavering voice.

But Malek had no time to wonder or to answer. A bright corona of white light rose up from the crush of bodies piled atop Halcyon. It flung some aside, inert and lifeless as the man who had fallen just before.

"Streets piled with the dead, and a world built on the backs of the frozen," Malek said. His weapon brightened again, as if it too could taunt his enemy.

She emerged in a halo of white, her sculpted face impassive. But despite her armor and the glowing blade she wielded, she wasn't quite pristine. Blood stained her other arm and smeared the gray armor. The gun was gone, and the hand that had held it dangled from her wrist at an unnatural angle. The blood ran from the wound and stained the ground.

Malek smiled, both at the handiwork of his allies and at Halcyon, who still faced him with the same implacable gaze. Her lips were drawn, no doubt in pain, but her altered eyes were bright, tiny pinpricks of the battle's fire.

Behind her the Skyknights' blasts rained down from the sky. She ignored them.

Perhaps you make a better adversary than you seem. Malek moved, slow and careful, his body packed tight in a fighter's crouch. He kept his eyes on her blade. Those arcs of paralyzing energy could reach further than his arm.

But apparently, recharging the weapon took time. It had glowed white before. Now the blade looked almost like normal steel, only the faintest pearly sheen hinting at its power. He would have to act quickly.

He darted in. Not a convincing move against someone trained in stealth, but she would have to do something. And soon. Stoic she might seem, but that arm had to hurt. And was bleeding.

She took the bait. The weapons clashed together, and the energy fields flared from the collision. Blue lightning wreathed Malek's blade, even as he drew it away to attack again.

Heads turned, watching them. Even here, it seemed, they all wanted their show. Malek watched the gray-armored frames grapple with his people, and wondered. Had any of them been fans of the fights, before they'd come to see him as a threat and an enemy?

He slashed out at Halcyon's abdomen. She skipped away with the grace of the assassin she had been, and he thought he heard her snicker. One of her men cheered.

What have you accepted? What have you become part of? Malek danced just out of her range. The blade she held brightened even as he watched, a moon-bright reflection.

But she was used to two weapons, two hands.

Two avenues of protection.

He roared, his best impression of the beast Vareth so often pretended to be, and lunged.

She spun away. He stepped to the side, facing her wounded arm, and swung hard at the shoulder it hung from.

Her armor offered some protection, but whichever of the mob had torn away the gun had already widened a crack in it. The energy-bite of the lightning glowed in the widening breach. Malek smelled blood and burning flesh.

Halcyon swayed. Malek thought she might fall, but she caught herself. She straightened her knees with slow, deliberate movement, and the light from the lasers above made her eyes gleam.

She raised the sword again in challenge.

"You fight well," Malek called as he darted away. "You might have been someone, if you'd let yourself. Why waste those talents? The people you serve aren't worthy of the person you could be."

There was no arc of energy, not yet. Only the pale promise of the blade's bite. "I came here with a purpose," she said, her movements graceful even as they slowed. "I came here to destroy you before you destroy us."

"You came here to die trying. Even the men and women in the pits know when that is what they've chosen."

Halcyon smirked, her expression all the colder for its bloodlessness. "And you will cut me down. Like any enemy. But these are not your pits. And I won't die for your delusions."

"No," Malek answered. Lightning coursed over the surface of his blade. "You will die so a world may be reborn."

The answer was a roar and a half-moon sliver of light.

CHAPTER THIRTY-FOUR

EVERYTHING WAS out of his control.

Ania had ripped through the tunnels. Her wing had followed. Soran could see them below, raining laser fire on Halcyon's soldiers.

He'd heard Malek had found Halcyon, too. That they were dueling down below. A whisper through the static at his ears said each had injured the other. Knowing Malek's undefeated record in the pits, he wasn't sure he believed it. Or sure whether to curse or to gloat.

Or to speed down to the gutted tunnels, blast whoever had hurt Malek, and gloat then. He thought of Malek below him, grateful hands and lips pressed to his flesh, and smirked. *How would you feel, Lord of the Pits, if you owed me for once?*

But four starfighters remained clustered around the tower. Three and a half, given the plume of black smoke pouring from one. The shot had come from a launcher. Soran's lips pursed. It should've come from the Skyknights. But even as he scowled, silver birds flew toward their injured prey and circled for the kill.

Three beams of light brightened in the weapons cores of three starfighters, lined up in a ring around the Seraph's tower.

"They were using six," Soran whispered to himself. "Are others coming?" It would take time for them to get here, if they were.

But wherever their allies might have been, apparently these three meant to try now. He roared after one, bright bolts of silver on his heels. Their fire lit the sky, bright enough he could forget the blaze below.

He fired in the direction of the enemy craft's engines, too far away to hit, too filled with rage and desperation to care.

It's not even moving out of the way. "They're concentrating on the tower," he called over the communication link. *Vultures. They don't belong in our sky.*

Was that what the Senate wanted? Pilots who knew they'd come here to die? Who would fall to charred and burning ruin still firing on the Seraph's tower? The thought turned his stomach. He'd expected it from Malek, with all his talk of war and its price, and the armies he assembled from the rejected and the lost. Malek wanted to win at all costs, and would throw anything at all in his enemies' way.

Somehow this was worse. A pack of bureaucrats and their minions, a mob of the unworthy. Thousands of dirty hands, uprooting and destroying what they could never build themselves.

"There are only three," he said. "They'll need more if they hope to make the tower fall."

"Three is enough," said a taut voice in his ear. A Skycaptain's voice, too young to be either of his best.

He fought to keep the bile from his voice. "If they want the tower to fall—the world to see it—they'll have to shoot in unison."

"Which means—"

"Which gives them less opportunity to aim at us." His lips curled in disgust, and he fired again. *You're making this too easy.*

The others followed his lead. A synchronized barrage flared out toward the starfighter's engine. Flame flared up from it, and it listed.

But even as his Skyknights cheered into the speaker at his ear, its weapons blazed to life. Streaks of white fire scorched black lines into the tower's filigree. The starfighter tumbled from the sky still ripping scars through the metal, a last act of martyrdom or spite.

Burnt lines, even and regular, like the claw marks of some great beast. Most were superficial, but one wound gaped, its center all fire. Soran felt it, somewhere inside him, a searing heat and then a chill that left him numb. His fingers moved, graceful as always, over the controls that fired his lasers. A gesture without meaning, in the face of desecration.

Then something else caught his eye: a glitter of light in the darkness.

The others.

Skyknight craft, slim and sleek, darting out to finish what he'd started.

I've waited too long. His engines roared, a shriek of despair.

He blazed after the second one. His warriors flew after him, men and women trained from birth to fight for his city, their very bodies sculpted into weapons, sleek as the craft they piloted.

Hope surged again in his breast. He thought of Malek's lips and hands on him and grinned. *We're warriors. Even more than you are, Destroyer. We were made for this.*

The starfighter hovered in front of him, hulking and silent. He fired at it, whirled away, and fired again. And again. And again. Sprays of light seared it, and it shuddered. Like its partner before it, it began to move. Crippled by its wounds, no doubt. Soran laughed, a high trill of mockery, and took aim again. *How much can you take? Why don't I find out?*

The square, hulking bulk stopped shaking. It didn't plummet to earth.

"What?"

The starfighter spun, still slow and heavy. Its weapons array feathered out, white-hot with energy.

Looking for him. The whole time, this one had been looking for him.

They hadn't needed six starfighters after all, or even three. Why take down the Seraph's tower when you could take down the Seraph himself?

He trusted to his skill and dove. Fastest of the Skyknights. Prince of the Air.

He felt the weapon's heat. Close, like before, but if he swerved to evade it, he would—

The blaze of white energy grazed his wing, and the sound of impact filled his ears. His craft spun, and the world tilted in front of him.

He clutched at the controls, his delicate body contorting as though he could force his craft to *stay up! Stay up!* Hands white and aching from his grip, he wrenched his craft upright again.

A message flashed on his display, overlaid on his view of the smoke-filled skies: *Left stabilizer damaged.*

His fingers danced over the console. That problem, he could solve. Any Skyknight in his first year of flight training knew how to handle that. His display flashed a message reading *Manual control engaged.*

A mortar whizzed past him. He twisted to evade it. More roughly than he would have liked. But then, his wing was damaged.

He hissed in frustration. Who'd done that? Some fool of Vareth's, so intent on the starfighters above that he hadn't noticed Soran? Or were some of them still in the enemy's hands? There was no way to know. His little excursion had blown him far off course. His tower gleamed in the distance, too far away, its tip an impossibly thin line of filigree.

And below the gleaming, a scorched hole.

Pride swelled in his breast. *The others did it! They drove the starfighters off!*

"Or they've abandoned it," he whispered.

But he couldn't celebrate for long. Ania had seen other starfighters, hanging back while their allies attacked the Seraph's tower. They'd been far away from him then.

At least one of them wasn't now. Headed for the tower, maybe, to try and do what the others hadn't managed to. But it had found Soran instead.

Now it advanced, slow and ponderous. Its weapons array flickered with the beginnings of new light.

He couldn't weave away from it. Not when it could fire a whole barrage of shots at him. Not with his stabilizer damaged, and not when he didn't know just what the hit had done to his wing.

Well then. He'd just have to shoot it down before its weapons powered up again, and hope he could get out again.

He smirked. Of course he could. He was the Seraph, after all.

His enhanced sight let him stare at the holes torn in the enemy ship's hull. Most hadn't done much damage, but a few had burnt through the outer layers. He focused on the largest of them, took aim, and sped toward the starfighter. No hesitation, and no regrets.

He fired directly into the hole in the hull. The hole flared molten-metal red and widened. The starfighter shook, this time for real.

Soran braced himself for one last blast and then peeled away, hard. His craft dipped and trembled, and he gripped the controls tight. The edge of the starfighter's hull filled his vision, coming closer and closer to the very wing the starfighter had damaged. *I have to–*

The edge of his wing grazed metal, and he saw sparks rise from the corner of his eye.

Then he was clear, racing away from the dying behemoth as it fell from the sky.

The tunnels lay below him. His tower was too far away, and they were too close. The torn innards of his city, ripped open beneath him. There was blood, the blood of many dead, and the warriors below, a squirming crush of activity.

In the center of it all, two figures. One massive and broad, his frame encased in black armor, his blade wreathed in blue lightning. The other was tall and slender. Almost a Skyknight, except that anyone dressed in that snow-gray uniform could only be a mockery.

One arm hung uselessly from a gaping wound in her shoulder. Blood ran over her armor. So much that it was a wonder she still stood. But her blade gleamed as well, pearled and bright.

I have no time for this little show. If the starfighters had abandoned their plan to destroy the tower, he could always come back, watch Malek kill Halcyon, and–

The flare of white fire was bright enough he wouldn't have needed his enhanced eyes to see it.

But they showed him Malek wouldn't evade it, even before he watched Malek try to twist away. The energy glanced off Malek's shoulder, and his arm froze, dead as Halcyon's. His blade fell from nerveless fingers. It lay on the ground in front of him, still wreathed in lightning.

Soran swooped down, his weapons blazing.

My city is burning. My First Skycaptain is hiding in a hole in the ground. I can't lose him too.

CHAPTER THIRTY-FIVE

HALCYON ADVANCED on trembling legs. Her sword wasn't glowing now. Only a slight pearly sheen attested to its power. To what it had just done to Malek.

That didn't make it harmless. No enemy was ever harmless.

Malek lay curled on the ground a few feet away. The weapon's energy had caught him in the arm, not the chest, but still knocked him back.

That near miss saved my life. Malek's own bitterness surprised him. Why should that matter? Years of victory in the pits meant countless close calls. And his enemy was wounded already.

Malek's wound didn't hurt. It didn't feel like anything at all. It hung from his shoulder, limp as the one hanging from Halcyon's wound. Only a tingle of sensation lingered in the joint. Not just numbness, but a sharp chill.

It worried him more than pain. Pain, he understood; one couldn't be a fighter in the pits and not get used to pain. This strange numbness was something else. He growled and tried to move the arm, and his shoulder twitched, a faint tremor the only hint of movement.

The roar of engines above him made him glance up. For a moment, he thought it might be Ania, diving down to look for Tanth in the blasted-open tunnels. But only one Skyknight flew like that.

"Damned fool," Malek muttered. He put out his uninjured arm to steady himself. "I don't need—"

A tall shape leapt from the silver craft anyway. A glitter of silver, his would-be rescuer beautiful even in war.

He didn't let himself savor it. *She's after me, Soran. This kill is mine.*

His sword lay on the ground in front of him, lightning still crackling over the blade. But without his hand to command it, it had already begun to fade. He kept a wary eye on his enemy and reached down with his good hand.

Halcyon's blade swept down toward him even as his fingers closed around the hilt. He raised his blade to meet the blow and turned it aside.

"Leave him!" called a familiar voice. A blaster buzzed. Its bolt shrieked and sped past him. Halcyon dropped to evade it, an exhausted mockery of a roll. But it worked. The blast passed by her, harmless.

Her soldiers cried out in fear and dismay and rushed toward Soran. *Good. You'll get them out of my way.*

Malek advanced, his blade flaring with light. Somewhere deep inside him, it felt wrong, holding it in the only hand he had left. But he'd fought so long in the pits that he'd grown used to injuries. If this one was strange, he could deal with the eerie feeling later.

Right now, he had to survive. Right now, he had to win.

Halcyon spat up at him and raised her blade.

"This isn't a fight," Malek told her. "Not anymore. This is—"

"My execution."

"Yes."

"And you take pride in it."

Not in the way you think. He brought down his blade. She countered with what fading strength remained to her. Lightning coursed from the point of impact. A faint gleam rose from Halcyon's blade, a last wisp of energy. But the lightning overwhelmed it. It enveloped not just her blade, but the hand that held it. She shuddered once, and her arm lowered.

Burning orange eyes glared up at Malek. Then, with a slow, deliberate movement, Halcyon arched her neck.

Malek blinked and raised his sword again. Blood and dirt spattered her armor, but her exposed neck was pristine. Altered and elegant, as if this battle hadn't touched it.

"You came here to die," he said. "Very well, then."

He brought down his blade.

"Another beheading." Soran's lip curled. "And you say you're more than a barbarian."

Malek smirked back at him. Blood stained his flight suit, and Malek doubted it was his. His chilled shoulder twitched, a stinging echo of sensation, as though his deadened muscles still ached to join the fight.

Soran leaned down to wipe his knife on the jacket of one of their fallen allies. One of the people from Ember City, Malek's symbol sprayed in silver on the cloth Soran was using to clean his blade. That meant he was angry. At the situation, or at Malek?

"You belong in the sky," Malek said. "Or did you abandon your tower after all?"

"All this fuss over you. Finding you, hunting you. For all I knew, you were dying."

Ah.

"I've won the greatest tournament in the pits for years running. Do you really think I was going to die in our first battle?"

Gray-carapaced soldiers rushed toward them, their cries cutting off Soran's reply.

Malek had only one arm to defend himself with. It would be best to face them now, before they took advantage of it. He rushed at them and sliced through two before they drew back, fearing his blade's bite. Another fell to one of Soran's daggers.

Some still approached, cautious, knowing it meant death for them to get too close. But most were wise enough to flee. Their leader had fallen already, and they would follow soon enough. They raced into a blasted tunnel.

Two soldiers fell to expert shots from above. Malek caught the glimmer of a golden reflection on a helmet. Its owner, his reconstructed legs still too delicate to leap, climbed down from a small hill of debris, still shooting. Malek's hand twitched around his blade. Without both arms, he couldn't hold his massive gun.

Don't come down, Kenn. Kenn could defend himself from high ground, but down here, in the middle of the maelstrom?

Malek growled at himself. Kenn was a victor. Kenn had chosen this war. Just like the others had. He risked his life now just like the others, with or without his lord's protection.

He looked at Soran and tilted his head toward a blasted tunnel. "If you're looking to go on a rescue mission, Seraph, others need it more than me."

Soran's too-blue eyes widened. "Tanth is—"

"—somewhere in there, yes. Vanguard hid him. But if they've breached the tunnel, that won't be enough."

Soran glanced up. "The tower." He tilted his head, listening. "They say it stands. For now."

"So they say. And that's enough for you?"

"Of course not."

"Then leave this to us. I've fought one-armed before."

Soran snarled. He looked at his fighter. Malek's gaze followed his. The sleek craft no longer gleamed, and a black line tore across one wing. Was that enough to keep a Skyknight down? He doubted it. And this was Soran, the Seraph. The fastest flyer, the best trained, the symbol of the city itself.

He raised an eyebrow and headed for the tunnel. Soran followed him.

Soran apparently took protecting Malek seriously. His blaster fire found anyone who tried to attack Malek from his numb side. Kenn skulked nearby, seeking out hidden alcoves and slipping from one to the next. People of the Below surrounded them, a wall of living bodies.

They passed the smashed center of a light globe, its innards still bright with eerie light. Kenn slipped ahead of them, his hands moving over the metal as if searching for something.

Finding it, he turned back to Malek. "Be careful," he said in an exaggerated version of the dialect of the pits. "We laid a trap here to protect the elders and anyone else who couldn't fight." He traced his fingers over the blasted wall again and ran them over a small groove.

Malek's lip quirked. *That's one of the symbols Vanguard uses to find his way.* Only now, it seemed, it was being put to a different use.

Kenn tilted his head. But whatever hidden clues his helmet showed him, Kenn wasn't projecting any holograms now. Which only made sense. If he projected anything now, enemies would see it too.

"Keep to the left," he whispered, still in dialect. Soran frowned, not understanding, and Malek whispered it to him. Soran echoed it in the ceremonial language of the Skyknights. But the people of the Below apparently understood Kenn already. They gave him indulgent little grins. Malek couldn't help but snicker.

The soldiers rushed in after them. The few defenders left on the far side of the trap engaged them, but there were far too few. The soldiers cut them down, cold and methodical, and red rage misted Malek's vision.

He'd known they would die, known many would. Some would have to, and he'd never hidden that from anyone. Least of all from himself. But seeing their blood stain the ground, knowing a trap already waited for them?

What a waste.

Then the trap took its revenge.

The ground fell away beneath their feet. It crumbled just like the towers above, as if the war in the skies had shaken even the tunnels below them.

Armored hands flailed for the edges of the pit. Most missed. The few soldiers who managed to grab hold lost their grip a moment later, their unlucky hands stung into letting go by expert shots from Kenn or his companions.

The trap opened on a profusion of spikes and jagged metal, jutting out from all directions. Some of it was humble, rusted scrap fallen or ripped from the walls and repurposed for a deadly snare. Some of it came from nobler sources, pieces of filigree fallen from the spires above. Some looked even more personal, small trinkets or rare treasures. Anything sharp enough to pierce, they'd installed here, repurposed for the defense of the city.

"That won't hold them all." Soran shot at the blood-spattered gray mass, already struggling to crawl its way back up.

"It will delay them," Malek returned. "That's all we need."

Kenn turned his head away. A gangly, pale-skinned man busied himself at the pipes, searching, as Kenn had been before. He grinned and slammed a hidden button with an exaggerated gesture. Then he whooped and laughed, apparently wanting to make sure no one missed his showing off.

Malek smirked. *Yes, you're the one who tripped it. You'll get to tell the others that, if you live.*

A bright light flared from the depths of the pit. Some of Malek's companions winced. Malek didn't. This was war, the war he'd wanted, and he couldn't be kind to his eyes.

He heard no cries of pain, no shrieks of dismay. *What exactly did they do?* Curious, Malek peered down. The makeshift spears and pikes glowed with energy, and even those soldiers who hadn't been pierced by the blades lay frozen.

"They are stunned," Kenn said, "but not for long."

Not for long. Malek glanced at his own shoulder, tried again to move it, felt the same chilled sensation as before, like someone had lodged a sharpened sliver of ice in the joint.

But a javelin of ice would hurt too. This still didn't. He snarled a curse in dialect. "Let's get moving."

Those lucky enough to avoid the trap were already easing their way along the tunnel. They clung to the walls for support, inching their way toward the defenders.

The globes hanging from the ceilings were whole here, eerily untouched by the ravages of battle. An elder ran out to meet Malek, his bronzed skin gnarled and wrinkled. "Malek! We didn't expect to see you, but of course we are pleased—"

"Don't be." Soran cut him off. "Malek is injured. And we've brought company."

The man's face fell. "My Seraph," he began, with an awkward bow.

"Save it."

"We heard that the Destroyer killed Halcyon. They'll run now, without her to lead them."

"She was an assassin before she was a commander. Some of them will run. I'm sure some already have. But these are the Senate's people.

Masses and gangs. This body will still move without its head."

Malek caught the familiar silver glimmer of the end of Vanguard's cane. "Then they're coming," he said, stepping out from the shadows of the tunnel.

"Get back inside," Malek growled. "You and the First Skycaptain both. They're already here."

The elders whispered to each other. The fittest, best-armed, and most determined poured out to guard their hidden place.

"They won't get past us," said one young woman, her voice the soft, high voice of a girl.

"The trap didn't catch all of them. And killed fewer than that," Malek answered. "Where is First Skycaptain Tanth?"

"Inside," said an elder. "With the medics." He cast a pointed glance at Malek's arm. "Where you should be."

Malek gripped his sword tighter. "The nerves need mending. Reconstructing, perhaps. Halcyon's weapon was powerful."

"My Lord, let them look," said someone else, an ash-rubbed version of Malek's symbol smeared on his face. "In the Belt, we have our own ways of healing. They should have their own too."

Malek favored the man with a grim smile. "Very well."

But their company, it seemed, had arrived.

Chapter Thirty-Six

Soran watched Malek emerge from the tunnel, and glared at Malek's useless arm. A small bandage on his shoulder testified to some kind of injection. Could they really do something for that wound down here? Kenn's little trap could only stun. Whatever Halcyon had done would last longer.

Malek turned to one of his victors and tilted his head toward the gun on his back. "Take this. I can't use it with one hand. And you'll only have one shot before the enemy gets too close. If you fire once they do, you'll blast the tunnel with it."

Soran's scowl deepened. Watching Malek wield that weapon before had made heat crackle underneath his skin. Now Malek's arm hung dead from his shoulder, and someone else was hefting the weapon off his back. A big man, a well-muscled victor with bronze skin and dark hair, his armor scratched and scuffed and stained with dirt and blood.

Soran might have found him attractive too, before this little war. But not now. Not watching him lift the gun off Malek's back with the kind of slow reverence more suited to a temple than a battlefield.

Sycophant.

Malek watched the man take aim. Then he nodded, apparently satisfied, and slipped away. A pale-skinned and gray-haired woman from the Below trailed after him. She wore an elder's shawl. A healer, Soran supposed, and frowned. Could a random old woman really heal a wound like that, made by a powerful weapon the people here had likely never even seen before?

He looked back at the victor with the gun, not feeling much more confident about him either. He would be lucky if he got off one shot with it.

Halcyon's minions came on. Far fewer than there had been before, but they came on. Soran snickered. They'd never take the City now. They didn't have the numbers. *All these dramatics. Crawling over the dirt just so you can die here.*

Near him, Kenn had climbed onto a makeshift hill of pipes and twisted metal. One shot blasted an enemy visor to shards. The next took care of his exposed head.

At least someone here has style.

The low hum of the weapon reverberated around him. The gathering energy rumbled under him, vibrating his bones.

The white pulse filled his vision. It swallowed up the men and women coming for them in scouring light. Soran couldn't see it well, not so close to the beam. He couldn't see them die, but down here he could hear it: the sizzle of burnt flesh, charred into ash. The beginnings of screams, and the distortion that ended them. The ring of energy bursting outward from the devastation.

It was beautiful and terrible, and all Soran could think was *That weapon belongs in better hands than yours.*

But he didn't have long to dwell on his revulsion. Not all of their enemies had died in the beam. Those who didn't rushed onward, their cries of challenge less eager than desperate. Some of the fighters bore the scars of Kenn's little pit, bloodied holes in their armor or bits of filigree still stuck in the chinks.

But for all that, they didn't turn back. And the great city around them was burning. Soran gritted his teeth

"Those who cannot fight, get inside!" Malek cried. The elders took up the cry and slipped into their own little hiding places, clutching guns or sticks. Or makeshift blades they'd twisted out of the bones of their own city.

Soran's keen eyes caught the flash of Malek's blade as the energy roared to life around its surface. Its tang filled the air around him. He stepped back. Better to let Malek handle the ones closing in on them when all he had was a blaster and a few knives.

But he could fire into them. One of the soldiers, either fearful of Malek's bright blade or just clever enough to avoid it, rushed at Malek's dead side. Soran shot a bolt of energy into a raw, exposed place where some sharp weapon had torn a hole in her armor. She snarled in rage and pain and fell back, clutching at the wound.

Emboldened, he shot at a few others. Someone lunged at him, but he darted out of the way with a Skyknight's agility, and one of Kenn's unerring blasts felled his attacker before he had a chance to do it himself.

Malek's blade flashed beside him, a flare of deadly lightning. A crowd of soldiers, big and brawny, rushed them all at once, and he blasted the visor off one only to twist away from a blade wielded by another.

They crashed into a line of victors and people from the Belt, brawn against brawn, the kind of thudding sound that would have sent a flare of heat through Soran's breast if he hadn't been down on the ground in the thick of it.

"They're breaking through!" one of the people of the Below called, his voice old and crackling. Soran winced. Even an elderly Skyknight would never let himself come to sound like that.

Malek's sword was a bolt of striking lightning. He couldn't focus on Malek now, but he could see the light, a bright spear to cleanse his city and purge it of its invaders. One of his little minions, a pale-skinned woman, had attached herself to his weak side.

One of the twins? Soran wondered. A hot spike of jealousy flared through his blood.

He willed himself not to look, shot some lumbering brute in the back, and slipped into the tunnel where Tanth and the others lay hidden.

He peeked into the entrance and caught sight of Tanth, the elder who'd served as the medic, and Vanguard.

"First Skycaptain," he said. "Are you well?"

Tanth rose to his feet with stiff, jerky movements. "Well enough."

Soran frowned. A Skyknight's agility was his greatest asset in close combat. Without it—

"Can you fight?" he asked, his voice curt.

"We can all fight," Vanguard said. His slender fingers gripped the hilt of an ornate, well-made knife that must have been crafted above. A Skyknight's weapon, sharpened and polished and gleaming.

"You're not afraid," Soran marveled.

"I've been afraid since they came after Malek, my Seraph." Vanguard answered, his voice soft. "But I was born for my city's defense. What happened to my eyes didn't change that. If I have to fight, I will."

"They are contained."

The voice should have been Tanth's. But Tanth was down here with him.

Failing that, it should have been Ania's. But Ania was somewhere in the sky above him, tearing open the tunnels with laser fire.

Soran looked up. He couldn't help it. "Then this is the last of them?"

"Yes, Seraph. There's still fighting on the ground. But no more are coming into the city."

"No more," he repeated, as if he could make himself believe it.

It seemed every time Soran shot one, another sprang up to take its place. Whatever he'd thought about his knife before, he'd drawn it now, just to have something in his other hand when they got too close.

That's how the Senate plans to beat us. Sheer numbers. Cannon fodder. He thought of Malek's speeches, all that flowery nonsense about those he deemed worthy. *What good is worth when they have thousands of bodies to throw at us?*

From somewhere above him came the shriek of a Skyknight's engines and a rain of orange flame.

He could see a crack of light in the tunnel above. He threw himself to the floor and curled up against a rain of dust. He knew before he looked up which insignia he'd see painted on the side of the craft. "Skycaptain Ania!"

"My Seraph. I will find them."

Soran scrambled to his feet, kept a wary eye on the others around him. Harsh-eyed men and women, probably from Ember City, formed a ring around him. *Protecting their ally.* It almost made him laugh.

"Skycaptain Ania," he said. "You have found them. And us."

"This tunnel—"

"Tanth and the elders are inside. If you keep blasting it open, you're as likely to hit him as the fools attacking us. Or our blind friend from the Below. Or their elders. Or me."

"Understood." Her voice was grim, the old laugh gone. He heard the whine of her weapons energizing again, saw the light from her weapons array, a dim glow through the smoke.

But he couldn't watch, not here, not now. Not when an armored man was barreling toward one of the elders, a slim woman whose pale face and once-bright shawl were covered in ash. Soran took aim and fired, but his shot hit the man's thick armor.

The man shoved her aside. Soran heard a sickening crunch and a cry.

In the corner of his eye, he caught the light-flash of Malek's lightning blade again. Too late, perhaps, for the elder. But Malek's sword cleaved two of the attackers, wrong arm or no.

The frail and the weak huddled in what darkness the last of the tunnel had left to them. Knives flashed in their hands, some crafted weapons, some crude shards of their own pipes and tunnel they had lashed together with wires and twine.

Some threw debris. Rocks, fragments of tile, twisted pieces of scrap that once had been filigree. A brown-skinned man, his hair as gray as the dust that covered it, hefted up a chunk of metal almost as big as his torso and flung it at the head of a soldier about to shoot at one of the twins.

And everywhere he heard their whispers.

He would have thought Malek would give most of the commands. But Malek's commands weren't the only ones. Even Soran's weren't. All around him, he heard the people of the Below, their voices soft: "Attack there." "Leave this one be." "Protect the elder." Words passed from one to the other, a chain of demands and advice.

Who were they coming from? If it wasn't Malek, and it wasn't Soran himself, and Vareth and her followers were still outside, then—

"Vanguard!" called a voice, calm and even, but taut with urgency all the same.

So Ania isn't the only one on a rescue mission. Soran turned toward the glint of light on a silver helmet and a golden visor, dusted with soot and dirt but otherwise undamaged.

"Where is Vanguard?" Kenn called again.

Where is Tanth?

Then Soran realized he hadn't just been thinking it, he'd heard someone say it. He looked up.

Ania stood in the blasted entrance to the hall, her hair hanging down and loose, the ribbons she always wore in it tangled remnants of torn gold.

"Where is Tanth?" she demanded again.

CHAPTER THIRTY-SEVEN

MALEK'S ARM tingled.

A good sign. But not good enough. If he couldn't use his arm again, it was just a distraction. An uncomfortable sensation that would only get in the way. And his enemies were still hunting him. Either the Senate had trained it all into them, or they had nothing left but killing.

He understood it. The City itself was their enemy, and if they couldn't kill Malek, anyone else would do. He'd felt it himself, in this very battle. He'd wanted to kill Halcyon, of course. But she wasn't the one he wanted, not really. She was only a proxy, just like her hapless minions. But the Senate holed itself up in the capital, and if he couldn't reach them, their foot soldiers would have to do.

And everywhere he did the dirty work of killing them, people followed him. Victors, people of the Belt, defenders from both above and Below. Elders looked up at him as they crawled out of corners they'd crouched in and clutched weapons with their trembling hands, as if he'd become a hero.

He snickered. If they saw him as a savior, they were foolish. Ania was saving just as many of them. More, probably, now that Malek's one arm could do nothing but sting.

But the people Ania saved looked at her with wide, fearful eyes. She cared only for the man she hoped to find, and would destroy anyone who got in her way. And although they owed her their lives, they knew it.

"Where is he?" she demanded of the very people who would have been hunted and killed without her to rescue them.

Malek frowned.

There were no more coming in, so Soran said. And so it looked. There were no more waves, no more endless ranks on ranks. Many of them had already been wounded, speared by Kenn's pit, seared by blaster fire, or struck by rock and pike and spear and blade. But Malek had been right when he'd called them desperate.

One of his victors ran forward. He saw the black blur of her tattoos against too-exposed light skin and smirked. She stopped in the middle of the blasted tunnel, too-pretty lips drawn back in a snarl of challenge.

He hadn't gone to her in a long time. Hadn't wanted her. Not with Soran a constant heat in his blood. But looking at her now, her skin decorated and clean in the midst of battle, Kiara was still beautiful.

She didn't look helpless, not to Malek. But their enemies, as gullible as new fighters in the pits, saw only an easy mark. She killed three before anyone even saw the flare of the force field's light.

Her painted skin flickered, the bolts of energy flaring and dying against it. She laughed, held out her arms, and threw back her head.

Malek's lip quirked. The picture of invincibility she'd always been in the pits, her power inked on her untouchable skin, shown off to men and women who were fighting their last.

But she couldn't absorb their fire forever. She shot another, kicked out at a third, then retreated into those very shadows herself to give her field time to recharge and blast anyone who got too close.

Some of the soldiers rushed after her. Most fell to Soran, to the twins, to Malek. To Ania, who ran on, still searching.

The others converged on Malek. He was their target, their nemesis, the doom of their commander. And he was injured. His allies rushed in to protect him and made a ragged, protective ring around his injured side. Anyone who came on from the other side would fall to his blade.

But Malek wasn't the only one here who needed protection.

Blaster fire blazed from a dark corner, but the soldiers who'd made it past Malek's dance of death—or the shield of men and women around him—weren't letting it stop them. It flickered out against armor, harmless as a display of light.

Malek saw a flash of movement. A blade's edge, flashing from the shadows, its movements aimless and desperate.

Tanth? He dashed away from his protective cocoon, concerned. Tanth had been injured, but he knew how to fight. He wouldn't miss like that. And he'd have a blaster, at the very least.

But when his eyes adjusted to the shadows, he saw not Tanth, but Vanguard. Vanguard crouched down, huddled in a corner, and struck out at his attackers with a small blade. Groping for a weak point he could not see.

Malek tensed, ready to spring. He heard a choked little gasp from the soldier Vanguard was fighting. Perhaps Vanguard had been lucky, after all.

Someone darted past him. There was something off in the movement, but urgency lent the figure speed. Malek saw a gleam of light off its helmet, and heard a familiar voice, its usual calm tone laced with worry. "Vanguard!"

A blast from Kenn's weapon aimed at a crack in the armor on a soldier's back. It widened, and Malek saw the woman shudder.

Kenn fired again, calm and precise as ever. His foe crumpled to the ground. Kenn's plum-dark lip curled, and Malek saw the white of his teeth. He shot again.

"That's enough," said one of the big victors. He shoved the soldier's lifeless body aside. Vanguard crouched in the corner, the weapon still clutched in his hand.

"Are you all right?" Kenn asked.

"I am," Vanguard said, and stood. Blood splattered his blue shawl.

He turned toward the sound of Kenn's voice. "But I'm sure I wouldn't have been if you hadn't come. It's not easy to fight someone who can see you when you can't see them."

Kenn nodded once and glanced over at the fallen soldier. "You did well enough."

"We'll have more to do than gloat down here," Soran snarled, glancing up at the sky and then at Ania, reproach in his too-bright eyes.

But you did the same thing he did, Seraph. You came down here too.

But this was no time to argue with Soran. A bright blast whizzed past them, a slim bolt from a delicate weapon. That hadn't come from a victor's blaster.

That was a Skyknight.

But Soran lurked just off to his side, just far away enough to pretend he didn't want to protect Malek.

Ania, he thought at first. But those blasts couldn't have been hers. She would never have let them drive her into a corner like that, not when she'd come here to deal death to the ones who had chased the First Skycaptain to the ground.

Tanth.

A group of soldiers were converging on his little corner. Malek growled a challenge to distract them and swept out with his blade. He cleaved an enemy through a chink in the armor at his neck. His blade's energy had faded, the lightning a thin crackle now, but blood poured from the wound he'd left.

He whirled around and the others stepped back, wary.

"People of the Below!" Vanguard called, his voice high and clear. "Defend the First Skycaptain!"

They surged through the corridor, threw their stones, brandished their makeshift blades. Some leapt at the armored bodies just as Kenn had. Unaltered fingers, gnarled by age and hard life down in the Below, dug into the spaces between armor plates, ripped and tore.

Someone ripped an armor plate clean off of one soldier, the fabric beneath as vulnerable as skin. By the time Kenn aimed, his helmet down and his precision inhuman, they'd moved on to another, and another.

And through it all wove Ania, a blaster in one hand and a blade in the other, making her way to the side of her First Skycaptain. Quick glimpses of blue fabric, and moving trails of blaster fire, told Malek that Tanth was moving too, slipping between the big bodies pushing to get to him.

To Malek, it was beautiful. As beautiful as any victor he'd watched in the early tournaments, his heart hammering in his chest, beating with fierce, possessive pride.

But they were closing in.

Malek lunged. His blade tore through another soldier's back. Ania glanced back at him and nodded, her too-blue eyes bright.

You're welcome.

Two more soldiers fell to Soran. A prince's vengeance for his shattered City.

But Halcyon's little minions had heard Vanguard's order. And any of them could see Tanth's sculpted body, his trained poise. Even if they didn't recognize the First Skycaptain down here in a tunnel, making his last stand, they had eyes. They could see how valuable this man was to the defenders.

And a Skyknight's bones were fragile as a bird's.

"We've got you!" called Tena. She and Tor rushed from their place at Malek's side to Tanth's defense.

"No. We do," came a voice, harsh and forbidding. Its source, a soldier, tilted his head, and the enemy converged.

With a blue blur of movement, Tanth tried to shift aside. But Malek knew even before he moved that there were too many. The graceful bird, its back already broken, was hemmed in on all sides.

Soran shrieked a protest, and another throat took it up.

"Tanth!" Ania cried. "I'm coming for you! Just hold on!"

Tanth. Not First Skycaptain.

Ania blasted her way between them. Blood poured from a throat her blade slit, and she whirled to face another, and another, and another.

Malek followed, engaging the few who hung back. But he was not the threat now. He was only the lurking death that took any the deadly Skyknight missed, her golden ribbons and long hair dripping with her enemies' blood.

"Ania! I can't!"

"Tanth!"

The soldiers only moved closer, closing the gaps between them.

Ania raised her blade in challenge. "He's not yours."

Soran looked over at Malek. The twins looked up too, a question in their hazel eyes, and Kiara, her force field recharged now, peeked out of the shadows.

Malek held Soran's gaze. *Wait.*

Ania lunged for the soldier, her blade flashing, her lips pulled back in a grotesque snarl.

"Now!" Malek cried, and surged forward with the others. His blade sliced through two, with a storm's blaze of lightning. At his side, Kiara was a tattooed blur, her force field bright. And on the other side stood Soran, his red-brown hair a swirl of color, his movement too fast for Malek to see.

When his own blade's light cleared from his vision, Ania stood over a decapitated body. Her blue-dyed eyes, darker than Soran's, glittered with cold light.

Tanth stood in the corner, his back still eerily ramrod straight. His gaze was steady, but his breathing labored, and the hand that held the blaster twitched.

"No!" cried a woman's voice. A soldier's visored head tilted down to stare at the body, then up to fix on her comrade's killer.

But she didn't lunge for Ania. She lunged for Tanth.

Tanth whirled around as quickly as his body would let him. But despite his alterations, it wasn't fast enough.

She collided with him and he crumpled beneath her. Malek lunged forward even as they fell.

Skyknight-agile and uninjured, Soran was faster. The bolt of light from his blaster flared over her armor, widening a crack in it. Pink flesh peeked from the breach, already singed by Soran's blast.

"Get away from him!" snarled a voice, cold with rage and hatred.

Ania leapt at Tanth's attacker and shoved her off Tanth's motionless body. They tumbled together on the ground, and Malek caught sight of a bloodstained blade in her hand.

She drove it deep into the crack Soran had made, an artless, desperate motion. Blood gushed from the wound, but she only drove it in deeper, snarling a curse in the high language of the Skyknights. A wail came from the woman, and then a gurgling cry, and then silence.

Ania lifted herself up. The gray-carapaced soldiers stepped back.

But whatever fear they'd found wouldn't save their lives. Malek's sword crackled with its eagerness to end them, and all around his allies advanced.

When the lightning cleared and the last body fell, Ania stood smeared with blood. She stared ahead, her eyes glazed over with rage, her hand still clutching her knife, as though she expected new enemies to spring forth from all sides.

Or hoped they would. Malek had seen that look before, in the pits. The look of someone who had lost everything, and whose only refuge was destruction. Someone who had lost herself in it, and wasn't sure how to come back once the enemy was gone.

"They're all dead," said Soran, his voice quieter than Malek had ever heard it.

CHAPTER THIRTY-EIGHT

ANIA RUSHED to Tanth's side. So did the elder in the medic's shawl, and so did Soran.

Men and women crowded around him. Hands held him up so the medic could examine him. The gnarled, tough hands of the forgotten. Soran winced.

And somewhere deep in him, something seethed, red-hot and molten. *After all this. All Malek's talk of the unworthy. This infiltration, this infestation.*

After so many towers, blackened and charred and fallen to the ground.

Now it was Tanth who was broken. His wheezing breaths filled the silence.

Silence, after so much fighting. Silence worse than the cries of the soldiers, the thudding explosions of the fire from the launchers, the crumbling of the towers.

He didn't have to guess what the medic had to say. Not with that sound echoing in his ears. Not with the blue fabric of Tanth's flight suit stained a deep purple with too much of his blood.

He lay at an awkward angle, propped up by many hands. Soran seethed at that too. More desecration. More defilement, when his First Skycaptain was so badly injured. What had broken when the soldier woman had collided with him?

Under the red fire of his rage he was cold again. So cold.

What does it matter if they touch him? The thought was bitter acid in his mind. If these people—these wretched people, battered by life, without even alterations to spare them its worst—hoped to do anything for that wound, they'd have to bring him back up.

To get him to one of the towers, where he belonged.

One that still stood, anyway. Soran's stomach turned.

The medic laid a hand on his shoulder. Gentle. Careful. He sprang back as if burned.

"Seraph," she said, pulling her hand away. "I can't—"

But before Soran could shove her away, Ania's shriek split the air, and even Soran went still.

She wrapped her hands around Tanth's face and slapped his cheeks to revive him. "Tanth! Tanth, please..."

His eyes cracked open, their altered blue gem-bright. "Ania—"

An engine roared overhead, and Tanth's neck craned to follow it.

"No," Ania said again, her voice choked. "I'm here. I'm right here."

The medic bustled around him. But all she did was press a needle into his arm. His eyes widened, and he took in the sight of Ania in front of him.

"Ania," he said, his voice clear with the energy the injection had imparted. "You came for me."

"Always." She lowered her head, tears pooling in her eyes. His arm reached out, shaky and slow, to wrap around her slim frame.

"The City needs you," he said. "Go defend it."

His head tilted toward Soran. "And you too. The Seraph should be in the sky." He cast a pointed glance at Malek.

"He should be," Malek agreed. "And I should be defending the City as well." His injured shoulder twitched, a first hint of movement.

You look like a fool, pit fighter.

But the mockery didn't make him feel any better. Instead, he watched Malek's arm with mounting anger. *Useless. Worthless.*

That cold chill, deep inside him. A frozen core at the center of his fire.

You.

You came here. You brought this with you.

Death. Destruction. Devastation.

He wrenched his gaze away. Toward the door to the tunnel, and his starfighter beyond it. Toward the freedom it offered. Somewhere in the distance, a Skyknight's engines shrieked, and something inside him howled with it.

I should be in the sky.

Tanth's hand slipped, sliding down Ania's shoulder. "Ania..."

She leaned closer. Her face, streaked with tears now, hovered close to his. His lips moved, but all Soran heard was his soft breath. Ania—still a Skyknight, still a warrior, even here—gave a strangled sob and pressed her lips to his.

His hand clenched again, tightening around her arm. Then it slipped again, fell to his side, and was still.

Ania stepped out of his embrace, her eyes wide, her cheeks wet with tears.

"Seraph," she choked, wiping the tears away with the back of her hand. She blinked, and when she stared up at him again, her lips were pressed together in a grim line.

"Skycaptain," he said. First Skycaptain, now. But that could wait. "We have a city to defend."

"We do."

"Go then." Malek's voice, from somewhere behind him. Somewhere impossibly far away.

He listened to the shriek inside him and whirled around, his lips drawn back in a snarl. He was cold, so cold, and he wanted Malek to feel the same. "This matter is ours, Destroyer."

Malek didn't gainsay him. That only made it worse, a white-hot curl of rage over an even deeper chill.

"If any are left here on the ground, they are already dead," Malek was saying. His blade glowed, the lightning running hungry over it.

Some part of him, some old part, some part he'd forgotten, smiled. A *Destroyer's reckoning.* It would be violent. It would be bloody. Not one of his City's invaders would be spared. "Very well. You owe us that much."

Under pitch-black and empty eyes, Malek's lips curled into a smile that matched his own.

But Ania wasn't so easily soothed. She stared directly into his dark-dyed eyes, and then spat in his face.

"They came after you," she snarled, and turned away.

Being in the sky again soothed him.

Not enough, no.

The grief and rage still lurked inside him, a hard, cold center beneath a whirling flame.

But for now, there was only flight.

His craft hadn't been damaged, not seriously. And the Below had its mechanics, who had done a fine if ugly job of repairing the small tear in his wing. He raced toward the tower, his engines humming, only the slightest hint of wobbling keeping his flight from being perfectly smooth.

Ania raced after him, the shriek of her engines a constant companion. The air crackled with their weapons, fully fed with energy and eager to take their vengeance.

"Seraph," said the too-young captain over his link. "Skycaptain."

Soran heard Ania's sharp intake of breath. *He doesn't know. But she knows.*

"The tower," Soran prompted. This battle gave him something to do. Something to focus on. Something to think about, besides the flame and the chill.

"It stands. But their starfighters are still flying."

Then there were more coming, after all.

"They shot some of us down already, and are keeping most of us away. They're fanning out their fire, so that we can't get close enough. And they still have a few tanks. Worse, they've wrested a few launchers away from Vareth and her followers."

Soran snickered. Had Vareth finally made a mistake? "Malek is coming, and has others with him. They'll take care of that, I'm sure. As for the rest—"

"—we'll handle it," Ania finished for him. She raced ahead. He gunned his engines and matched her, then slipped ahead. He was the Seraph, after all.

The tower rose above them, still tall, still proud. But the black line he'd seen before marred one side, gaping and charred. It wasn't burning or melting now, but the black twisted scar the blasts had left looked almost worse now than then.

A scar on the face of the City. Even if they repaired it and polished it until it gleamed, Soran would remember. His people would remember. No matter how well his builders might hide the marks of the new welds, they would be there. He would see them, and he would know.

And they would remind him of all this. Of a dark tunnel, where his best fighter had huddled, and hidden, and died. Soran gnashed his teeth and growled.

The starfighters had been scattered. But the faraway ones had made it here at last. Skyknights dove in to harry them and dashed out again, streaks of silver bright against their bulk. The starfighters drifted, trying to converge on the tower, but with the Skyknights circling, they could get no closer. White bolts of energy fanned out from their weapons systems, but by now the Skyknights knew the pattern of their fire, and evaded it with practiced grace.

"I'm on the left one," said Ania. "My Wings, you're with me. No questions. No hesitation. We bring it down."

The Skycaptains whose squads Ania had led cheered over the link. The sound stung Soran's altered ears.

"My Wings, follow me," Soran returned.

"Understood," came a voice. Then, after a moment, with a quaver only Soran's modified hearing might pick up. "The First Skycaptain?"

Soran waited for Ania, but her end of the line stayed silent.

"He was slain," Soran said at last. "Those wretches chased him down into the Below, hunted him, and killed him."

Gasps and cries filled the communication line. Wails of grief that became snatches of a mourning song.

When this was over, the Skyknights would sing it for their fallen captain.

"Chased him down into the Below," someone whispered. A place few Skyknights would expect to visit in their lives.

Much less die in.

"Stop talking and start fighting," came Ania's voice, hard and cold. "I have revenge to take."

The wail of their engines drowned out their replies. A shriek of despair and a roar of challenge all at once, their fighters saying what their mouths couldn't express. Soran gunned the throttle and added his craft's voice to the chorus.

He rocketed away from Ania, trusting to her rage, and dodged a blast from one of the launchers. *Do you really think that's going to stop me? Now?*

His Skyknights scattered to avoid the blast but regrouped almost as quickly. He watched their firetear red-hot wounds in the craft's hull, bit his lip, and sped toward it, tasting blood.

His blaster fire widened the wound. He saw twisted metal, torn cables, and finally light.

He smirked. Somewhere to his side he could see the one Ania had targeted, tumbling from the sky with a spray of aimless weapons fire. It caught a Skyknight in its wild path.

Soran couldn't let himself pay too much attention. The starfighter he'd targeted was damaged, but its weapons systems blazed to life.

"Target the cells!" Soran called. "Overload them before they can shoot at us!" He laughed over the link even as they flew off to obey. "We'll get out. If we're quick enough."

He raced toward the energy cells, keeping himself in the center of the group. He fired first, the impact an eruption of light that stung his eyes. He turned, sharp, and rocketed skyward, not waiting around to see what he'd wrought.

A moment later he heard the crackle of the other Skyknights' shots. So much heat and ozone filling the air that he could taste its tang even after darting away. And after the lightning came the thunder, the thudding boom of the enemy starfighter tearing itself apart. The light below him filled his vision, and the smoke rose to cloud it a moment later.

"One down!" Soran called. Death for death, destruction for destruction.

"I was about to say the same thing," Ania said over the link. "But it looks like this one will take a bit lon—"

Or not. Light flared in Soran's vision again. *And that makes two.* The fire inside him curled and wheeled, a wild consuming heat that drove away the worst of the chill.

For the moment, anyway.

He turned in a wide arc, trying to escape the thick smoke and get a better view of both his tower and the last of the starfighters menacing it.

He saw the fanning pattern of white light first, flickering against the clouds of smoke like a distant, gathering storm. Then he caught a glimpse of the starfighter's bulk. It had taken advantage of the Skyknights fighting with his brothers, and hovered just in front of the tower, too close, too close, its weapons perfectly aligned with its fragile target.

No!

But it was Ania who said what he was thinking. "Not again," she whispered, barely audible over the communication link.

This city isn't yours.

He called out the order to attack in the kind of voice Malek would use. But they were speeding toward their enemy the moment they heard his engines' cry and saw his thrusters flare.

There was no subtlety in this, no strategy, no careful maneuvers of the elegant and elegantly trained. There was only the flare of every laser from every craft left flying the skies above Aerix, all converging on one point.

The starfighter's weapons brightened too, a last desperate effort to take down the towerbefore it fell.

It didn't stand a chance.

It burst where it hovered, a blazing explosion, the white, charging weapons arrays the center of the ball of flame. A blossom of red fire spread out into the sky.

His rage, turned outward. Consuming, destroying. Leaving nothing but the empty chill that filled him.

So this is vengeance.

CHAPTER THIRTY-NINE

MALEK LOOKED up from the bloody body of a soldier. The flower of fire in the sky was fading now.

He smiled. *The last of your enemies. And the last of mine.*

Vareth and Dia had gone ahead, hunting for the few soldiers who still manned their launchers and their tanks, stubborn and alone. Their enemies wouldn't down any Skyknights now. He chuckled, a grim laugh.

Sweat and blood slicked his good arm, and blood stained his sword blade as well. He'd spent its energy for the moment, but he didn't care much about recharging it now. They'd all but won. Many of the stragglers they'd found had been injured already.

More than a few had asked for death at Malek's hand. Apparently the Destroyer was a legend to them now, too. The corner of his mouth twisted in a grim smile. A legend like that could only serve his ends.

Victory. Within their grasp. Malek forced himself to think of that, willed away the image of Ania, leaning down to kiss a dying man. Of Tanth's hand, tightening around her arm and then falling to his side...

He shut his eyes against the memory. *Every victory has its price. And every victory's price is worth paying.*

But the queasy feeling in his gut lingered, somewhere beneath the budding exultation.

"Is it over?" A young woman's voice pulled him from his thoughts. She raised a hand, dark brown and too gnarled for one so young.

"It will be," said someone else, before Malek could recover himself enough to answer. He bore a crudely painted version of Malek's symbol on his chest nearly obscured by ash and blood. "As soon as Dia and Vareth get back, there won't be any of them left."

Malek chuckled. Pride rose in his breast again, fierce and warm. He hoped it would be enough.

"The towers are still standing," another woman agreed. "Even with the launchers and a few tanks, what can they do? They have no starfighters now." She puffed out her chest. "And we have Skyknights."

Malek looked at her: slender, unaltered. She would never reach those towers herself – would only see them from the ground. They were not for her, and yet she still believed in what they stood for.

He turned, hearing footsteps. Vareth and Dia trudged toward them, bloodied and smiling. Behind them rumbled a tank, but it made no threatening moves. The windows rolled down, and the twins saluted, formal to the last.

"My Lord," Vareth said, pressing a dark fist to her chest in respect and homage. "The launchers are ours now. The Skyknights went after the tanks once the last starfighter fell."

"There's no one here but us and the dead," Dia agreed.

"Then that's the last of them," Malek said.

He looked at Dia, a strange thought compelling him. "Your pikeman?"

"My Lord?"

"A young man. One you brought with you from Ember City. He had one of Zarel's pikes, and guarded the tunnel behind us."

Vareth nodded and hummed, a low, sad sound that told Malek what she was about to say. "He fell defending the tunnel."

Malek closed his eyes and lowered his head. Would he have been a victor, before the time of war?

It didn't matter. It shouldn't matter. Malek had known the risk when he'd begun all this. And the pikeman had known when he chose to become a part of it.

He wasn't the first to die. And the Skyknights had lost far more.

But he growled in answer, and kept his eyes shut for a long moment. When he opened them again, he asked, "Did you retrieve the weapon?"

"I did."

"Give it to someone else from Ember City. It should belong to one of them."

Dia nodded. The edge of her lip twitched in a wry smile.

Malek cleared his throat and willed thoughts of death out of his mind. *Every victory's price is worth paying.* He opened his link to Soran. "Seraph. You saved your tower, it would seem."

Laughter over the line. "It's standing. Damaged, but standing."

"And that explosion was the last of your enemies? We're finished here. The hostiles on the ground have either died or fled."

"They won't get far if they did," Dia said.

"The battle is over," Malek agreed. "But Aerix will take time to rebuild. And Aerix is only one city. If the Senate attacked Ember City too, the rest of our world will feel their wrath soon enough."

"We'll be ready for them," said a familiar voice. Malek turned to see Vanguard, escorted by Kenn.

"The rebuilding of Aerix comes first," Malek said, his voice grim.

Malek looked out over Aerix from a window in the Seraph's tower.

He should have done it sooner. He should have done it long before all this. He'd dreamed of it, long years ago, when he'd first pored over the information he'd gleaned from Delen. When the old poems and ancient tales had first sung to him of war.

He'd been here once before, meeting and planning and thinking. But that hadn't given him much time to stare, and Soran would have gloated too much if he had. The brute, the rube, dazzled by the beautiful City. He snickered at himself, thinking of it.

And at Soran, who stood beside him now, his slim fingers curled around the filigree of the window, a grip tight enough to dent it.

Malek's eyes had grown used to the light. But below him lay a ruin, the gilded towers broken, their splintered remains barely touching the clouds, their tops fallen to the bloodstained ground.

He shook his head. He'd known what might happen when this all began. He'd never hidden it from his victors, or from the men and women who followed them. For all their planning, all their hope, all their need for this alliance, Aerix might have fallen in the end.

Malek hadn't expected it, of course. This world needed this war, like a plant tucked away in some greenhouse needed water. And sometimes only blood could nourish dead soil.

He'd hoped for exultation, but he'd always planned to settle for rebirth.

But Soran—

He willed away the thought. They'd driven back the enemy, and now he had as much right to stand here as Soran did. Now the City below him, battered as it was, stood as the first victory in his war.

And Soran stood beside him. They'd done this together, and he could feel Soran's nearness. The first stirrings of heat curled through his flesh.

But under it all lay something dark and cold, something all his reminders of victory hadn't been able to quell. He hadn't known Tanth, not as well as he should have, but the First Skycaptain of Aerix was a priceless jewel. And Tanth had bested Vareth. The mightiest of his warriors, and the best of his advisors.

And then there was Vanguard and the people of the Below. Malek and his victors understood them, of course. But most Skyknights never would have, because most Skyknights didn't have to.

But Tanth had understood everything. Malek closed his eyes, sucked in a long, shaky breath, and looked out over the devastation again.

Some towers still stood, but most had fallen, from the outer city to the inner. The ones that remained rose up from the rubble of their sisters, like the last men and women standing after some grim contest. Above it all the smoke of war still rose, a shroud over the devastation and a veil for the dead.

The sight reminded Malek of his pits, of the smog over the skies of Dis. But he could not have said that to the man standing beside him.

He turned away from the window. "You've won, Seraph of Aerix."

You rather than *we*: an appeal to Soran's pride. He would need it now, given what he'd lost.

Soran slid his fingers from the metal and edged closer. Malek risked the beginnings of a grin.

But when Soran opened his mouth, the words he spat at Malek weren't words of celebration. "You cost me half my city, King of the Barbarians. And the best of my Skyknights." His altered eyes shone, a shock of blue against the gray that had swallowed the City. "Even this tower. If we'd chosen some other room, the ceiling might fall in on us where we stood."

"And yet your city stands," Malek returned, fighting to keep his voice even. They couldn't stop now. Soran had to see it. "And yet this tower rises up to spear the sky. And to show your enemies they cannot crush you."

Soran's lip curled. "Easy for you to say. You've lost no one."

"I never promised this war would come without a price."

"A price? That's all you have to say? This defilement, this destruction. This City, untouched until you, and all you can say is 'a price?'"

"Soran, I—"

"Losing my First Skycaptain is a price?"

"Ember City fell. Five of my victors. Thousands of people."

"Five of your victors." Soran sneered. "And a handful more today. And that's all that matters to you, isn't it?" He jabbed a pale, impossibly delicate finger in Malek's face.

Malek growled and grabbed at Soran's wrist, clutching it until Soran gasped in pain. "You talk as though I don't care about your City. About your Skyknights. About Tanth."

The thin wrist twisted in his grasp. Soran's altered eyes blazed. "How dare you—!"

"He fought beside me as an ally. He fought my best victor in a sparring match and won."

"An ugly brute and a fool, who cares nothing for Aerix or its people. Only what she won in your pits, and what hell she can follow you into next."

Malek leaned closer. Soran backed away, but Malek still held him by the wrist.

"An ugly brute and a fool," Malek repeated, pronouncing every word, "who has been mourning for your First Skycaptain since we got back here."

"Because he bested her."

"Because she knew what that meant. Because she knew—as I know—that nothing can replace him."

Soran's fingers reached for him, blind and thrashing.

Malek let go. "What is it you want to do? Rip open my scar with your bare hands?"

Soran's hand latched onto Malek's numb arm, the nails digging in, a strange parody of that first night they'd met.

"I can't feel that," Malek reminded him, his voice soft. He almost wished he could.

Soran raised his other hand and held up his dagger, cleaned of blood but far less polished than it once had been.

"No?" he taunted. The word was more acid than teasing, but under the circumstances, Malek could live with it. He slipped into the closest approximation he could muster of a fighting stance, one fist held up as a guard. It would have to do.

"What are you going to do?" he asked again. "Kill me? Now that you risked your city itself to save my life?"

"Anything I can do." Soran lunged, too quick for Malek to evade. Malek could only twist away, let the blade tear through the fine cloth he wore and slice a line of fire in his side.

The wound wasn't deep. Malek wondered, feeling its sting, if that was by design.

As before, so long ago, he grabbed at the hand that held the blade. Soran didn't wait. He let the blade go, his lip curled.

Malek moved his hands to Soran's shirt, grabbed at the fastener, and unzipped it, not bothering to be graceful. The pink scar Malek had left on his flesh peeked out, indelible as a signature.

"You wear my mark," said Malek.

Soran watched him out of lidded, glittering eyes. He hissed, an animal sound.

"You knew the risk."

"I—"

"So did he."

Soran shrieked and shoved Malek, just hard enough to push his way past Malek's bad side.

He scooped up his blade and ran out of the room, leaving Malek staring behind him.

Chapter Forty

THEY BURNED Tanth's body on a funeral pyre.

They chose the highest platform they could find, as close to the center of the City. It hadn't been easy. They'd picked their way among the debris to find a place sturdy enough to hold a small gathering of Skyknights and victors.

Some sang, a traditional song of farewell. Soran was one of them.

The old religions said the voices, lifting into the sky, carried a fallen Skyknight's soul above and away. That here on the planets, their craft gave them wings, but the song would offer them real wings, wings of their own, no starfighter needed.

The mourners wore flowing blue clothes, instead of black, to speed the Skyknight's soul into—where? The song had never been clear. Somewhere out in the vastness of space, some deep and hidden sacred place among the stars.

Soran doubted it existed. Traditions had their value, but only some of the old tales made sense. But now that Tanth was gone, for the first time in his life, he found himself hoping there was something to the song.

Like all the others, Ania was trained to sing the mourning song. But her voice broke over and over and she cried out the notes in an aching wail.

Soran felt it too, a chill deep within. He'd played politics all his life, mocked those who couldn't keep up with him. Enjoyed those who could as opponents, until he got his chance to destroy them.

But his First Skycaptain was his right hand, and had been since their training together in their youth. It was like losing a part of himself, and knowing it would never be found.

This wasn't enough. It would never be enough. The whole city should have mourned with them, high-caste citizens gathered on all the nearby platforms, watching with bowed heads, the ceremony broadcast to the rest of the City below.

They were recording, of course. Broadcasting with what remained of the system. Kenn had helped, as had those of the Below who had stolen glimpses of Malek and the others. But it was still all wrong. He'd died protecting Malek and his thugs, but they weren't even singing.

He fought down a shudder and sang louder, a trill that ended in a wail of his own. It would be worse if they did. Worse to hear the words of his mourning song in Vareth's accent.

Or Malek's.

Even the flames made his hands curl into fists at his sides. A funeral pyre was only right; as the Seraph, he'd seen hundreds.

But seeing fire made him ill now.

Flames, consuming what was left of his First Skycaptain, after war had scorched his City. The smoke still rose around him, choking and oppressive.

But the alternative would be to consign Tanth to the ground. And that was unthinkable. Sacrilege upon sacrilege, and the ultimate disrespect for a Skycaptain who had given his life for his City.

Soran glanced over at Vareth and shuddered. No doubt they did such things in Dis.

He didn't look over at Malek. He couldn't. Every time he tried, his anger rose to choke him. He couldn't see the new wound he'd left in Malek's side. And even seeing it might not soothe him.

You wear my mark.

Soran hadn't gotten it erased. He hadn't had the chance.

You could have. An inner voice, whispering inside his head. *Just before this. If you'd really wanted.*

He clamped his lips shut to keep from snarling at himself. How could he have a thought like that now, with Tanth dead and his City shattered? He focused on it, how it itched. That might have meant healing, before all of this. Now, it served as a reminder of what Malek had done to him.

To all of them.

He welcomed that. It kept him angry. He closed his eyes and coughed, gave himself a long moment to collect himself. Then he opened his eyes, turned away from his First Skycaptain's body, and addressed the crowd.

"Skyknights. Warriors. People of Aerix," he called, in the trained voice of the Seraph. "We are gathered here today to mourn Skycaptain

Tanth, the greatest of our fighters."

A humming, mournful chord. Soran heard deeper voices in it now: Vareth and Malek, at least, and probably Kenn too, though his voice wasn't as loud or as deep.

A hot spike of anger curled through Soran. Who did they think they were?

An ugly brute and a fool, who has been mourning for your First Skycaptain since we got back here. Soran bit his lip. He could save the songs for his own people, but he couldn't stop them from joining in their mourning. *Fine.*

"He fell defending our City. From invaders, who broke their sacred promises to leave our skies alone. Who flew to Aerix as usurpers and destroyers. Who felled towers that had stood for generations."

He looked over at the pyre again. "And stole one of our greatest from us."

Another humming wail.

"I am your Seraph. But the First Skycaptain was our greatest protector. He watched over our skies with perfect precision and unfailing devotion. He saw these invaders when they first crawled to the doorstep of our city and cast their envious eyes on our skies."

There should have been silence. Silence, or song. But someone hurled a curse.

Soran let himself smile, wry and bitter. "And they found their excuse to attack us." He cast his gaze over at the group of victors, but did not let it linger on them for long.

"They stretched their grasping fingers into our skies. They took all they could from us. As we always knew they would, if they had their chance to try."

A memory, unbidden. Soran's own voice, sneering at Malek, cruel and dismissive: *Don't tell me you think that the fools in Feris or Corian could get close enough to Aerix to plunder it!*

Soran had called him paranoid. A conspiracy theorist. And yet.

As we always knew they would, if they had their chance to try.

He fought down a shudder and kept talking. "But our city is still standing - thanks to the watchful leadership of the man who died to defend it."

The hum became a cry. A roar of anger and defiance.

"First Skycaptain Ania!" he called. It was part of the ritual, the First Skycaptain's replacement speaking for her predecessor.

He shook his head. What could she say, her throat raw with wailing song and tears glistening in her eyes? The Skyknights knew what she and Tanth had meant to one another. How could they not? Even the people had guessed.

But could she speak of it now, with the wound so fresh?

She bowed her head, then raised it again. "I have nothing to say, my Seraph. Only that the ones who did this are dead. Even if it claims my own life."

Soran nodded. It would have to be enough. And from the rumbling wail that answered, it would be.

He fought down a snarl and turned to Malek. *None of this is right. You shouldn't even have the right to speak.*

But Malek had defended him at the last, and he had defended Malek.

Malek waited a long moment, his head lowered as Ania's had been. Then he spoke.

"Your First Skycaptain was a great warrior. Greater than my best. And he died defending me. Protecting my rights as a guest in your City. I am in his debt. And yours."

"Your world invaded ours," someone snarled, close by him. The same voice that had cursed him before.

The man leapt at Malek, his body a blur of movement, Skyknight-agile, leaping at his weaker side.

Soran's body twitched, automatic. He didn't even realize he had turned until he saw Vareth's bulk crashing against the attacker, his slender shape wriggling under her massive bulk. Soran's eyes widened. How had she moved fast enough?

How had she moved faster than Soran himself?

He willed away that thought and curled his lip at Malek for good measure. She must have been expecting this. Protecting her lord at all costs, from attackers that sprang up from all sides.

Even from their allies, Soran thought before he could stop himself.

Had he managed to sneak a weapon in here? Soran shook his head, not sure if that would please or anger him.

"Enough!" Soran called out, as angry at himself as at them.

The man stilled and glared at Soran with Skyknight-blue eyes.

Malek waved a hand. "He is right."

Heads turned. People whispered. Someone, abashed, hummed a mourning note. A few others took it up, quiet, halfhearted.

"He is right," Malek said again. "Your City is part of this world now, for better or worse. And my coming gave our enemies an excuse to attack it—and a reason to kill your greatest fighter. Your anger is only right."

They looked at Malek, expectant. Soran scowled.

"But we are part of this world as well. And we will rise up to avenge him."

CHAPTER FORTY-ONE

THE DAY after Tanth's funeral dawned bright. Blue sky peeked through the smoke of war. The filigreed window let in the light as if this tower knew nothing of the war outside. And nothing of the sorrow in the City.

Soran had been avoiding him since. Malek had followed him through the tower, but he'd just darted through the hallsand said nothing. He flitted past door after door, Malek on his heels.

"Wait!" Malek called, the word as calm a command as he could make it.

"Wait," Soran echoed, his voice cold and mocking. He turned on his heel. His brows angled hard and sharp over his eyes. But at least he was looking at Malek. Now maybe he would listen.

Soran spat at Malek's feet.

Or not.

"I understand," Malek said, his voice low.

"You understand nothing."

What could Malek say to that? He moved toward Soran, determined not to let him run away again.

Soran stepped back. Toward a corner, if Malek could catch him there before he twisted free.

"My First Skycaptain is dead because of you. Everyone knows it. And all you can say is that you will take our vengeance for us? As if vengeance for his death belongs to you!"

"Do you really think that I would take that from you? I only meant that together, there are enough of us to make this world burn for what they've done to you."

"You say I play games." Soran laughed. He stepped backward again. "Then you use my City as a piece in yours."

Malek saw his opportunity and lunged.

Soran's back slammed against the wall. Malek thought of Tanth and felt a flare of concern. Still, he pressed his bad side against the wall and put out the one arm he could still control. "You knew the risks when you made your choice."

"Did I?" Soran threw himself against Malek's bad side. But Malek was expecting it, and Soran's alterations had made his body light. Too light. Light as the man they'd just watched break.

Malek closed his eyes and took a slow, deep breath. "Regret is a luxury neither of us can allow ourselves."

"Regret. That's all this is to you. Some tiny, minor inconvenience, niggling at the back of your mind."

"No, Soran. No. But if we mean to win this—"

"Win. That's all that matters to you, isn't it?" Soran's face was inches from his. "Even if the world shatters under your feet!"

"Soran—"

"This is all another pit fight to you. Nothing you do matters," he said, pronouncing every word, "as long as your opponent dies first."

Malek winced. "We left our lives behind, Soran. Everything we valued. Everything we were." *And there will be more. I could tell you right now. All that it will cost us going forward. The price every victor I saved agreed to pay. But it won't ease your pain.*

He dropped his arm. It would give Soran a way out, if he wanted it. But this wouldn't end unless he offered it.

Soran's mouth opened in an O of surprise. He pushed against Malek. Malek let him.

"Go if you want," Malek said.

Soran froze.

Malek ran his hand over the smooth blue fabric of Soran's shirt. Soran trembled under his hand, but stilled.

Malek pulled the fabric up, exposing Soran's chest. Soran expelled a slow, steady breath. His hands twitched once, and he grabbed at Malek's wrist.

Malek stared at the exposed scar. Soran, too, was glaring at it, his lip curled in barely-checked rage.

"You're not going to erase it by staring at it," Malek said. "Or at me."

Soran loosened his grip, and Malek slid his fingers up to touch the scar. Soran flinched, but didn't pull away. Malek traced his fingertips over it. Soran stared down at his hand and said nothing.

"He knew," Malek said, still running his fingertips over Soran's scar.

Soran curled his fingers in, digging his nails into Malek's wrist. "He knew better than you. He flew the patrols that found Halcyon's army in Feris and in Corian." His other hand shot out to curl around Malek's side, seeking out the wound he'd made there and pressing in.

Malek gritted his teeth against the pain. "Your Skyknights won this victory. Tanth died for this victory. Can you not savor it, knowing your greatest and best bought it with his life?"

"He should never have died," Soran whispered. His mouth curled in a pout, like a lover's.

"Not for you."

"No." Malek leaned in and closed his eyes. "I promised you a world, Prince of the Air. I didn't know that it would cost Tanth's life. But I knew it would come at great cost. I never pretended otherwise."

"A world," Soran murmured.

Desire, or derision? Malek didn't let himself wonder which. He pressed his lips to Soran's before he could think better of it. Before Soran could pull away, or curse him again.

But Soran's mouth only opened wider. Slender arms wrapped around him and clung tight to his broad frame. They pulled him closer, and Soran gasped into his mouth, as if he understood the comfort Malek meant to offer.

Soran's lips slipped down to his neck.

"We've won," Malek whispered into his ear, like a secret, like a talisman. "Your City endures, as it always has."

Soran shuddered against him, and heat flared through his flesh, bright and fierce and proud enough to drive out the chill. "My City—"

Malek pulled away, just far enough for Soran to look into his altered eyes. "And the rest of the world will come at my call. You've seen it."

"Have I?"

Malek's lip quirked into the first hint of a smile. *There you are, my Seraph.*

"You have. All of Ember City and more of the Belt, coming to fight for me. How many more will come, now that the Senate tried to level Aerix and failed?"

Soran smirked. "All your people."

"Yes."

"So what happens now?"

"Now I return to Dis. Now I tell them—and Kenn shows them— what the real barbarians did to your City."

Soran laughed, high and wild. His hands moved on Malek's back, and he slipped closer. He whispered in Malek's ear, as Malek had in his. "And?"

Malek wrapped his good arm around Soran. His wrist stung where Soran's nails had pricked it. That was good. That was life, fierce and bright. That was the Soran he wanted.

And the Soran who wanted him.

"I told you already," Malek said at last. "I broadcast what happened in Aerix to the rest of the world. And the rest of the world rises up to avenge it."

ABOUT THE AUTHOR

A. M. Hawke lives in the Washington, DC, area where she works as a peer mentor and advocate for people with disabilities. She has a master's degree in philosophy from Georgetown University, but has always returned to her passion for writing. When not writing, she can be found gaming, seeking out new restaurants to try, or hanging out at a local coffee shop on Saturday mornings.

CPSIA information can be obtained
at www.ICGtesting.com
Printed in the USA
BVOW06*0743280717

490007BV00010B/15/P